No One Sleeps in Alexandria

No One Sleeps
in Alexandria

Ibrahim Abdel Meguid

Translated by
Farouk Abdel Wahab

The American University in Cairo Press
Cairo   New York

From delight to fury and from fury to light;
I build myself whole from all beings.

Paul Éluard

The Mediterranean is an absurdly small sea; the length and
greatness of its history makes us dream it larger than it is.
Alexandria indeed—the true no less than the imagined—lay only
some hundreds of sea-miles
to the south.

Lawrence Durrell

The gods were disturbed by their noise, which had
deprived them of sleep, so they sent a plague to them,
but they soon multiplied again and their din rose, so the
gods sent them a six-year drought and a seven-day great
flood. The flood was so horrific that the gods also were
terrified and withdrew further away into the sky.

Babylonian Flood Myth

Secret beloved voices; the voices of those who have died
or who, for us, are lost like the dead. They speak in our
dreams sometimes and sometimes in thought the mind
hears them; with their echoes, sounds of the poems of
our first life come back momentarily like a distant
music in the night fading away.

Constantine Cavafy

Translator's Acknowledgments

I would like to thank the following friends and colleagues for help with various aspects of the translation: Evelyn Anoya, Heather Felton, and Emily Teeter (University of Chicago); John Eisele (College of William and Mary); Gregg Reynolds (Datalogics, Inc.); Neil Hewison (The American University in Cairo Press), and Zora O'Neill.

Man is clay and straw; God is the potter.

Ancient Egyptian saying

1

Hitler is pacing around the chancellery in Berlin, stooped slightly forward and hands clasped behind his back, in a state of deep reflection. His lips are pursed, which makes his mustache appear a little askew. His eyes are open wide with vexation, which makes them twinkle all the more. But in fact, his chest and head are about to explode. He is totally oblivious to the Chancellery guards standing at their posts and to his own bodyguards following behind him. He is wishing he could wring the Polish president's neck.

Today is August 25, a clear day in Berlin. Hitler is thinking of old-time wars, which began as hand-to-hand combat between two commanders and ended in the defeat of one of them, whereupon he and his army surrendered to the victor. But he cannot risk that; he knows very well how small his body is—even though it is he to whom Austria simply offered herself last year like a practiced whore, even though it is he who did not hesitate to invade a well-armed Czechoslovakia and met no resistance. Only the Poles are obstinate; they don't want to return to the Reich what the Treaty of Versailles has unjustly given them. He will not accept anything less than what Germany had lost. This is exactly the right time: twenty years have passed since his time in the hospital after almost losing his eyesight in the war, which had ended catastrophically for the German nation. His old bitterness haunts him a great deal; it is time he reaped the fruits of his struggle, beginning with when he joined the German Workers' Party, organized the National Socialist Party and the stormtroopers, was jailed, and fought the communists, up to when he became chancellor and liquidated all his enemies, and the communists before them. The German people had supported him and cheered for him, so that he came to realize that he was the messenger sent by heaven to restore Germany's dignity. But he does not want to declare war so early. The obstinate Poles are forcing him to do it. He rushes into the chancellery.

It is now 3 p.m. sharp. Hitler signs the order to invade Poland, then heaves a sigh of relief. He orders something to eat in his office, then calls Eva Braun on the telephone and chats with her and tells her that he won't see her this afternoon. He remembers his former war minister, Blomberg, who had lured him, along with Goering the Luftwaffe chief, to be the witnesses at Blomberg's marriage to a woman who, as Himmler, the chief of the secret police, later proved, was a prostitute with a police record. He curses Blomberg and all whores and remembers how he removed him from office in a thorough reorganization.

But that was last year. He does not need anyone now. He must look forward, only forward to the future. He finds himself thinking of his friend Mussolini.

It is now 6 p.m. He has not left his office yet. Attolico, the Italian ambassador, presents him with a letter from the friend he had been thinking of a few hours earlier.

"In spite of Italy's unconditional support of Germany, Italy cannot intervene militarily unless Germany supplies her at once with all the war materiel stated in the list attached to this letter." Hitler looks at the list, resisting a tremendous urge to explode. Ambassador Attolico does not notice Hitler shaking his head in vexation; the man's neck is not long enough for the shaking to be noticeable—that would require shouting, which was what he did when he addressed the masses. But he will not give speeches now. He wants, on the contrary, to appear calm.

With sudden elation he remembers the day he entered Austria with his troops without facing a single shot. That was the morning of March 12 of last year. That day he went to Linz, where he had first gone to school as a child. There he excitedly delivered a speech to the frenzied masses. His envoy to Rome, Prince Philip of Hesse, had telephoned him the day before to convey Mussolini's warmest greetings and to intimate that Austria meant nothing at all to the Duce. Hitler responded to his envoy with overwhelming joy, saying that he would never forget the Italian leader's support, no matter what happened, and that if Mussolini ever needed him, he would stand by his side, even if the whole world were against him.

The day of his invasion, he had pondered the frenzy of the Austrians as he addressed them. He remembered how he had been born to a poor customs official and how, as a young man, he had wanted to be an artist but failed to gain entrance to the Arts Academy in Vienna, which caused him to leave Austria for Germany. Then he pondered his triumphant entry into his childhood home. Remembering the telephone conversation of the day before, he became ecstatic with joy. What more could anyone want, than to feel that providence was on his side? He had made his decision to annex Austria to the Reich. Today, however, Mussolini was letting him down before he even started the war.

Hitler becomes a bit depressed. He almost calls Eva Braun to summon her to his office. The arrogant Poles are standing like boulders in my way, he thinks. My dear friend who brags about my believing in his ideas is letting me down. What kind of people are these Italians? Real pirates! But these pirates can go into battle in the Mediterranean against the French and keep them busy until Poland is no more. Mussolini's letter was not a good sign.

Therefore, when the telephone rings, he hesitates before picking it up. He lifts it to his ear and listens as his foreign minister, Ribbentrop, tells him that a mutual defense treaty between England and Poland had just been signed.

At this moment, the Führer cannot think of anyone but Keitel, the chief of staff. He summons him at once and calmly tells him, as if dismissing the whole matter, "Stop everything at once. I need time for negotiations."

❖

It is not a long time, just five days. There is a blackout in Paris; leaflets urging women to volunteer in the army are distributed in French cities. France declares full confidence in her generals: Gamelin, Darlan, and Vuillemin, the chiefs of staff of the army, navy, and the air force. General mobilization is declared; troops and convoys pass through the streets of Paris on their way back to their barracks. In London, the platforms of Waterloo station fill with suitcases and luggage as women and children leave for the countryside. In Italy, Mussolini issues an order dividing the army in two: one branch commanded by Crown Prince Umberto, and one commanded by Marshall Graziani; the government confiscates coffee beans from the markets, declaring that the government will handle the coffee trade in order to supply the armies. All this despite the fact, as Hitler understood from the letter, that Mussolini was reluctant to side with him in the war.

Every country in the world is shaken and attempting to define its position if the war breaks out: to fight, to stay neutral, or to wait. Unrest continues in Palestine. A ship carrying twelve hundred Jews approaches the coast in order to smuggle them into the country. A few people in Germany take to the streets to protest the war; some throw themselves in front of trains rather than witness a new war annihilate the world. This happens in many European cities. The ship Maritt Pasha crosses the Suez canal carrying French and Senegalese troops to Syria and Lebanon to reinforce French defenses. In Cairo the commencement ceremonies for Victoria College are postponed, police patrols increased, anti-espionage measures intensified, and reserve officers mobilized. Mahmud Ghalib Pasha, minister of transportation, orders a number of railroad cars converted into field hospitals. Air raid sirens are tested; seven steamers are stationed in Bulaq to evacuate the inhabitants of Cairo if the need arises. In Alexandria,

Admiral Cunningham, commander in chief of the British Mediterranean Fleet, meets Prime Minister Ali Mahir Pasha in the Egyptian government's summer headquarters in Bulkely to discuss necessary naval procedures if war breaks out. The Committee for Protection against Air Raids, headed by the mayor of Alexandria, meets and decides to increase fire stations to three and to order car owners to paint their headlights dark rather than light blue. The air raid alarm system is also tested there. Metal nets are set up outside the harbor to repel naval attacks. Night tests of searchlights are conducted above the city to prepare against air raids. Mr. Miles Lampson, the British ambassador, arrives from London to meet His Majesty the King at the Muntaza Palace. Hitler proposes to the British government to settle the dispute by having Poland surrender Danzig at once and hold a plebiscite for the inhabitants of the corridor. He sets a deadline of two days and asks that the Polish president himself, or an official emissary authorized to negotiate, give him the answer.

This becomes the only way to prevent matters from deteriorating any further. The world waits with bated breath through the two-day reprieve. The question now: Can any person or any power save the inhabitants of Earth from the coming hell?

Protests and suicides do no good. The wheels of death are turning. It is decided to open the book of hell.

And he said to me: if you see the fire, fall into it, for if you
fall into it, it will be put out, and if you flee it,
it will seek you and burn you.

al-Niffari

2

On Magd al-Din's last night, he sat silently amid his family. They were looking at him, incredulous. But he simply sat there, seeming not to have changed at all. He was forty but looked twenty, with an elongated face, strong features, well-defined cheek bones, green eyes, and the hair blond but always covered by a white skullcap. His body retained the strength of a younger man.

"Why won't you let us fight?" One of his three sisters' husbands asked. "We can fight the whole village if we have to. We still have some old weapons, and we are men."

Magd al-Din told them all to go to bed. "Tomorrow is another day. We'll leave it all to He who is never overtaken by slumber or sleep"—his favorite words with which they, especially his young wife Zahra, were all familiar in times of crisis. They all went upstairs to their rooms in the big house. His mother, Hadya, who had lost her eyesight, went to her room on the first floor, leaning on the arm of Zahra, who carried her one-year-old daughter, Shawqiya, on her other arm.

From all corners of the house came that smell Magd al-Din liked, the smell of the mud walls baked by the heat of the day, mixed with the smell of dung from the animal shed and the smell of the cheese mats and butter churn hanging on the walls. Magd al-Din went up to the roof out of habit. He looked at the white dovecote, and, listening intently, he heard a faint, almost inaudible cooing. He heard nothing from the rabbit pen. He felt stifled; a heat wave had taken hold for days on end; it was getting more and more humid, as if the summer did not want to end. What had revived this old, dead affair now? Why, really, did he not want to resist?

❖

Like a sudden rain pouring down on the village, people began to talk, publicly and privately, about the old vendetta between the Khalils and the Talibs. The deputy mayor of the village came to ask Magd al-Din to leave the village by week's end.

The vendetta between the two families had been over for ten years, and none of the Khalils except Magd al-Din was left alive, and none but Khalaf of the Talibs—Magd al-Din, who had been exempted from military service because he had memorized the entire Quran, and Khalaf, his childhood friend. This friendship made each do his best to avoid facing the other in battle. Magd al-Din's five brothers were killed, and his father died of grief. Only he and his brother Bahi, who was always wandering somewhere or other, remained alive. His cousins, now wedded to his sisters, also remained alive. Khalaf's six brothers were also killed, and his father likewise died of grief. The whole village learned of the pledge that Magd al-Din and Khalaf had taken. They had decided, more than ten years ago, to stop the river of blood.

Magd al-Din had said to his friend, "And now, Khalaf, only I am left to die. I will not permit myself to fight you."

"I seek nothing from you, Magd al-Din."

"Then you will seek out Bahi. If that is the case, kill me instead, Khalaf."

"I won't seek anybody out, Magd al-Din. We are all covered in shame, the killer and the killed."

So the story had ended long ago. And Bahi, who ended up living in Alexandria, never appeared in the village again. Reviving the story of the old vendetta between the Khalils and the Talibs was nothing but a pretext to get rid of Magd al-Din. The mayor had simply succumbed to his weakness and hate. Magd al-Din was doomed, as were all his brothers, to pay for the sins of Bahi. What did Alexandria have for Bahi to love it so much? Would Magd al-Din join him there tomorrow or would he settle some other place on God's great earth? "Dear God, most merciful," Magd al-Din whispered as he sat down, his back against the dovecote. He took a tobacco case from his vest and rolled a thin cigarette. He never loved any of his brothers as much as he loved Bahi, and there they were, about to be united again.

"Your father died, Bahi, saying nothing but your name."

"I can't live in the village, Sheikh Magd. Prison has destroyed me."

"Our village is good, Bahi."

"You're a good man, Sheikh Magd. You see the world only through the lens of the Quran. Why do you really stay in this stinking village?"

Magd al-Din had no answer. He did not know then, and he still, to this day, does not know how to answer Bahi's question. That day Bahi had added, "Your father's dead, your brothers have been killed. Nobody's left except the women and me, and I am no good to you."

After that, Bahi left for Alexandria—ten whole years of separation. Magd al-Din made sure to visit him once or twice every year, quick visits, never more than one night, and on the following morning he would return with a lot of nice things to say to the mother, Hadya. He always found Bahi wearing clean clothes, a shirt and pants, since he had given up his village garb a long time before. He lived in a room that he kept clean and fragrant with frankincense and musk, and always carried in his pocket a little box of ambergris that gave off a captivating fragrance. But he looked pale and exhausted and hid from Magd al-Din the many pains that he suffered in the city. Magd al-Din never told his mother of his worries about his brother's pain, only gave her good news about her poor son.

That was the only lie that Magd al-Din told in his entire life. It always pained him to see the life his brother was leading in Alexandria, but he got used to telling his mother otherwise. He loved his brother and told her what he wished he would become. The age difference between them was five years, marching with them like a half-century of strange pain. Bahi was the older of the

two. His father would always look at him and say "God works in
mysterious ways! This is my son, from my loins, and these are also
my sons, all from the same mother. Some till the land and some
trade and some memorize the Quran—but this boy came into this
world bearing the sins of all creation."

From an early age Bahi came to hate any attempt to teach him
anything in a Quranic school, the village mosque, or at home, and
he hated nothing more than peasants and working the land. Some
said that was a result of being handsome; others said it was because
of fear in his heart. The father always said, with sorrow in his eyes,
"God made him this way."

The mother chose the name Bahi, or 'Radiant,' because she
gave birth to him on the twenty-seventh of Ramadan, the most
sacred of nights. As he was sliding out of her, she saw a beam of
light coming out with him and filling the room and the walls with
light. The midwife cried as she swathed him, telling his mother to
hide him from all eyes for, in addition to the beam of light that
came out with him, he was born already circumcised. He was a
child of purity destined for great blessings.

Because of this, no one saw Bahi until he was able to walk,
when he sneaked out of an opening in the big wooden gate and
rolled down the narrow alley, his face still encircled with that
wondrous light. The mother's apprehension ended only after she
gave birth to three daughters, then Magd al-Din—she was no
longer the mother of males only. The father's apprehension,
however, did not end. He had realized early on that Bahi's eyes
revealed a recklessness that was unusual in the family. For even
though Bahi's eyes, like all the children, were the same green as his
mother's, only his eyes had a strange blue tinge as well.

Once Bahi grew to adolescence he took to leaving the house in
the morning and coming back in the evening only to sleep, without
speaking to anyone. No one questioned where he spent his days.
The mother was filled with tenderness toward him, and the father
could not explain the weakness God had planted in his heart
toward the boy. Gradually Bahi became more like an apparition in
the family. The brothers would go to the fields early in the
morning, and he would leave after them, but no one knew where
he went. They would return in the evening, tired, to have supper

and go to bed early, but their mother would not sleep until she heard the squeak of the gate and Bahi's heart beating as he crept in.

Eventually he started staying away for longer stretches, and when he came back, he would sleep in the first spot he came across, with the animals or the chickens, on top of the oven, in the hallway between the rooms—anywhere but where his siblings slept. The father still could not figure out the cause of his weakness toward his strange son, and the peaceable boy had caused no harm yet.

Then Bahi's secret became widely known throughout the village: he was possessed with love. He followed the women along the canals and through the marketplace. The village women waited for him to pass through the alleys, so that they could look at him from the rooftops and from behind doors. They all learned his appointed rounds by heart. The halo of light that his mother said had slid out with him the day he was born was still with him, but only the women could see it. News of him reached the neighboring villages, and other women and girls began to sit and wait for him by the canal that separated the village from the fields. Women with special needs would rush up and touch him, but little girls were afraid of him. They would stand at a distance and giggle, as their bodies shook uncontrollably.

His father and brothers were surprised by what they heard about the boy. Then one day, they saw him at the edge of the field. His brothers Fattuh, al-Qasim, Khalil, Imran, and Sulayman were there, but Magd al-Din, the youngest, was not with them that day. At first they were surprised that he had made an appearance, but after he sat down by the water wheel, they got busy with their work. Moments later they saw him get up and walk around the old sycamore several times, looking toward the distant village, then they heard him start to yell. They stood up with their hoes in between the short cotton plants. In the distance, they saw a large number of men charging toward them, their hoes and clubs raised toward Bahi. "The Talibs!" the brothers shouted. There had been no blood between the two families until that day. The men of the Talib family drew together, and Bahi rushed to his brothers in terror.

"They're going to kill me!"

"Run away from here. Go tell your father and your cousins. Quick!"

Bahi raced past his brothers faster than a horse.

His brothers attacked the charging men, and a long battle ensued. On his way, Bahi saw his father and his cousins hurrying toward the field carrying hoes and clubs. He did not go back with them but kept running until he reached the house. His mother was standing there, terrified. He threw himself into her chest. He was barely sixteen. He burst out crying.

She patted him on the back and asked, her voice pained, "Why did you do that, my son?"

"Protect me, mother."

She took him to the nearest room, then changed her mind and took him upstairs—"So your father won't kill you when he comes home," she said under her breath and Bahi heard her. She closed the door and went downstairs to wait for the battle to end. That day, she realized that the gates of hell had been opened, and that it would not end before the fire consumed all of them, who were only the firewood.

In the upstairs room, Bahi realized what had come to pass. It was the bitch, the whore, the wife of Abd al-Ghani, oldest of the Talib boys, who had seduced him. It was she who, in broad daylight on market day, had reached out as he was passing in front of her door and dragged him inside by the back of his neck. "All this light!" she exclaimed, and he said nothing. He let her look into his eyes and run her hands over his chest.

She bewitched him. She placed her fingers on him, and it was as though armies of ants crawled over him and made him her captive. She dragged him to a nearby room as he succumbed to her, the glances of the chickens and the ducks in the courtyard pursuing them.

The dark, windowless room was suddenly illuminated. She perceived the light, while he did not realize that he had entered into the dark. "It's coming out of your body, my bridegroom. I must bear your secret. Light me and take me to hell." He heard her and let her do as she pleased. She lifted him to the seventh heaven.

He left her house feeling light as a feather. What had been weighing him down; what had he emptied into her that now made him so light? The narrow streets were no longer narrow, the black houses no longer black, nor did the dung in the streets have a repulsive smell.

She had been married to Abd al-Ghani for only a month. That was why she had not gone to the market with the family women that day; she was still a bride. Afterwards she still did not go out, and concocted excuse after excuse for a whole year. The Talib boys watched their eldest brother submit to his young, beautiful wife, and they marveled at the power of beauty over men.

But the women, the Talib boys' wives, schemed and were successful. One day, Abd al-Ghani lifted his wife off her feet then pushed her to the ground in the midst of his brothers, their wives, his mother, and his father. He placed his foot on her chest and a knife on her neck.

"Who, bitch?"

She did not hesitate.

"Bahi," she said in a faint voice.

"That wanton little boy?" Her husband spat in her face and pressed the knife deep into her neck.

Her laughter rang through the courtyard of the big house. Her husband was thrown down, falling onto his backside, and the knife flew from his hand. He groaned in pain, then his eyes turned away and fixed onto faraway space. He had driven the knife into the neck, he was absolutely certain, but no blood came out—just a beam of light.

She got up, still laughing. His brothers searched frantically for the knife but could not find it anywhere. Later they would find it in the courtyard and wonder how nobody had seen it that day. It was so rusted that as one of them rubbed it, it turned to dust. The brothers carried him to his room; he could not walk on his own. She stood in a far corner, laughing and crying at the same time. She aroused the women's pity and fear. The same women who had schemed against her took her to the shed and sat around her in a corner on the straw. She did not stop shaking. They said she would die that night. The men forgot about her, worrying instead about their incapacitated older brother. The women gave her a bowl of fresh milk, which she gulped down, letting half of it spill down her chest and never ceasing to laugh and cry. Then she fell asleep on the straw, and they watched her side move with her breathing, like a tired animal.

At dawn the men came out of their brother's room dragging their feet. The women wailed, "Is he dead?"

"He was murdered!" shouted the men. "His blood is on the hands of the Khalils! The life of the little dandy boy is not payment enough."

No one saw the wife sneak out of the shed at first light and disappear. In the morning the Talibs lay in wait for Bahi on the streets. The news had spread. Bahi was returning from a neighboring village. No one had realized that the women and girls washing their pots and pans in the canal had gone far outside the village, so that before Bahi entered the village, the women alerted him, and he turned to the fields, where his brothers were. The women then went back to their usual place along the canal in the middle of the village, where the ducks swam. But the Talibs had planted their own spies, so they knew where the boy was going.

Magd al-Din climbed down from the roof. He opened the wooden gate and went to the house of Khalaf, his one remaining friend from the other family; he too had been ordered by the mayor to leave the village.

"What have you decided to do, Khalaf?"

"Sheikh Magd, there's nothing left for me here. For a while now my money and my trade have been in Tanta. I know that I am not the the real target of this action—the mayor has just decided to retaliate for what Bahi did to him so long ago, so he dragged up this vendetta business, which has been over between us for years. I'm leaving the village tomorrow. I know I could just come back the next day, but I won't." He offered Magd al-Din a Cottarelli cigarette and asked, "I heard that your cousins, your sisters' husbands, want to fight the mayor. Is that true?"

"There will be no fighting. I forbade them."

"What are you going to do?"

"I'll leave the village tomorrow too."

Magd al-Din left Khalaf's house realizing for the first time that he was acquiescing to the mayor's order, not out of fear or submission, but out of a deep desire to leave the village and join his brother in Alexandria.

Two days before Magd al-Din's last night, the reply that Hitler had demanded came to him in the form of the announcement of the Polish peoples' speedy mobilization and the Polish president's appeal to his people to stand behind their army in defense of freedom and honor.

So the reprieve was over. The machine of evil had been switched on, and there was no escaping it. In the morning following Magd al-Din's last night in the village, at exactly 4:45 a.m., the full-scale invasion of Poland began.

It was Friday, the first of September, 1939. Magd al-Din did not usually go out to the field on a Friday; he preferred to spend the whole day in the small village mosque. But on this Friday he went out to the field. He did not want to go to the station directly from his house, and he had asked Zahra to go ahead to the station later that evening. The mayor had sent a number of guards to Magd al-Din's house, where they learned he was in the field and would leave the village from there. In the evening the chief guard and his men stood at the little bridge that connected the village with the road to the fields, in order to prevent Magd al-Din from going back to his house.

The mayor had not believed that he would leave the village so easily, but the guards watched him ride away from the village on a donkey so small that it looked like a she-ass. They fired some shots in the air to scare him. Magd al-Din chose not even to look back. He truly wanted to get out.

3

The railroad station that evening, like all evenings, was empty except for the poor stationmaster, who could not leave until after the last train, at ten o'clock. And as on other evenings the platform was a structure of wide, lifeless slabs of stone, and the sign bearing the name of the village was off-white, with faint black lines, and mounted on two rusted iron poles. Not a single sparrow perched on the sign or flew near it.

There were no sparrows in the nearby trees either. The four rails between the two platforms were black and shiny, but congealed fuel oil stained the crossties and the ballast beneath. Seen from above on summer days, the rails were always shiny, their surface almost white. The road connecting the station with the village was, as usual, a narrow dirt road, hot, with a few curves and a few eucalyptus trees. At that time of the evening there was usually only one man walking on the road. And at that time of day, it took a while for someone standing at the station to decide whether that man was walking toward him or away and toward the village. The truth was that the man always disappeared, as if he were a trick of the eye, and no one knew where he went. What is it in the summer that makes the eye see no change in the scene from one evening to another, or in the distance from the village to the station? Is it the heat and the refraction of the light on the dust?

The greenery too was the same as it had been every day, stretched out along the dirt road, with very few birds around or on it—a few crows on the fronds of the tall palm trees, the occasional egret in the branches of the ancient sycamores.

Through this lifeless landscape, Magd al-Din made his way to the station. The world appeared to him like something cast aside, something seen from a hilltop at noon on a day in the blazing hot month of Bauna. Was what happened to him a short while ago real? Was it really he who had complied with the mayor's order so easily, and left the village as easily—more easily, even, than a thorn pulled from dough? From a distance, he saw Zahra standing on the platform, her brother next to her, and their little daughter Shawqiya on her arm. At her feet were two small baskets and one large one. She was waving at him to hurry up. The donkey was slow, and he urged it on as much as he could. Before he reached the crossing, though, he left the donkey behind and continued on foot. The train had nearly reached the station, and Magd al-Din rushed on. He tripped over a wire stretched between the switches, and had to leave behind his shoes, which had slipped off, but he finally crossed the rails and climbed onto the platform. He saw the stationmaster in his official uniform, its brass buttons shining in the distance, and the red fez above his black face seemed to be floating in the twilight. The stationmaster looked to him like one of those fierce-looking border guards. He wished he could take his time greeting the man and shaking his hand, for it was his friend Abd al-Hamid from the next village who, like him, had memorized the entire Quran. They had met twenty years earlier at the governorate headquarters in Tanta when they were taking the Quran memorization test, on the basis of which they would be exempted from military service. Both of them passed the test, and both were exempted. By law, neither of them was supposed to do any work but recite the Quran. They both spent ten years without work, then they had to find other jobs—surely after ten years the government could not still be monitoring them. So Magd al-Din started working the land with his brothers, while Abd al-Hamid worked for the railroad. They became reacquainted, and then met every time Magd al-Din went to visit his brother Bahi in Alexandria. Why had neither of them worked as a Quranic chanter or a singer of hymns? It could be the voice: Magd al-Din's was faint and cracking, but Abd al-Hamid's was loud and strong. Magd al-Din had often thought of bringing it up with Abd al-Hamid, then changed his mind, or rather, forgot.

The train pulled into the station just as Magd al-Din joined Zahra. Magd al-Din saw his old friend coming toward him with one of the small baskets, which he put into the train car, then went back for the other one while Zahra's brother carried the big basket on board.

"Take your time, Sheikh Magd," said the stationmaster. "I'll keep the train waiting for a bit. I want to greet you properly, my friend."

They rushed to embrace each other. Magd al-Din wondered if his friend knew the reason for his trip today. The train let out white smoke and blew its whistle. The stationmaster also blew his whistle. Magd al-Din leaned out the window to tell Zahra's brother, "The donkey is just before the crossing." The train gathered speed, and the sound of the wheels grew louder.

It was only then that Magd al-Din realized that it was over, that he had been kicked out of his village, although he did have a secret desire to leave. This was something that had never happened to anyone before—at least he had never seen it in his lifetime.

The conductor came and Zahra showed him the two tickets she had purchased before Magd al-Din's arrival. When the conductor left, Magd al-Din noticed the terror in Zahra's eyes. He turned his eyes away from hers and noticed at the end of the car a woman around whom sat five boys and girls, barefoot and wearing old, tattered gallabiyas. He had seen this very woman and these same children on the train when he went to visit Bahi in the middle of last year. Merciful God! He did not believe it, but it had actually happened; he had seen her before that on yet another trip. It seemed that ever since he had started visiting his brother, he had seen this woman and these nearly naked, barefoot children. Despite the years that had passed, the woman and her children had not grown any older. The silence in the car was profound, with the exception of the sound of the wheels beneath them. Zahra had moved to the edge of the seat and spread out a gallabiya that she had taken from the large basket. She laid the baby to sleep on it and covered her with a black shawl from the same basket. She asked Magd al-Din to close the window tightly. It was now dark, and cold air was rushing in with the movement of the train.

How could the train ride continue? What could be said now that Zahra had laid the baby down to sleep and sat there looking at her husband who kept looking back at her, though his eyes did not seem as frightened as hers?

Zahra felt pained because she had no brother except the one who came to see her off at the station, and he was only her half-brother. Her sisters and mother could not fight the mayor. Yes, she wished she had many strong men in her family to fight the mayor, since Magd al-Din had forbidden his cousins to fight him. Magd al-Din must have feared that his sisters would become widows if their men died. But someone should have prevented them from leaving, even if he acted against Magd al-Din's will. Since she could not offer her husband the protection that strong men in her family would have provided, she was leaving with him, broken-hearted. But she had accepted what a faithful wife had to do. The frightened look in her eyes would soon disappear, without a doubt. And it did—it changed into a look of profound compassion. She wished they would let him go back home tonight.

At about this time, he would have come back from the field, washed up and had his supper, fed the animals and rubbed them down, changed their water and put out fodder for them. He would have helped Zahra milk the water buffaloes, then performed his late-night prayers and sat alone near the kerosene lamps in their room, reading the Quran.

"Anyway, that's what happened. Ha, ha, ha!" a coarse voice was heard.

Magd al-Din looked around to see where it came from. Zahra did not look but just sat still, silently annoyed. Magd al-Din saw the man who had spoken, a short, fat man with a faded fez. He was sitting on the edge of the seat, his feet barely touching the floor. He was speaking in utter surprise to a man who sat opposite him, farther to the side of the seat. Magd al-Din could only see his fez and the back of his neck and his white, slightly soiled shirt collar. They kept talking, and because they were close to Magd al-Din, he could hear them clearly.

"Neither France nor England would let him get away with it. It's the beginning of a new world war."

"That's why I'm laughing so hard."

"What do you mean, laughing like that? I tell you, it's a world war, and people are going to die."

"I mean, we've been transferred to work in Alexandria the very day Germany invades Poland. This can't be just a coincidence—it's been arranged with Hitler."

Magd al-Din listened, surprised. He knew, from scattered talk in the village and from the big radio he rarely listened to, that there were preparations for war, that Germany was creating problems with other countries, and that people were afraid that a new war, more devastating than the previous one, might break out. He had forgotten all that in the last few days. And here it was coming back. He listened to what the two men were saying.

"I couldn't get the evening paper in Tanta—people just snatched them away from the vendors. The radio said Warsaw has been bombarded heavily since early this morning and that German troops were invading Poland from more than one direction."

"This is because of the greed of the European countries. It's the war of the greedy."

"The problem is, this war will come to us."

"Because we've been transferred to Alexandria on the same day? No, of course not. There's no reason to be so pessimistic. What does Alexandria have to do with a war in Europe?"

The conversation took what seemed a strange turn to Magd al-Din, so he took out the little Quran from his vest pocket. But before he could open it, the two were talking again.

"Alexandria itself will be the reason the war comes to it. Yes, sir—don't forget, Italy is in Libya."

"You think Mussolini would do it?"

"He is Hitler's mentor—if he doesn't join him this year, it'll be next year."

"Well, we're only staying in Alexandria for a year. Besides, I doubt if the war will spread. Hitler swallowed up Czecho-slovakia and Austria before that, and nobody did anything about it. He will swallow Poland and no one will stand up to him. All of Europe is terrified, and the Soviet Union has signed a treaty with him. Besides, why should we go so far? I wish Germany or Italy, or both of them together would occupy Egypt and rid us of the English."

❖

The sound of the wheels died down as the train stopped in the Kafr al-Zayyat station. The two men stopped talking, the white ceiling lights came on, and the clean, yellow wooden seats now shone more brightly. A man and three little boys came into the train car. The man was well dressed, in a summer white sharkskin suit, a clean fez, and black-and-white shoes with thin, pointed tips. The boys wore blue shorts, short-sleeved white shirts, and blue suspenders with white pinstripes. They had calf-length white socks and black patent leather shoes with wide tips. They looked as if they had just stopped crying.

The man, who sat facing Magd al-Din, now placed his index finger to his lips, warning the children, who sat across from him, not to make a sound. Then Magd al-Din watched him take from his jacket pocket a golden cigarette case, which he pressed and a thin cigarette came out. He lit it and exhaled its blue smoke, closing his eyes in contentment.

The train started moving again. Magd al-Din was familiar with the following stops. In two and a half hours, the train would be in Alexandria. That's what he had learned from his previous visits to Bahi. Would he find him doing well this time?

On that long-ago day, the father and his sons came back from battle carrying al-Qasim wrapped in a gallabiya. The mother screamed. Magd al-Din, eleven at the time, sat alone in a corner and cried. Al-Qasim was the kindest of his brothers. He was also the bravest, and his courage was well known in their village and in the neighboring villages.

The Talibs buried their son, the one betrayed by his wife, in the late afternoon, and that night the Khalils buried their son who had been killed . The village slept in silence and terror. The following day no one left home. On the third day people went out after a rumor had spread that the Khalils had accepted God's judgment, that their dandy son had caused the eldest Talib son to die of grief, and for this the Talibs had killed the eldest son of the Khalils. Everyone was even and no one owed anyone anything. By week's end, though, one of the Talib sons was found killed outside the village. All attempts by the mayor, the county, and the governorate to reconcile the two families failed. No one accused anyone of murder. Everyone knew how it would happen: an eye for an eye, until the two families were extinct. It was no longer surprising for people to know which family harbored the next victim; the game was precise, no matter how much time passed between one victim and the next. Whenever another was killed, the people of the village shunned Bahi even more. It was he who had caused the conflagration of this quiet village that knew of vendettas only from old tales about old times, which no one alive had witnessed. Bahi wished one of the Talibs would kill him, but they paid no attention to him. They humiliated him. They did not kill him because they did not deem him worth it, and he knew it. That was why he frequently left the village and stayed for days on end in Tanta or Kafr al-Zayyat. Abd al-Ghani's widow took to singing at the edges of the fields and walking along the irrigation canal outside the village. If she entered the village by mistake, the children chased her away with stones and chanted, "Bahiya loves Bahi." That was what they called her now; her real name was Wagida. Bahi often heard the children and wished that one morning they would find Wagida—or Bahiya, as they called her— dead. But that did not happen, just as the Talibs did not kill him. They had killed five of his brothers, just as his brothers had killed five of them. The children eventually grew tired of chanting whenever they saw Wagida, so she started coming into the village, and the women opened their doors to her and offered her food and drink and followed her in pity as she walked through the village singing sweetly. Britain had declared Egypt a protectorate, and people began to see troop trains pass by the village and told strange stories about them. The county and governorate police forces went into the villages to pick out the best men and send them to fight in faraway lands. People forgot Bahi's story, and the vendetta between the two families abated. People were now more interested in the stories about the "Authority" and what it was doing to the peasants and in stories about the finest young men, the flower of youth, who had disappeared in mysterious circumstances, as well as the heroes who had come back from the war and those who had not. They wondered how Britain could have defeated Germany, and resigned themselves to God's will, which had not granted Wilhelm II victory, so that the pestilence of British occupation was not lifted from Egypt. Gradually the stories of the war also began to fade from memory, as did Saad Zaghloul's revolution after the war. The village, however, remembered its martyrs in the revolution and the war before it, and her lost children. Among them was Bahi, who had disappeared during the war years and had not returned.

❖

The train was leaving another station as the conductor scrutinized the tickets of the well-dressed man and his children. Magd al-Din opened the Quran at random, and his gaze fell on the seventh sura, "The Heights."

Out of the blue, Zahra asked him, "Why did they do that to us, Sheikh Magd?"

There were many verses preceding the point at which he had opened the book, and he did not think to read the chapter from the beginning. His voice rose a little, heedless of those around him, *"Moses said to his people: 'Seek God's help and be patient, for the earth belongs to God to give as a heritage to such of His servants as He pleases, and the end will be in favor of those who fear him.'"*

"Almighty God has spoken the truth," he murmured to himself and closed his eyes and the Quran.

He began to recite from memory in no particular order, *"And as the unbelievers plotted against you to keep you in bonds or kill you or get you out. They plot and plan but the best of planners is God. Say: 'Nothing will befall us except what God has decreed for us. He is our Protector...' And in God let the believers put their trust... The likeness of this present life is as the rain, which We send down from the sky. By its mingling arises the produce of the earth, which provides food for humans and animals until the earth is clad in its golden ornaments and decked out, and the people to whom it belongs think they have all power over it, our command reaches it by night or by day and we make it like a harvest, clean-mown as if it had not flourished only the day before! Thus do We explain the signs in detail to those who reflect…For to anything which We have willed, We but say 'Be' and it is. To those who have left their homes in the cause of God, after suffering oppression, We will assuredly give a goodly home in this world. But truly the reward of the Hereafter will be greater if they only realized it. They are the ones who have persevered in patience and put their trust in their Lord…Do not say of anything: 'I am going to do that tomorrow,' without adding, 'God willing.'"*

His voice was rising gradually, until it almost filled the whole car. *"And call your Lord to mind if you forget,"* he continued. *"I hope my Lord will guide me closer to the right road…And if you punish, then punish with the like of that which was done to you. But if you endure patiently, that is indeed best for those who are patient. So give glory to God night and day and give praise to Him in heaven and earth all day long."*

The short man turned to his friend and whispered, "That man is reading, but the Quran in his hand is closed. He is reciting loudly and seems not to be paying attention to what he is reciting. He must be truly troubled."

"You will see a lot more than that if the war goes on for a long time."

The short man, surprised at his friend's comment, said nothing and thought instead of the reception Alexandria was going to give them at night.

King Farouk performed the Friday prayers at the Mosque of Mustafa Odeh Pasha in Fattuh Street in Gumruk—as the morning papers announced. The king was welcomed by the prime minister, Ali Mahir Pasha, Abd al-Rahman Azzam Pasha, His Eminence Sheikh Muhammad Mustafa al-Maraghi and, of course, the mayor of the city. After prayers the king returned to the Muntaza Palace, as happened after every prayer. The morning newspapers also announced that the number of newborn babies this week was 520 for natives and 25 for foreigners. As for deaths, there were 100 for natives and one for foreigners. Causes of death for Alexandrians were old age, scarlet fever, meningitis, malaria, and pulmonary tuberculosis for adults; and for children and infants they were dysentery, whooping cough, and tetanus. The only foreigner who had died was a Greek, killed by a drunken Cypriot.

This little murderous world is against the innocents:
it takes the bread out of their mouths and
gives their houses to the fire.

Paul Éluard

4

"It's hard arriving in a city at night," said the short man to his companion as they passed Magd al-Din on their way to the door of the car. Magd al-Din did not listen to the response of the companion; in fact, he did not respond. "Wake up, Zahra. We're in Alexandria," said Magd al-Din as he shook his wife's shoulder. She awoke, slightly disoriented. "God protect us," she said to herself. She felt her head and found her black head cover in place. She felt her chest and found the money under her clothes. She stared at Magd al-Din, and indeed it was Magd al-Din!

She stood on the platform carrying the baby. He watched the woman and her five children and the well-dressed man and his three sons. What made him do that? The woman and her children disappeared before his eyes, even though the station was not crowded, perhaps because the lights were dim. But that happened every time he visited Bahi; he would see the woman and her children on the train, but they would disappear on the platform. The well-dressed man and his sons did not disappear. He watched them as they left through the nearest door. He stood for a long time on the platform until almost all the passengers had disappeared.

"Porter?"

"Yes?"

The strong, tall, barefoot man carried one small basket on his left shoulder, placed the other one under his right arm, and told Magd al-Din to follow with the big basket. The porter's strides were long and fast, and Zahra almost stumbled more than once. Magd al-Din was at a loss; he could not ask the man to slow down. His eyes were fixed on the two bare feet of the porter, he did not know why. He remembered that he himself could have been barefoot after leaving his shoes on the tracks when he was hurrying to the station, had not Zahra brought another pair in the big basket.

"It's hard arriving in a city at night." The words echoed in his head. When he went out the station door and into its big courtyard, he was met by a vast, profound darkness. The lights in the square facing the station were all out, and the trees were very black. There was no light except for the red glow of the lanterns on the horse-drawn carriages, lit in violation of security regulations.

There were a few carriages in the courtyard, as well as mule carts and taxicabs. The porter put the two baskets on the ground with Magd al-Din's help. Magd al-Din gave him a piaster.

"The war has started, my man. This won't get me supper."

Magd al-Din did not understand what that meant. Had it started just this morning, as he had heard the passengers say, and arrived here by nightfall? Had it come that close? He thought for a while and the porter, despairing of getting anything more, left.

"Where to?" asked the old carriage driver who approached Magd al-Din.

"Ghayt al-Aynab."

"Five piasters."

"Fine."

The driver brought his carriage closer and helped Magd al-Din load his luggage. Magd al-Din and Zahra climbed into the carriage and sat down, Zahra still carrying the baby, praying that she would not wake up in the dark.

The driver cracked his whip in the air, the horse lunged forward, and the whole carriage was jolted. Zahra fell back, then suddenly forward, and the baby almost fell under her feet. She got hold of herself and breathed, feeling the refreshing breeze caress her face and cool her body. "It's a merciful climate," she said to herself as the cool breeze soothed her. Zahra slept again as the carriage moved on. Magd al-Din marveled at that, since she had slept most of the way on the train as well.

"Where in Ghayt al-Aynab?" asked the driver.

"Twelve Street, house number eighty-eight," Magd al-Din told him.

"I know the street, but you'll have to handle the number. You know how to read, of course?"

The driver took out of his vest pocket a small dark bottle the size of his palm. He opened it and raised it to his mouth and took a quick gulp. "Care for a sip of quinine tonic?"

Magd al-Din did not answer, and the driver did not press him. They focused on the road.

There were only a very few passers-by and very few carriages. One or two taxicabs passed them. A while earlier, the driver had turned onto Umar ibn al-Khattab street. Candles in small, yellow lanterns cast a dim light in the small stores along the way. Rarely did they see a store with electric lights. At al-Hadari urinal the carriage entered Isis Street. The stores there were few and far between and most of them were closed. When the driver turned onto Raghib Street, the stores were slightly better lit and there were more pedestrians, taxicabs, and carriages. There was a streetcar ahead in the distance, and the lamps on the lampposts were painted dark blue so the light barely reached the ground. The few electric lights in the stores showed many broken tiles on empty floors. It was not yet 11 p.m. Magd al-Din had noticed only one coffeehouse, at the end of Isis Street. There the few customers sat around the light of a single electric lamp pushed into the farthest corner of the café. He saw another café at the end of Raghib Street, directly in front of the bridge to the left, a small café in which only three people sat by candlelight. In front of the bridge, the driver stopped.

"Seems the electricity's been cut off," he remarked.

Only a few moments before, Magd al-Din had watched as a black tent covered everything. The streetlights and the few store lights went out, and a black mass enveloped everything.

"Electricity's off, and the bridge's been raised for the boats to cross. We've got to wait. I could've turned on Karmuz Bridge, but going along the Mahmudiya canal at night and in the dark is dangerous, for me, you, and the horse."

Zahra had awakened at the very time that Magd al-Din wished she would sleep.

"Where are we?" she said

"In Raghib."

"Raghib? Who is Raghib?"

"Hush, Zahra. Go back to sleep. The electricity is out and the bridge is raised for the boats. We have an hour to wait."

But Zahra did not sleep. She took out her breast and gave it to the baby, who had also awakened in the dark. Magd al-Din was thinking about the times that he had visited Bahi and how the electricity would be cut off in the night for reasons unknown to the people, and they would talk about it in the morning. There were stories about the police pursuing robbers who had attacked boats going through the Mahmudiya canal, or the arrest of some young men who belonged to political societies. People also knew that sexual harassment took place in the dark; in the dark, a woman would be groped by passers-by who suddenly were behind or next to her, even though she was walking by herself. Therefore, as soon as power was cut off, every woman or girl would try to find another so that they could encourage each other. True, the groping hands would not stop, but the two women would be bolder and shout insults at the man.

A number of men had gathered in front of the bridge, and three women sought safety together in the doorway of the candlelit café. Magd al-Din reached for Zahra to make sure she was there, even though he knew she was. Carriages gathered and drew nearer to each other. The taxicabs, their blue lights barely shining ahead of them, headed for the Karmuz bridge. The driver took out the quinine bottle again and said under his breath, "The boats coming in are chock full of weapons, cannons, and cars. There're soldiers with flashlights all around them. Seems like the war is coming here." To Magd al-Din, he said, "Why did you come to Alexandria today? Aren't you afraid of the war?"

Just then, the streetlights came on, so Magd al-Din did not answer. The bridge began to lower to its normal position on the canal.

As the carriage crossed the bridge, it nearly fell apart going over the potholes. To the right, immediately after the bridge, a strong smell of flour came from a high-walled mill. Its wire-screened windows were covered with fine white flour, making them stand out in the dark. Before the end of the streetcar's winding tracks at the end of the street, and in front of the police station that occupied a commanding position in the square, the driver turned right onto Ban Street, which people called Twelve Street, because it was twelve meters wide. It was the widest and longest street in the area. Zahra saw several dimly lit streetcars sitting in the square and cried out, "What's that? A train?"

"It's a streetcar, Zahra. A streetcar," Magd al-Din calmly replied.

The driver laughed and asked if it was their first visit to Alexandria. Magd al-Din said yes and fell silent. Once again there was the smell of flour, this time from another mill to the left of the carriage on Ban Street, where the carriage was proceeding with great difficulty, greater even than on the bridge. The street was not paved, only covered with little white stones. A few moments later, Magd al-Din asked the driver to stop. The house was to the right, there was no mistaking it, a small two-story house stuck between two three-story buildings.

❖

"You're lucky you found me. I just got back from the café," Bahi said, as he made tea for them on a small spirit stove in a corner of the small room.

Magd al-Din, who was stretched out on a mat on the floor, leaning his head to the wall, asked, "What were you doing at the café so late?"

"Nothing, Sheikh Magd—just chatting and drinking tea."

He laughed as he poured tea in the little glasses. Zahra was squatting with her back to them in another corner of the room, nursing her baby, who had not had her fill in the carriage. How were they all going to sleep in one room? she thought, holding back her tears as she remembered their big house in the village. The baby opened her amber eyes and looked at her mother without letting go of the nipple, then she burst out crying. Did the pain the mother felt flow into her? Probably. Zahra's feelings, however, soon changed to surprise at how clean and neat Bahi's room was and at the fragrance of musk that permeated it. She was also surprised at Bahi himself, who wore pants and a shirt like city folk, and white shoes. This is a different man from the one she had seen ten years earlier, she thought. Did Alexandria do this to everyone?

"Why don't you tell me the real reason you left the village?" Bahi asked. "I didn't know you hated the village, or loved Alexandria."

"I told you I've been wanting to leave for a long time."

"And your land?"

"My sisters and their husbands will take care of it."

"Then you might as well kiss it good-bye."

Hearing faint moans coming from Zahra's direction, Bahi asked her, "What's the matter, Zahra? Why are you crying?"

Magd al-Din had no choice but to tell him the whole story. They all fell silent. Bahi's silence was the most profound. Had he been such a curse on his family? To this day? What did fate want from him? He had suffered more than enough all these years. Should he have killed himself early on? And all because he was born attractive to women? He had let himself walk anywhere, at any time, but none of the Talibs had killed him. He went through all the horrors of the last war, but fate had not given him a chance to die. He had left his village and wandered through the markets of neighboring villages. A woman selling ghee and butter from Shubra al-Namla picked him up. His reputation had preceded him to all the villages, and he still had those killer eyes that radiated allure. The ghee vendor picked him up while Bahiya was still stalking him, following him to the other villages. In these villages, too, the children no longer chased her—they had gotten tired of it. Bahiya followed him like his shadow. At night she disappeared in the fields, and he hid from her, thinking that she would never find him. In the morning, he would discover she was following him again.

"Don't follow me in the streets, Bahiya."

She would smile and run her hands over his chest with a distant look in her eyes. He would see her tears and turn his back on her, almost in tears himself. More than once he thought of grabbing her and standing with her in front of the train. But he could never bring himself to do that; he was too weak to commit suicide. He could see the lines of old age beginning to appear prematurely on her face, and a few thin hairs on her chin. When the ghee vendor picked him up, he let himself go, unafraid of anything. The fiendish thought that he might become the cause of another woman's madness even occurred to him; he wished he would become the cause of all women's madness, in all the villages. If only all the women all over the countryside would follow him, thoroughly besotted! It was as if Bahiya knew. She disappeared suddenly. The ghee vendor brazenly invited him to her house, and he went with her without fear, hoping to become the cause of her madness. He watched her introduce him to her father as a big merchant from Tanta who wanted to buy all their butter and ghee, all year long. He saw in her mother's eyes slyness and greed and doubts about his story. He thought of turning her into a madwoman too. They prepared a room for him to sleep in, and he asked them to collect all the ghee, butter, and eggs from the village. He learned from the beautiful, rather buxom woman that she was a widow, whose husband had been run over by a car in Tanta. She came to his room every evening. He had no doubt that her parents knew. He realized what was being planned for him. But he was not made for marriage and family life. On the dawn of the seventh day he sneaked out. The whole village, with its black houses, was enveloped in fog. It was a sight he would not forget: black houses made gray by the white vapor that stretched to the edge of the universe. Could hell be any different from what he was seeing? The houses appeared to him like mythical beasts writhing in torment, in utter blindness. When his feet hit the railroad tracks, he headed for Tanta, not to his village. When he came to an underpass, he sat down to drink tea from a shack that served it. He wanted to wait until the fog lifted so he could see things more clearly.

When it did lift, he saw in front of him a group of border guards on camelback dragging a group of peasants bound with a long rope. He had no chance to escape. One of the guards got down from his camel, grabbed his arm, and calmly bound him with the others. He did not object, question, or scream. They marched him with the others to the governorate headquarters in Tanta and from there to the army camps in Cairo. The 'Authority' had kidnapped him to serve and fight, against his will, as corvée in the armies of England, which had declared Egypt a protectorate.

*. . . feeling through the hot pavements the rhythms of
Alexandria transmitted upwards into bodies which could
only interpret them as famished kisses, or endearments
uttered in voices hoarse with wonder.*

Lawrence Durrell

5

It seemed that everything was ready to accommodate Magd al-Din
and Zahra. At night Bahi told them that the landlord, Khawaga
Dimitri, was a good man who lived on the second floor in two
rooms, next to which was a separate room that he could rent to
them. They found out from him that a woman by the name of Lula
lived with her husband in the room across the hall from his own.
Bahi told them also that he would let them sleep in his room that
night and that he would go out and sleep in the entryway of the
house, where it was cooler and where he would be more likely to
wake up early. Magd al-Din had to agree with him, even though he
was surprised at his brother's talk of getting up early. Then he told
him to wake him up early too, so he could go out to look for work.

They spent most of the night talking about the neighborhood
and its inhabitants. Nothing said that night stuck in Magd al-Din's
mind, for he knew it already. Zahra, though, was surprised to hear
about the tensions between Christians and Muslims and how they
had subsided now, and that the real tensions now were between
northern and southern Egyptians. Bahi said that the northerners
from Rosetta and Damietta and elsewhere were always peaceable,
but that the southerners from the Jafar and Juhayna clans stopped
them in the street and insulted them. There was always a conflict
between the two southern clans, but they united in their

opposition to the northerners. He said he was working for a day when he would lead the northerners to rout the southerners, and that day was going to be very soon.

Zahra found herself breaking in, "What do you do in Alexandria, Bahi?"

He looked at her for a moment and smiled. "Ask Sheikh Magd."He left them, took a blanket and a pillow, and went out to sleep in the entryway. Zahra was amazed that she slept without a single dream. She placed her head on the pillow in Bahi's bed and took her baby in her arms and slept. She did not even notice that Magd al-Din was stretched out on the floor next to the narrow bed. He had told her to sleep on the bed. As a peasant wife, she should have refused and let him take the bed, but she found herself, without thinking about it, getting into the bed and going to sleep, as if another woman was doing it. In the morning she sat, ashamed, in front of him and kept herself busy making tea for him and Bahi.

Magd al-Din went out without delay to look for work, and Bahi left after him, no one knew where. As he was having tea with Magd al-Din and Zahra, he told them, "Khawaga Dimitri passed by early, and I told him how you want to rent the room next to his apartment, and he agreed. He even went upstairs and told his wife to expect Zahra today. You can go up in an hour or so, Zahra."

Around ten o'clock, Zahra found herself alone in Bahi's room, so she decided to go upstairs. As she stepped out of the room, she saw before her a beautiful, blonde woman wearing a see-through nightgown with bare shoulders and arms. She was washing up at the tap in the hallway. She was startled, and Zahra said awkwardly, "Good morning."

"Bahi's sister?" asked the woman as she turned from the tap.

"Sister-in-law."

The woman looked her up and down. "Where's his brother?"

"He went out to look for work, and Bahi went out with him."

Zahra gathered her courage and looked the woman up and down, then went upstairs.

❖

Zahra sat in silence between Sitt Maryam and her two beautiful daughters, Camilla and Yvonne. Sitt Maryam was about forty years old. She had a white, round face and short chestnut-colored hair that she left untied and uncovered. Her daughters also wore their hair untied but long, hanging down their backs. The girls had their mother's chestnut hair and amber eyes and round face, though a little narrower at the chin. Camilla had two attractive dimples in her cheeks that were quite pleasing to look at.

Zahra was wearing the same long black peasant dress that she had worn the day before, a dress with a wide square neck that made it easier for her to nurse her baby. On her head she had a black shawl that hung down both sides of her chest to cover whatever might be revealed by the loose-fitting bodice of her dress. Under the shawl was a tight head wrap that covered all her black hair. Camilla and Yvonne kept looking closely at Zahra, as though she were from a different planet. It was Zahra's silence that surprised them, as well as her neatly trimmed eyebrows and her dark, almond-shaped eyes. Zahra was silently studying the icons hanging on the opposite wall. She knew them well. She had seen them many times in the home of Ata, the village grocer, whose wife, Firyal, was a seamstress. Zahra noticed that Sitt Maryam had a pedal-operated sewing machine in a corner of the room. Firyal's sewing machine was small and hand-operated, and Firyal had it on a low table and worked on it all night long.

Sitt Maryam's room was smaller than Firyal's house, but it wasn't made of mud. Besides, it was painted sky blue, so it seemed sunny, and the window opening onto the street bathed it in light, as did the door open to the hall. Zahra could see another door inside the room and figured that it led to another room for storage. Zahra sat on a sofa next to Sitt Maryam. Camilla and Yvonne sat on another sofa. The two sofas were covered with two clean kilims with geometric patterns of red, green, and blue circles and lines. On the floor was a kilim without any patterns. In the ceiling there was a small, idle fan next to which wires extended to a lamp below the fan. The fan most likely was never turned on, as it would have cut the lamp wire. The ceiling was made with wooden boards resting on strong beams and painted white. On the wall was an old photograph of Sitt Maryam at twenty, in a wedding gown, standing next to Dimitri. In the picture Dimitri looked slightly balding with black hair. She wondered what he looked like now. Zahra had not seen him yet. Under the photograph was a small wall clock, and under the clock was a glass china cabinet with closed drawers in its bottom half. On top of the cabinet was a wooden, broad-based semicircular Telefunken radio with two big buttons near the base. In the corner, next to the sewing machine, was a small, old table on top of which were several pieces of new fabric and unfinished new clothes.

The clothes and fabrics in Sitt Maryam's house were more than she had seen in Firyal's house in the village. People here like to dress up, she said to herself. This is the real Virgin Mary, and this is her son, Our Lord Jesus Christ, may peace be upon him. The face of the Virgin Mary is pleasant, snow-white, and full, and her chin is curved a little like Yvonne and Camilla's faces. Jesus' face is happy, but his face in the other icon, once he became a prophet, seems sad, in spite of the halo around his head. Did Bahi really have a halo of light? Yes, it went with him everywhere, but Bahi's face is not like the face of the Messiah. Lord have mercy, it actually looks a little like him! I ask your forgiveness, Lord Almighty!

The day before, Bahi had told them that Bahiya was also in Alexandria. She had appeared a year earlier. He had noticed her come into the café, look at him, and then go out and stand on the opposite sidewalk to watch him. He did not realize it was Bahiya until she had left in the evening. He froze in place. She still came during the day to observe him from a distance, then disappeared at night.

He said that one night he was taking a walk along the bank of the Mahmudiya canal when he heard a voice calling his name. He thought it was the mythical seductress, the siren of the village, but he could never forget her voice. After he had overcome his surprise he moved closer to the bank and found her standing in front of a hut made of old tin cans, holding a small kerosene lamp that she sheltered from the wind with her other hand. She made way for him at the door, and he entered the hut fearfully: a very harsh life. She slept on sackcloth and had a lot of bread, mostly spoiled, that people had given her. She had apples and bananas. She gave him an apple and sat watching him in silence. He took the apple home with him, debating whether to eat it or toss it away. He placed it near him in his bed and slept. It stayed on the bed until it became rotten, so he threw it out the window. He fell silent for a long time, then said to Magd al-Din "If I die, bury me in the village."

❖

"How old are you, Zahra?" Sitt Maryam asked.

"Twenty," replied Zahra.

Camilla, Yvonne, and their mother all asked at once, "Is this the first time you've seen Alexandria?"

"Yes."

"And your husband, why didn't he rest today after the trip?" was Sitt Maryam's next question.

"He's like that. He doesn't like to be lazy."

"God be with him. Nobody finds a job easily these days."

"God will provide."

Zahra paid 160 piasters, two months rent, for the room. She went in and found it to be a big room, but its window opened onto an air shaft rather than the street. "That's fine," she told herself. She felt close to this lady and her daughters. Sitt Maryam asked her if she had more money to furnish the room and she said yes. So Sitt Maryam asked her if she would like to do it that day. Zahra thought a little then said to herself, "Why not? It wouldn't be bad if Magd al-Din came back and saw the new room with furniture." She agreed, and Sitt Maryam got up and went into the inner room to put on her street clothes. Zahra, casting a quick glance at the inner room, saw a brass bed with high posts surrounded by a white mosquito net, exactly like her bed in the village, except that the posts of her bed had been discolored in spots. She would buy another one like it today.

Sitt Maryam closed the door quickly. The two girls were once again staring at Zahra. This time she felt embarrassed, so she lowered her head and stared down at the plain kilim on the floor, looking for lines and colors that she did not see. Camilla got up quickly and opened the little cabinet under the radio and took out a magazine, then sat next to Zahra and opened it to a particular page and asked Zahra, "Do you know Asmahan?"

"Yes."

"Do you like her voice?"

"When I hear it."

The girls burst out laughing. Camilla offered the magazine to Zahra. "This is her picture."

Zahra looked at Asmahan's splendid face, which she had never seen before. As she studied her beautiful eyes and the beauty mark on her face, she wondered, "Is she really that beautiful?"

Camilla had more questions. "Do you have a radio in the village?"

"We have three—one in the mayor's house, one in the coffeehouse, and one in our house."

A look of pain appeared on her face and everyone was quiet. Zahra wiped a tear before it formed in her eye. Camilla turned another page in the magazine to show a bright-faced woman, with brown lipstick on her full lips, wearing a tight dress that showed her curves in reckless playfulness. "This is Esther Williams," she said. "Do you have a cinema in the village?"

Sitt Maryam came out just then, laughing and saying to Zahra, who had begun to feel overwhelmed, "Camilla's mischievous, Zahra."

Zahra did not comment. Her attention was drawn to the black dress that did not reach Sitt Maryam's feet and the semi-transparent veil with the gold pin that draped across her nose. Zahra laid Shawqiya down on the sofa and said, "This is the first time I've ever left Shawqiya."

"We'll be back soon, before lunch. Camilla will look after her. Would you like to have lunch with us, or don't you like the food of the Copts?"

Zahra felt slightly at a loss. It surprised her that she had never eaten or drunk anything at the house of Firyal, the village seamstress. She had heard, as a young girl, women talking about the bad smell of Coptic food. "You are good. Your food must also be good," she murmured.

Sitt Maryam took her gently by the hand, and they went out.

❖

Sitt Maryam walked confidently along the sidewalk, but Zahra could not take her eyes off the unpaved ground. That was why she was two or three steps behind. It was hard to walk on the street covered with little white stones; the sidewalk, also unpaved, was higher than the street and lined with rectangular basalt blocks that were covered with sand and small stones in preparation for tiles to be installed. "Watch out, there's hole for a drain," or "There's a water main," Sitt Maryam said from time to time. Zahra would stop for a moment and cautiously step around what Sitt Maryam warned her about.

"This is the streetcar. Have you seen it, Zahra?"

"Last night."

"Let's get on it. Remember the number—it's eight. It goes to Abu Warda."

On the streetcar Sitt Maryam led her to the women's compartment. "Who's Abu Warda?" asked Zahra.

Sitt Maryam smiled. "It's a street in Bahari."

Zahra noticed that there were three women who had gotten on the streetcar before them who sat silently, their faces veiled.

"We'll get off at Attarin," Sitt Maryam told her. "This streetcar goes around in a circle, from here to Attarin, then Abd al-Munim Street, then Istanbul Street, and Safiya Zaghloul and the Chamber of Commerce, then Manshiya and Bahari from Tatwig street, and comes all the way back with the same ticket—something of a joy ride."

Zahra did not say anything. She could not understand how anyone could spend all that time on the streetcar. It seemed to her that women here had no work to do. She smiled. The streetcar moved and she was taken aback for a moment, her heart beating fast. How could she have left the house without her husband's permission? How could she have left her baby daughter with people she had just met for the first time? Was it enough that Bahi said they were good people? And since when did Bahi say anything useful? But she could not go back. The vast white space captivated her eyes, and she gave in to it. Where was this city taking her?

She let herself study the two- and three-story homes, with their narrow doors opening onto silent courtyards. The old facades had balconies on which a few items of wash hung haphazardly to dry. A few stores had opened their doors. She noticed that Sitt Maryam paid the conductor a half-piaster coin and took back a millieme and two tickets. Sitt Maryam saw her looking at the broad window of a store where the streetcar had stopped, a window displaying pots and pans and beautiful china and glassware. She told her these were Ahmad Ibrahim's stores, the most popular stores in Karmuz and Raghib, and that they could buy whatever Zahra needed on their way back from getting the furniture.

Zahra found herself adjusting to the slow flow of movement around her in the street, and to passengers getting on and off the streetcar. Suddenly, though, she was overcome by a strange smell, and they were in the middle of a street crowded with butcher shops, with carts piled high with cow, water buffalo, and sheep feet and heads and organs, lined with stores displaying small slaughtered sheep with clear red stamps, and filled with a crowd of women wearing black body wraps.

"Let's get off here. This is Bab Umar Pasha. We'll cross Khedive Street and go into Attarin."

They got off. Zahra's eyes could not settle on any one thing for long. A refreshing breeze in Khedive Street began to soothe her. She noticed that the first floors of the houses were predominantly dull. The stores in Attarin were now all open and showed long, deep interiors that looked like manufacturing shops. Zahra looked up several times at the balconies.

The houses here were huge, taller than any she had seen so far. The doors were wide and the spaces inside enormous, filled with cardboard boxes and other things she did not recognize. The balconies were beautiful, resting on supports shaped like animals—little lions, tigers, and rams. The balconies had railings of shiny, black and green wrought iron. A few women stood on the balconies hanging out laundry, while a few others sat in the sun. Many of them were old, with loose gray or henna-colored hair and flabby white arms that could be seen, bare, through the railings. Zahra smelled the water sprayed on the ground in front of the stores. In more than one small alley she saw small cafés in which one or two patrons sat smoking narghiles or reading the papers.

All at once, groups of beautiful young women appeared, laughing. They wore colorful tight pants and tight tops, and their faces were made up and their hair done à la garçon. Zahra was astonished that women would cut their hair in this boyish style. Sitt Maryam noticed Zahra's reaction and said, "Don't worry about it."

From inside one of the stores, Zahra heard someone comment, "Well, well, well! When are we going to become English?" Then she heard the young women laughing boisterously. One of them shot back, "When hell freezes over, buster! Not even if you became French!"

Zahra smelled the strong odor of tobacco smoke and saw in front of her a store with a red facade and big black lettering, with a scale on the counter, behind which a man sat smoking a narghile. On the shelves were small boxes and many cigarette packs. She saw several of these stores with red facades, apparently characteristic of tobacco shops. Sitt Maryam pointed to a street from which came a strong smell of ghee, coconut, and sugar.

"This is the piazza of the Syrians. They are all pastry makers," she said. "This is al-Laythi Street, the most famous street for antiques in Alexandria. Here they sell French objets d'art, Belgian chandeliers, Swiss watches, Italian chairs, and expensive things from all over the world." Zahra was reminded of the strong, European-looking face of the man that she had seen smoking the narghile in the tobacco shop.

A woman in a white nightgown came rushing out of a side alley, holding a man by the scruff of his neck. After giving him a smack on the back of his neck, she pushed him into the street, then stood for a moment looking around. She was barefoot, her hair disheveled, with sparks flying from her tired eyes. Then she went back into the little alley, and three scantily clad women, who had stood by the entrance and watched as she kicked the man out, followed her inside. A young coffeehouse boy carrying a tray with a coffee cup, a small coffee pot, and a glass of water almost ran into the man who had just been beaten. But he skillfully stepped aside, laughing, "In this place, it's sweet to be smacked on the back of the head." The man staggered toward Zahra, who was scared and hid behind Sitt Maryam. Sitt Maryam quickly bent down, took off her slipper, and waved it in the face of the man, who stepped back, giving her a military-style salute as the vendors in their stores laughed.

Sitt Maryam and Zahra went on through al-Laythi Street, where the antiques caught her eye, as did the men and women who moved slowly and gracefully among the wares, looking at and examining them. There was a strong smell of wood varnishes, paint, and alcohol.

"We've made it to the Arab street. You'll find all kinds of furniture here."

Zahra noticed that one alley was filled entirely with shoes of every style and color, on high tables and low tables and on the sidewalks. She saw another long alley filled with displays of used clothing, and shirts, jackets, and overcoats hung in the store entrances, giving off a faint smell. Then they entered a short street, neither wide nor narrow. In front of the shop doors were living-room sets and all kinds of chairs—wooden, upholstered, bamboo. Little boys were dusting them with feather dusters.

"Good morning, Blessed William."

"Good morning, Sitt Maryam."

He knows her by name, Zahra thought to herself. She realized that here she could sit down for a little while. She needed that, after having nearly screamed to leave the whole neighborhood.

Blessed William was about fifty, short with a strong build, wearing a clean gallabiya and a fez on his head.

"It's been a while," he said, offering two chairs to Sitt Maryam and Zahra, who sat down at once. The the smell of the concrete floor recently doused with water reached her nostrils, and the smell of frankincense burning deep inside the dark store soothed her nerves. A little boy appeared and the man said to him, "Quick, get a pitcher of carob drink."

Blessed William went to different points on the wall and lit up the big, long store, revealing shiny armoires, beds, tables, chairs, and other pieces of furniture.

"How are things, Blessed William?" Sitt Maryam asked.

"Things are bad. The war has broken out, and everything is going sky high."

"The war broke out only yesterday, Blessed William."

"We've been living in fear for the last few months. The

drunken English have chased the customers away. I swear by God, I considered selling the store to a Moroccan or a Greek. Only last night, some hoodlums caught three drunken Englishmen and beat them and stole their money. A police force from Kom al-Dikka came and dragged everyone to the governorate headquarters and beat them on the back of the neck until they almost went blind." He laughed and added, "I was there—I went to the governorate because they'd arrested one of my workers. There was this Indian soldier there who really upset me—he stood there saying 'Again, again,' as the the secret police were beating the men. Can you imagine that? An Indian! I wanted to tell him that Gandhi was starving himself to death so that people like him would become real human beings, not lackeys to the English."

"And then?"

"They let the people go, of course. The hoodlums were long gone."

"Everyone's turn will come," remarked Zahra.

Blessed William took a long look at her and said, "You are good-hearted."

An old woman with heavy make-up and bright yellow dyed hair passed in front of the store. She was carrying a cheap red leather handbag and wearing a short skirt and a pair of sheer red stockings, through which the green veins of her legs showed. Zahra recoiled and Blessed William said, "One day the land will be cleansed."

Sitt Maryam could not tell Zahra that in that neighborhood, at the end of the street where they had walked and in the narrow alleys, many women were prostitutes. Zahra must have figured that out for herself, but she had begun to feel a little pain in her breasts, and drops of milk were leaking from her nipples and staining her gallabiya. She had to buy what she needed quickly so that she could hurry back to her baby daughter.

"On our way back we'll buy the fabric and cotton for the mattress and pillows," Sitt Maryam told her. "Tomorrow you'll have the furniture of a bride, God bless it."

But Zahra, desperate for anything that would give her happiness, still felt ill at ease and afraid of the city.

"I want a sane man to consult about a problem."
"The only sane man in our city is this madman."

Jalal al-Din Rumi

6

Did Alexander know that he was building not just a city to immortalize his name, but a whole world and a whole history? Probably: he was concerned not just with immortality, but with changing the world.

The distance from Pharos Island, now Anfushi, to Rhakotis, now Karmuz, took one hour on foot. It must have taken the same amount of time in the old days, because there were no buildings to walk around. The land was flat and sandy. Therefore when Alexander stopped his horse in Rhakotis, he was able to see the farthest spot in the sea, Pharos, and he decided to connect the two points—but he died before that was done. It was Ptolemy I and his successor, Ptolemy II, who actually finished building the city. Alexander had laid the city's foundation stone and delegated the task of planning to Dinocrates, a skilled architect. He planned it like a chessboard, with streets running straight from north to south intersected by straight east-west streets. Why did he plan it like a chessboard? Did he intend for it to be a stage for playing and dying? Its inhabitants, under Augustus, after the death of Antony and Cleopatra, numbered three hundred thousand free citizens and an equal number of slaves. But Alexandrians were fond of cockfights and writing verses that made fun of the rulers. That was why, when Napoleon Bonaparte conquered it, its inhabitants numbered only eight thousand.

Since then, Alexandria has raced against time, expanding and becoming crowded with strangers from everywhere. It became a real port. Palaces were erected in the space between Ras al-Tin and Abu al-Abbas. Muhammad Ali dug the Mahmudiya canal. The Jewish architect Manshi drew up the plan to develop Alexandria, a process that continued under the reign of Muhammad Ali's sons, Ibrahim, Said, and Ismail. As the number of foreigners increased, they went east to the vacant land in Raml.

They bought the land and built palaces and magnificent mansions. On the small lakes to the south and east of the city, villages sprang up in Raml, Siyuf, Mandara, and Hadra. Eventually they eroded, becoming urban neighborhoods crowded with the poor who arrived from north and south.

The city kept expanding; the foreign strangers occupied the north, and the poor occupied the south. When the Raml streetcar line was established, development continued to the east and north. The railroad between Raml and Cairo became an easy route for the lost and the fortune seekers from the Delta and Upper Egypt.

Among the foreigners were hundreds and thousands of adventurers, who came to the cosmopolitan city and made it a virtual tower of Babel. Among the Egyptians were thousands of castaways, like Magd al-Din, who preceded and would follow him.

The north of the city was no longer enough for the foreigners, so the poorest of them—Greeks, Jews, Italians, and Cypriots—moved to some of the poorer neighborhoods, such as Attarin and Labban. They moved closer to and mixed with the Egyptians, who lived in the south of the city. Magd al-Din had arrived in an Alexandria that was on top of the world. In addition to the European residents, there were soldiers from Europe and all the Commonwealth—and he, the expelled peasant.

Magd al-Din was still going out every day to look for work in a world that was boiling on top of a volcano. Two days after the German invasion of Poland, Britain declared war on Germany, and a war cabinet was formed. Churchill became first lord of the admiralty. France also declared war on Germany. Young King Farouk, not yet twenty, was still moving between the Ras al-Tin and Muntaza palaces. The ministers were still in their summer headquarters in Bulkely. A reader of the newspaper al-Ahram sent an appeal to the king and the ministers to go to Cairo, because state officials, from undersecretaries to the lowliest employees in government departments, could not make any decisions. As a result, business had come to a standstill at "a difficult time," as he put it.

In Alexandria, the German ambassador presented the prime minister, Ali Mahir Pasha, with a letter declaring that Germany wished Egypt well. A state of emergency was declared throughout Egypt. Police and security forces were deployed all over Alexandria, perhaps also because Queen Farida celebrated her birthday on 5 September at the Ras al-Tin palace, at which high-ranking statesmen converged. Leaflets and posters in French and Arabic declaring a state of emergency were distributed everywhere. News came of continued tensions and skirmishes between Arabs and Jews in Palestine, after the police were able to arrest a thousand of the twelve hundred Jews who had arrived secretly on the coast by ship. The prime minister of Egypt announced that Italy's neutrality kept the danger away from Egypt, whereupon the Italian minister plenipotentiary affirmed his government's friendship with Egypt and its people. People were divided: some supported Egypt's entering the war on the side of England, and others opposed that; some supported England and its ally, France; and others supported Germany and its sly fox, Hitler. The Egyptian government declared that Egypt would fulfill its obligations to England under the 1936 treaty, but that its army would not take part in the war. That did not prevent the king from issuing a royal decree to form the new Territorial Army, commanded by Abd al-Rahman Bey Azzam, minister of religious endowments. That army was charged with safeguarding public establishments in peacetime and in war, supplying the regular army with provisions and equipment in war, and joining it in battle if the need arose. The decree establishing that army, the commander in chief of which was the king, stipulated that it would be composed of those who had reached conscription age but had not been accepted because of a physical defect or illness. That an army of invalids had been established—and that it was run by a ministry whose purview was charity—mystified the people. And even though people were certain that Egypt would stay out of the war, talk of inflation began, and prices on the stock exchange declined. An era of prosperous trade with British army camps began.

Life went on as usual; the king and the ministers soon went back to Cairo. In Alexandria, the Muwasa hospital lottery was as popular as ever. People crowded in front of Cinema Cosmo to watch Charles Laughton and Maureen O'Hara in The Hunchback of Notre Dame. Orphanages were placed under the supervision of the ministry of social affairs, in agreement with the Alexandria city council. Biba Izz al-Din announced that she would be back at the Diana Theater in Alexandria performing the following summer. Al-Shatbi Casino hosted a group of Lebanese young ladies who performed the dabke dance at the annual party of the Maronite Charitable Society.

The east harbor filled with military and merchant marine ships. Camps were set up along the beach in Mustafa Kamil and Sidi Bishr, and late afternoons saw a promenade of horse-drawn carriages carrying soldiers and Alexandrian prostitutes—native as well as Greek, Jewish, Armenian—on the corniche. The soldiers of the Empire did not go far into the city; the women came to them. There were taverns everywhere, big and small, rich ones on the corniche and poor in the alleys of Bahari and Manshiya. They were filled with Australian, New Zealander, and Indian soldiers, who mixed with ship captains, sailors, stokers, and pimps who knew the dark, decaying, narrow ways to the crumbling houses with dislodged tiles and wooden roofs where rats lived. In the entrances of those houses, old, red-haired women sat smoking narghiles. They permitted the customers to enter after they had inspected the young Jewish, Armenian, and native girls, whose white flesh gleamed through their short, flimsy nightgowns. The scene, with variations, could be observed in many quarters: in the houses of Bahari, open to the harbor, or in those behind Tatwig Street, or in the houses of Attarin, hidden behind the stores and shops, or in the houses of Farahda and Bab al-Karasta or Kom al-Nadur—the hill built at one time by Cafirelli, Napoleon's engineer, as a strong point in the city's defenses.

Every morning, very early, Magd al-Din would see more than one streetcar stopping at Sidi Karim Square. People would get on the

streetcars and sit in silence, looking out the windows fogged with
the dawn's dew. Every morning, Magd al-Din could not help
turning and looking at the police station at the end of the square
and reading the sign over it: "Ghayt al-Aynab Police Precinct."
Why could he not stop doing that? He did not know.

Many did not take the streetcar, but walked up the little slope
and across the bridge. A number of them stopped at the flour mill
there, as some had stopped earlier in front of the flour mill on Ban
street. Others continued on their way, a path now familiar to
Magd al-Din, splitting along the banks of Mahmudiya Canal.
From the south they went east to the Muharram Bey textile mill.
From the north they went east and west to the ice or oil plants or
the Ahliya textile mill in Karmuz. Later, Magd al-Din would often
go west, and would work at the oil, soap, or fodder plants, or at
the warehouses. He would even make it all the way to Mina al-
Basal to work in the cotton ginneries. All of that would be later on.
For now he knew nothing about the establishments in Kafr Ashri
and Mina al-Basal. For now he was stuck between Raghib and
Karmuz.

He did not like to stop at the two flour mills. What could he, a
peasant, do in a flour mill? And what could he do anywhere? It must
be that he just wanted to work somewhere away from home. He still
insisted on going out wearing a new, clean gallabiya and the black
patent-leather shoes that he always saved for special trips.

On the Mahmudiya canal he saw ships sailing slowly into the
harbor or going back south. Several tugboats stopped in the
distance, especially in front of the companies. Anchored on the
shore close to the bridge there was always a ferry, which ran back
and forth when the bridge was raised for ships to go through. He
rarely saw women in the early morning. Every morning he would
be certain that he would meet someone he knew, but he never did.
The truth was he wished for something like that to happen; he
needed someone to take him by the hand in the city.

Bahi was no longer good for anything—he spent all day at the
café. How he lived and where he got the money, Magd al-Din did
not know. Bahi said that in Ghayt al-Aynab there were more than
a hundred men from their village, and he knew each and every one.
He knew why they had left the village for Alexandria and what

scandals they had been involved in before they left, and he had imposed a five-piaster monthly tax on each of them, thus making five pounds per month. Two months earlier they had rebelled against him. They went to the police precinct and complained to the prefect, who looked at Bahi and could not believe that a hundred people feared the man standing before him. The prefect kicked them out. Once outside, Bahi raised the tax to ten piasters a month. Now they were his fighting force, and he wanted to lead them in battle against the southerners. Magd al-Din remembered but did not believe Bahi's words.

He kept listening for someone who knew him to call out his name, but that did not happen. One morning followed another, and the search for work never stopped. Every day he saw men with bare feet and bare heads walking or hurrying along with him to look for work. He noticed that one young man in particular, who looked lost and whose eyes rolled in a way that Magd al-Din had never seen before, had tried deliberately to stay close to him. When the young man spoke, saying "Every day it's like this," Magd al-Din realized that he had a nasal twang. He always looked angry when he did not get work, but would soon smile and hurry along with the others, following close to Magd al-Din who, for a moment, thought the reason he was not picked for work was because that half-idiot stood next to him. But he knew that these were the blessed children of God, so he asked Him for forgiveness. He was turning left now because most of the men seeking work were turning left after crossing the bridge. He stopped with the others in front of one plant's big metal gate.

"What kind of work do they do here?"

"Ice."

"What do we do with the ice?"

"We stack it or carry it to the delivery carts. This plant will close next month—it doesn't work in the winter."

A worker at the plant went out and looked at the crowd of job seekers. He picked a few among them, but not Magd al-Din, who noticed that most of those seeking temporary work wore tattered clothes and were barefoot, and so deduced that work was in very short supply. He decided he would not change his new gallabiya or shiny shoes; he was never going to appear shabby, and when he found work he would buy suitable new clothes. Zahra had already taken thirty pounds that he had saved over the last few years and spent twenty pounds to buy all the necessary furniture. Magd al-Din felt sad every time the job seekers jostled each other rudely and cruelly when a company representative would ask for five or less. He would choose a spot in the back of the crowd. In front of the Ahliya textile mill with the big green metal gate, he stood with the others. The black man who came out every day to pick the workers pointed to him and said in a confident voice, "You there—come here."

Magd al-Din approached.

"Tomorrow I will give you a job," the man said with a smile. "You have to come in pants and a jacket."

He got a job at the mill rolling the bales of cotton from the cars that carried them from the ginneries up close to the spinning machines. The job lasted three days, then he went back to job hunting with the others. Their rounds would begin at six o'clock and end at eight. By that time they would have passed all the companies on the north bank of Mahmudiya Canal, the oil, soap, ice, and textile companies. They would have demonstrated their strength for the tugs and ships anchored at close intervals, which came from Upper Egypt to unload their cargo of sugarcane, fava beans, cotton, grains, and earthenware jars and pitchers. Usually a contractor with his own crew of workers would get the job to unload the ships, and if Magd al-Din or any of his colleagues was hired, he would receive ten piasters for the day's work.

At eight o'clock in the morning, just getting over his disappointment at not finding work, he would sit down in the café next to the bridge and order a glass of tea. Moments later he would feel heartened and get up to buy al-Ahram from the little boy who sold newspapers from a small wooden stand in front of the café. He was always the only one in the café, but he would hear a voice calling out his name and imagine meeting someone he knew. One day he got the newspaper and gave the little boy a whole pound. The boy said he did not have any change. Magd al-Din did not know what to do and returned the newspaper, but the boy, who recognized him by now, told him he could read the paper in the café and return it when he was done. Magd al-Din sat down to read and realized that the world was a great big mess: sandbags distributed by the civil defense department to hospitals and public establishments; advertisements for Longines, Zenith, and Vulcan watches; this evening, on the radio, Fathiya Ahmad and her band; before that at eight-thirty, comic monologues by Husayn al-Maligi and Nimat al-Maligi, and before that a selection from the Sura of al-Hajj, recited by Taha al-Fashni; Queen Elizabeth arrives at Easton station from Balmoral on her way to Buckingham Palace; Warsaw wiped out; at least five million Poles perish in the war in one month; giant cannons, bigger than the world has ever seen, reduce Warsaw to rubble.

"The world is in a great big mess, Magd al-Din—where are you going?" he thought to himself. He got up to return the newspaper to the little boy only to find that the boy had picked up his newspapers and was running away as fast as he could. Alarmed, he followed after him, but a policeman grabbed him by the arm, saying, "And you're reading the newspaper, to boot?"

Two other policemen went into the café and arrested two people sitting there. They were all led to a police van originally used to transport criminals between jail and the courthouse. He dropped the newspaper and climbed into the van parked on the bridge. He noticed a car blocking Raghib Street and two others blocking the road parallel to the Mahmudiya canal, so that people were forced onto the bridge, where they were grabbed. Anyone who made any effort to resist was smacked on the back of the neck and kicked every which way.

In the lockup at the Ghayt al-Aynab police station, more than twenty people who were arrested that morning, including Magd al-Din for the first time in his life, were herded in. Before he could think of anything else, Magd al-Din saw that idiotic young man sitting in front of him, his gaze fixed on Magd al-Din and smiling as usual. Magd al-Din turned his eyes away to the yellow walls, visible through the high black bars of the cell. The walls formed a semicircle around them, with bars placed close together, like those on prison windows.

The police station was a rotunda with high yellow walls, and its main gate opened onto the square where the streetcar turned. Inside a corporal with thick eyebrows sat behind an old, black wooden table; three other policemen were milling about. In a corner some rifles hung on the walls; in another corner a closed door led to the prefect's room. The corporal fixed his glance on Magd al-Din and ordered one of the policemen to open the jail cell. He motioned Magd al-Din to approach.

"What's your name?"

"Magd al-Din Khalil Sulayman."

"You don't look like the rest of the riffraff, Magd al-Din. Why don't you have your identity card?"

"I forgot my card in the village."

"Village? What village?"

"My village. I've only been in Alexandria a few days."

"Are you a farmer?"

"Yes."

"Here for a visit or permanent residence?"

"Residence, God willing."

"Well, do you have five piasters? Anyone who pays the government five piasters can be released."

"I do. Nobody asked me before," Magd al-Din said with a sigh of relief and reached his hand into the vest under his gallabiya, took out the one-pound note, and gave it to the corporal. It was about 2 p.m. Six hours had passed since he had been thrown into the crowded cell to sit in silence with the other detainees. The corporal said he did not have change for the pound and sent a policeman to get change from a streetcar conductor. When the corporal saw that Magd al-Din had not moved, he asked him, "Why don't you go back to the cell? Are you afraid you'll lose the pound?"

"No," Magd al-Din found himself saying, "but this poor idiot boy, why is in there with us?"

The corporal looked at him for a moment then smiled. "We'll take ten piasters from you then and let him go, if that's what you want."

He got up from his desk, walked over to the cell, and dragged out the idiot boy, who kept staring and smiling at Magd al-Din, even twisting his neck to see him, until he was out of the precinct. Magd al-Din sat back down with the others, and the corporal locked them up again.

"Did he take a pound from you?"

"No. He asked for five piasters and sent for change. He'll give me the change."

"So, you have five piasters?"

"Of course—you saw I have a pound."

"Can you believe we're all being held here for five piasters each? Since the days of Sidqi Pasha, anyone caught without an identity card has to pay a fine of five piasters. If anybody here had five piasters in his pocket, he wouldn't have gone to work. And you, you're looking for work when you have a whole pound?"

Magd al-Din was surprised at what he heard. For a moment he thought of paying for all of them, then changed his mind. He needed every millieme now. "How are you getting out?" he asked.

"Same as every other time. Tonight the head of the neighborhood will come identify us and vouch for us, and we'll get out."

Once again silence descended. The policeman was taking his time coming back with the change. Magd al-Din squatted, his elbows on his knees and his head between his palms. Bahi was the only one who could get him out of this tight spot. He began to have the feeling that perhaps the corporal had intimated to the policeman not to return with the pound. What would happen if night fell before the policeman returned? How would Zahra feel? As he always did in times of crisis, he left it all to God. He sat down on the floor, found room to stretch out his legs, and closed his eyes for a moment. He saw himself walking on the roof of a fast-moving train, surrounded by troops of every complexion, speaking every language, carrying rifles as if they were spears, walking in sands into which their feet sank on the roof of the train. Above him and them were huge black birds, the names of which he did not know.

Magd al-Din opened his eyes, astonished by this fleeting vision. He saw the feet of the other detainees stretched out in front of him: feet resting on their heels, crossed one over the other, or spread apart, big feet that at first looked like shoes, then turned out to be bare feet, worn on the bottom, completely black on top. Some heels were so furrowed that folds of rolled, dried skin hung down from them. The toes had big outgrowths on top, more than two on each toe, with black nails grown long and bent downward over the fronts of the toes, thus forming a protective layer against unforeseen things in the street. One foot had four toes, another six, the sixth toe hanging straight on the side, like a baby tucked onto his mother's side, almost sliding to the ground. Amazingly, that sixth toe was clean. Nearby there was a foot that had no toes, a solid foot from which the toes had been cut by a knife, its front skin wrinkled, a foot that looked more like a rectangular block of old wood. To Magd al-Din it looked like a toothless mouth. On almost all the feet, the ankles were ringed with blue, black, or red blotches.

"These shoes on your feet, don't they bother you?" Magd al-Din was surprised to hear the man next to him ask. Had he seen him examining the bare feet? Maybe. Maybe he wanted him to take off his shoes so he could steal them. It was the same man who had engaged him in conversation earlier. He looked closely at his face: an exhausted face with a reddish complexion that did not look healthy. Closer examination showed malnutrition and emaciation. The gaunt face had a small, pointed nose, a mouth with a downy mustache, and narrow, amber-colored eyes. His hair was black, combed with a wide-tooth comb, with a few gray hairs. On the whole, the man showed signs of a mysterious anguish. When Magd al-Din did not respond, the man went on, "I saw you looking at everyone's feet. Being barefoot here isn't just a sign of poverty—sometimes it's a hobby."

Magd al-Din's eyes grew wider as the man continued, "You want to know why Egyptians are fond of going barefoot? You'd know if you took off your shoes. Aren't you more comfortable when you take off your shoes?"

"Of course," Magd al-Din replied with a smile.

"Well, some people like to be comfortable to begin with."

The man's voice was a little loud, so the rest of the detainees were following what was being said and laughing. "When you go into a house with no chairs, can you sit down on the floor with your shoes still on? Of course not. You take off your shoes. None of our houses have chairs."

Magd al-Din had to laugh with the rest of the men. The corporal yelled at them to stop. Magd al-Din remembered the pound and looked at the corporal, who yelled at him, telling him to wait until "that son-of-a-bitch of a policeman" came back.

"More importantly, shoes wear out, and a man's got to buy another pair," the man went on. "A barefoot person, on the other hand, is self-sufficient. Every month he gets new skin on his feet—that is, a new pair of shoes. If it weren't reprehensible, you could sell those new shoes. Remember, that's twelve new pairs of shoes a year, all gratis, compliments of God. You can't buy a pair of shoes for even twenty piasters."

The laughter got more boisterous, and once again the corporal yelled at them to keep it down. Magd al-Din was now totally drawn in by the gaunt man with his peculiar talk. This man would be his friend for a long time; he would run into him often on the road. It seemed he was the one whom Magd al-Din heard calling his name early every morning. Both of them, like the rest of the detainees, had tears in their eyes from all the cheerful laughter.

Again everything grew quiet, as if a moment of meditation had been sent from heaven. They soon heard the voice of the same man who had been talking to Magd al-Din earlier, reciting in a low voice words that he obviously liked, marveling at their sad meaning, "Council of Alexandria, I am at the end of my patience. Should I speak to you in Greek or Hebrew? You take the people's money and squander it on a bridge. Instead of sucking the people's blood, come suck my—"

He did not say the word that everyone had anticipated. He fell silent, but the silence was broken by laughter that shook the precinct to its foundations. The corporal became angry, and some policemen were startled. The laughter died down in hoarse spasms. Just then, three policemen rushed inside the precinct looking frightened, each holding the wide leather belt he had taken off his pants. It seemed they had been in a battle that they had lost. The corporal shouted at them, "What's wrong with you?"

"A big brawl, Mr. Corporal, at Ban Street."

"Muslims and Christians?"

"No. Southerners and peasants."

Magd al-Din's heart beat fast. The corporal said to the frightened policeman, "Peasants can't fight. It'll end peacefully."

"Not this time. Bahi Khalil fancies himself a big leader and has sworn to break the backs of the southerners."

"Any casualties?"

"Many."

Magd al-Din almost collapsed when he heard Bahi's name. The corporal ordered the policeman to get his colleagues from their room behind the precinct and for them to bring their guns. He called security headquarters on the telephone and requested a security detail. Then he got up, went over to the cell, and opened the door, yelling, "Get the hell out of here. All hell's broken loose, you sons of bitches."

The first one out was Magd al-Din.

From one town to another I set sail.
Why is the wind so contrary?
Why am I ever a stranger, ever on the move?

Folk song from Egypt

7

Ban Street was now almost deserted except for the police. A security force with clubs and shields had been dispatched and took up positions on both sides of the street. A big paddy wagon stood there, filled with peasants and southerners alike. The soldiers were still chasing the brawlers in the alleys and bringing some of them back to the paddy wagon. Women were watching through closed windows; men and boys stood in the doorways. The sound of an ambulance came from the direction of Karmuz. A woman collapsed on the ground near Bahi, crying silently. She was barefoot, her black clothes tattered, hair disheveled, eyes blank, but she did not seem insane. There was another woman, a younger one, weeping quietly in the arms of Magd al-Din, who kept patting her on the back, his eyes fixed on his brother's beautiful face covered with blood, his eyes still open, gazing at Magd al-Din in sorrow and fear for his destiny. There was a look of apology to his younger brother in his eyes.

"Go inside, Zahra."

It was obvious that the blow had split Bahi's skull from behind. Nothing could be done. The battle had taken place right in front of the house, as if Bahi had wanted someone to see him fighting. No one had believed his old stories. Only Magd al-Din did, always. Today he no longer had to fight anyone.

Magd al-Din stepped forward, then sat down, placing his brother's head on his thigh. He shook with a pain that no human alive had ever felt.

The paramedics and a young police officer went over to him. The woman who had collapsed near the body and whom Magd al-Din had not noticed until now was frightened by the police officer. She got up and walked away quickly.

"Who's this woman? Anybody know her?" the officer asked a policeman.

"She's some crazy woman who was always following the dead man."

The officer did not understand, but Magd al-Din's eyes grew wider as he remembered Bahiya.

"You know the victim?" asked the officer.

"He's my brother."

"Do you accuse anyone?"

Magd al-Din did not reply.

"After the burial you can make a statement or a charge," said the officer.

He motioned the paramedics to carry the body. They removed it from the lap of his brother, who could not stand up. He stretched his hand to the man standing next to him.

"Give me a hand, brother."

It was the gaunt man who had been his lockup companion a short while earlier. The man extended his hand.

"Dimyan. My name is Dimyan. Get a grip on yourself," the man said as Magd al-Din got up.

A man Dimyan recognized came over to them. It was Khawaga Dimitri Faltaws, Magd al-Din's landlord and one of the neighborhood's educated Christians, who worked as a labor supervisor at the municipal garage in Hadra. Dimyan had asked him to get him a job, any job in the city, but the man apologized nicely after a month for not finding him a job.

"Do you know him, Dimyan?" Dimitri asked.

"Yes. He's my friend," replied Dimyan, pleased that Dimitri had not forgotten him.

"Then ride in the ambulance with him. I'll catch up with you at the government hospital in a cab. He's a stranger in town."

Magd al-Din listened as his eyes followed the woman who had been sitting near Bahi's body. It was none other than Bahiya. Now she was at the far end of the street. God have mercy.

❖

The ambulance drove off, with the body laid on a stretcher between two long seats on one of which sat Dimyan and Magd al-Din, while the two paramedics sat on the other. The ambulance was not going fast, and did not blow the siren that would have cleared the way through crowds. The road was not crowded, and the ambulance was carrying a corpse.

The slow movement of the car resembled that of a gentle horse or a boat on calm waters. Magd al-Din was now smiting the sea with his arm since he had no staff, and it parted, and in the middle was a grassy pathway on which the gentle horse moved gracefully. Magd al-Din, vexed, smote the air and it parted, and on each side was a smooth, white, glass wall on which pearl-like snowdrops gathered—white tears, white blood and pain. He walked in the space that the air had deserted and was drenched in sweat. He took off his gallabiya, his vest, and his undershirt, leaving only his underpants, which now stuck to him, becoming part of him. Everything rolled down the walls in front of him. Beautiful women and maidens and stones and monkeys and old women clad in black and a familiar face that he did not remember, a face he had often seen and heard calling out his name, "Come, come, Magd al-Din." He followed the voice without knowing where. He could not go back and could not break the kind voice's spell. In front of him rolled all the images he had seen before: his brothers who had been killed, his dead father, his blind mother, his sisters and his cousins, all the Talibs, and the mayor. But they were all children, running and laughing. He wanted to catch one of them, anyone, but could not. The kind voice would not let him go back until he reached the end of the road, the edge, from which white vapors rose and where he could see only tortured arms flailing and hear only groans. He rose up, nearly on the tips of his toes . . . then he collapsed.

"Don't cry, friend. You'll kill yourself."

The thin Dimyan patted Magd al-Din on the shoulder and put his arms around him. He had been crying in pain. Bahi's story had ended. Bahi himself had put an end to it.

He had returned after the Great War. The country was gripped by the revolution for years afterwards. Bahi told Magd al-Din "This village of ours does not move at all. It's like a big beetle that never leaves its hole." It was he who had to stir it back to life.

His mere appearance on the scene was enough to rekindle the fire. He had come back stronger than he had left, his features scorched by both the sun and the cold. He now had a thick mustache, had become taciturn, and early wrinkles showed under his eyes. His face had also acquired a new pained look.

The family did not believe that he had been in the army all that time. "Where did they take you?" "From the road." "Why didn't you tell them who you were and what family you came from? They would've let you go." "I told them, but they didn't let me go."

No one believed him except Magd al-Din, who knew that some people have been preordained to endure great pain. Job was one, and now Bahi. That was why Bahi chose to sleep in Magd al-Din's room. At night he told him a lot about the war, about the boat on which they shipped him with the other soldiers to Europe. He described to him the trenches and the snow in the mountains, the battles at the French-German border, countries that he did not know and cold that he could not bear and beautiful women who came to the soldiers during their rest or to whose villages the soldiers went.

"I was afraid, Magd al-Din, but they dragged me, physically pulled me. Is God going to punish me for the foreign women also? Was it really me who went there? Listen, I know lots of English words and French ones too: bonjour, which means 'good morning,' that's good morning in English, and comment allez vous?, meaning 'how are you?' and how are you? in English, and à demain and à bientôt, which mean 'until we meet again,' and also bye bye and see you, and ça va bien, meaning it's going well, and fine, which also means all's well.

"A year later we were taken to Palestine to fight the Turks. May God forgive me, I fought with the English against the Muslim Turks, but it was against my will."

Bahi's reappearance was not enough to close the books on the past. It meant that he was still there, which meant that the vendetta would be rekindled. All hell broke loose. Of the two families, only Magd al-Din and Khalaf remained. Bahi never counted, and that was the root cause of his great pain.

Of course, there were the sisters, as well as the mother, after the father died of grief. Bahi and Magd al-Din inherited a large chunk of the family land. Magd al-Din's share was three feddans. Bahi also got three feddans, but he sold them secretly and disappeared again. The mother's silent crying caused the light in her eyes to grow dim. She loved him very much without showing it; she had never forgotten the beam of light that had come out of her when he was born. He came back from the war without his halo. It seemed that everything about him had been extinguished. How had the life of that pure child turned into darkness? Magd al-Din was certain that he would come back one day. The mother was about to lose her eyesight completely, when Bahi appeared in the middle of the house. As soon as he got off the train, first the women then the children spread the news. Before Hadya's daughters could bring their mother down from the second floor, Bahi was on his way up.

"Light of my eyes!" she cried and threw herself in his arms, but he was cold. He kissed her cheeks and hand in silence.

In the evening he told Magd al-Din about the city where he had spent all that time, white Alexandria, where foreigners from all over the world and poor Egyptians from all over the land went. He chose not to give his address to anyone. He said he would visit them from time to time. In the morning they could not find him at home. Hadya entered into a phase of more profound silence. Magd al-Din did his best to give her courage and urge her to preserve whatever light remained in her eyes. Little by little the mother was reassured, for Bahi was making an appearance from time to time, though sometimes at long intervals.

Then the people of the village noticed that a new building was being constructed with red bricks brought over from the kilns of Kafr al-Zayyat. They asked the construction workers about the house and its owners, and they said they knew nothing except that it was a government building. The house was being built outside the village limits on deserted land that no one owned. Then the mayor received an official letter stamped by the Islamic civil court in Tanta, requesting him to render assistance as it was requested of him by the representatives of justice in the new court that would be built in the village. By the end of the year the court had been built, and the mayor eagerly awaited the representatives of justice. When a sign was erected reading "The New Courthouse for Civil Law," with the emblems of justice—the scales and a hand placed on the Quran—beneath it, the mayor saw that the time had come for him to render assistance to the representatives of justice. The court judge, usher, and clerk came to him, and the clerk presented the mayor with a new letter in which it was requested that the mayor assign two watchmen to guard the court. The mayor gave the representatives of justice an elaborate banquet.

The courthouse was a one-story building. It had three rooms, a hall, and a bathroom. The court began to accept cases. The first complaint came from an extraordinary woman. Khadra, daughter of the deputy mayor, was complaining that her husband had beaten and insulted her.

Khadra was one of the village's beauties. Her husband was her dreaded cousin. To the amazement of the villagers, the court summoned her husband. That was the first time in their life that they had heard of a woman taking her husband to court. It had never happened once in the history of the village. The husband did not go to court, and he decided that the wife would not come back to his house, even if she were to withdraw her complaint. The court, through the clerk, summoned him again to appear within a week. He did not, and the judge ordered that Khadra be granted a divorce. The village was shaken to its foundations by this unheard-of verdict. The judge disappeared from the courthouse for a week. Bahi appeared in the village streets for a few days, then disappeared again. People saw Khadra's father, a broken man, walking in the street in shame. How could a woman complain to the government about her husband? What courage! And what heresy!

It was natural after that that men would give their wives strict orders not even to pass in front of the courthouse. A whole year passed without a single complaint or verdict. So people were reassured, especially since Khadra had disappeared from the village and her ex-husband had married an even better wife. The truth was slightly different. It was simply that the story of Khadra and her husband was now past history. Another woman lodged a complaint asking for justice against her husband, who had seized her inheritance. The judge ruled that she be given her inheritance back and granted her a divorce since the husband was not faithful to his legal duty. The village was shaken again.

Then, at intervals over a long period of time, a number of men were surprised to receive summonses to appear before the court. The husband would go, not knowing what awaited him. Before going, he would beat his wife, pressing her to admit that she had lodged a complaint against him. The poor, helpless wife would deny doing anything of the kind. Then the husband would go and be surprised not only that his wife had complained, but that the judge knew intimate details about his personal life as well. Thereupon the husband would fall to pieces and not wait for the verdict, which in a number of cases was simply that he should go back and treat his wife better. He would go back and divorce his wife without any discussion. In three years, twenty women were divorced. Bahi would disappear and then reappear riding a gray horse along the canal or the edges of the fields. The painful story of the vendetta was over and done with. The village's biggest preoccupation now was the court that had so shaken families and homes and whose activities extended to the neighboring villages, especially in matters of inheritance.

It turned out that dozens of women had lost their rights because of husbands or strong brothers. The court always found in favor of these wronged women. Then came an ominous day when the court summoned the mayor himself.

The mayor went, thinking that at most, the court needed some help carrying out the verdicts. But the judge did not receive him in his chamber, but rather in open court, and did not permit him to sit down. True, he was a mayor, but the court had its own traditions that applied to great and small alike. The shocking question to the mayor was whether he was abusing his wife. It was she herself who had lodged the complaint that he did not treat her well, that he did not take her the way the sharia, the Islamic civil law, ordained, but that he took her from behind.

You can imagine the mayor as he sprang forward, as he attacked the judge and the usher, held back only by the guards who had gone with him. They prevented him from making that mistake. They were in a state of great surprise and fear. The mischievous among them hid their smiles.

The mayor left the courthouse without answering any questions. He rode his horse and raced the wind. Halfway home he stopped. The vast open space and the green fields around him restored his feeling of calm. This village had been calm throughout its history. The calm was broken only by the vendetta between the Khalils and the Talibs, which was over and now remained only as a memory. He did not think that similar events would befall any two families after the tragic end of the Khalils and Talibs. Then came this court, which had shaken the village and unearthed all its heinous deeds. The judge, usher, and clerk must be killed and the courthouse demolished. He must contact the authorities requesting that the court be moved somewhere else. It was Satan's court. But his wife could not have done that. Or could she have? He had tried more than once to sleep with her in a non-customary manner, but she kicked hard and he never tried it again. He had been an impetuous young man. It was impossible that his wife would remember that now and complain against him.

In a few minutes the mayor reached his house. He stood in front of his wife, shaking with anger, nearly breaking into thousands of little pieces. He would die if he did not do something about it. Those dogs, the guards, would spread the news. But she was his beautiful, rich wife from a great family, and he truly loved her. He broke down in tears before her and said nothing. He slept, asking God for death.

His wife was the daughter of one of the notables in the next village. The news made it there instantly. In the evening, her father and his men came. The father said in an almost inaudible voice, "In the morning, we'll go to the court. If there is a complaint, we'll kill our daughter and that'll be the end of that."

In the morning there was no one in the courthouse. Its doors were wide open. Even the sign on the door had been taken off and was lying on the ground. By noon, policemen from the governorate were there, and the village was filled with laughter and crying. It was not a real court. It was just a trick invented by a devil to ruin the village. The village went to sleep that night wondering who that devil might be.

The people said, "The government is lame, but it can beat a gazelle." The police were able to track down the first woman who had gone to court, Khadra—who had disappeared from the village after her divorce. They found her in Tanta living with Bahi, who was now dividing his time between Tanta and the village. She said she had tried many times to prevent him from continuing, but that he was intent on wrecking all the homes in the village. People shunned Magd al-Din's house and family for some time, but because of Magd al-Din's Quranic education and piety and Bahi's past, people eventually were friendly to Magd al-Din again. Bahi became a mere memory in his jail cell in Tanta. No one but Magd al-Din knew that when Bahi finished his sentence, he left for Alexandria. No one ever knew what became of Khadra. "No way could she get away with it. She's probably already been killed by her father or her brothers," was the comment anyone who brought up her name would get. Several years passed without Bahi making an appearance in the village; he was now totally forgotten. The mayor, who could have looked for Bahi anywhere in Egypt, remembered him suddenly. When he thought of something to do about it, he kicked Magd al-Din out of the village, and to make sure the people would not remember the unpleasant story, he said the expulsion was related to the vendetta. With him he expelled Khalaf, the last of the Talibs. But the people of the village remembered vividly what Bahi had done to the mayor and secretly laughed. And there was Bahi, laid out helplessly before his brother, now devoid of strength, weakness, or rashness. He had chosen his own death in the city that he had said was white.

And deliver us all from high prices, the plague,
earthquakes, drowning, fire, being taken captive
by the barbarians, the stranger's sword,
and the rising of heretics.
Kyrie eleison.

Coptic prayer

8

Pompey's Pillar is the name of the huge column erected by
Alexandrians to immortalize the memory of the Roman emperor
Diocletian. They dedicated it to him as a gift, in appreciation for
the prosperity they had enjoyed under him, forgetting that it was
Diocletian who had persecuted them most, and persecuted the
Christians in Egypt and Palestine in general.

Pompey's Pillar is in the middle of Rhakotis, almost in the
exact midpoint of Karmuz Street. The pillar is separated from
the street by a wall that surrounds the whole archaeological site.
To the left of the relics of Kom al-Shuqafa lies the Muslim
cemetery, which takes up a large portion of Karmuz Street,
extending to Rahma Street. The cemetery is called 'the pillar
tombs,' in reference to Pompey's Pillar. The tombs end on the
north side at Italian School Street, a quiet, narrow street seldom
noticed by pedestrians or cars. For this reason, many lovers go
there in the evening, lured by the dark to make out and
sometimes, take their love-making farther without fear of being
discovered.

Behind Pompey's Pillar extends the hill of Kom al-Shuqafa,
where some Nubian families and gypsy clans live. The Nubians
usually sell peanuts and seeds in little paper bags on the street. The
gypsies go out on short trips to the city to do their usual things,

reading palms and shells, telling fortunes, dancing, and selling cheap costume jewelry.

The streetcar runs up and down Karmuz Street, beginning at the bank of the Mahmudiya canal, halfway between Karmuz Bridge, which leads east to Ghayt al-Aynab, and Kafr Ashri Bridge, which spans the canal near the harbor. In front of the point where the streetcar route begins, on the southern bank of Mahmudiya Canal, lie the houses of workers who work in the railways south of the city. Behind these railroad tracks lies Lake Maryut, which extends farther than Alexandria, reaching as far as Amiriya in the west and Idku in the east. Magd al-Din will have to discover all these places, but that will be later on.

Every day, Magd al-Din went to the cemetery, where he sat in front of his brother's tomb and recited the Quran as long as he could. On his way to the cemetery he would see Pompey's Pillar high above and realize that it was a relic from a bygone era. A strange thought would occur to him. He wished he could go up and sit on top of the pillar, and spend the rest of his life there, without food or drink, ceaselessly clamoring the name of God, exactly as the great Sufi saint al-Sayyid Ahmad al-Badawi did on the roof of a house in Tanta, until he died.

"You can't go on like this," Dimyan told him, after following him to the cemetery one day.

"What should I do, Dimyan?"

"Come with me to look for work. I usually get work most days now. Besides, you can't spend your life sitting in the cemetery. This, God forbid, is an act of godlessness."

Magd al-Din looked at him for some time and finally said, "You are right, my man."

Since the day Bahi was killed, a great friendship between the two men had developed in no time at all. Everything at the hospital was over quickly thanks to the presence of Khawaga Dimitri and Dimyan. The following morning the public attorney's office gave permission to bury the body, and by noon it was interred. As the shroud-wrapped body was lowered into the grave, Magd al-Din realized the great wrong he had done his brother: he had disobeyed his wish that he be buried in the village. That night Bahi had laughed and said that if he died and was buried in the village, he wouldn't cause anyone any problems. It was impossible for Magd al-Din to change what had happened. He could not go back to the village, and his mother should be kept in the dark, at least for now. God alone knew how helpless he was.

Khawaga Dimitri paid ten pounds for the tomb and the burial expenses and told Magd al-Din in a whisper, "You can return it to me when things are better." Magd al-Din was sure he could repay it, for his land in the village produced income, and he was sure his sisters would send him his share every season. What puzzled Magd al-Din was the affection show-ered on him and his wife by Khawaga Dimitri and his family even though they had only known each other for a few weeks. Sitt Maryam told Zahra, "Your brother-in-law was a prince." Dimitri told Magd al-Din, "Your brother was a good guy." Magd al-Din surmised that Bahi must have done them some favors when the need arose. He told Zahra to empty Bahi's room out so Khawaga Dimitri could have it back.

Nothing in Bahi's room was needed, so the furnishings were sold to the secondhand-goods merchant in the morning. Magd al-Din took Bahi's clothes and gave them away to the poor at the cemetery. Zahra found an envelope in the armoire containing twenty pounds and cried when she gave the money to Magd al-Din. Bahi was saving from shame before Khawaga Dimitri—Magd al-Din could now return the ten pounds Dimitri had loaned him so magnanimously.

Even though he had not asked about it, Zahra told her husband the story of how Bahi took part in the battle and how he died. She said she heard shouts on the street. At the time she was in Sitt Maryam's room, and they looked out of the window. She saw Bahi moving as fast and as gracefully as a horse, brandishing his club, and he felled everyone he hit. He was completely different from the Bahi she had known. He was like a supernatural force, throwing men to the ground right and left. There were many peasants on his side, but the southerners were more numerous. Her eyes could only see Bahi. Just as the battle was about to end, after most of the southerners had cleared the street, a group of them appeared from one alley, heading straight for for one man, Bahi. All the clubs came down on his head. At once, she went down to the street screaming, but Bahi was already dead. It seemed that he looked at her as if he were asking her to be a witness to his courage. Magd al-Din asked her if the woman Bahiya had reappeared in the street since then, and Zahra said she had seen her only the day Bahi was killed. She had seen her that day, but did not believe it, and looking at Bahi, who had just been killed, she soon forgot about her.

Magd al-Din continued to go out to the cemetery every afternoon, giving money to the poor, and reciting the Quran. By nightfall, he would go back home and have supper, his only meal since breakfast, then he would recite the Quran until the night's last prayer, when he would go to bed. He seldom spoke to his wife. He became even more silent when he began to notice one or more women in front of Bahi's tomb, crying and placing roses and cactus flowers on the tomb. When he went closer, they would move away and leave without a word. He decided to discover the secret of those women, so he went to the undertaker in his shop across the street from the cemetery and asked him. The man smiled and said, "This is the first deceased whose relatives are all women. They come to me and I point out the tomb to them. I didn't see them the day of the burial, but they haven't stopped coming yet." He fell silent for a moment then went on, "It seems he was a decent guy. The women give me money, generously." Another pause, and then he said, "Strangely enough, a man came to me a few days ago and asked me about the tomb. I took him to it, and he immediately fell upon the woman who had come there just before him and beat her bad, dragged her by the hair, and he swore a sacred oath that he would, God forbid, divorce her." He asked Magd al-Din if he knew anything about that man, and Magd al-Din left him without a reply.

"The only thing you know about me is that I am Dimyan Abd al-Shahid. But I know that you come from a good family and I too come from a good family. My grandfather used to own slaves—no lie. That's what they say about him in our village, Dayrut. You're from northern Egypt and I am from southern Egypt. There are many notables from the north and many from the south. And in both north and south, the poor are of course more numerous. Somebody's got to take from somebody! Make sense? Do you hear me, Magd al-Din?"

"I hear you," replied Magd al-Din, as he did every time Dimyan asked him. Dimyan was now passing by every morning to accompany him on their job hunt. On the days without work, which were usually more than the successful days, they would sit at the café by the bridge. Magd al-Din would buy the newspaper and astound Dimyan with news of the German submarines and torpedo boats that blasted the British ships then disappeared like demons into the waters of the Atlantic Ocean. Dimyan learned a lot about Magd al-Din's life. The most important thing he learned was that Magd al-Din had been exempted from military service because he had memorized the Quran.

Dimyan was now calling Magd al-Din "Sheikh." He once told him in jest that there was no law exempting those who memorized the Bible from military service. Then he laughed, "But who could memorize the Bible?"

Every time they met, Dimyan would tell Magd al-Din something about his life until the story was rounded out. He told him that one day, out of the blue, one of the village people announced that Mr. Baskharun was an infidel. Baskharun was Dimyan's grandfather, not the great-great-grandfather who had owned slaves. Why was Mr. Baskharun an infidel? The accuser said that as a child, he had not been baptized. The truth was that there was a dispute between two families over a piece of land, and one of the adversaries was able to spread that rumor about Mr. Baskharun.

"What is baptism, Dimyan?"

"Baptism means becoming Christian. Without it a man stays in limbo, between heaven and hell."

"That means nobody holds him accountable?"

"Exactly."

Magd al-Din smiled and said, "How can that be bad for the person?"

"Of course it can. Don't ask me how. But it's a very difficult situation. I don't know exactly the nature of the difficulty, but I feel it. It's like falling off a mountain but never landing anywhere. You remain suspended in space, in total emptiness, neither hot nor cold, not even air of any kind. Do you know, Sheikh Magd al-Din, that that happened to me once?"

"You stood between heaven and hell?"

"Yes. I felt it when I rode an elevator. Only one time in my life I rode an elevator in a building in Manshiya. I was cleaning the roof of the building. It was very hard work. The roof was a pigsty. I couldn't go down the stairs. Can you imagine? I was too exhausted. Anyway, I stepped into the elevator and pressed the button. It went down so fast that I felt I was in a place that had been emptied out completely. I remembered the story about heaven and hell and being stuck between them. If I hadn't seen through the glass door each floor going by in front of me, I would've screamed in fright."

Magd al-Din looked at him in amazement and admiration, and felt genuine warmth toward him. Dimyan continued his family's story.

"My grandfather went to the church in Asyut, Dayr al-Muharraq, the largest church in Asyut, and brought back the priest who had baptized him as a child. He was a blind man on crutches. But nobody believed him because the priest himself had committed many sins in his youth before he entered the monastery."

Magd al-Din, honestly wishing to learn, asked, "Is it necessary for a person to be baptized young?"

"It's more proper. But, no. A person can be baptized any time. Baptism is very simple: the priest holds the child and plunges him into a marble basin filled with water. Of course there's also music and hallelujahs and hosannas—it's a real party!"

"Well, your grandfather should've been baptized again."

"He adamantly refused," Dimyan laughed. "He insisted that he'd already been baptized and would not submit to those machinations. Deep down he was sad. He went to sleep and hasn't awakened to this day."

"There's no power or strength save in God!" exclaimed Magd al-Din.

"Anyway. My father and his brothers came to hate the village. They divvied up land and left the village. My father went into business until his money was gone; he left my mother, myself, and two daughters, and another son who died later of typhoid. My sisters have married and are living with their husbands in Suhag. My mother is living with me, hardly ever moving except to sleep. So this was how a big family was ruined because of a little lie. But thank God nobody said that the reverend was rendered incapable of baptizing my grandfather, or that the water in the baptismal basin had dried up when he was about to baptize my grandfather. That would've meant big sins, an old curse in the family. Yes, sometimes as the reverend baptized a child, he would be surprised to see that the water had suddenly dried up or that the child clung to his hand and couldn't be wrenched away."

Magd al-Din did not know how to comment on this story of his good-hearted friend.

"You're a pious man, Dimyan," he said as he looked him in the eye.

"It only seems that way," Dimyan laughed. "I haven't been to church for many years. The church of Mari Girgis is only two steps away from my house, and your house too, but I haven't been to it on Sundays or during the holidays. You know why?"

Magd al-Din was not sure what to think, so he ventured a guess, "Because of what happened to your grandfather?"

"No. I just forget. I always forget. Sometimes I say to myself, Dimyan, you're unemployed—why don't you go to Georgius the Martyr, that's Mari Girgis, he might find you a permanent job. Then I forget, even though I know about Mari Girgis's many miracles. Muslims sometimes come to him on his anniversary and ask him for help. Mari Girgis is a big saint. You know the saints, of course. You know that the Alexandria city council once tried to demolish the mosque of Abu al-Darda to make way for the streetcar line, but anyone who raised a pickax against the building was paralyzed. So they left it in its place, and now the streetcars go around it. And, as the song tells us, I know that al-Sayyid Ahmad al-Badawi used to liberate the Muslim captives from the enemies. You're from Tanta, so you know the story better than I do. Besides, brother, I'm confused: Mari Girgis has performed miracles and al-Sayyid Ahmad al-Badawi and Abu al-Darda all have made miracles. They're all right. So why the distinction between Copts and Muslims?"

Dimyan fell silent for several moments then said, "I have an idea. What do you say I go to Mari Girgis and ask him for work, and you go to Abu al-Darda or Abu al-Abbas and ask for work? Or, how about the other way around—maybe Mari Girgis is angry with me because I've stayed away from him too long."

❖

Magd al-Din did not expect Zahra to cry in such sorrow when she heard the cannon fired in the evening to announce that the following day would be the first day of Ramadan. He felt the same sorrow and the same need to burst out crying but he pulled himself together. He knew the difference between Ramadan in a big city and Ramadan in their village, where everyone and everything was sympathetic and friendly. A light tap on the half-closed door made Zahra quickly dry her tears.

Khawaga Dimitri and his wife came to wish their neighbors well on the occasion. As Khawaga Dimitri sat down on the sofa next to Magd al-Din, the latter said, "You're making me fall in love with Alexandria."

Khawaga Dimitri said with pride, "Alexandria is an ancient city, Mr. Magd al-Din."

Magd al-Din felt the profound meaning alluded to by his neighbor. It was the tenth of October, and today he had begun work at the Ahliya Weaving Company, a job he hoped would last a long time. Who knows? Maybe this city would open up her kindly heart to him, though he had yet to see it.

"How about a walk now?" asked Khawaga Dimitri. "Ramadan is the month for staying up late."

"Come and listen to the radio with us," suggested Sitt Maryam to Zahra.

Magd al-Din went out with Dimitri, and Zahra went with Sitt Maryam into her well-lit room. She saw the room glowing white and the two daughters radiant with delight. The sewing machine was in the middle of the room. Sitt Maryam sat on the chair in front of the sewing machine, while Zahra sat on the sofa with Yvonne. Camilla sat on the opposite sofa looking at Zahra with surprised delight.

Zahra no longer felt shy. She asked Camilla why she was looking at her with such surprise, and Camilla answered, "Because you're so beautiful!"

Everyone laughed. Sitt Maryam, obviously pleased, said what she usually said about Camilla, "Watch out, Zahra—Camilla's mischievous!"

There were some light taps on the half-open door. There was a cool, refreshing breeze. Camilla got up to open the door, then shouted happily, "It's Sitt Lula!"

Sitt Maryam's face lit up and so did Yvonne's. Zahra found herself gazing at Sitt Lula, the well-proportioned blonde with a ruddy complexion. She was wearing a green batiste gown with a floral design and green velvet slippers, but nothing on her head. Her hair shone like radiant amber. As she sat down, Lula said, "My old man went out to spend the evening with his friends at the café, using Ramadan as an excuse."

"Us, too—our men went out," said Sitt Maryam with a smile "We're all in the same boat."

Everyone laughed, including Zahra this time. Camilla turned on the radio and Abd al-Wahhab's voice flowed from it. It was obvious that Camilla loved him. The song, "His eyelids teach the art of love" made the girl sway her head to its Spanish swing and laugh. Suddenly she shouted, "Chestnuts!"

Everyone fell silent. Zahra was surprised as everyone listened for the muffled voice echoing in the street. It was the voice of the chestnut vendor, whose words were jumbled, but everyone knew that it was he. He was gone for most of the year, then reappeared again with the beginning of winter. Yvonne went down and bought five piasters' worth, and Camilla quickly set out a large spirit stove and began to roast the chestnuts. Zahra knew what they were; Magd al-Din had often bought them in Tanta. When Lula took a chestnut and placed it in her mouth for a few moments, her mouth looked very beautiful and her teeth very white. Zahra felt she was in front of an extraordinary woman and watched her as she ate the chestnut slowly with great delight.

She closed her eyes for a few moments, then said, "How great it would be to have chocolate-covered chestnuts! They call it marron glacé, Camilla."

"Oh, I love *marron glacé*."

That was the first time that Zahra had heard the word. She did not show any surprise, but kept it inside. She wondered at Camilla being so merry and full of joy, and her sister Yvonne so quiet and poised. The Lord really works in mysterious ways!

Abd al-Wahhab's song came to an end, and Camilla got up to turn the tuner knob on the radio, saying "I'll find some more Abd al-Wahhab," and indeed found him on another station. She recognized the music. "Oh, what a wonderful song! Sitt Lula!"

Zahra surmised that there was familiarity between Lula and Camilla. She did not understand the difficult song. She had often heard it in the village and would move away from the radio or turn it down or off. She never understood the song. Camilla volunteered to explain it to her. All that Zahra got out of the explanation was that Sitt Maryam was happy with her daughter and her boldness. But Zahra herself did not understand Camilla's explanation, and could only pretend to be impressed, "Really, all of that in the song?"

Everyone laughed, then Camilla shouted "Amm Mahmud!"

"Again, even in Ramadan?" Lula said.

Amm Mahmud's voice rang out from the street, "Latest! Latest! Read all about it!" Camilla took half a piaster from her mother and went out quickly. Yvonne explained to Zahra that Amm Mahmud came around whenever an extraordinary event took place, selling a printed sheet with the details of the incident before the newspapers published it. Zahra made the gesture of warding off evil by pretending to spit down the front of her gallabiya and said, "God protect us!"

Camilla came in silently.

"Read it," her mother said, smiling.

"It would be better if Yvonne read it," Camilla answered.

Yvonne held the printed sheet and read silently, then blushed and said with affected nonchalance, "It's nothing. A lady's married to two men at the same time." Lula hit herself on the chest in fear and made the same gesture to ward off evil more than once.

"Tear up the sheet and throw it in the garbage," was Sitt Maryam's calm reaction.

❖

Magd al-Din noticed that there were many children who had gone out in the street despite the dark and the absence of streetlights. He walked with Khawaga Dimitri in the other direction toward Karmuz.

"A plague on England and Germany on the same day," said Khawaga Dimitri. "We get nothing out of it but inflation and darkness."

The stores were open, doing business by the light of candles or small kerosene lamps. Some owners were bold enough to turn on one or more electric bulbs, but the lights were all inside. What little light escaped outside enabled the children to play and the passers-by to walk. Most people came out to buy food for suhur, the late-night meal of Ramadan, and for the following day. Magd al-Din saw a European-style bakery and thought of buying some bread, but Dimitri told him that the bakery stayed open all night long; they could buy the bread on their way back. For now they should go first to Karmuz Bridge to buy tobacco.

Immediately after the bridge was a store with a white facade and windows of shining glass. The light came from a small white lamp. The salesman had a white, ruddy face and wore a white coat. Magd al-Din noticed that the store carried many brands of cigarettes, molasses-cured tobacco for the narghile, and regular bulk tobacco. Dimitri bought tobacco for a piaster and remarked, "Fresh Turkish tobacco with a refreshing taste."

Magd al-Din bought the same and decided he would be a regular customer at the store, since bulk tobacco was better than that in packets.

On their way back, Magd al-Din looked from the bridge to the Mahmudiya canal, now dark on both banks. He saw many barges and ships moored there. He realized that there would be many work opportunities for the unemployed the following day. In Ban Street the kids had lit their lanterns in disregard of civil defense instructions and went door to door asking for the customary treats, or sat in small groups chatting and playing. Dimitri did not wish to go back so soon and suggested to Magd al-Din, "How about a cup of coffee? This would give the women the chance to stay up."

Magd al-Din thought it would be a good opportunity for Zahra to overcome her sorrow. He went into the café adjacent to Gazar Pastry Shop. It was filled with patrons drinking tea and coffee and playing backgammon, dominos, and cards by the light of small lamps. Dimyan was playing dominos with another person, while three other men sat with them. As soon as Dimyan saw Magd al-Din and Dimitri he got up to welcome them. Magd al-Din said, "You're staying up too, Dimyan?"

"Ramadan encourages one to stay up, Sheikh Magd!" was his reply.

As they all sat down, Dimyan shouted, "As of tomorrow, with the beginning of the month of Ramadan, the people's restaurants will open their doors to the poor to break their fast. That's the king's order. So the poor can be guaranteed to eat for a month. Long live the king and long live Ali Mahir too!"

A man sitting in the far corner added his own dedication: "And long live the singer Muhammad Abd al-Muttalib and Sitt Fathiya Ahmad!"

The advent of the month of Ramadan did not cause the Egyptian government to relax the emergency and civil defense measures. On the contrary, they were tightened. Alexandria, like other municipalities, instituted nighttime and daytime air-raid drills. The prices of some commodities, especially fuels such as kerosene, gasoline, and natural gas, were raised. Some commodities, such as cooking oil, were removed from price-control lists, and people complained loudly. Flour mills began to add more than the legal limit of corn meal to wheat flour. As a result of the strict enforcement of civil defense regulations, no permits were issued for the erection of the tents or temporary pavilions for entertainment or religious events that people were used to having in the squares, outside the mosques, or other such places during Ramadan. For city dwellers, this year's Ramadan was less cheerful than usual.

In the big world outside, the naval war was still raging. The exploits of the legendary German battle cruisers *Scharnhorst* and

Gneisenau, which attacked British convoys, filled the world. The two battle cruisers seemed like ghosts; no one knew when they would appear, and after they had struck, they disappeared in the deep waters of the Atlantic. And so did the two pocket battleships *Admiral Graf Spee* and *Deutschland*. During reconnaissance flights, the Luftwaffe launched the first raid over France. French fighter planes chased and shot down some of the German planes. That new development caught the world's attention; German planes were now capable of going beyond Alsace-Lorraine. Fears increased when German deployments extended from the French to the Dutch borders. The Germans said the French borders were too narrow and that they needed to reinforce their troops. They also said Germany had no designs on the Netherlands. Jaffa oranges appeared in the markets in Alexandria. It was said that the abundant crop in Palestine could not be exported to Europe because of the war, and that was why the fruit was so cheap.

His Majesty King Farouk bestowed the rank of general on His Excellency Baker Pasha, Alexandria's police superinten-dent. People were cautioned against going beyond the streetcar route in the suburb of Sidi Bishr at night; there had been many murders, strong-arm robberies, and rapes. For the first time, it was decided that army officers would travel on the railroads first class, in recognition of their prominent place in society and to safeguard their dignity. His Royal Highness Prince Muhammad Ali left Alexandria for Cairo at the end of the summer season. The Teatro of Biba Izz al-Din performed the vaudeville play *An Aristocratic Thief*. The Egyptian gold pound coin was worth 185 piasters, and Craven cigarettes were three piasters for ten and six for a twenty-cigarette pack. It was decided that the officers of the Territorial Army should be recruited from the ranks of physical education graduates, who were always unemployed. The Egyptian film *Determination* was screened for the first time. The US Neutrality Act, also known as 'cash-and-carry,' was passed, removing the ban on arms exports to the Allies. Three German soldiers who had murdered General von Fritsch during the fighting near Warsaw were executed. The king continued to perform the Friday prayers at a different mosque every week; so far, he had prayed at the Kikhya mosque in Cairo and al-Dikhayla in Alexandria. The public safety report was issued, stating that fires had destroyed 858 houses, causing five thousand Egyptian pounds worth of damage. The Border Guard Corps began training on the use of anti-aircraft artillery in Marsa Matruh. Colonel Ali al-Sharif Bey was appointed director-general of the border adminis-tration.

The famous Nazi field marshal Hermann Goering, chief of the Luftwaffe, visited Italy, and the world awaited the outcome of the visit with bated breath. Ismet Inonu, the president of the Turkish Republic, gave a speech in which he declared his country's neutrality and its intention to stay out of the war. An embargo on foreign theater troupes was enacted, in order to cut down on expenses and to show appreciation for Egyptian troupes. Some cynics commented that international travel routes were already cut off because of the war. Serge Bujolosky, a foreign artist living in Paris, returned Watteau's painting *L'indifferent*, which he had stolen from the Louvre the previous June. He said that he loved the French eighteenth-century painter and especially that painting, which he had wanted to restore. The experts said that in fact he had damaged it, which earned him a two-year jail sentence. Memorial services were held at the French cemeteries in Alexandria for the French casualities of the Great War. The Consul General of France and notables of the French community attended the services. It seemed that Hitler was not going to attack the French front before the following spring.

Izz al-Din Abd al-Qadir, who had fired shots at Nahhas Pasha's car, filed an appeal to overturn the ten-year jail sentence he had received. The appeal was continued. Royal birthdays were celebrated, one for Princess Fawziya upon her reaching nineteen. The celebrations were held simultaneously at the royal palace in Cairo and in the imperial palace in Tehran, since she was the wife of the Iranian crown prince. The sixty-fifth birthday of the Egyptian crown prince, Muhammad Ali, was also celebrated, as was the sixteenth birthday of Princess Fayza. The Romanian embassy celebrated the coming of age of Prince Michael, son of King Carol II and Princess Helena of Greece. The biggest air battle yet between the French and the German forces took place over Alsace. The French shot down nine German planes. King Leopold of Belgium and Queen Wilhelmina of the Netherlands tried to reconcile the warring powers and made an initiative to that effect. Advertisements for Re-Zex pills announced, "Men of Egypt, science has come to you from faraway America. Perform like a twenty-year-old even if you are fifty. For eleven piasters, the price of one bottle of Re-Zex pills, you can say good-bye to being ashamed of your declining physical ability and vigor."

Hitler gave a speech at the Munich beer hall where in 1923 he had shouted, "The National Revolution has begun," and where he had announced that Germany was fighting for her *Lebensraum*. Then in 1937, he announced that Germany's *Lebensraum* was Eastern Europe, and that Poland, White Russia, and the Ukraine should be wiped out of existence, along with their populations, and become part of Germany. That was why, when he invaded Poland, the Russians did not hesitate to invade it from the other side, to safeguard the Ukraine and White Russia, and if Hitler turned on them, the Russians would share Poland with him. After Hitler departed, a bomb exploded in the beer hall and its roof collapsed, but there were no injuries. His Majesty contributed the sum of three hundred Egyptian pounds to the charity fund managed by the ministry of social affairs. Belgium and the Netherlands began to fear that Hitler might violate their neutrality. The price of Egyptian eggs rose from 180 piasters per thousand to 280 piasters. Turkey observed the anniversary of Ataturk's death. Amsterdam began to flood parts of its borders to slow down any German attack. Belgium declared universal mobilization. Joint maneuvers between the Egyptian and British armies were conducted in the Western desert.

Two automatic telephone exchanges were built in Alexandria, in Ibrahimiya and Glymenopoulo. Owners of match factories complained about the government-imposed prices, which did not take into account the rise in the cost of wood and other raw materials. Near Victoria in Alexandria the body of a young man, about twenty-five years old, was discovered in the well by a water wheel. Laurel and Hardy split. The newspapers showed Hardy acting in a new film with Harry Langdon. People were depressed because of this. The students of the Princess Fayza School for Girls distributed clothing and underwear to the students in girls' elementary schools in Alexandria on the occasion of the birthday of Her Royal Highness. A poor woman reported to the public prosecutor that her daughter, whom she had introduced to an employment agency seven months earlier, had disappeared. After a search it was discovered that the girl's first employer had sold her to a woman who ran a brothel in Qina and that the woman in turn had sold her to another brothel in Minya, who in turn had sold her to a brothel in Alexandria. Then she was sold to a brothel in Tanta. For seven months, she had been sold to brothels from south to north.

9

During the feast at the end of Ramadan, Magd al-Din found out for sure that he had lost his land. His brother-in-law visited him and learned of Bahi's death. Magd al-Din told him to spare his mother the trouble of coming to visit her son's tomb or better still, not to tell her at all. His brother-in-law told him about a project for an expressway that would go through the village and many people's property, including Magd al-Din's, and that no one could expect adequate compensation, and the mayor was behind the project. Magd al-Din remembered Bahi telling him to kiss his land good-bye and was silent for a long time, until he heard his cousin and brother-in-law say, "Emergency laws are in effect. The mayor can banish anyone—he can kill anyone, too. The emergency laws give him the right to do whatever he wants. May God protect the country and the people."

So Magd al-Din can easily be killed. That is what his brother-in-law is suggesting.

"Anyway, if you happen to get any compensation, please send it to me."

His brother-in-law gave him twenty pounds, his share of the year's crop. Magd al-Din realized that that was the last money he would ever see for his land. He also realized that he had to stay in Alexandria for good.

Alexandria was getting colder. Rain had fallen off and on for several nights in a row. The alleys and streets south of the city had become muddy. Zahra did not know how she would spend the feast days in her new city. Camilla and Yvonne promised to take her on a boat ride on the Mahmudiya canal and then to visit the zoo, but Zahra said she could not do that. Sitt Maryam said she would take her to the fish market in the afternoon before the feast to buy fish, and that the fish of Alexandria were irresistible. Zahra agreed to go out with her, especially since Magd al-Din had told her to celebrate the feast as if she were still in their home village, that grief was not called for, was useless even. He used to buy the traditional nuts and raisins from Tanta. This year he bought very little, less than he used to, from the square. Zahra needed to get out of the house one more time. True, her life at home passed quietly, and the two beautiful girls gladdened her heart with their beautiful spirits, as did Sitt Lula with her shapely figure, overpowering beauty, and merry character. But that was not enough. In the village she used to go out with Magd al-Din or by herself in the sun and the breeze in the fields, or into the shade in the heat of the day. Her feet were crying out for a walk, and her body ached for fresh air.

She took the Abu Warda streetcar with Sitt Maryam. They got off at the end of the line and walked a little on Tatwig Street up to the coast. In front of them was the king's white palace with many windows and the tall palm trees swaying with the wind and the guards with arms at the ready. A few men and many women, their plump bodies wrapped tightly in shawls, were walking along. A few Citroen and Packard cars had stopped with the people in front of the fish market. The fresh smell of the sea dispelled the fishy odor and filled their lungs with a refreshing breeze. The air was cold; dark clouds hung over the sea as the sound of the waves, which they could not see beyond the market and the police station, reached their ears. In front of the fish market, the vendors sat on the sidewalk or stood in their black or white vests and loose Alexandrian pants, also black or white, with hand-woven round, white rimmed hats. On the low tables were fantastic displays of fish in many varieties and colors ranging from silver to white, red, gray, and black. Sitt Maryam pointed to one type of fish and said it was called pigeon fish—big-bellied red fish that she said was not good, but that the poor bought to make fish soup. Zahra shied away from it; she did not want to be poor and buy it, in spite of its beautiful color. Red snapper was more beautiful and better. She bought some of that. She also bought some striped mullet. Meanwhile, Sitt Maryam was explaining to her the different kinds of fish and what they were good for. Of a particularly small fish she said that even though it was very cheap, it could be used in a delicious stew, which she would teach her how to cook, and would also teach her how to make fish casseroles with red rice. For some inexplicable reason Zahra suddenly thought of the statue of Muhammad Ali on his horse in Manshiya and whether it would be possible for him to get off the pedestal and take her and Magd al-Din back to her village. Sitt Maryam must have guessed that Zahra had been preoccupied for a few moments, so she offered, "How about a little walk on the corniche? It's still too early for sunset."

"The fish will go bad."

"It's cold and the fish is fresh."

Zahra walked like a little child following her mother.

During the feast, Magd al-Din realized that he had lost his land and that he had to stay in Alexandria. As soon as his brother-in-law left, he felt he had to get out of the house. It was not enough to visit Bahi's tomb and distribute alms. He had no work during the feast; none of the temporary workers had. He wished that Dimyan would visit him. On the morning of the last day of the feast, Dimyan did visit him, and just in time, as he was at his wit's end. He did not know anywhere to go in Alexandria farther than the Mahmudiya canal and the tombs in Karmuz.

"How about giving your wife a chance to visit with the neighbors and coming with me?" Dimyan said as soon as he sat down, and Magd al-Din agreed without hesitation. He noticed that Dimyan was now wearing shoes, had been wearing a new pair for a week, and this time he had on clean woolen trousers and an old, but clean, wool jacket.

"We've been working for a month now," Dimyan said to Magd al-Din. "I bought new shoes in the hope that I'll keep my job. But rolling those bales is hard work, Sheikh Magd, and I'm skinny."

"You'll get used to it, Dimyan. Hang in there until we find better work."

"I also bought the shoes in the hope that I'll find a better job, but I don't know what kind of work is better than what we're doing."

Magd al-Din laughed quietly, then went out with his friend to take the streetcar. They walked through the hubbub of the children on Ban Street, with their bright new clothes and colorful bicycles, which they dragged with difficulty on the unpaved street, and through groups of children gathered around vendors of balloons, candy, and, despite the cold weather, ice cream.

At the streetcar roundabout at Sidi Karim, where the road was paved, there were more children and even greater noise. Magd al-Din and Dimyan got on the streetcar.

The parade of children was uninterrupted even by the streetcar, which was moving slowly. They looked like joyous, colorful little birds. Magd al-Din and Dimyan got off at Khedive Street, where most of the stores were closed. They turned into Station Square.

A military band in the middle of the park was playing the songs of Muhammad Abd al-Wahhab and Umm Kulthum, surrounded by crowds of children, young people, visitors from the countryside, and inhabitants of the city.

"Watch out for the thieves in the crowds," Dimyan said to Magd al-Din, as they approached the audience. They stood there for a whole hour without feeling the passage of time. Magd al-Din had not thought that music could transport a man to such heights. They walked away in silence, as if they had just finished saying their prayers. The circle around a juggler enticed them to stop.

"Here thievery is very real. Half the people standing here are thieves the juggler knows," said Dimyan.

"I have fifty piasters in my pocket. They can steal it if they like," said Magd al-Din.

"You're smart, Sheikh Magd. But I am smarter," Dimyan replied with a smile. "I have nothing in my pocket."

They burst out laughing and pressed into the circle.

In the middle was a man in his fifties wearing tight old trousers and a tight jacket under which he wore a white turtleneck. He had on a pair of cheap black shoes that were too big for him and had no laces. It looked as though he had never polished them. The shoes looked even bigger because his trouser legs were tight and slightly too short, and his legs were thin. The socks rested on top of the shoes.

"Look—it's Charlie Chaplin's shoes, and his mustache too," Dimyan said excitedly. The man had Chaplin's mustache, which was still black. Magd al-Din did not know who Charlie Chaplin was.

"Been to the movies yet?" asked Dimyan.

"No."

"One of these days, I'll take you to see one of Charlie Chaplin's films."

The juggler was explaining what he was about to do, the miracle that no magician in the world had done, not even the infidel Houdini. No one knew who this Houdini was. The juggler said that he would use a person as a water pump, and would make water come out of his mouth and nose. He motioned to a barefoot peasant with disheveled hair and a dirty gallabiya to approach, which he did. He told him to bend over and he did. When the peasant raised his head a little from his bent-over position, the juggler rebuked him, telling him not to do it again or he would obstruct the flow of the water: "The water doesn't go up, jackass!" The audience laughed. The juggler stood right behind the peasant's rear end and began to operate an imaginary pump with his hand, as everyone watched in silence. Suddenly the bent-over man spread open his hands under his mouth and water poured out on his palms. He got up, choking and coughing, as the juggler hit him hard on the back to help him breathe. The juggler then went cheerfully around the circle among the spectators, who were laughing in surprise. "Did you see this great act?" he proclaimed. "I challenge any magician, I challenge Hitler himself, that same Hitler who'll teach the English to behave and who'll do bad things to them, I mean—"

The audience laughed louder after he said the obscene word. He had a small tambourine in his hand that he used to collect the piasters and pennies that the spectators were giving him. The peasant who had taken part in the show had gone back to the audience. Then the juggler began to speak of another trick that he would perform. But Dimyan shouted to him to do the pump trick again. It seemed that the juggler did not hear him or that he ignored him, so Dimyan continued to shout, requesting that he do the trick again, and several others joined him.

The juggler stood with a confused look on his face. He had taken out some ribbons with different colors from a cloth bag on the ground, so he returned them to the bag and looked at Dimyan defiantly. "You want the pump? Okay, come on over."

Dimyan had followed with his eyes the man who had taken part in the show and saw that he had moved away and disappeared. He let himself be led by the juggler, who said to the audience, "If no water comes out, it's because he's stuck up."

The audience burst out laughing and Dimyan was annoyed. Some members of the audience kept shouting, reassuring him that water would come out. The juggler told him to bend over, using an obscene word, and Dimyan complied, realizing for a moment how wrong the whole thing was. He had wanted to embarrass the poor juggler in front of the people. But he was not as smart as the juggler, and perhaps the latter would make him the laughingstock. But he did not back down. He bent over, and the juggler moved back a little, pretending to examine the middle of Dimyan's buttocks closely as the audience laughed. Then the juggler began turning his index finger in the air in front of Dimyan's buttocks, and the audience laughed more. The juggler kept saying, "We've got to clean it out," and each time, the audience laughed. Blood was now rising in Dimyan's face, and Magd al-Din felt sorry for his friend for putting himself in such a situation.

"Here goes!" shouted the juggler and turned the imaginary arm of the pump but no water came out of Dimyan's mouth.

"Wait for the surprise," the juggler went on. "No despair with life, in the immortal words of the great Saad Zaghloul!"

Then he backed down a little and kicked Dimyan in the buttocks as hard as he could, making him fall to the ground on his stomach, his face almost hitting the ground, had he not leaned on his arms.

The juggler stood back, saying to the audience, "His pump's empty—it gave the jinn a hard time for nothing. That's why I hit him in it."

As the audience laughed boisterously, Magd al-Din stepped forward to help Dimyan up, but Dimyan suddenly leapt on the juggler's back, sitting on it in such a way that the man was forced to stoop. Dimyan rained blows on the back of the man's neck, then jumped off and stood waiting for a fight. But the juggler looked at him, then ran and gathered his pile of things in his cloth bag and ran away.

The money that he had collected was scattered every-where, and everyone in the audience, young and old alike, rushed to pick it up. Magd al-Din and Dimyan left in silence, turning into Nabi Danyal Street toward Raml Station. After they had moved far enough away, Magd al-Din could not help asking Dimyan, "What did you do that for? We all know that the juggler's a trickster, but it's a show and a livelihood for him."

"I don't really know why I did it, Sheikh Magd. I only meant to have some fun with him."

Magd al-Din had never seen the world as colorful as it was that day. In the village, the feast also had children playing games, watching puppet shows, and engaged in other distractions. In the village, children's clothes were also new, but something there always made them appear old, perhaps because of bad fabrics and poor designs. Certainly the dull colors of the houses there and the dust kicked up by the donkeys that the children rode had something to do with making things appear older than they were. He did not want to remember the village now, anyway—let Alexandria take him to her heart. The open space here was whiter than Ghayt al-Aynab; the expansive blue sea inspired a feeling of serenity and rest. The clouds had left the city today, the wind calmed, and people were told to go out and have a good time.

"Battleships all the way to Bahari and Maks—English, French, Australian, and otherwise," said Dimyan to Magd al-Din when he saw him staring at the eastern harbor in the distance, and the military ships that filled it, with their foreign flags and big and small cannonry on board, and a few soldiers moving on the decks. Next to the ships, their shadows moved, up and down with the movement of the waves. Could Hitler actually make it all the way to Alexandria? Everything around Magd al-Din seemed to suggest that, ever since he had arrived. It was noon, and the statue of Saad Zaghloul loomed tall and awe-inspiring as he looked at the sea, pointing downwards. In the park below him, the children were having fun, and young men and women were sitting in peace. It was a splendid autumn day on which the rain-keeper kept the rain away from the happy people.

"Those are Australian soldiers."

Magd al-Din was looking at a number of tall soldiers with blue berets.

"They speak English like the English soldiers, but they're taller," Dimyan continued. "If you see two soldiers together, the taller one is usually the Australian. Their country is big."

Magd al-Din wanted to tease his friend. "What good would it do me to tell the Australian from the English?"

Dimyan looked at him for a moment, then smiled and replied, "True. What good would it do you or me? Perhaps just speaking about things has uses that we don't know."

They laughed and kept walking. As they passed some African and Indian soldiers, Dimyan said, "Soldiers from all over the world . . . The Africans have little tails—everybody says that. The Indians are so full of themselves, they walk like they're lords of their own manor. You know something? I wish I could go up behind one of them, slap him on the back of the neck, and run."

"These are poor men, Dimyan. They left their countries against their will, and none of them know whether they'll go home or not."

Dimyan fell silent, truly touched. A number of English soldiers appeared on the corniche, and a few of them were women. Some of the men had put their arms around the women, and some kissed quickly as they walked. Out of nowhere, many horse-drawn carriages appeared from behind, engaged in a mad race, carrying local lovers, foreign lovers, and drunken soldiers, both

men and women. The pedestrians tipped their hats and berets to
the riders, and the air filled with boisterous revelry.

"We are now in Manshiya. This is the statue of Ismail Pasha,"
said Dimyan, pointing to its semicircular pedestal. "Ismail Pasha is
King Farouk's grandfather, or his relative, anyway. He was the
one who built the Ismail Maternity Hospital. They say he's the
one who built the city of Ismailiya, that he was the one who first
moved to educate girls."

Magd al-Din did not need to hear anyone talking, but he let
Dimyan continue. He really wanted to drink in the light, the
refreshing breeze, and the water of the sea. He felt his chest
expanding, and his spirit revived. He would postpone the noon
prayers until mid-afternoon, or even wait until he went home at
sunset. Dimyan had told him that they would walk to Anfushi,
and he was happy for that. Dimyan must have sensed his friend's
secret desire and stopped talking. They walked in silence.

When it had rained during Ramadan, some streets, as well as the
untiled sidewalks, became muddy. In the early morning, people
going to work and students going to school walked as close as
possible to the walls. At the Sidi Karim roundabout, Magd al-Din
saw the water collecting near the sidewalks; it was so high people
had to wade through to cross the roundabout or to reach the
streetcar. The road there was paved, but it lay at the bottom of the
slope that began at Raghib Bridge. The narrow sewers could not
handle all the water.

Magd al-Din saw three barefoot young men standing on the
sidewalk, their pant legs rolled up to their knees, wearing old, tight
pullovers torn at the elbows and shoulders. For two pennies per
person, they were offering to carry pedestrians from one sidewalk
to the other or to the streetcar stop. Some pedestrians had placed a
row of stones, a sort of bridge to cross the street, but the three
young men removed the stones so that they were the only bridge.
The women and girls had to walk all the way to Raghib Bridge and
cross at the other side, where there was barely any water, then go
back to the streetcar stop.

One of these young men was Hamidu, the only son of the woman who sold vegetables at the entrance of the house opposite Dimitri's, and who had an amazing story to tell Zahra every time she bought anything from her. Hamidu had a long scar on his cheek and looked quite strong. After finishing this odd work, he would lug his shoeshine box and tools on his shoulder and head for the public squares or the cafés. Hamidu's hair was always disheveled, giving the impression at first that he was crazy. He never talked to anyone on the street and was never seen without his shoe brush in one hand and in the other a falafel sandwich, which he would wolf down part way, then place whatever was left of it in the first crack in the wall that he came across.

Magd al-Din saw Hamidu carrying people across the street for a few pennies and asked Dimyan whether this strange kind of work was common in Alexandria. Dimyan told him that only happened on the hungriest days.

Hamidu's image haunted Magd al-Din as he walked with Dimyan along the coast in Bahari and Anfushi. The wind made the tops of the tall, elegant Indian palm trees sway, their lush green fronds waving in front of the baroque balconies and facades of the old apartment buildings. The air here had the taste of cool, fresh water; the corniche curved gently, and the small fishing boats rested on the shore, nets piled high or stretched out, and no fishermen in sight. Today was the feast, and God was watching over everything and everyone.

Magd al-Din looked at the crowd of young men and women, taking in the refreshing smell of the sea and the grass, the sight of the vendors of peanuts, seeds, and roasted sweet potatoes. The horse-drawn carriages that had been going so fast were still speeding along, carrying lovers to the vendors of fried fish and shrimp, clams, and crabs. Magd al-Din decided that the whole scene did not suit him. How could he, a pious sheikh, be a witness to all these displays of love, coquetry, and mischief? So he asked Dimyan if they could go back as soon as possible, since the mid-afternoon prayer time was approaching, and in the winter, the time between that and the sunset prayer passed in the twinkling of an eye.

"We need a glass of tea in some café," Dimyan said. "What do you think?" Magd al-Din thought sitting at a café was more proper than being in the midst of all the revelry.

Dimyan took him away from the coast, and away from Tatwig Street, busy with the streetcar, decorated stores, and children running in every direction.

He must have sensed what was bothering his friend. In no time at all, they found themselves in Manshiya, which opened up before them, dazzling light pouring through the spaces between its broad, low buildings with capacious balconies and wrought-iron railings. Most of the stores were closed because of the feast, but restaurants and bazaars were open for business, as were the money changers on the sidewalk, their glass counters filled with coins and banknotes from all over the world. Despite the feast, many of them were busy at work, always wearing their eyepieces. The statue of Muhammad Ali stood high in the middle of the square. Magd al-Din and Dimyan sat down at the Nile Café.

"This is the brokers' café," Dimyan told his friend. "The stock exchange is right in front of you." He pointed to the middle of the square, where there stood a splendid white building with long, high windows and an imposing balcony. "And this," he added, "is Tawfiq Street. The exchange is closed today. How many homes it has supported and how many it has ruined!"

Magd al-Din pondered briefly what Dimyan said, his eyes involuntarily scanning the patrons, staring at their prosperous faces and thick white or dark glasses with golden frames. Those who did not wear glasses seemed to be focusing on something not quite there. A strong smell of tobacco smoke filled the air. Magd al-Din lit a cigarette and rolled another for Dimyan. He saw Hamidu come into the café carrying his shoeshine box. He watched him stand there studying the patrons, tapping the box lightly, then quickly go over to an English officer in military uniform who had taken off his green woolen cap and placed it on the table. The officer, about thirty years old, had a strong, ruddy complexion.

Hamidu sat in front of the man and, placing the officer's feet on his little stool, began to shine the black boots with white buckles. The officer was busy reading a foreign newspaper.

Magd al-Din did not take his eyes off Hamidu. As he watched him, he finished shining the boots, then started feeling them with his fingers. Magd al-Din did not know what exactly Hamidu was doing. Then Hamidu pulled the little stool from under the man's feet and lowered them gently onto the floor and stood up. Magd al-Din saw clearly that the officer gave Hamidu a one-pound note. Hamidu took it, then reached out and took the officer's baton, which the officer had placed on the table. The officer looked very puzzled, and before he could speak or protest, Hamidu had run away with the baton and the pound. The officer tried to overtake him; he got up, but as soon as he tried to move, he came crashing down, almost breaking his head and injuring his face. Luckily for him, there were several chairs in front of his, which helped break his fall, so he did not hit his face. He ended up on his back on the floor, writhing in pain and raising his head trying to see his feet. When Hamidu was feeling his boots, he had been tying the laces together—that was why he had lowered the officer's feet gently to the floor. There was a commotion in the café. An English officer stood up and took his gun out of its holster. An Indian soldier stood, befuddled, watching Hamidu run away on Tawfiq Street. The café patrons laughed for a moment, then were silent again out of pity for the young officer lying on the floor in pain. The waiter then quickly went over to him, untied his shoelaces, and helped him up to his seat. All the patrons were now looking on in silence, awaiting his reaction. The officer, too, was silent, then in broken Arabic he swore, "Bastard!"

Everyone laughed, and he got up and left the café in embarrassment.

The last few days of the year passed quickly. Rain came down hard, almost flooding the city—which during the winter suffered torrential rain for days and days, then the rain would stop for several days, then it would rain again nonstop, and sometimes the rain changed to hail. Work opportunities were now scarce. The textile mill laid off Magd al-Din and Dimyan, and once again they had to go job hunting every day. The ships arriving in Mahmudiya

Canal were few and far between. Sitt Maryam had told Zahra that
during the last few weeks of the year, Alexandria suffered
successive, almost continuous storms, until Epiphany, and then
the storms would increase in frequency and fierceness in the
following month, the last of the year. Camilla said, laughing, that
the thunder was going to sound like bombs and would shake the
houses, and lightning would dazzle the eyes. Zahra looked at her
admiringly as she added that the best thing to see in Alexandria
was the coastal road, the corniche, in the winter when the waves
rushed in and crossed the street, crashing against the apartment
buildings. She said the winter weather had prevented her from
going to see Abd al-Wahhab's new film, *Long Live Love*. The
dark, cold, and rain made Amm Mahmud, vendor of the crime
sheets, appear only rarely. News of crimes and scandals, however,
still circulated among the people, who learned, for instance, about
the young man killed by his colleague at night in the Labban
neighborhood, and another young man whose body was found in
a closed kiosk in the Farahda neighborhood. They found out
about the second incident of a woman marrying a man while still
married to another, and the man who had killed his own father a
long time before, and on the day of whose execution the black flag
flew above the Hadra prison.

On the clear days when he did not work, Magd al-Din was
now spending most of his time at the café by the bridge. Dimyan,
who kept him company most of the time, would ask him to read
the paper out loud, even though he frequently expressed surprise
that Magd al-Din kept buying the paper whenever he was not
working. "How can you pay five pennies for useless words and
lies?" he would ask. Magd al-Din had grown fond of knowing
what was going on in the world. He only read the big headlines
about the state of war in the world, then the crime section and the
obituaries. Why? He did not know.

Hitler had liquidated his enemies in the German aristocracy
and the remnants of the empire, as well as all who opposed him
after the incident in Munich. The Italian legation celebrated the
birthday of King Victor Emanuel III. The Egyptian government
banned trade in cigarette butts, which was common among street
children, who collected the butts in cafés and clubs, and on public

transport vehicles and in the stations. They collected them as quickly as sparrows collected grain and then sold them to poor peoples' smoke shops. The sly fox Mr. Churchill, first lord of the admiralty, gave a speech in which he talked of the Allies' losses at sea over the ten weeks since the outbreak of the war and how England would not be intimidated by threats. The Wafd party leaders visited the tomb of Saad Zaghloul on National Struggle Day, which the government did not observe. Al-Ahli Cinema screened Ali al-Kassar's film *Lend Me Three Pounds*. New camps were established to train the Territorial Army, which paraded before the minister of religious endowments at camps in Sidi Bishr and Damanhur. Despite the cold weather, the troops paraded in khaki shorts secured by wide suspenders and short-sleeved khaki pullovers over long-sleeved khaki shirts, with caps on their heads, and long Enfield rifles on their shoulders. The Monsignor nightclub opened the winter season by playing Argentinean music and Spanish songs. Forms were distributed to inhabitants of Karmuz, Mina al-Basal, and Gumruk to determine whether or not they wanted to be evacuated from Alexandria if the war reached it and where they would like to be evacuated to. No such forms were distributed in the poorer Ghayt al-Aynab neighborhood, which was part of Karmuz, even though it was separated from it by the Mahmudiya canal. The king inaugurated the new session of Parliament. A bullet discharged by a soldier's gun killed an officer on guard duty in front of the governorate building. The officer's funeral was marked by an official procession, then he was sent to his village of Quwaysna, where he received another official funeral procession. The soldier was executed. The lawyer in Alexandria had appealed the sentence, since the court had not given the soldier sufficient opportunity to defend himself, even though he had insisted that his rifle discharged accidentally. The black flag flew over Hadra prison for the second time in less than a month.

The Dutch steamer Simon Bolivar was sunk, and war with Germany loomed on the horizon. The appeal for peace made by the king of Belgium and the queen of the Netherlands failed. It was announced that Britain was now spending six million pounds a day on the war. Poland was now in total ruin, and Jews there were gathered in one neighborhood surrounded by barbed wire. No

sooner had December dawned than news came of the Russian
attack on Finland. German mines were sinking more and more of
the Allies' ships. The world was taken aback by the viciousness of
the Russian attack and the aerial bombing of Helsinki. English
cruisers had laid out a plan to sink the fearsome German pocket
battleship *Admiral Graf Spee*. The cruisers *Achilles* and *Exeter*
baited it in a battle that people followed every day. It was a bloody
match between wolves that went on for a few days, after which the
Graf Spee entered the port of Montevideo in neutral Uruguay. The
two cruisers lay in wait for it just outside the territorial waters.
What was *Graf Spee* going to do, and how would it break out of
this blockade? There were casualties on the pocket battleship, as
well as British prisoners of war that the *Graf Spee* had picked up
after their ships had sunk, but now it could not make it to the
Atlantic. Its captain was ordered to scuttle his ship outside the
territorial waters. The captain and his crew sank the ship in front
of spectators who had come from all over to Montevideo to watch
the deadly battle and record it. Laurel and Hardy got back
together, and their many fans were happy. A British army car
struck an Egyptian citizen on Maks Street, killing him instantly.
No next of kin was found. A certain Muhammad Musa threw
himself out of a window in the government hospital and died. No
one knew whether he had been killed, committed suicide, or was
overcome with hysteria. Fighting between Russia and Finland
continued, and the Finnish army stood its ground and scored
surprising victories. *The Graf Spee* captain Hans Langsdorff
committed suicide. He had held a press conference in which he
told the journalists that he had nothing to offer them, but that on
the following day he was going to give them something big; he
kept his word and gave them his suicide. Hitler threatened that he
would wipe out England by sending out a thousand planes every
day. In the Far East, the war between China and Japan flared up,
and the whole planet appeared to be one big fireball, on an
unknown part of which Magd al-Din, Dimyan, and dozens like
them were looking desperately for work. Magd al-Din was
puzzled by that half-crazy young man whom he always saw
appear out of nowhere near him at the doors of companies, or
hurrying alongside him from place to place. No one ever gave him

any work. Magd al-Din got used to his twang, and always took pity on him and more than once gave him a five-piaster piece. Occasionally, Magd al-Din would see the young man following him, until he would enter a café and sit down, whereupon the young man would go into the café too and sit at a distance, looking at Magd al-Din with his mouth open. Magd al-Din would then order him a glass of hot tea. Dimyan would say, "This is your jinn brother, Magd al-Din, who came out from underground." Magd al-Din would look at the idiot boy and see him as one of God's little children, lost but also blessed. Who could know?

The year was nearing its end. Zahra was very afraid of the thunder and the torrential rain. Sometimes it would be dark all day long. But her visits with Sitt Maryam and her two daughters, who frequently stayed home from school because of the rain, made her feel an intimate warmth, especially when Lula joined them with her jokes about vendors, merchants, and other people in the street. Lula's husband was now beating her more frequently. They would hear her screams coming from downstairs, but that usually subsided after a while and calm returned, only to be broken by her laughter. It was now a nightly occurrence. No one asked her anything about it.

Umm Hamidu's latest story to Zahra was about Count Zizinya, who was suing the city of Alexandria because it had seized his property in Raml. There was actually a lawsuit filed by Count Zizinya in which he accused the city of Alexandria of seizing land belonging to him along the coast from Glymenopoulo to Saba Pasha. She told Zahra that as a young girl she had worked as a maid in the count's palace in Raml, that she knew he was in the right, as the whole coastal area of Raml belonged to him, but he was a miser, so God sent someone to take everything away from him.

Unexpectedly, Umm Hamidu asked Zahra if she knew the poor woman that used to follow Bahi around in the street. Zahra said she did not know her. Umm Hamidu smiled and said that in Ghayt al-Aynab many people from Zahra's village knew her, that in her youth she had been in love with Bahi and that it was he who had caused her to lose her mind. Zahra fell silent, but Umm Hamidu kept on about how she had known many women who were madly in love with Bahi, that his face was fatally attractive to women, and that she believed that woman was one of his victims. Zahra said quietly, "This is old history, Umm Hamidu."

In the meantime the undertaker had found the body of Bahiya near Bahi's grave, stretched out in the mud, drenched by the rain and clasping her cane tightly with both hands. He had seen her a few days earlier sitting motionless in front of Bahi's grave, paying no heed to the rain and the cold. He tried many times to send her on her way, but she would give him a frightening glance and he would go away. That night he went to the graveyard to steal the shroud of a wealthy woman who had been buried that morning. On his return he saw Bahiya's dead body. He thought a little about what he could do and felt pity for the bereaved woman. He thought that if he notified the police, she would end up in a pauper's grave, since she did not seem to have any family; besides, the police were sure to make a big fuss about stolen shrouds and corpses in the rain. So he asked God for forgiveness, wrapped her in the rich woman's shroud, and buried her in the same grave as Bahi.

The year ended without a truce between the combatants. There were visits to the fronts by the various commanders, kings, and presidents, a message from King George V to the people and the army at Christmas, a message from General Gamelin to the people of France. Hitler himself went to spend Christmas with his troops on the western front. Everyone wished victory for their peoples and their armies. The Finns were still scoring surprising victories. The League of Nations expelled Russia from its membership. Yusuf Wahbi screened his film *Street Children* in Cairo, where there was an increase in cases of typhoid fever. Many bottles of cognac, champagne, and whisky were sold in Alexandria, where nightclubs stayed open by candlelight to bid farewell to the old year. Soldiers of the world danced with women of the world, and some cried, hoping for a better new year. Two days before the end of the year, a devastating earthquake reduced many villages in Turkey to rubble and obliterated the town of Erzincan. Zahra was hoping that the cold month of Kiyahk would soon come to an end. Magd al-Din and Dimyan would find work for a day and sit at the café for a week. On the morning of the last day of the year, the idiot boy sat in front of Magd al-Din, who ordered a glass of tea for him. But the boy suddenly burst into tears. Magd al-Din got up and sat next to him and asked him why he was crying. He said in that twang of his, his tears mixing with his snot, "My father killed my mother last night."

Pray for the salvation of the world,
our city, and all cities.
Kyrie eleison.

Coptic prayer

10

The bells of the church of Mari Girgis on Rand Street rang for the Christmas Eve mass. On the following day, Copts began celebrating Christmas. Young people went out dressed in their best, and so did the adults. The air was filled with the smell of cheap perfume, worn by people on their way to church or looking out of the windows of many houses. The joyous mood spread to young Muslim men and women, and many Muslim families went out to visit their Coptic neighbors to wish them a merry Christmas. Zahra saw Camilla, Yvonne, and their mother—three angelic roses whose faces were filled with a joy that she had never seen before. She wished them happy returns of the day, as Magd al-Din had instructed her the day before. He had heard about it from Dimyan, who told him, "Tomorrow our fast ends—forty-three days without meat, except fish. And we cook all our food using vegetable oil, Sheikh Magd. Our stomachs have had it, and they let us know it."

"So you fast forty-three days a year?" Magd al-Din asked him.

"Oh, Sheikh Magd," Dimyan laughed. "Almost the whole year is a fast. You have one month of fasting—we have several. It's an agony made bearable by poverty, which makes fasting the rule, not the exception."

After a moment he added, "Sometimes I think the fast goes back to the days of persecution. Take Lent, for instance—a fifty-five day fast, and the most important because it was observed by Lord Jesus Christ Himself. He fasted for only forty days, but we've added two weeks to it—one week before the forty days to prepare ourselves for it, and the other one after as a symbol of Christ's Passion."

"Dimyan, you're a devil!" Magd al-Din smiled.

After a pause, Dimyan asked, "Will you visit me the day after tomorrow? We're having a holiday, Christmas."

Magd al-Din was truly touched and decided to visit him more than once during the holiday. He heard Dimyan murmur, "Glory to God in the highest and peace on earth to men of good will."

That night he told Zahra about the whole conversation, and she realized the reason Coptic cooking smelled differently from Muslim food: "They fast all the time and they cook with oil—their whole life is an ordeal! God Almighty forgive me."

Camilla told Zahra, almost jumping for joy, "We're going to the mass, Zahra. It means prayer. We will sing praises to the Lord and say hallelujah and meet our friends!"

Zahra was surprised and baffled by what Camilla said, but figured it must be real and beautiful, because the mother and Yvonne also smiled. Zahra did not know why she was overcome by the urge to go with them to church, but her face turned pale for a moment at the unusual thought. She shook hands with them again, then heard Sitt Lula's voice and decided to spend some time with her. Magd al-Din was out late today. Maybe he had found a new job, since work here usually began early in the morning and did not end before seven in the evening.

The Christian holiday continued. It rained so hard on Epiphany that it seemed like the sky was just dumping huge buckets of water onto the earth. At night Zahra sat with Sitt Maryam, her daughters, and Lula, chewing sugar cane. Zahra discovered that the Christians did that just like the Muslims. Yvonne said confidently, "This is an ancient Egyptian custom— it's neither Islamic nor Christian. Our ancestors, the pharaohs, used to chew sugar cane on this occasion. It happens to coincide with the baptism of Lord Jesus Christ in the River Jordan. He was baptized by John. Do you know who he was, Zahra?"

"No, I don't understand."

Camilla laughed and said, "John is Yahya, son of Zakariya. Every day I hear Uncle Magd al-Din say when he recites the Quran, "*O Zakariya, we bring you the good news of a son whose name is Yahya.*"

Zahra appeared shocked by this girl, who had eavesdropped on Magd al-Din, as he recited the Quran in the evening in a very soft voice—but apparently they could hear it clearly.

"Let's stick to sugar cane," Lula said with a laugh. "We don't understand anything."

Khawaga Dimitri was working the night shift at the city garage. The Feast of the Sacrifice was approaching. Lula said with joy in her voice, "May God make every day a holiday!" The rain began to let up, and the black clouds stayed away. Yusuf Bey Wahbi's play *The Murderer* ended its run at Brentania Theater in Cairo. A big counterfeiting ring was apprehended with thirty thousand one-pound notes. Cosmos Cinema screened a new film featuring the singer Malak, *Back to the Countryside*. The Egyptian government sent the victims of the earthquake in Turkey twenty-four hundred wool blankets and vaccines for fifty thousand people. Dimyan said to Magd al-Din, "Do we have to have an earthquake here to get some blankets?" Then he smiled and said, "Dying of cold is better than dying in an earthquake, in any case." Construction of the chest hospital in Abbasiya, Cairo, was completed. It was announced that the Czechoslovakian army was formed in France. The Feast of the Sacrifice passed, and no one from the village came to visit Magd al-Din. It had started the day after Epiphany, and there were some murmurs among the Muslims: the rains, a blessing for the Christians on Epiphany, would, if they continued, not be a blessing for the Muslims on their feast days. People were surprised to see the feast start on a clear day, on which the sun rose early, and the earth drank up the water that had been pouring down until the previous midnight. After wishing Magd al-Din a happy feast, Khawaga Dimitri told him, "God has bestowed his mercy equally among the people, Sheikh Magd."

Magd al-Din was confused by this remark, especially because Dimitri had called him 'Sheikh Magd.' Dimitri explained that he was referring to how the rain had been pouring down non-stop for the last two days, Epiphany and the day before it, and it could have ruined the celebration of the Muslims' feast—they would have had to stay home and not go out to pray and visit. But God saved the day.

"God be praised," Magd al-Din assented. "Everything that comes from God is good."

"I was kidding you," Dimitri laughed. "I know you're a good man and that you don't treat Copts any differently from Muslims. This country, Sheikh Magd, has a slogan that goes back to the days of Saad Pasha Zaghloul: 'Religion belongs to God, and the country belongs to everyone,' but there are some bastards who like to kindle the fires of discord, especially in poor neighborhoods like ours."

Magd al-Din fell silent. He remembered Bahi, who had told him that the strife between the Muslims and the Christians had greatly diminished.

"There's always strife between different communities," he finally said to Dimitri. "Somebody must have given our country the evil eye, Khawaga Dimitri. Thank God the war is keeping everybody preoccupied."

The Feast of the Sacrifice was over. The Piaster Project Committee was still collecting donations for the Egyptian national industry in Cairo and the provinces. A new and unfamiliar type of mosquito descended upon Alexandria from the environs of Lake Maryut. The laboratory at the city's Center for Epidemiology studied it, and concluded that it was not a mosquito but some kind of feeble fly that the cold weather would take care of, and that it did not pose any threat. And indeed the remaining days of the Coptic month of Tuba wiped it out. The Muwasa Society conducted its annual lottery. The Opera House dedicated its shows to the Commonwealth troops. Queen Farida and Queen Nazli were keen on attending these shows. News came that Charlie Chaplin had finished *The Great Dictator.* Muhammad Abd al-Wahhab's film *Happy Day* was shown in Alexandria, and Camilla and Yvonne attended its last screening and told Zahra about penniless Abd al-Wahhab and the charming new child actress, Fatin Hamama. In the newspapers, Mrs. Aziza Amir thanked the Egyptian people for making her film *The Workshop* such a success and gave special thanks to the army and the art critics. Joint Egyptian-British maneuvers were conducted in the east at the eightieth kilometer on the Suez Road. Rita Hayworth was crowned Miss Hollywood for the year 1940. A new tomb dating back to 4500 B.C. was unearthed near Saqqara. King Farouk donated a movie projector for the entertainment of the troops and the people of Marsa Matruh. Three bodies were found in the Mahmudiya canal in the month of March. Among them was the body of the boy who spoke with a twang. The police apprehended the perpetrator, his own father, who had gone crazy. He also admitted to killing the mother. Magd al-Din stayed in his room for three days, blaming himself for the murder of the idiot boy, because he had not believed him the day he cried and said his father had killed his mother. Dimyan had advised him not to go to the police, saying that if there was a crime, it would be discovered. And it was, but it claimed the poor boy as its victim.

Dimyan saved Magd al-Din from his sorrow by taking him one evening to a faraway café on Mahmudiya Canal between the Raghib and Karmuz bridges, where lupino bean vendors lived in the houses scattered along the street parallel to the canal. They would place the lupino beans in sacks, which they secured firmly and left in the running water of the canal for a few days until the bitterness was gone. They would then pull the sacks to the bank of the canal and load the beans onto pushcarts and start selling them in the early morning in the neighborhoods of Raghib, Karmuz, Mahattat Masr, and Muharram Bey to the east and Qabbari and Kafr Ashri to the west. In the evening they would return exhausted and leave their pushcarts safely on the bank of the canal. In the morning they began their rounds again. A few of them sat in the remote café, in the empty area that was a good place for murder and love, as well as prayer and devotion.

Magd al-Din and Dimyan sat every evening in the very small café on the bank of the canal, which was really no more than a few wooden tables and straw chairs outside a small tin-sheet kiosk in which the coffee and tea were made. A pleasant breeze blew from Mahmudiya, laden with white mist, as if winter wanted to breathe its last breath there. In front of them passed boats with their sails unfurled, pulled from the bank by strong men with ropes tied between the masts and their chests. Around the big boats were small, colorful feluccas, in which young people were singing and making merry. The boats came from all over, ended their route at Nuzha, then went back.

Magd al-Din felt that everything around him was free except him, who had been shackled to Alexandria indefinitely. He was doomed to stay in the very Alexandria where yesterday he had seen Ghaffara, the sawdust vendor, stand in front of his cart and donkey and exclaim, "Please God, let Italy get together with Germany so Alexandria might be lit up with foreigners and sexy dames!" Everyone laughed—the passers-by as well as the store owners who bought sawdust from him to strew on the floor before sweeping their stores at the end of the day.

Ghaffara had a wooden cart with a wooden box about one meter high extending the length of the cart, about two meters. The cart was drawn by an old donkey that always looked exhausted. On both sides of the cart Ghaffara had written "Capacity: four tons; nationwide transportation; will take telephone orders and deliver sawdust." People would read the sign and laugh, as the whole cart—the wood, the donkey, sawdust, and Ghaffara himself—could not weigh a quarter of a ton. Ghaffara had appeared the day before with a fez on his face. He had removed the tassel of the fez and attached a rubber band that secured it behind his head. He had attached a round water filter to what had been the top of the fez and cut two small holes, into which he fixed two pieces of glass that stuck up to protect his eyes. He told everyone that he had heard an educated man reading from the newspaper about a proposal submitted by a doctor to the ministry of health to use fezzes as gas masks, since there were no gas masks in the market. Since the face and head had the same circumference, the fez could be secured to the face by means of a rubber band and a person could then make mica eyes for the fez. Ghaffara did not know where one could buy mica, so he used glass instead. The doctor suggested placing an air filter through which to breathe. In the stores in Attarin, Ghaffara could find no air filters, so he bought a small water filter. But there were no gases, or even raids against Cairo, or Alexandria, or anywhere else in Egypt. Ghaffara knew that and countered that the air in general was dirty and full of poisonous gases. One did not have to wait for the raids to get the gas.

Cannons were fired in Alexandria and throughout the country to bring the good news that a new precious gem had been added to the royal crown, as Princess Fawziya had given birth to a baby girl on the eighth of April. When the news was broadcast, a large number of Egyptians went to the royal palace in Cairo to offer their felicitations. Contrary to what was expected, Hitler did not attack Holland, Belgium, or France. He attacked Norway and Denmark instead. Russia was now done with Finland. The northern seas witnessed the fiercest battles over Norway, but the king of Denmark surrendered quickly and called upon the people to be calm. The Germans increased their pressure against the Allied forces in Norway. Troops from Rhodesia arrived in Egypt and were welcomed in Suez harbor by Ahmad Rasim Bey, the governor of Suez, whom the newspapers did not mention was also a great poet who wrote in French, and also a great lover of women. Joining him to welcome the troops was the British minister plenipotentiary, who delivered a speech welcoming them on behalf of the soldiers of the empire, not just in Egypt but in the "greater fatherland, from New Zealand to India."

Dimyan was beset by fits of dry coughing. He told Magd al-Din that he was afraid he might have developed asthma, in which case he would undoubtedly die, since a bottle of Mendaco pills cost thirty piasters, and besides there was a shortage since it was usually imported from England, and that was no longer feasible because of the war. Then Dimyan looked sad and told Magd al-Din that he had decided to go to church, confess his sins, and go regularly on Sundays. The Prophet's birthday had already passed in silence. People listened to the Quran on the radio, but there were no nighttime celebrations with the usual pavilions. Huge amounts of traditional sweets and sugar dolls and horses were still sold, however. Dimyan was observing Lent, which he believed was two weeks too long. He went to church without much thought and came back with tired eyes. "I cried a lot, Sheikh Magd," he said, "and the reverend father blessed me. I asked Mari Girgis to find a permanent job for you and me. And, as you can see, I am no longer coughing. The reverend gave me oil that got rid of the cough. Faith is sweet, Sheikh Magd. It's thanks to you that I've found faith, even if you didn't mean for it to happen. I had forgotten that faith, and men of faith, were still around."

Sitt Maryam gave Zahra a jar of 'Hazelin Snow,' a compact of powder and some lipstick and taught her how to use it. She told her, "You're still young, so why not do this for Magd al-Din's sake?" Magd al-Din saw her and realized what had happened but did not say anything at first. His wife was going to learn the ways of the big city whether he wanted it or not, and he had to keep quiet about it, otherwise she would seek it even more. He knew that forbidding something only made it more desirable. He even went out of his way to say to Zahra, "You've become more beautiful than before." And he knew he was not lying. He would come home exhausted after making the rounds of the factories along the Mahmudiya canal. He had made it all the way to the warehouses of the credit bank in Kafr Ashri. He had carried heavy sacks on his back all day long or worked at the cotton ginneries in Mina al-Basal amid hundreds of women who carried the raw cotton before the seeds were extracted, and he saw the collapsed chests of men with respiratory diseases as a result of inhaling the cotton dust, especially those men who oversaw the initial ginning process. And yet work was not always available, since the little cotton at hand had been left over from the previous season. So he made the rounds of the boats anchored in Mahmudiya Canal to load or unload cargo. From time to time he would catch himself looking around for someone and always found Dimyan, who never left his side. But he was not looking for Dimyan, but rather the murdered idiot boy of whom he thought quite often. And so as days passed, employed or unemployed, that huge area in the south of Alexandria became the daily arena of Magd al-Din and Dimyan, a painful arena from which he came back longing for something beautiful. And he was not lying when he told Zahra that she had become more beautiful. Biba Izz al-Din opened her summer season at Teatro Diana at Raml Station, as she did every year, but earlier than usual. Cinema Metro screened *The Wizard of Oz*, and the music caught on with the soldiers in the trenches and battlefields in Europe. Early khamasin dust storms blew in from the Western Desert for one whole day. As the month of May arrived, the Muwasa Society had finished building its hospital in Mina al-Basal. The city of Alexandria banned swimming in Anfushi this year, and future years if the war continued. The Christians celebrated Easter and seemed more joyous than at Christmas. The final examinations in schools started, and Zahra noticed that Camilla was looking paler, that she was not her usual cheerful self. Zahra asked her what was the matter, and she said she really loved school and that this happened to her every year with finals and the beginning of the long summer vacation. Zahra was surprised, and continued to notice Camilla's pallor, and saw her more than once struggling to hide her tears. She was surprised to see Yvonne also look pale. She talked about it to Sitt Maryam, who seemed baffled. Lula got into the conversation, saying, "If it was just one girl, we'd have said it was love." Zahra looked at her, annoyed, and Sitt Maryam blushed. At night Zahra thought a lot about the two girls and told herself that one of them was in a tight spot and the other knew about it. She immediately added to herself that Camilla, who showed more pallor and who had an angelic face like that of the Blessed Virgin Mary, was the one in the tight spot. She was like a flame that would not quit until it was extinguished. She asked God for forgiveness and to protect the two girls and the good family. The streets and gardens filled with lettuce leaves, green chickpea plants, green onions, and remnants of herring, sardines, and onion skins. True, all of that was in the garbage bins, but the passers-by and even people indoors could smell it. Zahra went out for the first time on a felucca in Mahmudiya Canal with Camilla, Yvonne, and Sitt Maryam, and they went to the zoo. Everything around them appeared cheerful, even the two girls. But their laughter was not as joyful as usual. Besides, Camilla left them and disappeared for more than an hour, then returned. Zahra noticed a new color in her cheeks and a joy that disappeared only minutes after her return. Those days, Camilla was never seen without an English book in her hand. She and her sister were enrolled in the most famous secondary school in Alexandria, the Nabawiya Musa School.

Shamm al-Nasim (the spring festival) and the other feasts were over. Finally Norway surrendered, and the Allies were beaten. The world waited with bated breath for Germany's next blow. The

German battle cruisers *Scharnhorst* and *Gneisenau* attacked the British aircraft carrier Glorious and sank it in less than ninety minutes. The Egyptian minister of national defense issued an order prohibiting marriage for second lieutenants in the Egyptian army so they would not be distracted from military affairs by family obligations. Opening Marsa Matruh as a summer resort was postponed indefinitely this season, in view of the war and because there was no place for people to stay anyway. The United States began exporting to the Allies the fighter jet Bell Airacobra, which flew at a speed of seven hundred kilometers an hour, at a price of twenty thousand pounds apiece. Fishing was banned in the western harbor in Alexandria, just as swimming had been banned in Anfushi earlier. General Baker Pasha, Alexandria's police superintendent, issued orders declaring May eighth an emergency day, so air-raid drills were conducted as were mock rescue operations. There was a call for volunteers to be trained, and the locations of public shelters and their capacities in the neighborhoods of Gumruk, Manshiya, Labban, Attarin, Mina al-Basal, and Muharram Bey were announced. Fifty prominent figures in the city of Sydney, Australia, agreed to a proposal to give, free of charge, tracts of land in the northwestern part of the continent to the Jewish Colonization Society for Jews fleeing Europe. The police superintendent's office in Cairo formed a six-hundred-man force of different ranks from the police and the army and placed it at the disposal of the political section. The dawn of the tenth of May brought the world the news it was afraid would happen one day. The Germans struck their biggest blow: their armies invaded the Netherlands and Belgium and part of France. The invasion of Norway was accomplished, and the world realized that the most horrific military revival in human history had taken place in Germany, which was now spreading terror everywhere in Europe. Mr. Chamberlain resigned, and Winston Churchill formed the new cabinet and stood in the House of Commons to say that his policy would be to wage war from the sea, the land, and the air, that the goal was one word: victory. King Farouk unveiled a statue of Mustafa Kamil, a young king dedicating the statue of a young leader. The newspapers published his now famous words, "Free in our land, hospitable to our guests. My soul, forged from the shining light of patriotism, cannot live in the dark of oppression and despotism." Preparations were begun to evacuate Alexandrians, if necessary, to the Bihayra governorate. The world discovered that Germany had deployed 126 divisions in its invasion of France. The Netherlands surrendered, since resistance was futile. Queen Wilhelmina broadcast a speech in English, in which she said that all prayers for détente and understanding had been in vain, that her nation had been defeated because of the enemy's superior forces, but that it would not be defeated morally, that the Dutch spirit would remain sound and strong. The newspapers in Egypt announced a new line of defense, comprising the Delta from Alexandria to Port Said as well as Cairo, and it turned out to be a line of defense coverage offered by a life insurance policy sold by the Sun Life Insurance Company. The area around the Muhammad Ali barrages was closed to the public as of May 15. The pricing commission of Alexandria met at the city hall to set the prices of staple goods and decided to keep the current price structure in place, with the exception of the price of matches, which was raised. The Postal Authority issued a five-millieme commemorative stamp bearing a picture of the year-and-a-half-old Princess Faryal. The Germans were able to open a fifty-mile-wide breach in the French lines of defense. Through it they placed their armored divisions sixty miles behind French army lines, thus encircling about half a million French soldiers behind the Maginot line, which the Germans did not attack directly, but in which they opened two breaches and went around it. The Belgian army laid down its arms after losing three quarters of a million of its men. In Alexandria foreign nightclub *artistes* were deported on a boat, and it was announced that all foreign artistes would be deported for fear that they might be recruited as spies. The number of English recreational women members of the ATS (Auxiliary Territorial Service) in Alexandria and Cairo increased. A special camp was set up for them on the Mustafa Kamil section of the beach and anyone who wished could get close and watch them in their swimsuits. Some malicious liars even said that sometimes they went into the water without said swimsuits. The first evacuation from Alexandria took place when a thousand orphan children were evacuated to orphanages in Mahalla al-

Kubra and Mansura. A man in whose possession were papers written in code was arrested and taken under guard to the main police headquarters in Cairo. There was only one merchant in Alexandria who violated the official pricing code, only one burglary, of a jewelry store in the goldsmiths' row. There were fifty traffic violations and one attempted murder. Britain was now like a dignified man with his pants down, trying desperately to pull them up but failing to, then finally managing to do it, after his heart had almost stopped. Britain had to withdraw its forces from France with the least possible losses, and it did manage to evacuate the troops from Dunkirk and Calais and other locations using all available vessels, big and small, and volunteer boats— the biggest escape operation by sea in history with about four hundred thousand soldiers evacuated back to their island under German bombardment on land and sea. Magd al-Din would read the news to Dimyan, who could not believe that human beings could wreak so much destruction. Dimyan asked him, are people in Europe human like us, or or are they devils? How could the Earth bear all of this without exploding? When Dimyan saw a picture of Laurel and Hardy, he asked Magd al-Din about the name of the film. He told him it was *The Air Devils*, and Dimyan suggested that they watch it together, give up a lunch or a supper and watch it, so long as the cinema was not screening any Chaplin films.

Magd al-Din was surprised at the idea, and Dimyan asked him if the cinema was proscribed in Islam, and Magd al-Din said he didn't mean it like that, but that he thought if he ever got into a movie theater he wouldn't be able to get out of it. Dimyan, who had become like a meek little child since going to church and confessing and praying to Mari Girgis, laughed.

The raids of Paris had begun to intensify and the world waited with bated breath. Was Hitler going to enter Paris? Was the most beautiful city in the world about to fall? The newspapers published the poem written by the Egyptian poet Ahmad Shawqi after the end of the Great War:

You are the beauty and majesty of this epoch
The very cornerstone of its solid edifice

*The people of the epoch have taken up the banner of right
from you
Its civilization marched on in the light of your sons.*

The situation in France appeared quite bleak. A German armored division captured eight thousand British and four thousand French soldiers. That armored division was under the command of an intelligent German soldier whose name, Erwin Rommel, would become very familiar to Egyptians later on. His panzer division was nicknamed "the phantom division" and was the spearhead that penetrated the Somme, advancing toward the Seine, capturing all the French and English troops in its way until Rommel occupied Cherbourg which, together with its troops numbering thirty thousand, surrendered to him. The roads in France were filled with refugees chased by the machine guns of German planes. The French army collapsed and De Gaulle was appointed undersecretary for national defense. The Soviet Union seized the Baltic republics. But who had the time to think about that? Paris fell, and the people's hearts were wrenched by the horrors of war. Camilla wept, and when Zahra saw her she figured that Paris must be something so big as to cause Camilla to cry. Camilla said her life's dream was to travel to Paris one day and that she could not believe that the capital of beauty could fall.

General Pétain formed a new government, which laid down its arms and signed an armistice agreement with Germany. De Gaulle suddenly fled from Bordeaux to Britain, carrying the honor of the French nation with him. In the evening Khawaga Dimitri came into Magd al-Din's room. He told him that he had learned from a relative of his who worked as a supervisor at the Railroad Authority that the Authority needed some new permanent employees. They were needed to face the pressure of work these days, when dozens of cars loaded with provisions, weapons, and soldiers were arriving every day. Magd al-Din could go the following day to the administrative building of the Railroad Authority in Qabbari to submit an application.

The first person Magd al-Din thought of was Dimyan. He did not ask Khawaga Dimitri about that. He figured that they probably needed more than one worker. Quickly he made his way to Dimyan's house. In the morning, both of them applied for jobs and were accepted right away. They only had to have the usual medical check-up. This was the government job that would guarantee them a decent life.

Around them a state of the highest emergency had been announced. A few days earlier, on the tenth of June at 4:45 p.m. to be exact, Italy had declared war on England and France.

The world was shaken, and Italian mothers sobbed as they saw their sons called up for active military duty. The American secretary of state announced that Italy's entry into the war was a major catastrophe for humanity. Egypt immediately severed its relations with Italy. Real evacuation of many Alexandrian families to the countryside began. Thousands of gas masks were distributed and were used by falafel makers to protect against the vapors of frying oil and by the bakers in front of the big ovens. Ghaffara refused to change the mask he made himself out of the fez, as he did not trust anything that the government distributed. Dimyan said to Magd al-Din as he received the letter of appointment, "Georgius the Martyr has sent us this job as a gift, Sheikh Magd. I implored him for it."

"I also spent long nights reciting the names of God, until the Prophet came to me in a dream and my heart was reassured," Magd al-Din said in agreement.

At night, as Magd al-Din lay awake next to Zahra as she slept, he thought of his new job. He thought that no one in the world knew anything about him. What if he were to die? Would anyone care? Italy entered the war, and people began to flee Alexandria, but he had to stay. It had been an involuntary trip decreed by God, and now he had to sleep in the city whose eyes were now looking upwards, to the sky.

The cruel and ravishing bears
Born on the very day of war
Utter innocent wishes.

Paul Éluard

11

This day has a different flavor, and it is whiter than any other day before it. This is what Magd al-Din felt, the light pouring down on his face as he left the house in the morning.

He paused for a little while on the threshold and looked right and left. The street was deserted except for three persons, one at the end of the street to the right and the other two heading for Sidi Karim. People were still asleep or were awake but had not left their houses yet. Every day the summer sun brought the morning in surprisingly early. Yesterday at the headquarters of the engineering section of the railroad, they were given directions to their job location. They were to leave Ghayt al-Aynab and walk along the bank of Mahmudiya Canal to a point midway between Karmuz Bridge and Kafr Ashri bridge. There they would find a big housing compound for railroad workers, next to which they would find a smaller housing compound for traffic workers who also worked for the railroad. Between the two compounds they would find a small road ending at a gate to the railroad tracks, the vast, complex network of the "Zaytun" area, as they were told. After passing through the gate they were to go back left for a distance of two kilometers to reach their job location, Post Number Three. They did not understand why it was called a "post," since the postal authority was not hiring them. Neither of them bothered to ask about that. On their way back Dimyan said, "These are crazy people. They want us to walk all the way from Ghayt al-Aynab to the railroad housing compound along the Mahmudiya canal, then go back the same distance through the railroad?"

"What can we do?" Magd al-Din asked him.

"The job location is just in front of Ghayt al-Aynab and Ban Street. Two alleys away we'll find the fence separating Ghayt al-Aynab from the railroad. We'll find an opening in the fence, or we can make one ourselves, or jump over the fence."

Today they would do that and they would do it every morning, for this was a permanent job, a government job. Magd al-Din stood in front of Dimyan's house and called out his name. The whole house, even the walls, seemed asleep. The door was low and dark and out of it came a draught of warm air laden with the breath of the crowded dwellers. The morning air was truly refreshing, and the dew that had gathered on the streets and the houses at dawn was still sending forth a cool breeze, if one kept away from the doors of the houses. The smell of soap rose from the streetcorners, bath water poured out on the street by fulfilled, satisfied women at dawn before anyone could see them. Only the houses looked tired and drab, their main entryways without wooden or metal doors, the narrow staircases emitting the smell of fatigue. But Magd al-Din was happy, feeling the cool of a winter morning even though it was summer. Dimyan emerged out of the dark door into the light of the new day.

"Look at you in that khaki suit!"

Magd al-Din smiled without comment, looking at Dimyan's head now covered with a blue beret that looked like a train engineer's hat. The two proceeded like two merry children toward the fence in the south.

They stopped in front of the stone wall, which was about two and a half meters high. Magd al-Din thought that jumping over the wall might be forbidden. He was confused for a moment, then heard Dimyan say, "It's not that high, as you can see. I'll clasp my hands together, and you can climb on them, then you get to the top and sit down, then give me a hand up to join you—then we'll get down on the other side."

Dimyan clasped his hands together, but Magd al-Din hesitated. He lifted his foot from the ground then put it down again.

"It's hard for me to step with my shoes on the hands of one of God's noble creatures."

"What?"

"How could I step with my shoes on a creature that God has exalted?"

Dimyan looked at him incredulously then saw Magd al-Din actually take off his shoes and throw them over the wall. Dimyan smiled and shook his head at his friend's meekness. He clasped his hands, and Magd al-Din stepped on them with his right foot then jumped up and grasped the top of the wall, feeling the hard stones of the wall, which could not have been more than twenty centimeters thick. Dimyan pushed him up, and finally Magd al-Din was able to sit on top of the wall. He suddenly said, "The wall is shaking!"

"Don't be afraid. It's very solid."

Dimyan stood wondering how he was going to climb. It would be hard to grasp Magd al-Din's hand and jump; that might pull Magd al-Din down. Magd al-Din himself must have thought the same thing. He said, "You can step on my foot. Think of it as a stair and then give me your hand."

Dimyan took off his shoes and threw them over the wall and jumped up until he held on to the top of the wall, pushing down a little which helped him to get a little higher. That made it possible for him to place his foot on that of Magd al-Din, who held him by the jacket to help him up. Dimyan's torso was now higher than the top of the wall. God in heaven! What happened? Crash! A big chunk of the wall collapsed with them on top of it; it fell down in one piece, and quietly.

Magd al-Din fell down on his backside, and Dimyan's chest hit the wall, and both felt great pain where they fell. But a few moments later after they overcame the shock of the fall, they were now facing each other, and they both laughed happily: two solitary men in a huge open space laughing without an echo. They both got up, leaning on their hands, and started looking for their shoes. Neither of them had looked around nor seen anything until now. The first thing they saw was the vast, open space and the sun rising strong to their left and the faraway blue sky. But the land appeared dreary, lime and sand and little rocks, two old and rusty rails, beyond which stretched land covered with thorny plants and short cactus, then a few rails, between which were pebbles and evaporated fuel oil that appeared to have separated from the soil, its black color turned gray by the eddies of dust. At intermittent distances they could see a few small thickets of unkempt thorny plants.

They walked to the right. Dimyan was quite surprised at how vast the land was as it opened up before him. How could he have missed all of this even though he had lived for many years in Ghayt al-Aynab? Why had he never thought of going beyond the wall so close to Ban Street, separated only by two alleys? This vast open space to the south was matched only by the vast sea to the north.

Some of the railroad tracks seemed to end at new bumpers attached to short concrete columns. There were many cars lined up on more than one line. They appeared to have been lined up carefully, for on every line there were for the most part cars of one kind only: the flatbed cars on one line, the boxcars on another, and the semi-closed ones on a third. All the cars were dull brown, with the exception of the boxcars, which were dark gray. The floors of the flatbed cars were covered with thick wooden boards, planks attached together by wide, thick iron ties nailed to the boards. But despite all the obvious care taken in storing the cars, the place appeared deserted. Magd al-Din thought that perhaps they had been duped, that Adam, peace be upon him, when he descended from heaven must have descended to a place like this one, that God who sent Adam to earth in the care of providence, would forsake them here. There was not one single bird in the sky, but they saw in the distance a pipe rising from the ground, with an oilcloth hose that almost reached the ground, attached to it. Next to the pipe a man sat next to a big green mulberry tree under a canopy made of bare tree branches.

"So there are people here," exclaimed Dimyan, who must have been thinking along the same lines as Magd al-Din.

"Come on. Let's go ask him."

The man was about their age, but his clothes were tattered and he was barefoot. He was so dejected that he seemed not to have heard their footsteps. When they got close to him both of them thought they probably should just keep going and leave him alone, for he seemed totally oblivious. But in the way that one sometimes thinks of doing something, changes his mind, yet still does it, Magd al-Din asked him, "Where do we find Post Number Three?"

He pointed with his index finger, indicating that they were headed in the right direction. But Dimyan, who did not like the man's silence, exclaimed,

"What's with you, man? Speak, the day's just begun!"

The man looked at him for a long time, and Dimyan was at a loss and began to shrink back in fear. Magd al-Din almost burst out laughing, not believing what was happening to his friend.

"Get out of here," the man said in a faint voice.

"Yes, sir," said Dimyan meekly and walked despondently in silence as Magd al-Din tried to muffle his laughter.

After they were far enough away Dimyan said, "That was a jinn, Sheikh Magd."

A big wooden kiosk appeared, its walls made of wooden planks planted close together in the ground. On top of them was another row of planks, attached to the lower row by broad metal strips, and on top of it all was a pitched roof of corrugated iron.

Next to the kiosk a man was crouching over a little fire holding a big tankard with a long handle made of braided wire. "Greetings," they both said. The crouching man raised his head. He was making tea, which had begun to boil in the tankard. They could smell its pleasant aroma.

"You must be the new workers, Magd al-Din and Dimyan. I'm Hamza. We've been waiting for you."

Today should be considered a feast day. Zahra went to the market at Sidi Karim, behind the police station, and bought a pair of pigeons for five piasters and a chicken for ten piasters. Sannusi, the butcher on Fawakih Street, slaughtered them for her. She cleaned them and boiled the chicken and the pigeons, then she stuffed them with southern Egyptian hulled wheat, which she had bought from Bishri, the grain and spice dealer on Raghib Street.

The pleasant aroma filled the second-floor hallway and also the first floor. So Lula too went out quickly and bought pigeons and chicken and came back and started cooking them. She did not forget to go up to the second floor and tell Zahra that she could not resist the delicious aroma of her cooking and so had to do like her. She asked Zahra, who was quite surprised, to forgive her. Zahra insisted that Lula taste the chicken gizzards. All the while Sitt Maryam followed the exchange smiling, for she understood the intricate meanings of women's little games!

Zahra's little girl, Shawqiya, was playing in the hallway between the two rooms, and Camilla was teasing her from behind the open door and their laughter could be heard. A kitten came up from the first floor and stood in front of the hallway meowing and looking around. This frightened Shawqiya and made her run to her mother, and as she did she stumbled on the door's low threshold. Her mother held her up to her bosom, patting her on the back and calming her down.

Shawqiya had screamed, which made Camilla hurry into the hallway. She figured out what was happening and shooed the cat away. The sun bathed Camilla, who stood there in a tight, short, light dress. Her strong, svelte body was bursting with femininity. She had a small frame that was filled with yearning to rebel and break free like a mare, and a body that imposed itself on your eyes so that when it approached from a distance you could not see anyone else. The fragrance of that body, like the aroma of aged wine, filled the nostrils and stirred the soul. Anyone who spoke with Camilla had to fight a real desire to take her in his arms without any preliminaries. Her slender waist and unbound, inviting chest appeared like a natural harbor for every hungry ship. Little, gentle Camilla had a body sanctified by an aura of warm allure. Zahra saw Camilla under the sun and exclaimed to herself, "Praise the Creator, she's a gazelle!" Camilla heard her and did not say anything because the sound of drums and brass and wind instruments playing a military march drowned out everything else.

"The cinema!" Camilla shouted and ran to the window of their room. Zahra followed her, smiling. Quiet Yvonne gave up her place at the window to Zahra and went into the inner room to watch from its window. Sitt Maryam stayed in her place behind the sewing machine, working quietly now.

The cinema cart was a large wooden box with posters on its four sides. It was pushed by a man wearing a military uniform, which in fact was the uniform of all the popular street musicians, most prominent of whom was a man who carried a huge drum about one meter across that hung from his neck by a leather strap and rested on his belly. In his hands he had two drumsticks covered with cloth with which he beat the drum on both sides. Around him was the rest of the band beating smaller drums or cymbals or playing the same military march on their saxophones. Around everyone was a group of children dancing and laughing.

"Look at Clark Gable!" Camilla said to Zahra.

"Who?"

"Clark Gable."

"Is that the man or the woman?"

Camilla laughed. "The man, of course. The woman's name is Joan Crawford."

Zahra fell silent for a few moments then, washing her hands of the whole affair, said, "These are difficult names."

"The name of the film is *The Sinful Desire*," Camilla told her.

"Behave, girl!" Sitt Maryam shouted from behind her.

Everyone fell silent. Zahra thought about this indomitable girl who had been so sad the past few months and who had cried when the Germans entered Paris. What was it that made her regain her gaiety? She must have gotten out of her predicament. Zahra suddenly realized that she should not have looked at these posters for the movies this time. She had decided that the last time, when she saw in the picture an almost-naked woman jumping into the sea. This time she saw the actor with the trimmed mustache embracing the actress, boldly bending over her and almost kissing her. How could they take these wanton pictures and display them in the streets for every woman and girl to see? She backed up from the window and said, "Come with me, Camilla."

Camilla walked behind her to Zahra's room. Zahra had been holding her daughter by the hand all that time. She let go of her hand and uncovered the pot and with a ladle took out the chicken liver, put it on a saucer, and offered it to Camilla. Camilla was surprised but did not turn it down. Zahra told her, "Your uncle Magd al-Din has started a new job today."

"Congratulations! So that's what you're celebrating!"

After a few moments Camilla asked, "Does every wife love her husband the way you do, Sitt Zahra?"

"The way I do? No. But who else does a wife have besides her husband? Do you learn something else in school?"

"We learn that exactly in school, and then some."

"What is it that you like about that actor with the difficult name?" Zahra asked her suddenly.

Camilla was chewing the hot chicken liver fast and blowing on her hands. After she was done she answered, "His eyes—his eyes are so deep, Sitt Zahra."

They both fell silent. Zahra thought about the age difference between them, only five years. Zahra was twenty-one, but Camilla was too daring for a sixteen-year-old girl. What would they do to a girl like that in the village?

"I'm afraid for you, Camilla."

"What for?"

"I don't know. I'm just afraid."

"Don't be afraid. The mischievous live longer," Camilla laughed and left the room.

The end of the school year was the reason Camilla had regained her gaiety. The ordeal was over. Perhaps she had needed no more than one other meeting to fall forever. How could she permit herself to get into this relationship, doomed to end in failure or death from the very beginning? Whoever said that one could joke about matters of love? But they were good days anyway. It all began in a contest between the boys of Abbasiya and the girls Nabawiya Musa held at Ras al-Tin school. Whose fiendish idea was it? The headmistress of Nabawiya Musa School was challenging society. She was a woman of liberal ideas, though she was strict with the girls. She asked for the impossible and was confident that she would get it. She would have the girls compete against the boys and was confident that the girls would hold their own. What happened was that he was paired with her. The literary and scientific questions were hard, but he was amazingly capable. He recited verses from Keats in English and Baudelaire in French, helped his teammates out, and was the reason the boys of Abbasiya school scored such a stunning victory that the Nabawiya Musa girls cried in agony. She could not deny that she thought about him for a few moments that night. She was haunted by his sad, pale face, by his simple clothes, clean but suggesting poverty, as did his slightly yellow face. His eyes were always moist, almost tearful the whole time, sad but contented eyes. That was what attracted her. He was a truly charming young man.

She went to sleep thinking that she would not see him again. But the following day she saw him standing on the sidewalk opposite the gate of her school. She froze for a moment. She realized that he had come to meet *her*. She held onto Yvonne's arm and would not let go. When she got off the streetcar at Karmuz Bridge she saw him getting off from the other car. He stood for a little while, watching them as they walked down the slope leading to Ban Street in Ghayt al-Aynab, then he walked along the Mahmudiya canal in the direction of Kafr Ashri.

He started stopping by her school everyday, just to look at her. Whenever she changed her route on her way home, he would be there. Finally she stood at some distance from the school and looked back at him. Yvonne was sick that day. It was as if he had prepared everything in advance. He came over to her right in the middle of the street with a necklace of white jasmine and in front of the passers-by, he slipped it over her head and around her neck. She stood totally still and he took her by the hand, and they walked to the Shallalat gardens.

"Where did you get the courage to do that on the street?"

"Poetry. I love all the crazy poets. Do you know the love story of Yesenin and Isadora?"

"No, I don't know Yesenin. I know that Isadora was an extraordinary dancer."

"Do you know anything about the French surrealists?"

"A little."

"Well, those surrealists do whatever they want, without fear."
They sat under the old, thick, tall laurel trees.

"I don't know how I gave in to you," she said.

He was looking at this meek hen with wide eyes and could believe neither what was happening nor what he was saying.

"But—" she added.

"I know, you're Christian—you're wearing a cross. I'm a Muslim. That's how it is. Where will it lead ? I don't know."

That day he read to her some of the poetry of Baudelaire, Rimbaud, and Éluard, of whom she was hearing for the first time.

He said to her, "My beautiful one, we must see the rose of your white milk bloom. My beautiful one, hurry, be a mother and give me a child in my image." When he saw that she was embarrassed, he said, "All the flowers of the fruits light up my garden, the trees of beauty and the trees of fruits. I work alone in my garden as the sun burns, a dark fire on my hand." He told her that what he had just said were verses from a poem entitled "Poems for Peace" that Éluard had written after the Great War and in which he was celebrating the soldiers' return home. That they were not love poems. She was surprised at herself: how could she be listening to this sad lover of poetry when she herself was a merry free spirit, he the Muslim and she the Christian? But she knew that the end was near at hand and that she herself had better end it.

She gave in more. They went together to the gardens of Nuzha and Antoniadis in the midst of the winter flowers. Yvonne now knew the story and begged her sister to spare her and to spare herself. Camilla would hide for a while, then find herself looking for him when she got out of school. As they were walking among the camphor, oak, towering Indian palms, and the bare acacias that would come into full bloom with the advent of spring, he asked her, "How old are you?" "Sixteen," she said. He told her that he was seventeen, that his life's dream was to finish secondary school and university, then go to the Sorbonne. Taha Husayn's educational journey was what he wanted to model his life on. It was not particularly important that he get a doctorate—what he most cared for was to walk in the Latin Quarter, visit the Louvre, Orsay, the Pantheon, the Eiffel Tower, and Montmartre, and on the banks of the Seine, to read poems that soared in the air. In the gardens that day, she let him give her a quick kiss, after which she asked that they go back without delay. The naive lover did not realize that her body almost burst free and held on to him, almost betrayed her and defeated her ability to control it.

For a week after, she did not go to school. She fell ill and had no will to move or eat. In the few moments that they were alone, Yvonne cried and told Camilla that she had pleaded with him to put an end to the relationship, to disappear from Camilla's life. She told him, "You're from northern Egypt, Rushdi—you don't know what southern Egyptians are like. Besides, in this case it's a compounded problem, a difference in religion, and violation of southern Egyptian customary behavior." She asked Camilla to forgive her for her desperate action. Rushdi disappeared. He no longer stood in front of the school to wait for Camilla, who now started going more frequently to the school library to borrow the books of French poetry translated into English. She read Victor Hugo's *Les Misérables* three times and memorized the streets of Paris, forgetting that that was a century and a half ago.

She soon recovered and laughed as she remembered how madly she had gone along with Rushdi. She also found that as soon as he disappeared, she was rid of any feeling of closeness with him. Was it the difference in religion that helped her to forget? He reappeared during exam period. She saw him waiting for her, holding a red carnation. He told her that after the exams he was going to his village, that his family was originally from the countryside. He also told her that he was sad that the Germans were attacking France viciously, that he was afraid that Paris might fall and Hitler would destroy it as he had destroyed Warsaw. Then he said, as if to himself, that Hitler could not destroy Paris; no one in the world could do that, even if they occupied it. Paris possessed a spiritual force that would stop the worst possible evil in the world; Paris had the power of beauty. He said he had come to say good-bye, to shake her hand quickly, as Yvonne was standing, tensely, at a distance. He apologized for any unease he had caused.

Camilla shook his hand. She remembered him only when Paris fell. She cried because she imagined him in his village, crying over the city that he loved. She had said she wished to visit

Paris only because he had said that himself. Then she soon forgot everything. But she asked her mother to give her permission to learn French at the Berlitz School on Saad Zaghloul Street. The mother said she did not mind, on the condition that she went in the mornings, accompanied by Yvonne, who also wanted to learn the language.

When the foreign teacher was explaining the French verbs, she wrote 'aimer' on the board and, addressing one of the girls, she said, "Je t'aime." Camilla found herself involuntarily repeating to herself, "Je l'aime."

He said, "Sit on the throne and I will present everything to you." I did, and he presented everything to me.

al-Niffari

12

Magd al-Din came back from work, as he did every day since he had started the new job, his hands stained with fuel oil, his back, arms, and legs exhausted, and aching all over. As usual he sat down on the bed, his feet dangling, as Zahra sat on the floor and pulled off his shoes and placed his feet in a small washbasin filled with hot water and salt.

"Are you going to bathe now?"

"Yes. Give me some kerosene, too, to clean my hands."

She poured some kerosene from a can into a small jug and gave it to him. She also handed him a bar of soap and put the towel on his shoulder and his slippers outside the door of the room. The bathroom was in the hallway for common use. When the water from the shower hit the floor tiles, it was audible to all, but there was no way around it; he had to bathe, since he came back so dirty he could not stand his own skin. He could neither eat nor sleep until he had washed away all the day's fatigue and dirt.

That day, like all other days, he had to dig into the hard earth under the old crossties, remove the old tracks and ties and, with his co-workers, install new ones—all for for more than one railroad line that needed maintenance or replace-ment. The many trains coming to the harbor left loaded with equipment and troops. The trains coming from Suez carried the African, Australian, and Indian soldiers of the empire all the way to the desert. The trains stopped in front of the pipe with the hose attached, next to which sat the silent man that he had seen the first day. There was an underground water reservoir to supply the steam locomotive; the pipe and the hose were connected to the reservoir, separated by a huge round knob that when turned would release water to the pipe and hose and ultimately to the locomotive. This whole apparatus was called 'the Raven,' no one knew why. As for the man sitting there, Hamza, Magd al-Din's co-worker said he was an insane man who had planted the mulberry tree a long time ago and sat waiting for little birds that never came.

Magd al-Din and Dimyan saw their co-workers leave their jobs and approach every train as it stopped to get fuel and come back carrying little cardboard boxes filled with chocolates, tea, and cookies. The Indian soldiers, with big turbans and long rifles, were more generous than the others. Hamza said of them, "Even though the Indian soldier is Indian, he is smart. I tell him 'English is good,' and he says 'Indian is very good' and gives me more cookies."

The workers would laugh at the way Hamza pronounced the English language and wondered where he had learned the many words he used with the soldiers. As soon as they moved away on the trains, Hamza would stand in the middle of the tracks and speak in verse:

> *The punishment meted out*
> *To humans, big and small,*
> *Is deserved. Many a sin and cruelty*
>   *they commit*
> *And the angels, they write it all down.*

Then he would look at the cookies and the chocolate or whatever he had gotten and exclaim,

> *If it were just one worry I could handle it,*
> *But I am assailed by three kinds of worries:*
> *One inside, one outside, and*
> *One at the door waiting for me.*

❖

The long iron rail is dislodged at a leisurely pace; it rises in a deliberately slow manner, tearing up the wooden flesh of the crossties, raising the long, spiral-shaped nails that leave behind deep round, glowing holes filled with splinters of wood. The rail elevates itself for a short distance then extends and expands, and out of it to one side come other, less thick rails that keep extend into space, shiny brown. Then they turn into large coils that quickly shrink but increase in number, as does the original rail. Then it rears its head and sticks out a forked tongue, stinging Magd al-Din's leg. He leaps up, into space, but does not come down. He settles on the roof of a train hurtling forward at a crazy speed as the wind makes his hair fly and tears away his jacket, undershirt, and pants. He holds on fast to the train's shiny roof, with nothing on except his underpants, but he slides down the side of the train and clings to the high edge and cries out, but no one can hear him. The train slows down gradually until it comes to a complete stop in the middle of two rows of people with unfamiliar features. They are laughing hysterically, ceaselessly and their bulging eyes never stop rolling. He falls in their midst. Some of them grab him and scrutinize him viciously, still laughing. The train keeps going, spewing its blue smoke. He sees Zahra in a panic behind the train, calling out to him, "Magd al-Din! Magd al-Din! Sheikh Magd!" while he is hoisted behind her on the hands of the people with strange faces and eyes, who are laughing ceaselessly and viciously. He screams, but his voice is lost in the hundreds of laughing faces. Zahra falls on the crossties and the fuel oil and turns back in pain, limping as the departing sun hurries to leave and the darkness hurries forth. The men with strange features leave him crouching in the dark, moaning faintly and long, feeling like an orphan. Then torrents of rain come down, with successive claps of thunder, as he shakes violently.

"Magd al-Din! Magd al-Din! Wake up! There's a raid!"

Zahra was shaking him hard. He leapt up, frightened and swearing, "I bear witness that there is no god but God and that Muhammad is His prophet! Zahra, you've saved me from a horrible nightmare!"

Actually Zahra had not heard his moaning but was awakened when Sitt Maryam knocked on their door and told her about the air raid and that they had to go downstairs at once.

"I take refuge in God from Satan the damned. This is the sound of real cannons!"

During the past few weeks, the city of Alexandria had built a number of open shelters in the poorer neighborhoods, but the inhabitants used them to relieve themselves. That forced the municipality to assign policemen to guard the shelters, and stopped the building process. The military court in Alexandria, under the emergency law, held a session to try a poor girl who was practicing prostitution without a license. She was fined three Egyptian pounds. A house in Karmuz was raided for being an unlicensed brothel. When the police surrounded the house, the owner shouted, "Where's Goebbels? Where's the Gestapo? I am Hitler!" But the valiant policemen were not fooled. They arrested him and gave him a sound beating on the back of his neck. The newspapers received a great number of letters asking about the beautiful Hollywood actress Norma Shearer and whether she would remarry after the death of her husband. The answer was in the affirmative, that the prospective husband was the actor George Raft, with whom she had a close relationship while her husband was still alive. People were also wary and cautious, as the Italians were a stone's throw away from Alexandria. That was why, when the air-raid sirens were heard several times in the daytime, they realized immediately that these were no longer drills, and when they saw anti-aircraft guns blasting away, they were certain that the time of drills was gone.

Strict orders were given to drivers to paint their headlights dark blue, after it was noticed that they had become lax about it in the past few months. People were instructed to paint their windows and to apply adhesive gauze strips vertically and horizontally to the glass from inside so that it would not fly around if shattered. People were also warned not to assemble on the streets during raids, and that all vehicles must come to a stop and passengers get out of the cars. Landlords were instructed to vacate the ground floors of their buildings and to convert them to shelters for people without access to the public shelters. People

whose property was damaged as a result of the air raids were told
to apply as soon as possible to the city of Alexandria to get new
building materials—wood, steel, and cement—to repair the
damage or to reinforce old buildings.

That night when Magd al-Din awoke, people heard the
intermittent sound of the sirens and felt it was different from
earlier ones. It was accompanied by unusual scurrying about and
panic; there was more worry in their hearts. The daytime air raids
the previous week had been shorter and had not caused any
obvious casualties or damage. Tonight it seemed that real war
would come to the sky over Alexandria.

It was midnight and very hot. A few people walking on Ban
Street quickly went into the nearby houses and stood in the
entrances. Two taxis stopped; one of the drivers did not leave his
cab. One of those standing in the entrance of a nearby house
looked at him and invited him to come in to be safe, but he said,
"If the house falls on top of me, will I live?" It seemed to make
sense. Those standing in the entrance looked at each other, but
they could not violate the civil defense regulations. Standing in
the entrance of a house was safer than being out on the street in
the open.

Even though the moon was not full that night, it was bigger
than a crescent, and it lit up the streets and betrayed everyone.

Khawaga Dimitri, his wife, and his two daughters had gone
downstairs to Bahi's empty room and turned off the light. Lula
had also joined them. In the confusion, she did not think to wear
something to cover her shoulders and arms. Her husband did not
join her there. He was the solitary type. Besides, he lived on the
first floor, so what good would it do him to move to another
room? The truth was slightly different. As soon as the air raid
sirens sounded and the guns began blasting away, Lula shook with
fear and moved closer to her husband, who hugged her tight and
reached to take off her panties. She heard the footsteps and voices
of Dimitri and his family and tried to break away from her
husband, who held on and wanted to have sex right then and there.
He thought that was the best way to overcome fear. She resisted
him and also resisted her own desire, which lit up as soon as he
touched her. She was thinking of what would have happened if the

sounds of their lovemaking were to reach the ears of Dimitri and his daughters. That was why as soon as she was able to break away from her husband, she dashed out and joined them in her long, white nightgown, her shoulders and arms lighting up the eyes of those standing in the dark.

Magd al-Din was guided in the dark by Dimitri's voice and did not let go of the hand of Zahra, who screamed as soon as she got in the room, "My God! Shawqiya is upstairs!" Magd al-Din had to go up to bring the little girl while Zahra stood with the others in Bahi's room.

The guns fell silent but the all-clear was not sounded. The silence lasted for a long time, and so did the people's patience. They all pricked up their ears to hear a slow, calm droning sound like rains coming from far away. The buzz grew in volume, as if swarms of killer bees were coming to the city, like a storm gathering on the horizon to overrun the desert, or armies of locusts homing in on green plants: ZZZZZZZ. That was sound of the German and Italian planes coming in for their targets in large formations, coming in close to the city and close to the ground. The sounds of bombs and explosions and the flashes of lightning passed quickly in front of the closed windows, penetrating the shutters and the glass.

"Open the windows so we'll know what's happening," Dimitri exclaimed. Magd al-Din was close to the window so he opened it. In front of them the night looked like daylight, white and red, and engulfed in a river of blue smoke. The sky was burning to the north and people on the opposite side of the street screamed as they saw the smoke. Magd al-Din, Dimitri, and the women watched the light come in from the north and burn bright into the south, like a sword brandished by a celestial warrior. Magd al-Din began to recite the beginning of Sura 36:

"*Yasin. By the Wise Quran, verily you are among those sent on a straight path, a revelation of the Mighty, the Merciful, to warn a people whose forefathers had not been warned, so they are heedless. Already the word has proved true of most of them, for they are not believers. Verily We have placed yokes around their necks to their chins so that their heads are forced up. And we have put a bar before them and a bar behind them and so We have covered them*

up so that they cannot see. God Almighty has spoken the truth."
Then he repeated, "And We have put a bar before them and a bar
behind them and so We have covered them up so that they cannot
see." He repeated the verse, his voice growing louder, and as he
swayed the moonlight revealed him to everyone, though he was
completely oblivious.

"And We have put a bar before them and a bar behind them
and so We have covered them up so that they cannot see." Zahra
began to repeat after him, and his voice kept getting louder. Sitt
Maryam kept repeating, "We ask you God, the Father, lead us not
into temptation but deliver us from evil," while Dimitri repeated
with her, "We ask you God, Our Lord, lead us not into
temptation, which we cannot endure because of our weakness.
Give us help to avoid temptation, so that we might extinguish
Satan's fiery arrows." His voice and Sitt Maryam's voice grew
louder, "And deliver us from evil Satan by Jesus Christ, our Lord.
Amen." Magd al-Din raised his voice even louder, "O God I ask
you to lift every veil, to remove every barrier, to bring down every
obstacle, to make easy every difficulty and to open every door. O
God, to whom I appeal and resort in hard times and in easy times,
have mercy on me in my exile. Amen, Lord of All Creation."
Magd al-Din, still swaying, began reciting the Quran again after
his prayer. Dimitri continued his own prayers. The words
intermingled in such a way that one could only make out that they
were the prayers of sincere souls devoting every bit of their being
to God, the Savior:

"By the wise Quran, . . ."
"O God, our Lord, . . ."
". . . on a straight path . . ."
". . . lead us not into temptation . . ."
". . . a revelation of the Mighty . . ."
". . . deliver us from evil . . ."
". . . whose forefathers had not been warned . . ."
". . . because of our weakness . . ."
". . . true of most of them, for they are not believers . . ."
". . . us from evil . . ."
". . . and we have put a bar before them . . ."
". . . that are Satan's . . ."

". . . that they cannot see."

Amen. Amen.

Voices come from the street, men, youths, frightened women, and crying children.

"Where's it coming from?"

"The searchlights or the bombs?"

"The bombs."

"From Mina al-Basal, Bab Sidra, and Karmuz."

"All the bombing is in Karmuz—the houses are shaking."

"The searchlights are not stopping. The guns in Kom al-Nadura, Kom al-Dikka, Maks, Qabbari, and Sidi Bishr are all going at the same time. More than a hundred planes!"

"The sky is full of the blue flies of death!"

"Where has all of this been hiding, so that it appears all at once?"

"Khawaga Dimitri, get out, the houses are going to collapse," a voice came from outside.

"Who's that?"

"Ghaffara."

The voice was nearby and muffled. Ghaffara looked in on them from the window. The women had gathered in a corner close to each other. As soon as Camilla and Yvonne saw him, they screamed, "Mama!" They heard a muffled voice coming from behind the fez-mask that he had tied on his face.

"Have no fear, ladies. This is Ghaffara's anti–air-raid mask. Khawaga Dimitri, Sheikh Magd al-Din, please forgive me. I know you, and I was friends with the late Bahi. The houses in Karmuz are falling down and they are shaking here. You'd be better off coming out and standing in the street."

He was looking from behind his glass eye-pieces at Lula's arms and shoulders gleaming in the dark as if they had black covering in the daytime. Dimitri and Magd al-Din came out but the women did not.

Zahra had said, "No one dies before his appointed time. If we die here, at least we'll be protected from the eyes of strangers."

Khawaga Dimitri liked this logic, and he asked his wife and daughters to stay with Zahra. Lula of course stayed with them.

"Merciful God! Most Merciful! The fire is burning in the sky!"

The sky over the buildings to the north was red with thick clouds of smoke. The planes were buzzing and circling over the city like wasps as the searchlights followed them over Bab al-Karasta, Kom al-Nadura, the harbor, Manshiya, Qabbari, and all around, with bursts of gunfire following closely. People assembled on the sidewalks shouted, "God protect us," when they saw the numerous planes dropping their bombs, and they covered their ears as the sounds of nearby explosions were heard. They shouted, "God is great!" when the guns hit a plane and it fell down quickly in the distance, filling the sky with black smoke. The whole place smelled like a colossal fire.

Lula's husband, his hair disheveled and a cigarette in his hand, had joined the people on the street. A young man rushed up and hit Lula's husband's hand, knocking the cigarette to the ground, and gave him a strong look. Lula's husband apologized, scratched his head, and said, "The confusion made me forget the civil defense instructions."

Suddenly it felt as if the earth and everyone on it rose up, then fell, and their hearts dropped. The houses had also risen and fallen, or at least they thought so, but because they were low and small they did not collapse. They heard the sounds of houses collapsing in Karmuz, though.

"That's a bomb that just hit Karmuz!" a man shouted, and the earth rose and fell again.

"Another bomb! God have Mercy!" another man shouted.

Cries resounded at the entrances of the houses, then the whole place rang out with the screaming of women. Women, children, and men were now out on the street, as the earth shook and the anti-aircraft guns poured fire into the sky. The huge black planes dropped phosphorous strips over the city, making it look like a nighttime celebration. Everything was now very visible. The planes circled over the city in calculated maneuvers that seemed never to end. Every time a plane went down, another joined the formation. Many of the planes came very close to the ground and hit their targets dead on. Terror reigned.

Ban Street was now filled with people running aimlessly to Sidi Karim then rushing to Karmuz Bridge. As they approached the end of the street and saw the open space extending in front of

Raghib Street and Karmuz Bridge, they were horrified by the extent of the fire north of Mahmudiya over that well-known neighborhood. The fire had reached Raghib and Masr Station, and the world was a giant trap, filled with screaming, fear, and tears. Zahra's strength was the only reason Sitt Maryam, Camilla, Yvonne, and Lula stayed in the room in the house, even though it did not stop shaking, and the ground did not stop moving. Yvonne was sobbing quietly, but Camilla had lost consciousness in her mother's lap. She had stretched out on the floor, placed her head in her mother's lap, and slept—or so Sitt Maryam thought. The truth was, she had fainted a long time before and only came to in the morning after the raid was over. There were dozens of women and children who had fainted in the streets and alleys, and neighbors were kept busy taking care of their neighbors, until that long night that no one thought would ever pass, had passed.

At dawn, Hamidu the shoeshine man appeared. He stood in the middle of the street, a barefoot giant shouting at the faraway planes, "You sons of bitches!" Then he called on the young people to go with him to Karmuz to rescue people. He ran down the street followed by dozens of young people, as well as Ghaffara, who could not catch up with them but did not stop nonetheless, and had to hold up the fez with his left hand so that he would not lose it. Magd al-Din thought of going with them, but he was afraid to leave Zahra alone. What would happen if he were to die there or she here? He saw Dimyan, his face pale and his eyes unfocused, coming toward him. As soon as Dimyan saw him, he sat down on the sidewalk, placed his head between his palms, and started weeping.

"Don't cry, Dimyan. This is God's will."

"Thousands of people will leave Alexandria tomorrow. Where would I go, Sheikh Magd?"

"Stay with me. I am not leaving."

"You'll stay?"

"Can I leave a job like the one we've got, Dimyan? Besides, death is in the hands of the Creator, my friend. Where's your family?"

"In the church. They opened the door, and lots of people went in. The Sidi Karim mosque, too. The bombs fell just a few steps behind us in the Mahmudiya canal."

"*Say: 'Nothing will befall us except that which God has decreed for us,'* Dimyan. Ask God for mercy."

"Kyrie eleison. Kyrie eleison. Kyrie eleison."

*If a window or a house is filled with light,
be certain that only the sun is illuminating it.*

Jalal al-Din Rumi

13

The whole city was busy worrying and talking about the six-hour air raid. The morning saw corpses on Rahma Street, lined up peacefully as if someone had arranged them lovingly on the ground during the night. Fires continued to burn in Bab Sidra for a whole day, despite the efforts of the fire fighters and rescue workers who converged on the site, but it took too long to extricate the bodies from the rubble. Karmuz Street and the side streets filled with people from all over the city who came to help with the rescue or to see for themselves what could happen again or what could happen to them. Massive migration out of the city began. The king and princes donated money to the victims, hospital space was set aside for the wounded, and Don Bosco School was opened to those recently made homeless. Gloom descended upon the city, as neither daytime nor nighttime air raids stopped. Little by little the city grew accustomed to the new realities. New stories began to fly in the alleys and among the men who stayed up at home or in the few cafés that still opened in the evenings. Teenagers talked about love stories in the public shelters or about women surprised by the air raids in the bathroom or in the arms of their men, wearing nothing at all or, at best, nightgowns. Men talked about Ali Mahir Pasha forming the new cabinet, how to drink iced tea with limes or milk or just straight in

this heat, and how Britain recognized General De Gaulle as a
representative of free French people throughout the world. The
women and girls talked about volunteering for the Red Crescent
and moving out of the city. After that six-hour air raid, the
summer was never the same. In the commercial district of Ghurbal
a fishmonger lusted for the wife of a southern Egyptian merchant.
She was a white-skinned woman of dazzling beauty. The
fishmonger could not figure out how she had ever lived in
southern Egypt. When he could not have her, he started a rumor
that she was having an affair with the young teacher who lived in
the opposite apartment and that she seized the opportunity
afforded by the air raids to make love with the young school
teacher in the dark shelter. The houses kept the ugly rumor alive.
One day the husband grabbed his beautiful wife by the hair and
dragged her to the small alley named Moon Street, adjacent to
Stars Street and parallel to Sun Street, in that quiet area for which
its developer had chosen these beautiful names. In front of a
shocked crowd, the merchant stabbed his wife and stood over her
corpse. Hardly a week had passed when the fishmonger, returning
drunk one night, told some people that he was the one behind the
rumor. He immediately became the object of contempt, and the
woman's father and brothers appeared and, in front of everyone,
killed him on the very spot she had been killed, then drank his
blood, or so people said. The women in the city cried twice, once
when the beautiful wife was killed, after which they stayed out of
the shelters, and again when the loathsome fishmonger was killed,
when they realized the injustice done to the beautiful woman.
They started going to the shelters again, more bashfully than
before. On the banks of the Mahmudiya canal, more than one
abandoned baby was found, and people fished out two bodies in
sacks from the water. The two bodies, both girls, were bloated.
The water had carried them from the south. The first one was
discovered under Raghib Bridge, and the other, a week later, under
Karmuz Bridge. In the world beyond, the Germans started their
epic air battle over England. The Battle of Britain began on July 10.
Hundreds of planes took off from the French coast and from
airports in nearby Belgium to attack British convoys in the channel
and the airports between Dover and Plymouth.

The raids were so intense that in one of them, eight hundred planes attacked at the same time. Hitler announced that he was going to wipe Britain off the face of the earth. Now the fate of Britain was truly in the hands of its valiant pilots, of whom Churchill said in a speech in the House of Commons, "Never in the history of human conflict have so many owed so much to so few, as we all do to our pilots."

Zahra's mother came from the village and brought her daughter ghee, butter, cheese, and bread. She tried to persuade her several times to leave Magd al-Din behind and go back with her to the village since even people who had no villages to go back to were leaving, so how could she hesitate? Zahra said she would never leave Magd al-Din, but if Magd al-Din were to return she would return with him. Her mother said that the mayor had sworn that if Magd al-Din returned, he would kill him, that he could do that without any fear of retribution during the war. Zahra said that, now that he had his new job, her husband would not go back. Then she asked her mother whether the mayor had really expelled them on account of Bahi. The mother said that the mayor wanted Magd al-Din's first wife, the one who had died before giving him any children. But Zahra was not comfortable with that explanation, since that wife had died only one year after she had married Magd al-Din, and no one remembered her. Bahi was the only plausible reason. The mother told Zahra that Hadya, Magd al-Din's mother, almost died when she got news of Bahi's death and the fact that Magd al-Din could no longer return. Zahra asked her mother to tell Magd al-Din only good or ordinary news, even though Magd al-Din would not really believe anything good.

The mother's visit did much to alleviate Zahra's loneliness. She cried a lot the day her mother left. Sitt Maryam, Camilla, and Yvonne took her with them to Shatbi beach to watch the bathers—who were not many, mostly women and girls. Camilla and Yvonne took off their dresses and stood before Zahra in shorts and low-cut cotton blouses that revealed most of their backs. A small number of girls went into the water and so did a few women, still wearing their gallabiyas. Sitt Maryam said that she did not like to get in the water and so did Zahra, who added that she really could not. She kept watching the two girls, who

ran on the beach and played in the water. Early in the afternoon
Zahra asked to go home when she saw at the end of the beach a
foreign-looking young woman being kissed by a foreign-looking
young man, both of them almost naked.

The number of foreign soldiers in the city was on the rise.
Some went to the desert and others to the beach for rest and
recreation. The Italian school in Shatbi was set aside for Italian
prisoners of war. As their numbers increased, they were held in a
camp outside the city and in several camps outside Cairo. The
land war had begun on the borders. The Allied forces began to
wage offensive raids against the Italian forces in Libya, in addition
to air raids. On June 14, four days after Italy declared war, the
British and Commonwealth forces began to attack the Italian
troops in Fort Capuzzo and Maddalena and took more than two
hundred prisoners. On August 13, the Italian forces began their
march against Egypt under instructions from Il Duce himself.
Intensive shelling began on the borders near Sallum, and when the
dust settled and the smoke cleared, the Italian forces appeared,
beautifully arrayed: in front were motorcyclists in formation,
followed by light tanks and armored cars. The British changed
their plan, and instead of retreating before the Italians, they
poured cannon fire on them and caused so many casualties that
Graziani had to change his frontal attack plan and instead tried to
encircle the British and their allies, who retreated. The Italians
could not go beyond Siddi Barrani, sixty miles behind the
Egyptian border, and stayed there for a long time at the mercy of
sporadic British land and air raids. In three months, Italian
casualties numbered thirty-five hundred, and seven hundred were
taken prisoner. The big question everyone in Alexandria was
asking was, why were the Italians, normally such a peaceful
people, fighting? Even their planes could be distinguished from
German planes in the sky: the Italian planes did not stay over the
city for a long time—they dumped their bombs haphazardly and
returned to base—whereas German pilots seemed to know their
targets and went straight for them. Many Italian planes were shot
down quickly; German planes took evasive action in the sky. It
seemed to people that the Italians really did not want the war, that
they had been pushed into it, especially when people heard about

the number of prisoners taken on land and who arrived in the city every day. The people were reassured that the Italians could not occupy the city. But Germany had to be defeated in order for them to be really reassured. A large segment of the population, however, wished for the defeat of the British forces in the desert and for Italy or Germany to enter Alexandria. What they wanted most was for the English to leave.

Early one morning, Zahra saw Camilla and Yvonne standing in the hallway in their beautiful school uniforms. Summer vacation was over, and the girls looked like two merry butterflies in gray skirts, white shirts, and blue neckties, lending a childlike innocence to their sweetness.

Magd al-Din had left for work a little earlier. He was the first to leave and, during those weeks that Khawaga Dimitri worked days, he would leave with him.

"Is school so wonderful, girls?"

"Of course, Zahra. Especially the first day, it's like a holiday. We meet our classmates and teachers, and we talk about the vacation and the summer. The most beautiful thing in the world is the first day back to school, Zahra. After that, school is bad."

They laughed like two little doves. And since Zahra could not go back in time and go to school and live in the city, she hoped to see Shawqiya, one day, as happy as they were. Yvonne had turned the radio on to the Voice of London, which was playing beautiful music that Zahra had never heard before, music that made you want to fly or swim in the air like an angel. How was it that she had never heard music without lyrics before? Can such music be so beautiful?

The girls left for school. The cool morning breeze gave Zahra a feeling of heavenly happiness. She was not going back to sleep. She lay down next to her daughter on the bed, and looked up at the white wooden ceiling. Could Alexandria be so beautiful without her realizing it? Yesterday she had gone to Anfushi again with Sitt Maryam, for the first time in a long time. On the streetcar, people were looking healthier and happier than they had the last time she had gone, in spite of the ceaseless air raids. When she saw the statue of Muhammad Ali Pasha, she did not think of complaining to him. She was afraid that the air raids would demolish the statue and laughed at the idea that he might run away on his horse. She was truly surprised by the awesome apartment buildings with decorative balconies on both sides of Manshiya Square. Why had they not looked so majestic to her before? When the streetcar approached the end of Lisan Bahari on the coast, she began to hear the peaceful melody of the waves and smell the refreshing smell of the sea. When the streetcar emerged from the long cold street into the open air, Zahra saw the endless blue sea as its froth-capped waves gently caressed the beach. Along the coast, brown nets were stretched over a long distance with pieces of heavy, silvery lead holding them in place. Next to them were boats with furled sails and little rowboats, stopped or neglected on the sand. In the distance were huge gray ships with long and short cannons and masts and flags casting shadows on the breaking waters. On land Zahra could see crowds of lively women surrounding fish vendors. She had come here before but had not seen what she was seeing now. That was during the feast days after Ramadan. Summer here was really quite different from winter, and there she was, seeing things with new eyes, imbued with an energy she had gotten from the city whose own sons and daughters were deserting but in which she was now living and loving. True, it was crowded, but in a cheerful way. There were women swathed in long wraps that they let fall off their heads and shoulders and held under their arms, revealing rosy shoulders and soft arms, their hair showing under their head covers with red, yellow, or black edges. They got into long conversations with the vendors, and laughed spontaneously as the vendors raised their voices, and happiness showed in their eyes and faces. Many of the women were moving in a deliberate manner. One would let the body wrap slide off her head, revealing her bare shoulder. Then she would lift the wrap deliberately, raising her white, enticing arms as far up as she could so the vendor would see her armpit, plucked only the day before, silky smooth, and wake unmentionable desires in the hungry vendor. Many women, accompanied by little girls with rosy cheeks that they wanted to remain rosy forever, drank the blood of tirsa, which the vendors sold in cups.

"Don't be afraid, Zahra. Tirsa blood is very nourishing and fattening."

"What's tirsa?"

"It's a sea turtle. The fishermen bring it in and they slaughter it, cut up its flesh, and sell it by the kilo. People also drink its blood—it's the cheapest kind of sea food."

Zahra saw the other kinds of fish that looked more splendid than what she'd seen on her last visit. She kept trying to remember their names and asked about the ones she did not know. She also noticed more kinds than before. She saw red shrimp; orange crabs; silver sea bream; speckled red snapper; white mullet; white and red grouper; silver sea bass; long, white swordfish; fish that looked like fat little white bananas; long, strong green eels; dark red mullet, dark gray, almost oval fish; fish that looked like sweet potatoes; and white and black and silvery-white sardines—all displayed on dozens of wooden tables with crowds of women around them. Sardines were a very cheap fish, now in season, and many women bought large quantities to salt and use during the winter. The day before, Zahra had bought crabs, shrimp, and eels, more than a kilo of every kind. She spent a whole half-pound note from the ten pounds that her mother had given her. She also bought five kilos of sardines to salt. What made her splurge so much when she knew that her husband's salary was no more than three pounds a month? Undoubtedly it was the ten pounds that her mother had given her, but one more certain reason was that she had weaned her daughter the day before and she knew that one did not get pregnant while nursing—she knew that from her mother. Today she was going to become pregnant, she told herself. Her body shook and was shaking now, as she lay awake on the bed. Could a woman know that she was becoming pregnant as it was happening? Maybe. She felt that last night; she felt a little thing inside her attach itself to some other little thing. She felt an inner tension inside, ending in a profound calm coursing through her blood. Magd al-Din would be happy with her since she was going to bear him a son this time. He never expressed a preference of sons over daughters, but he grew up like all peasants, and perhaps like all men, preferring and hoping for male offspring. She was going to give him that, and this big white city, which accommodated all these people from all over the world without complaining, would help her.

No sooner had Magd al-Din finished his lunch, which he usually had late, after returning from work, than a loud woman's scream was heard from downstairs.

"It was Lula, that was her voice!" exclaimed Zahra. "I know her voice."

When another scream was heard quickly after the first one, Zahra went out of the room and met Sitt Maryam in the hallway. As the screams continued, Sitt Maryam went downstairs ahead of Zahra, who quickly followed with Camilla and Yvonne. After a moment, Sitt Maryam and Zahra were calling out to the exhausted Magd al-Din, since Khawaga Dimitri had not come home yet. Magd al-Din put on his gallabiya, to be ready for any development; he had eaten his lunch while in his underwear.

On his way downstairs, Magd al-Din saw Camilla and Yvonne coming up. They said nothing to him because they were hurrying. He heard men's voices at the foot of the stairs and the sounds of a large crowd standing in the street in front of the house. He heard Lula in her room screaming, "Have pity! Have pity!" Sitt Maryam and Zahra were standing in front of the door.

"What's happening?" Magd al-Din asked, and they did not answer but motioned him to enter the room. As soon as he did he closed his eyes. Lula was wearing a sheer white slip, almost naked. True, her hair was disheveled and her eyes swollen from crying, but, in the final analysis, she was an almost-naked woman. As soon as Lula saw him, she collapsed at his feet and held on to one of his legs and said, "Please, Sheikh Magd al-Din, I kiss your foot,"—and she actually did, since he was barefoot—"protect me, protect me from those sons of bitches."

She said the last sentence in anguish. He looked at the men standing in the room: her husband, a policeman, and a thin, sickly man. Zahra and Sitt Maryam had come close to the door, and Magd al-Din asked them to bring something to cover the lady's nakedness. But the policeman said, "No," and the thin man added, "She must come as she is."

"What's the story, exactly?" Magd al-Din inquired as Lula crouched on the floor next to his feet, quietly crying now.

"This man is not her husband—this man is," the policeman said, pointing to the thin man. Zahra had gone upstairs and brought down a white shawl that she placed on Lula's shoulders. As soon as she heard what the policeman said, she went out, terrified, and stood shaking by Sitt Maryam.

"Is that true, Sitt . . . ?" Magd al-Din asked, and he could not utter her name.

"You sons of bitches!" Lula screamed.

There were two policemen at the door of the house to prevent the angry mob from entering. The thin man rushed to Lula, trying to lift her up to go with them, while her lover stood there, his mouth agape, seemingly in total disregard of the situation. Lula got up and started to go with them. Magd al-Din yelled at the policeman to wait. He looked at Lula's lover and asked the policeman, "Why don't you drag this lout to the police station?'

"He'll come with us as a witness to the crime of adultery."

"There is no power or strength save in God," said Magd al-Din sarcastically. "Is the crime of adultery committed by the woman alone?"

"That's the law."

Magd al-Din could not help moving forward and, as hard as he could, he slapped the lover, who, to everyone's surprise, did not resist, or protest, or slap Magd al-Din back.

Lula saw the big crowd outside the door and gripped the wooden banister. "They're going to kill me, Sheikh Magd al-Din. Please help me, may God help you!"

The thin man, her real husband, began to pull her and try to pry her hands loose from the banister, but he could not. The shawl that was covering her fell to the floor, and she left the banister and turned to the thin man and screamed at him, "It's all your fault, you son of a bitch!"

Then she hit him in the chest as hard as she could. He reeled back, hit the wall, and fell to the floor. She turned to the policeman to hit him too, but he had pulled his gun and was aiming it at her. Frightened, she backed away and collapsed on the floor crying.

"Please, let's wait and solve this problem calmly," said Magd al-Din, who was thinking of the mob outside, which might actually kill her. Then he addressed Lula's real husband, "Take your wife and divorce her before a marriage official, away from the police. If you leave it to the police, they'll divorce her from you, but they'll also put her in jail. What good will that do you? Leave her be."

The man did not answer. In the meantime, Lula had rushed into her room and quickly closed the door behind her. The policeman tried to break the door down, but Magd al-Din held him back.

"Where would she go? She'll open it up in a little while."

Her voice came from inside, "I'm coming out, you sons of bitches!"

The door opened and Lula appeared in a beautiful dress, looking at everyone defiantly, then quickly bent down and kissed Magd al-Din's hand, crying all the while.

"Please don't believe them, Sheikh Magd al-Din," she said. She looked at Zahra and Sitt Maryam and said the same thing. Zahra was now crying, while Sitt Maryam was fighting her tears.

"Let's go—to hell, if you like," said Lula to the policeman.

It was obvious that once she was covered, after she had put on the dress, she feared nothing. It all seemed strange to Magd al-Din. How could she, an adulterous woman, be afraid to walk in the street in her slip, but now that she was covered, she was no longer afraid, even of death? He said to himself, "Who knows? Maybe this woman is as sinless and pure as a saint."

Even when iron is red, red is not its color;
its radiance comes from a fire that heats it up.

Jalal al-Din Rumi

14

Lunch break is from noon to 2 p.m. Workers who live in the Railroad Authority housing one mile away usually go home for lunch and a short rest, then come back to work. On many days Magd al-Din opted not go home for lunch even though his house was closer to work than those of his co-workers. As a peasant he was used to eating his lunch in the field. Now he was bringing lunch with him most days and staying alone at the post, whose location and wooden walls made it a comfortable place to rest in both summer and winter. The two hours gave him a chance to read from the little Quran that never left the vest pocket next to his heart. He would also nap for a few minutes, sometimes half an hour, on the long, low bench. At first, Dimyan did not like to stay during lunch break. Like most workers he liked to have lunch and relax at home. But he found the trip without Magd al-Din more tedious than it already was. So he decided to stay with him, lunching and relaxing and talking, but not for long, because of Magd al-Din's Quran reading.

The post smelled of dust and tea. The dust of the floor was moist, since there were no windows or openings except for the open door and the narrow gaps between the planks that made up the walls. And since the structure was more than fifty meters square, it seemed that the light pouring from the open door or the thin rays of light breaking through the gaps in the walls were not enough to dispel the humidity. As for the tea, they never really stopped making it, from when they first arrived in the morning to when they came back in the afternoon and during their breaks. They made it on a wood-burning stove outside the post, then drank it and poured whatever tea and leaves were left on the floor next to where they sat, for the soil to absorb it at its own pace. Today Dimyan, who was sitting facing Magd al-Din, said, "What's to be done, Sheikh Magd al-Din?"

"About what, Dimyan?"

"About this damned job of ours—it's breaking my back."

"You're complaining now, Dimyan, after we've gotten used to it?"

"The three pounds' salary we get is hardly enough, with this inflation."

"But it's better than nothing, or spending time in the police station lockup," said Magd al-Din. He was responding to Dimyan in a perfunctory manner, for they had had this conversation many times before. Magd al-Din reached into his vest pocket and took out the little Quran, then leaned back against the wall, extended his legs, opened the Quran, and began reading.

"Listen to me!" Dimyan said. "Every time I talk to you, you open the Quran and begin to read. Don't you read enough at home? At this rate, you'll make me bring the Bible and read it every time you speak to me."

Magd al-Din started laughing at Dimyan's exasperation and the way he talked. He also laughed because of what Dimyan had said about reading the Bible, when he was actually illiterate. When he had started the job, there was a condition that he learn how to read and write within a year. Now it was four months later, and he had begun to go to school only a week ago.

After he stopped laughing, he closed the Quran and asked, "What do you want from me, Dimyan?"

"I'm dying to know the real story of the man sitting at the Raven. Every time I pass by him, he just gives me this strange look. Am I the one who told the birds not to come to the tree? It seems like he wants to kill me."

"He looks at me the same way too."

"He must want to kill us both, Sheikh Magd."

Magd al-Din thought for a little while then said, "Leave creation to the Creator, Dimyan."

They were both silent for a long time. Then Magd al-Din read a few pages from the Quran, and he spoke aloud as he finished the Sura of the Believers. "*He will say: 'How many years did you stay on earth?' They will say: 'We stayed a day or a part of a day, ask those who keep count.' He will say: 'You stayed only a while, if only you knew. Did you think that We had created you for naught and that you would not be returned unto Us?' Therefore exalted be God, the King, the Truth! There is no God but He, the Lord of the Throne of Grace! He who invokes any other god besides God has no proof thereof. His reckoning will only be with his Lord. And verily the unbelievers will not be successful. So say: 'My Lord, grant your forgiveness and mercy for You are the best of all who show mercy.'*"

Under his breath, Dimyan said, "Kyrie eleison, Kyrie eleison, Kyrie eleison." Then he asked, "Why is it, Sheikh Magd, that every time I get into a conversation with you, you say, 'Leave the creation to the Creator'? For starters, I don't have anything to leave to Him."

Magd al-Din laughed, and Dimyan continued, "And you don't either, Sheikh Magd. Do you know what I'm thinking now?"

"No, I don't."

"This open door, if somebody were to come and lock it, with us inside, in this godforsaken place—would anyone know? This could happen while we're napping after lunch. Somebody comes, locks the door, and leaves. Then nobody comes in here or passes by. So, we die. Sheikh Magd, you've done something serious in the village, and you've managed to escape. You're very complacent, you accept whatever might happen. It's as if you want to die."

Magd al-Din was quite surprised by this strange talk from his friend. He felt sadness well up in his chest and into his eyes, and he would have cried, had it not been for a shrill train whistle, which made Dimyan jump up and go out to look. Magd al-Din waited for his return. When he did, he said, "An endless train, Sheikh Magd, filled with Africans. The caboose is black and so are the soldiers—everything is black except the cars, which were white to start with, but they're gray now."

Magd al-Din got up and went out with Dimyan and indeed
saw a very long train with dozens of black faces with broad, flat
noses. Dimyan said in a soft voice as if thinking aloud, "The whole
world is with the English. Hitler will never win the war."

The train had stopped for a short time to get water at the
Raven, then moved slowly again, down the middle of the complex
network of tracks in front of the post, where there were several
switches. The train was so slow that any soldier, or anyone else for
that matter, could have jumped off and then on again.

"They have tails, Sheikh Magd. If one of them got off the train,
you'd see the tail poking out of his shorts."

Magd al-Din laughed and waved to the soldiers, who were
waving to him from the windows of the train and making the "V"
sign that Churchill had invented and that had become famous all
over the world. One of them appeared at the door of one of the
cars carrying a small cardboard box and gesturing to Magd al-Din
and Dimyan.

"You run, Sheikh Magd, and get the box. I'd die if I saw the tail."

Magd al-Din laughed and ran up to the train and reached his
hand to catch the box that the smiling soldier handed down. Magd
al-Din hesitated for a moment, because the soldier had descended
a step and held the box in one hand and with the other held on to
the shining metal bar of the car door. It would have been easy for
Magd al-Din to look at the soldier's bare legs under the shorts and
to see if he had a tail or not. But he did not look but rather focused
on the box and on the black hand holding it, which seemed even
blacker when he reached out his white hand to take the box. What
frightened him, however, was a strange idea that occurred to him
as he reached his hand to take the box: what would prevent the
soldier from grabbing his arm and pulling him onto the car, which
would take him with the soldiers to the battlefields? Bahi had been
grabbed from the road during the earlier war. He could very easily
be kidnapped too, even though the corvée system had been
abolished. Nothing saved him from his thoughts and fear except
feeling that the box was light.

"It seems to be a box of cookies," he told Dimyan.

Dimyan fell silent for a moment as Magd al-Din opened the
box and found it indeed filled with cookies.

"You know what I really crave, Sheikh Magd?" Dimyan said.
"No."
"A can of Australian corned beef."

The workers doubled up with laughter at Dimyan's fear of getting too close to the African soldier. They were drinking their afternoon tea after coming back to work at two o'clock. There was nothing important to do that afternoon. The foreman, Usta Ghibriyal, never joined in their laughter, content with a smile. This supervisor was Dimitri's relative who had told him of the job opportunities in the railroad. He was of a diminutive build, with a graceful and gentle demeanor, and always kept to himself in a far corner looking at a small notebook that he had with him at all times. He could always be seen scribbling away in that notebook with an indelible pencil, adjusting his beret that he never took off, even while seated, pulling it closer to his eyes or pushing it back a little. When not writing with the pencil, he always placed it, with its shiny metal holder, in the upper pocket of his green jacket, in such a way that it poked from the edge of the pocket, a constant reminder that the pencil was always ready, at a moment's notice, to write. The workers knew that he took down notes on the progress of the day's work, prior to copying them in an official report to the administration at the end of each week, yet they never ceased to be surprised at the way he wrote, imagining, perhaps, that it was some form of magic, especially since he took such pains with his penmanship. Hamza commented on that once by saying that Usta Ghibriyal loved to write in that minuscule script of his, that at night when he did not have anything to do, he would erase what he had written during the day. That, he added, was confirmed by the fact that he always used the same notebook.

Today their co-worker Hamza laughed the most at Dimyan's fear, but he did not double over because he was too short. Hamza walked in a strange way, with his legs bowed. And even though he was not yet forty, he looked older. He had a ruddy complexion and blue eyes, like so many people from Rosetta. He

was so excessively polite that it made people uncomfortable. He
always greeted everyone he met, and if it happened that he left
the post and returned in a short while, he would greet his
colleagues as if he had not been with them only a few minutes
earlier. He was also constantly apologizing for any mistake, no
matter how trivial, such as standing up before someone else did.
At the beginning, Hamza's demeanor surprised Magd al-Din and
Dimyan, but little by little they grew used to it. Magd al-Din
concluded that he was a good man, whereas Dimyan thought that
he was almost an idiot. Hamza had a bad habit, though, that
caused his colleagues to make fun of him; no sooner would
someone say something or tell a story than Hamza would say
that the very same thing, in exactly the same manner and at the
same time, had happened to him. This became such a well-known
trait that some of them made up stories so that Hamza would
retell them as things that had actually happened to him,
whereupon they would burst out laughing, declaring that they
had made up the story. But he would counter by saying that his
was a true story, and he would laugh with them, proud and
triumphant. Thus he was the hero of all stories, both fantastical
and true. If a killer in southern Egypt escaped and hid in a corn
field, forcing the police to burn down the whole field to capture
him, that same thing happened to him, but in the Daqahliya
province, not southern Egypt. As for the man who went out at
night to relieve himself on the bank of the Mahmudiya canal and
was pulled down by his ass into the water by a female jinn, never
to come out again, Hamza had seen someone pulled into the
water in the same way. The man cried for help, but Hamza stood
there, nailed in place, unable to move at all to rescue him; he
could only move after the man had settled down at the bottom of
the canal. As for the white donkey that more than one person had
seen in their villages at night and that then disappeared as they
approached it, Hamza had met innumerable white donkeys and
ridden them all.

The strangest story was the one about the man who went at
dawn to the Mahmudiya canal to perform his ablutions there.
When he was done and as he stood up, pulled his pants up, and
started walking, he felt something moving between his legs and

under his buttocks, something giving him a little squeeze. The man pulled up his gallabiya and undid his waistband to see what was there, and found a number of white baby rabbits, dozens of them that looked like little mice playing in his underpants. The man ran home but could not stand still afterwards because of the strange movements of those rabbits. Then he could not sleep; what would he do about those rabbits that had taken up residence in his pants? He had to go down to the street again, and stopped screaming only when he noticed that everything around him was silent. He was so unable to get a grip on himself that finally he fainted and people saw dozens of rabbits running out from between his legs, white rabbits running every which way. The man died of fright. Hamza swore the most solemn oath that that had happened in his village also. Dimyan bent toward Magd al-Din one day and said to him, "This Hamza, for sure, is an inveterate liar."

"Why should that bother you? Leave creation to the Creator, Dimyan."

Dimyan could not stay quiet. "Nothing annoys me more than your forbearance and patience, Sheikh Magd!"

"You cannot change him," Magd al-Din said with a smile. "He's used to it, and the men have gotten used to him."

Today, as Hamza was laughing at Dimyan's fear, his face looked very red because he had just finished making tea on the wood-burning stove. He almost choked while laughing; blood gathered in his face as a result of the laughing, the fire, and the choking, and he almost ignited. When he was able to speak again, Hamza said, "Me too, the first time I saw an African, I was afraid of his tail. He was handing me a can of choice Australian corned beef, but I was afraid. I moved away and told him to throw it to me, but he didn't respond, so I said to him in English, "Throw it!" and he did. The strangest thing was, he understood the English and not the Arabic!"

Dimyan looked at him, barely concealing his annoyance, and asked, "Did you see his tail, Hamza?"

"Yes, I did, but I was afraid to grab it, yes, sir."

The workers burst out laughing and Dimyan remarked, "Maybe you were afraid, when you grabbed it, it would turn out to be something else!"

At that point the laughter was hysterical, and Hamza joined in, once again choking, which only annoyed Dimyan all the more.

Usta Ghibriyal smiled faintly and continued his magical scribbling.

Hamza asked Magd al-Din, "What do you think, Sheikh Magd—is it true that Africans were originally monkeys?"

Magd al-Din thought a little, and the workers waited for him to answer.

"Only God knows," he finally said. "What I heard was, the monkey was originally a man who wiped his ass with a loaf of bread, so God changed him into a monkey. That's what we heard as children. But I don't believe it, because God has ennobled man, so God would not change him into a monkey. Also, it could not be that man was originally a monkey."

The workers looked relieved, and so did Usta Ghibriyal, who said, "You speak wisely, Sheikh Magd. What do you think, Hamza? Did you see a man turn into a monkey?"

The workers laughed uproariously because this time the speaker was the usually silent Usta Ghibriyal.

Hamza composed himself and replied, "I am afraid that if say I did, nobody would believe me. I'd better keep quiet, Usta."

Everyone fell silent in the manner familiar to Egyptians after they laugh; a sudden quiet descended on everyone and everything. One of the workers said, "May God make it good."

"I have a curious story to tell you," Magd al-Din spoke up.

They looked at him expectantly. Hamza was particularly attentive—he pricked up his ears and was the first to speak, "Go ahead, Sheikh Magd. Perhaps you'll tell us something new that I don't know or haven't seen."

Magd al-Din smiled and winked to Dimyan to follow the situation. Dimyan was surprised at his friend, who began, "Once when I was a little boy, a young peasant man grabbed me and had his way with me in the field."

Everyone fell silent in shock. What was Sheikh Magd al-Din saying and why? What exactly did he mean? At that point Hamza got up holding the empty cup of tea and headed for the door as if he was going to make some more tea.

"Why are you silent, Hamza?" Magd al-Din asked. "Why didn't you say that that happened to you too?"

They heard Usta Ghibriyal laughing loudly for the first time. Dimyan jumped up and exclaimed, "God is great! God is great!"

As for Hamza, his red face turned a yellowish blue. Magd al-Din stood up and went over to Hamza, embraced him, and kissed his head, saying, "I didn't know it was such a bad joke, my friend."

When they stopped laughing, Usta Ghibriyal went back to scribbling in his notebook. They noticed that from time to time he was casting furtive, sly glances at Magd al-Din. As for Hamza, he went out to make tea that no one wanted.

A little while later, Magd al-Din went out and saw him sitting away from the wood-burning stove. He had not even put the teapot on. Magd al-Din sat next to him, and Hamza looked at him with a smile and said, "One does not usually make enemies with decent folk. A free man, no matter how poor, never forgets a good deed."

Magd al-Din felt a great relief. "I don't know how I got carried away joking like that. When I saw you were embarrassed, I was quite upset with myself."

"We say more than that everyday, Sheikh Magd." Hamza answered. "Look at that train!"

It was a freight train. Its flatbed cars were loaded with military equipment and made such a deep grating noise on the tracks that all the workers came out to see it. On every car was a tank or an armored car covered with netting, with one or two soldiers standing next to it. The train was coming from Suez or Cairo and heading for the desert, where there were great concentrations of Allied troops in al-Alamein, Bir Fuka, and Marsa Matruh. The soldiers were not African this time, but English or Australian and wearing khaki shorts in the middle of winter. They were perhaps coming from the south, maybe South Africa. On top of the shorts, they wore khaki short-sleeved shirts and vests without sleeves. The ruddy complexions of the soldiers and their white arms and legs meant that they had not seen the desert before, and since they looked young, perhaps they were new to soldiering.

The train was too fast. The workers saluted the soldiers and shouted, "Hello! Welcome! English is good. German is no good. Churchill is right. Hitler no right," and other such things that they said on this and other occasions, words that most of them did not understand but which guaranteed good results. The soldiers began throwing packets of Lucky Strike cigarettes, cartons of cookies and chocolate, cans of Australian and New Zealand corned beef and cheddar cheese. Usta Ghibriyal cautioned them to wait until the train cleared the post. They had gotten used to that and also, after the train had left the post, to running and gathering up the goodies on the ground, then bringing them into the post and divvying them up equally, according to who wanted what. Usually the catch was more than enough for all ten of them, and now everyone knew what everyone else wanted or liked. Usta Ghibriyal, for instance, liked Ceylon tea. Hamza, on the other hand, liked cookies and chocolate, which he handed over to his three children and to his co-workers' children, since they all lived in railroad housing together with workers from posts one through six, whose job sites were not far from them. All the workers would get together for big jobs or when there was an accident. When accidents happened there were no disputes about the goodies. The trains went through more than once every day; the soldiers liberally threw candy, food, and tea. It seemed the war would last for a long time.

On the way home, Dimyan asked Magd al-Din, "Why all these weapons today?"

"Don't you see the trains loaded with Italian prisoners coming from the desert? The war there is quite hot."

"It seems like the war will go on for a long time, Sheikh Magd."

"The weapons come from Suez and from the harbor in Alexandria, and the soldiers come from all over the world, Dimyan. It seems to me it's not war, but Judgment Day."

They both fell silent for a long time. Magd al-Din started thinking about Hamza, whom he had mocked today, and how Hamza now seemed noble in his eyes. Then he remembered Lula and what had happened a few days earlier and he grew tense. It was not easy for Zahra to be acquainted with a woman who turned out to be an adulteress. It was not easy also to live in the house of good Dimitri, who since that day had felt ashamed every time he saw Magd al-Din because he had not carefully screened his tenants. What were people saying now about good Dimitri and his children? Could Dimitri have turned down a tenant paying sixty piasters a month? And Bahi, his brother, had he known about Lula? And if he did, how could he have chosen for him to live in the same house? He smiled sarcastically at this last question and heard Dimyan say, "Look, it's Wahid the plainclothes policeman!"

Wahid was walking toward them in a blue gallabiya with vertical white stripes and a khaki overcoat. He had a white skullcap on his head and a gray scarf around his neck. In his hand he held a long bamboo stick that he waved around from time to time. They knew him well and met him almost every day and shared some of the goodies that the soldiers had given them. He was used to that and did it to all the workers he came across. And even though he was well dressed in clean clothes, and despite his pleasant, placid face, when he spoke he sounded like an uncouth, brutal clod, as Sheikh Magd al-Din described him all the time. Wahid was notorious in the whole neighborhood for shaking down everyone and for having no scruples whatsoever when it came to framing someone. He saw them as he saw them every day, and shouted as if he had just noticed them, "What are you carrying?"

"As you can see, some English canned stuff," Dimyan answered, smiling, and Wahid said, "You mean from the English warehouses?"

Neither of them knew where the English warehouses were, but they figured that today he wanted to get more than he usually got from them.

"What warehouses! Here, just take a couple of packets of tea, Wahid," Dimyan said, as his smile grew broader.

But Wahid shouted, "I have to take you in—this is larceny!"

He raised his stick, threatening them. Magd al-Din gave him a long savage look. He had looked around and saw the open space, as the sun was quietly setting, a cool breeze blowing and the dark gently beginning to cover the ground. He could hardly see the rails on top of the crossties, as everything was the color of dust.

"You know, Wahid," said Magd al-Din, "I could knock you to the ground and slit your throat on the track without anyone seeing you."

"What did you say, Sheikh Magd? Slit my throat?" Wahid asked in a more subdued voice, and he lowered his stick.

"Yes," Magd al-Din replied. "and the train will come, and in the morning people will see that it cut off your head."

Dimyan was genuinely frightened by what his friend was saying.

"We have two cartons, as you can see," Magd al-Din went on. "In each there is tea, cookies, corned beef, and cheese. We will give you a whole carton, and the two of us will share one, on condition that you never bother us again. Every time you think of doing it, remember that I can slit your throat without anyone seeing. Take the carton and leave in peace."

Wahid, as if in a daze, took the carton.

Dimyan and Magd al-Din walked in silence, then Dimyan asked, "You were really going to slit his throat, Sheikh Magd?"

"Yes. Today I can slit anyone's throat."

They continued on their way home in silence.

I did not hold myself back
I gave in completely and went.
I went to those pleasures
That lie on the edge
Between reality and imagination
I walked in the brilliant night
And drank the strong wine the valiant
seekers of pleasure drink.

Constantine Cavafy

15

Japan attacked Indochina, expanding its war along the western and
southern coast of Asia, since it was already at war with China. The
Japanese giant was restless, and it began to stretch and spew forth its
fire. America saw Japan's military power and ventures as a threat
and began to stand on guard. People everywhere began to realize
that the entire globe would soon be engulfed in the flames of war.

In Egypt, British planes attacked the new Italian positions in
Sidi Barrani, in raids that lasted four hours and extended into
Benghazi to hit the Italians' lines of communication. The ministry
of supply decreased the amount of coal sold to ironers and
pressers, since no coal was being imported from England and a
large number of trains were being used for military transport.
Ironers and pressers complained vociferously. Some brazen young
men started going out at night, wearing frightening gas masks to
take girls and women by surprise in the dark alleys. Groups of
such masked youth appeared at times like herds of bulls going to
their bullpens or leaving them for the faraway grazing pastures.
The Italians started using a new kind of bomb that looked like a
thermos bottle, which did not explode on impact but afterwards,
when moved or touched. A campaign began to warn Alexandrians
against such bombs, which had shiny surfaces that could not be
seen clearly in bright sunlight. People were distressed because for

the second year in a row, the month of Ramadan came and no lights or public celebrations were permitted. The price of many commodities went up, and kerosene was rationed. The price of potatoes rose from fifteen milliemes an English kilo to twenty-seven and from ten milliemes an Egyptian kilo to twenty. A large section of the wall of the corniche at Sidi Bishr collapsed as a result of water seepage. The royal banquets of Ramadan were no longer enough to keep the poor happy. In Alexandria there was only one banquet, held in front of the Mursi Abu al-Abbas mosque, whereas in Cairo, people said, they were held everywhere. In that banquet, taro root, meat, rice, fava beans, vegetables, and pastries were served for free. The deputy-governor himself inaugurated the banquet and ate with the poor, apologizing for the absence of the governor, who had gone to Cairo to congratulate His Majesty the King on the advent of the month of Ramadan. The ministry of social affairs formed a commission to study the increasing immodesty of women, as a result of the increase in the number of foreigners and their need for entertainment and the need for money among many segments of the population.

For Magd al-Din, Ramadan was no different from the year before, only now the women stayed up without Lula. Zahra noticed that Camilla had once more become silent and oblivious to others. She spoke once and said it was no longer permitted to stay in the cinemas during raids, night or day. Maryam asked Zahra why she did not leave Alexandria when everyone was leaving, especially since she was now pregnant and it would be better for her to give birth in her village. Zahra said that was a long way away, but that she would surely do that. She was lying, for she could never leave Magd al-Din. But she had no choice, as she could not explain how her husband had been expelled from his village.

As the feast celebrating the end of Ramadan approached, the world watched with bated breath as Italy started its predations of Greece. On October 28, which coincided with the feast in Alexandria, Italy invaded Greece from Albania. The Greek prime minister, Metaxas, displayed great courage in rejecting the Italian ultimatum, and Greece launched a counterattack. The Greeks in Alexandria rose up against the invasion. Young Greek men gathered in front of the Greek consulate, volunteering to fight in defense of the country of Achilles, Agamemnon, Hercules, Zeus, Hera, Aphrodite, Apollo, the Muses, Oedipus, Electra, and Pygmalion—the country that no one had ever disliked or could dislike now. The Egyptians admired the courage of the Greeks and began to greet their Greek neighbors with admiration and respect. The Greeks continued to be optimistic: "Il Duce is a miserable fellow," they told their Egyptian neighbors. They held enthusiastic poetry readings and sang and danced fervently.

Hitler had met with Franco a few days earlier at the French-Spanish border, but there was no indication that Spain would join in the war. New instructions were issued in France to exclude Jews from working in administrative and government posts, the press, cinema, or radio. Exceptions were made for those who had performed distinguished scientific services or who were decorated veterans of the previous world war.

In Alexandria, a train arrived from Suez carrying troops from South Africa who were said to be young Jews escaping the Nazi inferno. Those who survived, it was said, would go to Palestine after the war. They were welcomed in Alexandria at Sidi Gabir Station by the notables of the Jewish community, Sidnawi, Cicurel, Salvago and others. Young Jewish women showered them with flowers and blew kisses from their windows, and many Egyptians in the station greeted and applauded them. The train left for the desert in the evening, made no stops, and did not come across any workers until it arrived at Marsa Matruh two days later, when it dropped off the soldiers and brought back a batch of Australian soldiers for rest and recreation. A car was set aside for Italian prisoners of war, including a number of Libyans who were released later in Alexandria after it was established that they had been forced to serve with the Italian forces, and after they said that they were looking forward to the Allies entering Libya to rid them of Graziani, representative of the crazy Duce.

In Alexandria the fame of the new dancer Lula spread like wildfire. She danced to the Greek tunes of her doting accordion-playing husband, who never took his eyes off her. A drummer, who also sang, mainly to point out how curvaceous she was, accompanied her. She now only danced for the pashas at their mansions. A war had been raging over her among the dancing and singing women. She had previously been working with Usta Naima al-Saghir in Bahari and Sayyala, but she had disappeared with her lover until she was found by her husband, who had left the troupe and joined that of Bata al-Salamuni, whose turf extended from Karmuz to Kom al-Shuqafa and Qabbari. Usta Suma al-Nagili from Farahda and Labban entered the fray, as did Usta Fawziya al-Massiri, Naima's archrival in Bahari. But the impresarios, who were out of work because of the ban on public nighttime celebrations and whose only job was to organize parties for the pashas, arranged a meeting among the Ustas and stopped the war. "The world war is enough," they said. Bata al-Salamuni paid twenty pounds in reparation to Naima al-Saghir and the rest of the troupes agreed that Lula would dance for them once a month at any place they chose. The same terms were made available to the men's troupes: Hamama al-Attar from Bahari, Said al-Hadrawi from Hadra, Anwar Salama from Karmuz, and Sayyid al-Halawani from Bacos. Thus Lula became a boon to the dancing and singing troupes in Alexandria. The only thing left for her to do was to dance at the Atheneos or Windsor or other such corniche nightclubs, which were always full of soldiers and ATS women.

The story of Lula reached Sitt Maryam and Zahra, who were surprised at the wiles of women and also of men, for Lula's husband, who had seemed so jealous the day she was arrested, was now the very one accompanying her as she danced in the mansions. They had forgotten all about her, until the day they went out to the piazza in Karmuz. In the midst of the fishmongers and greengrocers and the stifling smells of the market, Sitt Maryam and Zahra saw a taxicab parked at the entrance of Sultan Husayn Street and a woman signaling to them from inside the taxi. They looked at each other in hesitation as they heard her voice, "Sitt Umm Camilla, Sitt Umm Yvonne." It was unmistakably Lula's voice. They went toward the taxi after looking around. What made them respond to her call in spite of their fear of being seen?

"Come on in. Don't be afraid."

She was sitting in the back seat and they sat next to her.

"Drive on," she said.

"Where to?"

"Home."

"The house is right there."

"Drive to the door, buster. These are respectable women—do you want them to be seen in public with me?"

The driver fell silent, as did everyone. Zahra crept closer to Sitt Maryam and clung to her.

Sitt Maryam regretted getting into the taxi. Zahra must have gotten in because of her. "Here we are," said the driver, as he entered a side alley and stopped.

They got out. Lula looked at him and laughed as Sitt Maryam smiled, but Zahra looked frightened. They heard the driver say, "Sitt Lula, are we not respectable folk, too?"

"Get a move on, you son of a club-footed woman," Lula shouted, and the driver drove away laughing.

"Please pardon me, I would like to invite you to a cup of coffee at my place to see my apartment. Please, Sitt Maryam, Sitt Zahra. Sure, I may be bad, but I'm married. I'd even say I am good."

As if hypnotized, they went in with her through the dark entrance of the house. They went up the stairs to the first floor, hardly able to see in the dark. Lula placed the key into the keyhole of the wooden door and opened it, then went ahead to open the windows, through which a little light entered, just enough to see one another and talk. Sitt Maryam and Zahra sat on the first two chairs they came across in the living room. Lula came back after a little while with a small spirit stove, a coffeepot, three cups, and a pitcher of water and sat in front of them on the floor. Lula looked prettier than she had in Dimitri's house. "It feels like I kidnapped you from the street, right?"

Zahra did not answer, and Sitt Maryam told herself that silence was better.

"How are Sheikh Magd al-Din and Khawaga Dimitri?" asked Lula. "I used to hear Sheikh Magd's voice as he recited the Quran at night—his voice went through the walls and came to me, a beautiful and soothing voice. Two days before my husband found me, I had intended to repent and go back to him because of Sheikh Magd al-Din's voice, even though I didn't understand anything from the Quran, but every time he said, '*Which of the favors of your Lord will you deny?*' I would cry—really cry."

Zahra said to herself, "I ask God Almighty for forgiveness."
She felt that it was not proper for the word of God ever to be
uttered by that woman. They sat for a long time as Lula told them
about the fight over her by the women's troupes and how it was
settled by the men: "The men can handle anything; you get
nothing from women except lies and deceit." She told them about
the nights of the pashas, which rivaled those described in *One
Thousand and One Nights*.

"Like who, Lula? Of course Abbud Pasha was one of them,"
asked Sitt Maryam.

"All of them—Abbud, Farghali, Spahi, and Tawil. I once
danced at Tawil Pasha's mansion in the presence of Nahhas Pasha
himself. Yes, he had just had an abscess removed and had come to
Alexandria to recuperate. But, to tell you the truth, he was always
looking at the floor. Maybe once or twice he raised his eyes to me.
I felt he was afraid of me, not of the other political parties. How
many parties are there in Egypt, anyway? At any rate, all pashas
are generous, even Salvatore Cicurel and Salvago, who own the
streetcar lines. He bought me a streetcar."

They all laughed for the first time. Caution and regret were
now gone.

"The only one left is His Majesty the King," Lula went on. "I
danced for the princes. He's the only one left. If I danced for him
I'd work in films with Abd al-Wahhab and go to Cairo, and leave
behind Alexandria and all these air raids. There's hope next
summer I'll dance at Muntaza. The war would surely be over by
then—it must! I've asked Sitt Didi, who lives here on Sultan Street.
She's the best designer of dance outfits. I told her to cut an outfit
for me, open on all sides, from behind, front, and at the waist and
along with the spangles and the beads and the rhinestones, to add
some genuine diamonds. You know, Sitt Maryam, sometimes I
miss you all very much."

They drank the coffee. Zahra noticed that the living room was
clean and the seats comfortable, not new but shiny. She also
noticed some musical instruments—a lute, a tabla, a tambourine,
cymbals, an accordion—scattered all over, some shiny, some old
and dusty, but on the whole it was a comfortable place and
appealing to the eye.

After they drank the coffee, Sitt Lula got up to bring some dance outfits to show them. Zahra looked at Sitt Maryam in dismay, but the latter calmly said, "Let's see the outfits and leave without looking at anything else. We'll never come to the piazza again."

As they were hurrying down the stairs, Lula shouted, "Please send my greetings to Khawaga Dimitri and Sheikh Magd al-Din and to Camilla and Yvonne. I promise you I'll dance at their weddings—I surely will!"

She had also told them about the foreign impresario who had promised her a trip to Europe, adding that there she would make good *ubbayyig*, and when she saw that they were puzzled, she said it meant she would make good money.

"The women who run the dance troupes have their own lingo," she explained, laughing. "You say, for instance, today it is *megamema*, which means you're out of work, and *abriz* means going to the bathroom, *arkhi* means food, and ayma means a big profit. There are many harder words that no one except these women can understand, because it's all inspired by hashish."

That strange meeting remained engraved in Zahra's mind for several days. She looked at Sitt Maryam in confusion and fear; she had committed a sin against Magd al-Din.

One day Sitt Maryam surprised her by telling her in front of her daughters, "Why are you tormenting yourself, Zahra? You can go ahead and tell Sheikh Magd about our meeting with Lula. There's no problem. I told Dimitri about it, and he laughed. But he said we shouldn't go to the piazza, exactly as I had told you, and to buy our things here from Sidi Karim or from far away, from Bahari."

So, it was not very serious; she could tell Magd al-Din. But she never did. Magd al-Din appeared to be in a state of constant silence. She wondered what he was so preoccupied with.

In that regard, he was not any different from Camilla, who returned to silence and despondency. She only spoke a very few words to Zahra—"How are you," "Good morning," "Good evening," and nothing else. Zahra now saw her eyes always welling up with tears. The truth was that Camilla had become certain that she had taken a road of no return. She had advanced in her study of French in the Berlitz school in the summer, and when her regular school started she had not stopped her French lessons, changing her schedule from a morning to an afternoon one, as evening classes had been banned since the beginning of the war. There were two days on which she left Nabawiya Musa school, went to Berlitz, and returned home at about four o'clock. Yvonne had stopped taking French, deciding to resume it the following summer. Camilla asked herself many times why she was persevering in her study of the French language and longing to read the great poets—Baudelaire, Verlaine, Rimbaud, Éluard, André Breton, and Aragon—but she had no answer. She once found herself during a lesson repeating to herself the sentence that she had uttered unintentionally during the first lesson, "Je l'aime," and discovered that she repeated it to herself frequently. Then she added, also without much thinking, "et il m'aime aussi." Her eyes opened like two flowers and her small, rounded breasts quivered as fire swept through her tender body and she felt her nose catch on fire. Two days later, after she got out of school and had reached Fuad Street and was walking in the cold shadow of the big buildings on that wonderful Alexandrian autumn day, she felt that someone was walking along with her on the other side of the street, neither going ahead nor falling behind her. She felt rays coming from his direction, hitting her right cheek, waking up her blood. She turned and saw him. Fainting was not a sufficient solution. Her feet almost let her down, and she would have collapsed had she not leaned on a wall for a few moments. Then she saw him in front of her, smiling and happy.

"How is French?"

Strength came back to her. She answered with a question, "How did you know?"

"You wouldn't believe me if I told you that before I left you I had seen in your eyes a desire to do everything that I liked to do."

They walked. She left her hand in his. He was back, with that strange talk that she did not understand. He seemed to her like a rainbow in the sky. She did not understand what that feeling meant; she did not know if she had thought about it before, but that was how he seemed to her, really: a rainbow crossing the sky in a fire chariot drawn by rainbow horses.

"Woe to you, Camilla, woe to you," she said to herself after silence had descended for a short while.

"What did you say?"

"Will you wait until I finish my lesson?"

"I will wait for you until the end of time."

"You talk funny, Rushdi," she laughed. "I don't understand you at all."

"What do you say we change the lesson this·time and walk for a little bit?"

They walked to Raml station. They stood on the corniche, invigorated by the cool breeze and the sea spray. He feared the lecherous eyes of the soldiers, white from England and Australia and black from all over the world, so he walked quickly with her to the opposite sidewalk, with its old, typically Alexandrian cafés filled with Greeks, sailors, and soldiers as well. A number of drunken soldiers came out from the Windsor, hurrying together with a number of young women who wore short khaki skirts that reached above their knees despite the cold. Each soldier had his arms around one of the young women as they walked and sang, opera style. He told her, laughing, that students were now saying that after the war the English should leave the country but leave behind the young women of the ATS. Camilla knew that they were conscripts, but he told her that their official jobs were as secretaries and telephone operators in the English camps and establishments, that they had different military ranks exactly like the men, but that their real job was to entertain the soldiers. He said they were not just English but French, Greek, Cypriots, New Zealanders, Indians, and South Africans and from all over the British Empire. Camilla never thought beyond the literal meaning of these pretty young women in the Auxiliary Territorial Service, abbreviated by the press to ATS and pronounced al-Atsa by the Egyptians. They stopped in front of the statue of Ismail Pasha in Manshiya.

"Let's stand here like a couple of European tourists," he said.

"Have you been to Europe before?"

He had put his arm around her and she felt his ribs under his shirt and light pullover, and he felt her fleshy warmth.

"I must go one day."

"You'll take me with you?" She clung to him even more closely.

"We may very well find that to be the only option available to us," he said, reminding her of what she had managed to forget in the summer. If only she had never studied French!

They kept on walking. Many fezzes appeared in the square, with its cafés that attracted brokers; merchants; stock-exchange experts; seekers of fame, fortune, glory, and happiness; would-be pashas and beys coming from the countryside to do business; and sailors who had gotten tired of the cheap bars of Bahari and the cheaper women of Haggari and who came here in search of better bars and prettier women. The square was also filled with horse-drawn carriages that raced along with their human cargo. And above it all was the statue of Muhammad Ali Pasha, ready to take off as the wind mirthfully played in the wide open space and on the ground where it kicked up the little leaves that had fallen indolently from the tree in the middle of the road.

"Where do you live?" she asked him.

"Not far from you. You live in Ghayt al-Aynab. I followed behind you once all the way to your door."

She looked very surprised as he continued, "I live halfway between Karmuz and Kafr Ashri bridges. There's housing for railroad workers there. It's an isolated, quiet place in front of Mahmudiya Canal and a big, empty stretch of land—completely safe."

"I know the place well," she said. "It's a really beautiful place, and the most beautiful thing about it is that no one can spot it or get to it easily."

He stopped and looked at her very closely, holding her shoulders without fear or shame. "Listen to you, you're saying beautiful things."

She laughed and started to walk again after gently removing his hands from her shoulders. "I've gone there with mother many times to buy fish from the salt works," she said. "There's a long, dark tunnel you go through, and then you find yourself right smack at the salt works."

"Exactly."

She did not want to tell him that she had gone several times to that very housing compound with her father, mother, and Yvonne to visit their relative Usta Ghibriyal, whom Rushdi surely knew and who surely was his father's boss.

"A man who lives in our house works for the railroad," she said.

"I don't know him. He doesn't live in our house," he said, and they laughed. She felt regret for her indiscretion but soon overcame it, for she had not mentioned the name of their tenant or that of Ghibriyal in any case.

Camilla went home that day like a free sparrow flying in a magnificent space. But as soon as she sat down, a gloom that she could not shake descended upon her. Her mother could not figure it out, nor could anyone else except Yvonne, who realized that her sister was at it again. Every night now Camilla would decide to break it off with Rushdi for good, and in the morning would wait for the afternoon when he came. He was very considerate. He asked her to let him follow her four days a week, and two days a week go out with him to some place far from home.

The priest, with his ruddy complexion, black beard, and black cassock, appeared at the house, and Zahra saw him for the first time, even though he had been to the house many times before. Zahra started hearing long speeches that she did not understand, and prayers and chants that she did not understand either. Every time the priest came, silence descended on the house, and Sitt Maryam closed the door of their room without looking at anyone who might be there, even when Khawaga Dimitri was present. An hour or more later the priest would come out, and Zahra would hear loud voices bidding him farewell, "Good-bye, father, may the Virgin protect you!" She also heard sobbing, but she could not tell whether it came from Camilla or Yvonne. She also rarely saw Camilla and Yvonne now, as they no longer sat out with their mother but stayed in the inner rooms after returning from school.

That continued to be the case until one day the air-raid siren sounded ominously, heralding imminent danger. True, the siren sounded intermittently with every raid, every day, and it sounded the same, whether the raid was big or small, but somehow, people had developed a sense, a sort of intuitive feeling about particularly bad raids by hearing the sound of the siren. Did that sound actually change, or did the war unite people and sensitize them in such a way that they were able to prophesy, like prophets or mystics? The feast at the end of Ramadan had ended ten days earlier with a big raid that lasted from six o'clock in the evening to ten, but it was scattered over various neighborhoods, so it did not leave a large number of casualties concentrated in one place. Today, however, people in Karmuz, Ghayt al-Aynab, Raghib, Masr Station, and Attarin felt that they, the very heart and pulse of Alexandria, were the targets.

That day Zahra had asked Magd al-Din several times about the priest and his visits, which occurred sometimes more than twice in one week and about the silence, the crying, and the mumbling, but Magd al-Din told her, "Leave creation to the Creator, and take care of what's in your womb."

When the siren sounded, she clung to him, and her daughter Shawqiya cried, as she sensed that the intermittent siren was bad from the way people around her panicked. She had also figured out that the long, uninterrupted all-clear was good and would clap her little hands when she heard it. Zahra hurriedly put a shawl around her shoulders, for the shelter was cold and humid, and went downstairs, followed by Magd al-Din, who carried Shawqiya. Zahra saw Sitt Maryam, the two girls, and Khawaga Dimitri going downstairs in silence. Zahra's fear did not prevent her from seeing how Camilla was withering away like an ear of grain left in the sun too long. They all went into Bahi's room, which was always open since no one had rented it, or Lula's room, which was also open since the migration of people from Alexandria left behind many vacant apartments and rooms. As soon as they got into the room Sitt Maryam said, "Turn off the light, Dimitri."

It seemed to Zahra that the woman said this because she did not wish anyone to see her daughter in her bad condition, rather than because of the raid, even though civil defense instructions clearly specified that all lights be turned off. It was the second half of the lunar month of Shawwal, and the moon had waned almost to a crescent, but its light was enough. Magd al-Din opened the window of the room to hear people's comments and to see them. Then he suggested to Dimitri that they go out on the street and join the men. Dimitri thought it was a good idea and they went out.

Magd al-Din saw the searchlights from the harbor and Kom al-Shuqafa filling the sky. Then he heard the loud droning noise of approaching planes, and as they flew within range, the anti-aircraft artillery in Alexandria let loose a barrage of red missiles from all the highest points in Alexandria. The sounds of the guns reverberated intensely from all directions. Boys and young men on the streets cheered as they saw some planes catch on fire, but the sounds of explosions were soon heard, and smoke could be seen in various quarters of the city in the west, east, and north. Then the explosions were concentrated in the downtown area. Children could be heard crying loudly in many houses, and various people began to recite loudly verses from the Quran. Ghaffara's voice boomed from behind his fez-mask, "That son of a bitch Graziani doesn't like us. What really kills me is, how come the planes come over from Italy to hit us? Why don't they go to England? Isn't England closer?"

The voice of a young man was heard to reply, "The planes come from Libya, idiot."

Suddenly Dimyan appeared. It looked as though he had just come from a strenuous race. His voice shook as he spoke.

"I didn't come here to hide, Sheikh Magd. The piazza, Karmuz, and Bab Sidra are all on fire, sky-high, worse than the six-hour raid. We've got to run and help our brothers."

Magd al-Din was silent, thinking how he had failed to heed the call before, that it would not be right to do that again. Then he heard Ghaffara say to the youth gathered there, "It's a black night, young men. Come on—let's go to Karmuz. Houses have fallen down, and people have died."

It was a night beyond the limits of the human mind. In the dark, frantic feet trotted like horses, and eyes hung on every explosion that filled the sky with fire and showering missiles. When they approached the Mahmudiya canal, they saw only pitch dark over the water and a few barges on which sailors stood watching the battle raging in the sky. In record time they covered the distance on Karmuz Street and entered the piazza by the clock tower. Magd al-Din saw fires the likes of which he had never seen, a huge mass of red, higher than the tallest buildings and houses. He stood helplessly reflecting, "God, most merciful!"

"Kyrie eleison. Kyrie eleison," Dimyan repeated, and Ghaffara exclaimed, "God, have mercy on your servants!"

Magd al-Din had seen many fires before in the countryside in which he could smell burning dung, straw, and firewood. This time however, he was smelling burned flesh, hearing cries from all directions, and watching as women ran through the streets in their nightclothes and men carried children from their homes to stand at a distance. Everyone was crying, the sound of planes droned ceaselessly over the city as the guns chased them and the searchlights raced all over the sky. He could hear the fire trucks coming from Kom al-Dikka and saw some parked in the distance in front of the burning houses, as the fire fighters in their helmets scrambled to the fire hydrants on the sidewalks to which they attached their huge water hose and began to put out the fires.

The bombing had moved to Mina al-Basal, and Magd al-Din could see Dimyan standing helplessly in front of him, and Ghaffara as usual wearing his fez-mask, and Hamidu and the young men running to the collapsed houses to pull out people pinned down or just lying there. There were many musical instruments lying scattered everywhere on the ground—lutes, drums, tambourines, accordions, saxophones, and flutes that looked like snakes and serpents. There were groups of almost-naked women who had been surprised by the raid, the destruction, and the fires. Some women from the houses that were not effected began to hand the others robes and gallabiyas to cover themselves. Curses poured forth against the Germans, the Italians, and the English who were behind it all. The air was filled with the smell of human sweat mixed with dust. They all began to remove the corpses from the debris. Then the all-clear sounded as the planes moved away, but the fires still lit the place, as did the headlights of the fire trucks. There were screams coming from the ruins and sounds of faint moaning as if someone was gasping a last breath. Every time someone alive was brought out, shouts of "God is great!" rang out. Magd al-Din had not expected to meet anyone he knew here, let alone find them in the ruins. He saw three men carrying a women on a stretcher and running; two were carrying it from the front and one from the back, and he heard a voice call out, "Sheikh Magd al-Din."

They were placing the wounded next to each other on the far pavement so the ambulances could transport them. The person carrying the stretcher from the back was his friend Dimyan, who came back and told him, "We took out a woman from the rubble. She saw you and called out to you. Didn't you hear her?"

"I heard her and didn't believe it. I don't know anyone here."

"She's right there with the wounded, anyway, so you can go over to her."

Dimyan ran off again to help rescue others. Magd al-Din made his way to the wounded. When he drew near, he saw her looking at him with a trace of joy in her eyes. It was none other than Lula. Merciful God! She motioned him to sit next to her, and he did. "Please forgive me, Sheikh Magd, I tried to seduce your brother Bahi, but he wouldn't give in. Dozens of times I came up to him at night, but he wouldn't do it."

"He's the one to forgive you, Sitt Lula."

"He did. But I need for you to forgive me also. I've thought a lot about you."

"I ask God Almighty for forgiveness."

"Then please forgive me."

"God is the One who can forgive you. I forgive everything, even though I don't think you've done me any wrong."

"Even my infidelity to my husband?"

"It's fate, Sitt Lula. Where's the injury?"

"My legs are broken."

He noticed that her legs were very swollen under her nightgown—a sure sign of severe internal hemorrhaging. As soon as the ambulance appeared, he lifted the stretcher at one end, and Dimyan saw him and ran over to help. They placed Lula in the ambulance, then carried over three other wounded women, and the ambulance rushed them to Muwasa Hospital. Before the ambulance had arrived, Lula was raving, "I've loved no one like King Farouk, nor desired anyone as I desired him. Now I won't dance in front of him. I don't think I'll ever go back to dancing."

Tears poured down her cheeks, and she held Magd al-Din's hand and kissed it. He let her do it.

As he went out to wash the next morning, Magd al-Din passed Khawaga Dimitri, who was just finishing up, in the hallway.

"Are you going to work today?" asked Magd al-Din. "I don't think anybody's going to work today. I'm going to the café, to meet people and find out what's happened to the city after that raid. Do you want to come with me?'

Magd al-Din went with him. Ever since he had started working for the railroad, he had not once sat in the café in the morning. In the café, Dimitri told him about Karmuz Street and Rhakotis, which Alexander connected with Pharos, now called Bahari. He told him that Rhakotis was a dangerous area, full of drugs and criminals, but that in the past it had been a place where Christians were tortured. He said that Pompey's Pillar was built on the hill of Bab Sidra, which in Roman times had temples and stadiums where gladiators fought to the death and where lions were set loose upon converts to the new religion. Dimitri told him that it was an old martyrs' field; that, in honor of the martyrs, the Coptic calendar began the same year that Diocletian massacred hundreds of thousands of Christians; that it had been a bloody area from time immemorial; and that the blood would not be washed away by Pompey's Pillar, which the Alexandrians had built to immortalize an oppressive ruler.

No one sleeps in heaven
No one sleeps in the world
No one sleeps
No one
No one.

Federico García Lorca

16

The year was nearing its end. Rain came down on Alexandria in buckets. It seemed that Alexandria was not going to celebrate the new year, that the lights would not be turned off exactly at midnight—they were already off. Nobody was going to throw empty bottles or old pottery and ceramics from the windows to bid the old year farewell and to hope for a better new year. It seemed that neither the Monsignor, Excelsior, and Louvre nightclubs nor casinos like the Shatbi, the Miramar, the Windsor, the Hollywood, the Kit Kat, or any of the others would celebrate the occasion. It was possible that people would spend the last night of the year in the shelters. The previous month, November, had been really bad. Two big air raids in one week, on the eighteenth and the nineteenth at six o'clock and eight o'clock in the evening respectively. Traffic to the railroad station multiplied; caravans of cars, horse-drawn carriages, and old taxis pushed their way through, carrying people and a few belongings. The platforms of the station filled with people waiting, sitting and lying down, filled with patience, fear, and a profound uncertainty. The smell of human sweat mixed with that of fuel oil and the smoke of the trains; the air became heavy, almost palpable. Few trains were moving; most trains had been set aside to move troops and military equipment. At the station you could also see people scurrying

around for a reason, or for no reason at all, as well as people
screaming because of the crowding or the hardships of life, and
people crying from disease, abject poverty, or fear. All these
sounds, the voices of males and females, old and young, mixed
with those of vendors of pretzels and cheese, peanuts and oranges.
Shells and rinds mixed with the broad bean pods and other litter
from various food products. Litter filled the corners and fell into
the cracks between the tiles, lay on top of the tiles, around those
sitting and under the feet of those walking or scurrying, and
around those screaming, jesting, or those in a complete daze.
Those were the days of the 'great emigration,' an unforgettable
event in Alexandria that people would later use as a landmark to
date events in their lives.

Magd al-Din could see the question in Zahra's eyes, but he
never gave her the chance to ask it. He avoided the fear in her
amber-colored eyes, and whenever he turned his face away, she
was somewhat relieved. What would really happen if she asked,
and he said yes? If she asked to go back, he would go back with
her, and the mayor would kill him. He would be leaving war for
death. Alexandria was now a safe haven, despite the heavy raids
and the long darkness. The desire to leave that was gently waking
in her must be suppressed, and she must remain as she had been, a
woman who would never leave her husband.

But one night, a particularly cold night at the end of the year,
she clung to his chest more than ever before, and he felt her smaller
than ever before, despite her rising belly; she was now a child
clinging to his chest. She said, having forgotten everything, "I'm
afraid, Magd al-Din."

"Don't be afraid. The air raids are far away now—most of
them are in Dikhayla, the harbor, and the English army camps in
the suburbs."

"I don't mean the raids. I'm afraid to give birth alone, and I'm
afraid to go back to the village."

"If we must go back, I'll go with you."

Zahra was silent.

"Is Sitt Maryam still keeping to herself?"

"Very much so, and she looks worried all the time. The priest
is always there, and Camilla is withering away."

"Keep Sitt Maryam company—don't let her be by herself. You can make up reasons to go with her to the markets."

But Zahra, who had been in Alexandria more than a year and now knew how to go to the markets by herself, did not find the prospect of going out to market as appealing as it used to be. Goods were in short supply, and fewer people, vendors or buyers, could be seen in the streets. Only Umm Hamidu relieved her loneliness now. She was still setting up her produce stall at the entrance of the house across the street. Zahra liked to sit with her for a while every time she bought something from her. Umm Hamidu also liked the clever young peasant woman who was always full of questions, so she often asked her to stay, sometimes offering her a small bath stool to sit on. But Zahra sat on the floor most of the time. Umm Hamidu would ask her how her husband Magd al-Din, whom the people of the neighborhood hardly knew, was and why he was always seen in the company of Dimyan, the Christian. Why, really, was he friends with a Christian? Umm Hamidu would ask, then she would remember that Zahra and her husband lived in Khawaga Dimitri's house and would say "Ah-ha!" Zahra always said, "We were all born after nine months." Or she said, "The One who created the Muslims also created the Copts," and Umm Hamidu, seeming to be convinced would say, "You're right," but would ask the same questions another day, then would go on and talk about things in Alexandria that Zahra did not know much about. She asked Zahra if she had seen the statue of Muhammad Ali Pasha, and Zahra said she had. So she asked her if she had seen the statue of Ismail Pasha by the sea, or that of Saad Zaghloul at Raml Station, or the English women soldiers, riding colorful bicycles on the corniche or the drunken English soldiers harassing girls on the corniche and in Bahari and Attarin, and sometimes even kidnapping them. She told her amazing stories about families that had lost their fortunes in the Cotton Exchange, about the people of lowly origins who had made great fortunes in no time at all by doing business with the English camps, or those who had won the Muwasa Hospital lottery, which at that time had just been won by one of the notables, a certain Effat, who won a whole ten thousand pounds.

"Ten thousand pounds went to someone who didn't need it," Umm Hamidu commented. "And they're always fancy names— Effat or Hemmat, or Tal'at or Dawlat or Bahgat. Never real Egyptian names like Bahlul or Shahhat, or even Mustafa or Ali. It doesn't have to be Hamidu."

She also told her a lot about King Farouk, who loved to pray in the mosque of Mursi Abu al-Abbas during the day, but at night people could hear the dancing and carousing in the gardens of Muntaza Palace all summer long. She told Zahra that if she had seen the Ras al-Tin Palace in Bahari, then the Muntaza Palace was at the other end of Alexandria, on the last, farthest east beach, a palace surrounded by five hundred feddans, which had beautiful trees from all over. She told her that Ismail Pasha, the grandfather of young King Farouk, had built it. "Everything beautiful in Alexandria was built by Ismail Pasha. They say that he was a spendthrift, that he loved life and built the Suez canal so that a queen from France named Eugénie would come and open it. He made the canal so he could see the queen. He was in love with her, and he gave her the canal." Zahra's eyes and mouth opened wide when she heard those stories, and Umm Hamidu would continue, "He built the opera in Cairo for her, a big theater so she could hear the singing of Si Abdu and Sitt Almaz. Ismail Pasha was a really generous man."

Talk would also turn to the new corpses, often of little girls, that began to appear in the Mahmudiya canal, or to the many new foundlings noticed wrapped in old rags and lying on the bank between the Raghib and Karmuz bridges, their cries barely heard by a passer-by or by someone out for a ride in a small rowboat. Usually such foundlings were handed over to the government, which placed them in orphanages. A few of them lived; the others died of neglect.

"But God is capable of protecting them—maybe one of them will grow up to be famous, a singer or a ruler. Men with unknown origins, the ones they called Mamluks, ruled our country. Maybe they found them abandoned near the canals like that."

Laughing, Umm Hamidu then asked Zahra if she had seen the soldiers of the Territorial Army stationed on guard duty around the mill, the bridge, and the police precinct. "The poor cripples,

lepers and one-eyed men—the best among them is no better than
a club-foot. They'd come to me and play all kinds of games and
maneuvers just to buy a millieme's worth of tangerine. I take pity
on them. One of them is very cute, he comes here and sings to
me." Umm Hamidu's mounds of flesh shook as she laughed. "He
really sings and moves his shoulders like a dancer: 'O tangerine
vendor, please tell me how much for ten.' I look at him and laugh
and give him a tangerine for free. The next day and the next he'd
come and dance and sing and so on until one day, I shook my
shoulder as I told him 'Ten tangerines, darling, cost ten piasters.'
He laughed and that made me laugh, and now because he's my
friend, he asks me how I am every day. He told me that he didn't
want to go back to his village after the war, that he wanted to live
in Alexandria. He asked me to marry him, I swear. I told him,
why do you want to marry a woman who can hardly move? Why
do you want to bury yourself alive? But he wasn't convinced. He
comes and sings to me everyday and says that he's patient and will
get his heart's desire."

Umm Hamidu expressed surprise at the German and Italian
raids against Alexandria, guarded as it was by the Territorial
Army, which could not fight an ant. "They should have pity on
them and send them food," she reasoned.

Umm Hamidu never missed a chance to talk about the
scandalous police behavior in Kom Bakir, Attarin, Mina al-Basal,
Mahamil, and Marsilya Street. She noticed that Zahra was not
particularly fond of that line of talk, especially after she heard it
the first time. But Umm Hamidu loved to discuss it, if only
briefly. She would tell her about the many respectable families
whose daughters went to those places during the day, then went
back home, chaste and honest for all intents and purposes, and
about the many poor women whose men sent them there also,
"Filthy men." There were also widows that sold themselves rather
than marry, so they could raise their children alone. That was, of
course, in addition to the divorcées and peasant girls who had run
away from home. "The whole country is throwing women at
Alexandria these dark days, when it's filled with soldiers from the
white world and the black world." She told her that Hamidu, her
son who worked as a shoeshine boy in Raml station, Manshiya,

Bahari, and Attarin, came to her with stories that would make one's hair turn gray, about the women, the soldiers, and all the foreigners. Hamidu was always upset at what he saw, and he did bad things to the English. "He'll either end up dead or banished to Mount Sinai." Zahra asked her where Mount Sinai was, and she said it was in the faraway place where they banished criminals. Zahra, who still had not learned where Mount Sinai was, fell silent. Umm Hamidu asked her once if she had noticed how in the Rashidi family, which lived in the house next to Khawaga Dimitri's, the men were very short and the women very tall. "Each woman needs two men, end to end, one to kiss her and the other to fuck her. Why aren't you laughing?" she asked Zahra, who was always shocked at the audacity of this fat woman who seemed, as she sat there, as if she had been planted, who seemed not to be able to stand up, as if her waist and huge posterior were part and parcel of the earth.

Zahra was even more surprised that she was so fascinated by what Umm Hamidu had to say. Zahra told her only one story, about the raid that took place the previous month and how her husband Magd al-Din and his friend Dimyan, when they ran to Karmuz to help with the rescue, found Lula in the rubble suffering from a severe injury. Umm Hamidu, who looked genuinely sorry, said that Lula was a poor woman who had not run away with her lover, but that her husband, the accordion player, was a pimp, that she had heard about her fame the last few months in the mansions of the pashas and hoped to see her, but God's will was done. She said that she herself had worked for some time with the troupe of Naima al-Saghir in Bahari. "A dancer?" Zahra asked in surprise. Umm Hamidu realized why she was so surprised, for who has ever heard of a fat dancer who cannot get up off the ground all day? She said no, that she was a dresser, and explained to her how she used to dress Sitt Naima al-Saghir for singing and dancing, and for the pashas' parties. Sitt Naima, she told her, had a short fuse. Every time she met a movie producer, she asked him to find her a role in a movie, and he would promise, but not deliver. So Sitt Naima took it out on her helpers, and Umm Hamidu left her service.

She talked to Zahra about the world of the *awalim*, the singing and dancing women. She told her that the piazza where Lula died was their headquarters in Alexandria. There were the artists' cafés, the houses of impresarios and leaders of the troupes, and the workshops for teaching singing and dancing girls. Any girl who ran away went to the piazza, for dancing was more honorable than prostitution, and, "as the proverb says, 'Every bean finds her measurer.' But the awalim say, 'Every dancer finds her drummer.' The dancer always marries a drummer or a tambourine player, seldom an accordionist or some other instrument—those love the singers. Each leader of a troupe has her own girls and her turf. So Naima al-Saghir, for instance, cannot enter Karmuz—Bata al-Salamuni would kill her—and so on. And now, after the movies, each dancer wants to be another Hikmat Fahmi, and every dancer who used to dream to dance in the corniche nightclubs is now dreaming to dance in front of the king. King Farouk is a handsome man whose face is as beautiful as the full moon; all the dancers are in love with him and women hunger for him!"

Then Umm Hamidu takes her spiel in a different direction. "Alexandria is a happy city, and its earth is saffron, as people say. They say that Alexandria was built by a crazy man named Alexander who filled it with wineries, and people danced and sang all day and night and cavorted with women. To this day they still find relics of Alexander and ancient Alexandria, just like they find treasures under collapsed houses after the air raids. After every raid the rescue workers find a lot of money and gold and jewelry under the rubble. They once found a clay vessel filled with gold coins stamped with the name of the Greek queen Naisa, who ruled Alexandria a long time ago. Yes, that's why they call the area Mount Naisa, because the queen lived there. They say she was a mighty queen, so the folks who live in Mount Naisa are mighty drug dealers and robbers that the government can't do anything about. In front of Mount Naisa on one side is the piazza, and on the other side Pompey's Pillar. The piazza is a very old neighborhood, and Pompey's Pillar is even older. It's surrounded by Kom al-Shuqafa, which has catacombs underground where the Nubians and Sudanese live. These Nubians and Sudanese spend their days selling seeds and peanuts, and at night they sleep in the caves like bats. The caves are full of relics known only to those blacks and to the gypsies. The gypsies also live there, but since the war started, nobody sees them on the streets any more. Where did they go? God only knows!"

Thus, after having seen the sea and the big squares with Sitt Maryam, Zahra entered Alexandria's magic world. Umm Hamidu's stories have given the city, whose inhabitants were leaving, a warm soul in a winter that now appeared truly frosty. But after the rain fell, warmth prevailed, spaces grew wider, and the sky moved higher, bluer, happier. Alexandria has always been a happy city, despite the apparent malaise because of the migration. Umm Hamidu's stories made it twice as happy. The rain, which had not stopped in days, would surely let up with the beginning of the new year, when the Christian and Muslim holidays would coincide for the first time in many years: the Orthodox Christmas would be on the same day as the Feast of the Sacrifice. If the rain did not stop, however, it would fall on Muslims and Christians alike, and there would be joy for all and rain for all, and even Epiphany, which Yvonne had said the previous year was an ancient Egyptian feast, would be for all.

Orders were given throughout the country that the new year be celebrated, but without lighting up the streets, and people were warned about the possibility of surprise air raids. For even though the combatants in Europe had announced a cease-fire on the last day of the year, no one could guarantee the actions of Hitler and Mussolini, especially since "our country has no interest in the European celebrations of the birth of Christ, it being an innovation that came with the occupation." At any rate, the raids had stopped in Europe on the penultimate day of December, in view of bad weather conditions, so people in Europe enjoyed two days in a row without raids. That was a particularly welcome respite for the British, whose cities Hitler had vowed to wipe out. The night of the thirtieth of December, however, witnessed intensive British air raids on the Gazala and Tobruk airports in Libya. Italian airplanes in turn attacked the British bases in Malta.

The world was still following the surprising advances of the Greeks in Albania, at the Italians' expense and amid the confusion of the Albanians themselves, who had not yet settled on one occupier of their land. The Führer addressed a message to the German army in which he enumerated Germany's triumphs during the past year and promised final victory in the new year. "The German Army of National Socialism has achieved brilliant victories in the year 1940. This army, on the threshold of a new year, has prepared itself with armaments hitherto unknown to humanity."

In Cairo, Biba Izz al-Din announced that she would open her new program at the Majestic Theater with the play *Who Are You Kidding?*, which would include singing monologues by Muhammad Abd al-Muttalib, Fathiya Mahmud, Thurayya Hilmi, and Sayyid Fawzi. The Shatbi Casino announced it would open its doors for new year's celebrations. Celebrants, mostly Commonwealth soldiers, danced to love serenades at the Monsignor in dim lights that did not show outside because of the tinted glass and heavy curtains. Neither Magd al-Din nor Zahra understood, for the second time, why people threw their old things from the windows at year's end, even though it was a small number of people who did, as most had left in the great emigration.

In Cairo, King Farouk attended a new year's party at the opera house for the entertainment of the English soldiers in the Middle East. The Wafd Party submitted to him a statement of opinion on internal and external affairs in Egypt, criticizing both. The Royal Air Force in the Middle East resumed its bombing of Gazala and Bardiya in Libya. The month of December had witnessed a ferocious surprise attack by the suntanned British and Allied armored forces on Sidi Barrani, where they captured "Italian officers who filled five feddans and soldiers who filled two hundred feddans." People once again wondered, as they saw the prisoner-of-war trains coming from the desert, whether the Italians were really fighting, or whether Il Duce and Graziani were doing the fighting alone. By the middle of the month, the Italians had been thrown out of Egypt, and the Allied forces chased them to Bardiya, which had been penetrated by the Australian soldiers in their long heavy coats. They captured five thousand Italians. Air raids started again with the new year in Europe. The Germans used a new type of incendiary bomb on London that started infernal fires everywhere and left behind, after each raid, three to four thousand casualties or more. One bomb fell on the House of Commons and caused serious damage, though there were no politicians in it. The German city of Bremen was totally destroyed by British air raids. In Libya, the Australians, together with the English, had invaded and routed Tobruk, and thirty thousand Italians were taken prisoner, bringing the number of Italian prisoners of war to one hundred thousand. Thus the huge army collapsed and became a negligible military force. The Allied forces spread along the coast from Sallum to Buqbuq.

Yusuf Wahbi's play *The Air Raid Siren* opened. Cinema Olympia screened the film *Dananir*, starring Umm Kulthum; Cinema Misr showed Mary Queenie's A *Rebellious Girl*; and Cinema Cosmo was playing One *Million Years B.C.*, which starred the new actor Victor Mature and which Camilla saw with Rushdi and saw in Rushdi's eyes the same sadness as in Victor Mature's. The Commandant of the Traffic Police, Muhammad Shukri Bey, issued an order requiring all cab drivers to wear a uniform as they did in European countries, a khaki coat over their clothes. In Alexandria the Israelite Sports Union had a gala party to benefit victims of the air raids, which was attended by Salvatore Cicurel and many other notables. Marshal Wavell's reputation spread. In disbelief, people watched the sweeping British offensive on Libya and the defeats raining down on Italy.

But Magd al-Din believed, for he saw the weapons being shipped by train to the heart of the desert every day, weapons that only red demons could make and only devils and giants could use. Hamza expressed amazement as he saw the young Italian prisoners of war, barefoot and heads shaved, shipped in open and closed freight trains, looking more like homeless children, and sleeping without a care. Some of them even smiled at the workers or waved to them. Commenting on their great numbers, Hamza sang, "If time deals you a bad hand, son of noble ones, bow your head, but follow not the ignoble ones." His co-workers, who could not see the connection between what he said and what was happening, laughed.

"Aren't they the ones who were fighting?" Dimyan asked him.

"My heart tells me these are good-hearted men who don't know how to fight in Egypt or Greece. It's all the devil Mussolini's fault," was Hamza's reply.

Roosevelt delivered a speech in which he said that America was going to be "the great arsenal of democracy." The licensed prostitutes of Alexandria complained about the dwindling number of patrons after the great emigration from the city. They requested that they be used to entertain the English soldiers in their camps in return for a fixed income, since Commonwealth soldiers who went to the brothels went there drunk and did not pay. Besides, the local customers, knowing that they had become a rare commodity, were no longer going to the poor brothels in Farahda and Kom Bakir, but to the posh ones in Hamamil, and were paying there what they used to pay in the poor ones. The newspapers announced that mentally retarded persons in Germany and countries under German occupation would be executed: "In Germany alone, one hundred thousand wretched creatures, idiots, and incurably insane creatures will be executed in the next few days." The workers laughed when Hamza said that only today he did not wish the Italians to enter Egypt because that meant that "the Germans would enter too, and execute all railroad workers like us." When he saw Ghibriyal's fox-like glance, he immediately added, "Except foremen," and everyone laughed even more. Dimyan began to feel a spiritual affinity with Hamza, and Magd al-Din forgot his previous insult to him.

Churchill gave a speech in which he praised Anglo-American cooperation, saying that they were in the sentinel tower guarding history. The air raids against Alexandria since Italy entered the war numbered one hundred, the most vicious of which was the six-hour raid and the two of the previous November. But the Italians had not come to drink Nile water; rather, they came as prisoners of war, as lost souls walking hundreds of miles on foot from Libya to Marsa Matruh. Many of them died on the road in the sun, the rain, and the desert winds. From Marsa Matruh, they were shipped by train or boat to Alexandria. The newspapers also reported on the trial of those accused in the case of the defective helmets supplied to the Egyptian and the British armies. It was a *cause célèbre*, widely covered in the papers and talked about everywhere,

especially in cafés and bars. The Royal British Army and the Royal
Egyptian Army had, at the beginning of the war, announced an
invitation to bid on supplying fifty thousand helmets for
Commonwealth soldiers and twenty thousand for Egyptian
soldiers. The bid was won by a team of Egyptian and Greek
contractors, who delivered the helmets on time. It turned out
afterwards, however, that the helmets were fake, that they were all
made of tin rather than steel, as was customary. In trying to excuse
himself, one of the defendants said, "What good would a helmet,
tin or steel, do against bombs from the air or against the big guns?
Would a helmet protect a soldier or prevent his death if God had
already decreed his death?" The case, and news of it, proved to be
a welcome diversion for the Egyptians during the war. The trial
was continued, as the defendants and the Egyptians had hoped.
Kassala fell to the English, and Ethiopian troops and the Italians
retreated to Eritrea, and Emperor Haile Selassie prepared to enter
Ethiopia at the head of his national army. Al-Azhar celebrated the
new year of the Islamic calendar. Ghaffara still put the anti–air-
raid fez on his face; he no longer traded in sawdust, as most lumber
yards had closed down after the cessation of maritime trade with
Europe. His customers, mostly shop owners, had also dwindled as
a result of the great emigration. So Ghaffara removed the wooden
box from his cart, leaving only one side panel, on which he wrote,
"Capacity: ten tons. Ready to move migrants to the station with
luggage or without." He started to salute people in the manner of
Goebbels, as he said, by raising his arm and saying "Heil Hitler"
to everyone. At the end of January, Muhammad Mahmud Pasha,
the former prime minister of Egypt known as "the Iron Fist," died
in Cairo. The soulful singer Malak opened in *Butterfly* in
Brentania theater on Imad al-Din Street. In Greece, the great
Greek leader General Metaxas died, and mourning was declared in
the Greek Consulate in Alexandria and all Greek clubs. An order
prohibiting bicycle riding in some streets in the capital was issued.
Italians retreated to Benghazi and Churchill spoke in the House of
Commons, saying that Egypt and Suez were saved. Cinema Misr
screened the film *Salama's All Right*. The English began advancing
on Tripoli. Italian tanks and armored cars were burned, Italian
casualties and prisoners of war since the beginning of the British

offensive totaled 150,000. Grief and muffled resentment of its mighty leader gripped Italy. Decorations went up everywhere in Egypt on the occasion of His Majesty's birthday; music played in public squares, gala parties were held in Zaafarana palace, police-officers' clubs, and the patriarchate. Restaurants were opened for the poor, and school children sang for our happy king. The dreams of Graziani to rule Egypt as a viceroy were shattered. A sublime royal directive announcing the campaign to combat bare feet was issued: "Barefootedness is not a cause but a consequence. It is better for the citizen to buy, with his own money, shoes that would protect his feet. Giving him shoes out of charity takes away from his dignity and increases his humiliation." At the same time the king donated the wild coney that he had caught to the Giza zoo. The newspaper *al-Ahram* published an article to explain what a "coney" was:

"We have received from the Reverend Boulos Roman, from Asyut, a description of this animal. He said that it resembled a rabbit, that it chewed its cud but that it did not divide the cloven hoof, that it was one of the beasts that God ordered the Israelites not to eat, since they were unclean. He added that it was sometimes known as "the sheep of Israel," that it lived in the rocks, and therefore was known for its wisdom. Solomon mentioned it in 'Proverbs,' saying, 'There be four things which are little upon the earth, but they are exceeding wise: the ants are a people not strong, yet they prepare their meat in the summer; the coneys are but a feeble folk, yet make they their houses in the rocks; the locust have no king, yet go they forth all of them by bands; the spider taketh hold with her hands, and is in kings' palaces.' When the prophet David enumerated God's mercy toward man, beast, and bird, he said that He created the rocks as shelter for the coneys. In some translations, the word 'rabbits' has been used, and even though they resemble each other, each was mentioned separately in the Bible, first the coney, then the rabbit. The fact that it was mentioned in the Bible tells us that it is found in abundance in Palestine."

Humans, no matter how numerous, who among them knows anything about himself?

Babylonian saying

17

There was a lot of work the last few days of winter, as cold air seared the faces in the early morning. The wind grew worse, especially after Magd al-Din and Dimyan went beyond the wall to the wide open space above the railroad tracks. There the month of Amshir had a chance to show itself in its true colors, as eddies whirled the dust suddenly, letting loose the cold wind, after which crazy rain poured down from a cloud that had raced in from some distant place. On their usual morning route, Magd al-Din and Dimyan no longer felt provoked by the silent operator of the Raven, who still stared at them. Dimyan noticed that the man had grown a beard and now was rarely ever seated, but instead was constantly walking back and forth. Dimyan asked Magd al-Din whether the man had actually gone crazy. Magd al-Din gave him his usual, vexing response, "Leave the creation to the Creator, Dimyan."

The workers had the task of completing a two-kilometer extension of the rail line, as the present lines could not accommodate all the trains waiting to enter the harbor. The two direct long-distance lines to and from the desert also had to be clear of all other trains.

The open area extending behind Alexandria, from Muharram Bey to Qabbari and passing by Ghayt al-Aynab and Kafr Ashri, was crowded with hundreds of cars and dozens of black steam engines that never stopped moving. They carried weapons from the harbor to the desert, or weapons and soldiers coming from Suez, or those that had been on furlough in Alexandria, as well as prisoners of war. Several trains arrived from the Cairo warehouses with dozens of flatbed cars carrying crossties, rails, and thousands of huge screws and nails, as well as the square steel plates placed between the cross ties and the rails. Trains coming from the Western Desert brought huge amounts of ballast. The area was suddenly filled with railroad policemen in their distinctive yellow uniforms, stationed near and around the equipment unloaded by the workers and the winches moving on rails. The workers, numbering over a hundred, gathered from all the posts to take part in this giant task that had to be finished in record time, even if they had to work day and night.

Despite their woolen outfits, the cold assailed the workers at the neck, sleeves, and hems of their pants. The heat of working was no longer enough to give them warmth, as the wind and the open space gave them no shelter. No one was allowed to take a lunch break, now reduced to one hour, at home. The workers accepted all this hardship, bothered only by the intermittent downpours. The rain forced them to run and take shelter next to or under the nearest car, but as soon as they returned to work, it came down again. On several occasions they made light of it and stayed at their work posts, but it would surprise them by coming down longer and harder. They found themselves obstinately matching wits with the rain.

They divided themselves—actually, their foremen, who were traditional experts at that kind of work, divided them into teams. One team was assigned to level the ground. Their tools were pickaxes and shovels. Another team poured and leveled the ballast in the spots where the crossties would be placed. Their tools were baskets and shovels. A third team was charged with arranging the ties. Their tools were their shoulders, on which they carried the ties. Another team had to carry the rails and place them on top of the crossties and the plates. One team was to fasten the rails to the crossties, using the spikes, which went through the steel plates under the rails and into the crossties, and which secured the two

sides of the rail from the bottom. The last team tamped the ballast
under the ties. The foremen's task was to measure precisely the
gaps between the rails horizontally and the bends to make sure
that the exact number of millimeters was left between sections of
the same rail, so that when the rails stretched in the summer or
shrank in the winter, they would not buckle. And, like all workers
in the world, it was impossible to endure the hardship of long,
arduous work without singing rhythmically, "Haila hop haila,
haila hop haila." This was especially true of those who carried the
rails, each of which was eight meters long. Each of these was
carried by ten men, who sang as they carried it, then gently
lowered it to their feet, and then, all at once, let go of it on top of
the plates and the crossties. Then they moved back, leaving the
place to the fastening team, which placed the huge screws that
went through the crossties, using a long key in the shape of a tube,
at the bottom of which was a square cavity the size of the screw
head. All the while they sang to the saints about the pain in their
backs, about their children, and about the English, who abducted
the women. Then they would laugh as Hamza watched.

Hamza was always among the rail carriers, despite his being
shorter than his colleagues. As Hamza watched the fasteners
spread around the rails, they seemed to him like desert hornets, as
they hovered close together and moved their arms all the time. He
sometimes imagined that they had sprouted wings and flew in the
sky, holding the rail then riding it as if it were a magic carpet. Then
he would laugh. From time to time, Dimyan would stop tamping
the ballast under the crossties and look at Hamza in the middle of
the line of men carrying the rail. He would realize, in surprise and
admiration, that his short colleague was very smart, that he did not
carry anything since the rail supported on the shoulders of his tall
colleagues barely touched his shoulders. Hamza must have
realized the meaning of Dimyan's occasional glances at him, so he
would sing:

> *I am a hardy camel,*
> *my only trouble is the camel driver,*
> *A grouchy man who's not up to his task.*

Or:

An orphan whose family is lost
Is lost in this country.

Or less loudly but with more feeling:

A prisoner of war in time
Can be sold to the nobility
But the people of a free country
Employed him as a servant.

"Bravo, Hamza. May God inspire you," the workers would say, only to be silenced by the downpour and run to take shelter in the cars.

The workers did not have fixed duties, but changed them every two days. Usta Ghibriyal was of the opinion that they should change every day, as that was more restful for the body and did not tax the workers' abilities. But Usta al-Bayya, foreman of Post Number Two, said the change would be better every two days. Al-Bayya was an old foreman, and his recklessness was so widely known that the workers nicknamed him 'the crazy one.' So no one could argue with him. Al-Bayya said, "Two days is better for the workers—they are as strong as donkeys." When he spoke, al-Bayya sprayed, a fact that made anyone speaking with him end the conversation as quickly as he could. In reality, all the jobs were equally hard, despite the apparent differences. Dimyan was of the opinion that all the jobs were so horrible that he prayed silently to Mari Girgis, the Martyr, who had given him that job, to fill the sky with black clouds so the rain would never stop, and the rails would come undone, and the trains would overturn, and the Allies would stop fighting the Axis. Then he would find time to learn reading and writing, subjects in which he had not made much progress, even though he had to take a test in a few weeks, otherwise he would not get a raise the following year. He would say to himself, "Lord, Most Holy, who created us and put us in heaven, but we disobeyed you by the counsel of the serpent and fell from life everlasting. But you did not abandon us but sent us saints and

prophets to look after us. Then one day you appeared to us, who
sat in the dark, with your only son, our savior Jesus Christ, who
died that we may live. Make us worthy, Lord, to partake of your
holiness to purify our souls and our bodies. Have mercy on us,
God the Father, Kyrie eleison. Kyrie eleison."

Other workers were quite content with the area, which
resembled paradise in its expansiveness and seclusion. No matter
how tiring the work was, all it took was a few moments of rest, in
which they would stretch out and take in the mysterious expanse,
for them to forget everything: the world beyond, which might
actually be better, or their homes and families. The passing trains
loaded with soldiers and weapons and other things looked as if
they had descended from the sky and were going back there. The
moments of excitement and talk about soldiers and receiving their
gifts soon gave way, vanishing into another imperceptible world
and time, far more mysterious than either. All their thoughts of the
world were centered on the vast open space, which gave them an
exhilarating sense of eternal contentment.

The black clouds, low and heavy like German planes when
they attacked the city at night, approached. The weary sun moved
and hid behind the massive black clouds, promising rain. One
moment later the downpour began, and everyone left everything
and hurried to the cars. Merely seeking shelter beside one of the
cars would do no good, for the rain did not come from any one
direction, so groups of workers looked for empty, closed cars.
Dimyan said to himself, "Have I really become that close with
Mari Girgis?" His eyes welled up with tears as he felt serenity
flowing into his soul. Did the Lord really love him that much?
Dimyan got into a nearby caboose, where he found al-Bayya,
Hamza, Usta Ghibriyal, Magd al-Din, and a number of other
workers. Ghibriyal immediately sat down on a side seat, took out
his notebook and indelible pencil from his upper pocket, and
began writing in his elegant manner, without taking off his beret.
Al-Bayya, on the other hand, removed the scarf around his neck
and took off his skullcap, revealing a totally bald head that was as
red as his face, probably from running for cover. The sound of a
distant train was getting nearer, as was the sound of English
soldiers singing and Scottish bagpipes. It was impossible for any of

the workers to leave the cars where they had taken cover, as the rain was coming down in buckets, soaking the dusty ground in a few seconds. They looked from the doors and windows of the cars at the soldiers, some of whom were also looking at them through the train windows. "They're getting drunk on the train, I swear," Hamza said, laughing in amazement. But no one paid any attention to what he was saying as the sky suddenly darkened, then lightning was followed by incessant thunder, and it seemed that the seven heavens were going to come crashing down on the bare ground. The men were afraid and fell silent for a few moments, until al-Bayya said, "It seems the English are planning something, Usta Ghibriyal."

The latter raised his head from the notebook, stopped writing, and said, "The English are always planning something, Usta Bayya."

"The English have defeated Graziani and now feel secure," Hamza blurted out. "What they're planning now is not to leave Egypt. I hoped Graziani would defeat them, but the idiot let me down, may there be a curse on his house!"

Al-Bayya looked askance at him and said, "So, you prefer Italy to England, Tumbler?"

Dimyan and the other workers laughed at 'Tumbler,' which al-Bayya was the only one to use, but which fit Hamza. Magd al-Din, who had taken out his Quran and was reading silently, smiled and noticed annoyance and anger in al-Bayya's eyes, which were very strange, as they looked at you and past you at the same time. The fact that they were blue helped strengthen that feeling.

"Why don't you answer? Talk to me," persisted al-Bayya.

The dark outside was compounded by a dust storm, even as the rain kept pouring down. Pebbles and flying sand were now audibly hitting the sides of the caboose. Magd al-Din hurried to close the windows, but the wind carried the dust through the open doors.

"I knew from the first that this was a black and dusty day," coughed Hamza.

Everyone, including al-Bayya laughed. Magd al-Din, no longer able to read, put the Quran back in his pocket. He remembered Zahra, whose time was approaching. Will God give him a son this

time? He decided that she would give birth in the village even if he
did not go with her. He could not bear to be separated from her
now, but he would be able to bear it when the time drew nearer.

Everyone fell silent, and eventually al-Bayya said, "I was
hoping Graziani would win, too, Hamza. I hate Churchill."

They had forgotten the conversation that had taken place
earlier, and now al-Bayya brought them back to it.

"I hate him, too, Churchill," Hamza said cheerfully, no longer
afraid of al-Bayya. "I know that you met him, Usta, when he
visited Egypt in '36. I met him, too, but I didn't like what he had
to say. He's full of hot air. He fooled Nahhas Pasha and made him
sign a meaningless treaty."

An ominous silence descended upon everyone, for what
Hamza was saying was total rubbish, but they were surprised to
hear al-Bayya say, "You're right, Tumbler."

Dimyan could not hold back his laughter, and everyone joined
in except Usta Ghibriyal, who smiled to himself, as did Magd
al-Din.

"Do you remember, Usta Bayya," Hamza went on, "what the
poet Bayram al-Tunsi said about Churchill and Nahhas in '36? 'If
Chamberlain's a greedy man who wants to pull a fast one on
Tharwat, he'll be lost. Let His Excellency know that we'll make
trouble—we've got nothing else to do.'"

Everyone looked around in disbelief, wanting to laugh but
unable to. Exasperated and barely suppressing his laughter,
Dimyan burst out, "What Chamberlain and what Tharwat
balderdash, man? That was way back when we were kids. What
does Chamberlain have to do with Churchill or Tharwat with
Nahhas?"

Hamza did not reply, did not even bother to look at him, but
rather looked at al-Bayya with humility in his eyes. Everyone
waited for al-Bayya's response. He calmly said, "Everything you
say is right, Tumbler. Those were the days."

Nothing was heard after that except the thunder and the
downpour, which continued until the evening. The rain stopped
then, as if to give them an opportunity to go home. They came out
of the cars like little chicks shivering with cold. They decided to
leave everything in place until the morning, but two long trains

filled with white, black, and Indian soldiers appeared, moving
slowly one after the other. As usual the workers lined up on both
sides, and the usual voices were heard: "Welcome Johnny,"
"Welcome Indian," "English good," "Germany no good." The
laughter of the soldiers could be heard through the open windows
and doors. That night the soldiers threw the workers many cans of
tuna, corned beef, cheese, and cartons of chocolate, tea, and
cookies. The workers were now running back and forth alongside
the trains. Magd al-Din was content with what the soldiers threw
to him, so he did not run. Neither did Dimyan, who was watching
Hamza, whose short stature made him look comical as he
approached the steps of the train cars and raised his arm to the
soldier standing there, but not quite being able to reach to get the
goodies, which forced the soldier to go down one step. Hamza
took what he was given, then put it on the ground and quickly
moved to follow another car and another soldier. Hamza knew
that no one would touch anyone else's loot and that, had it not
been for the dark, they would have divvied it all up equally.
Hamza was energetic that evening. Dimyan saw him reach out his
hand to an African soldier who suddenly let go of the cookie
carton and grabbed Hamza's hand, and in one quick move lifted
him on the steps of the car, then pushed him inside. Dimyan
shouted, "Hamza," but no one heard him. The trains passed, and
the workers began to gather their loot, but Hamza's remained on
the ground. "I saw the African soldiers carry Hamza into the car,"
Dimyan shouted. The workers laughed and al-Bayya said,
"Hamza is an acrobat—he'll defi-nitely get off the train near the
house. Gather his things and take them to his house." But Dimyan,
who had moved closer to Magd al-Din, sensed something else,
which Magd al-Din also understood but did not want to believe.

The hearts of the lovers have eyes that see
what others cannot.

al-Hallaj

18

It was Mahmudiya Canal that created Alexandria in the modern era. Muhammad Ali Pasha issued his sublime decree to dig it in the year 1819 and ordered the governors of the various provinces to round up peasants to work on it. The governors would tie them up with rope and bring them by ship. Many died of exhaustion and hunger. Those who died were buried where they fell, dirt was piled over them, and the rest were marched on. Many of those buried were still alive, only exhausted, and the governors ordered them buried. So the earth claimed bodies whose souls had departed, and bodies with souls still clinging to them. The dead and buried numbered about ten thousand every year. The digging of the canal took twenty-one years, bringing the number of the dead to more than two hundred thousand. The number of those digging was never less than four hundred thousand. The boats sailed or steamed into the canal on top of two hundred thousand life stories, maybe more. Those stories made their way to Alexandria, where the canal emptied into the harbor. Did any nation need more than two hundred thousand dead to acquire a history of myths, ghosts, madness, and demons? Alexandria flourished, thanks to transportation between the harbor, the Delta, and Upper Egypt. The population rose to sixty thousand. The city continued to flourish, the population to increase, and Mahmudiya continued to be a repository of secrets.

During the day, Mahmudiya is a waterway for ships, commodities, and work opportunities. In the late afternoon, it is a river for excursions and fun in feluccas and rowboats. At night, it is a place for thieves and smugglers, who raid the ships and steal what they can carry, and a place for police raids against them, a place where gunshots ring out night after night. Now thievery had increased because of the blackout all over the country. Mahmudiya is also the resting place of corpses, of those killed rightly or wrongly, coming in closed sacks from the countryside, never making it to the harbor, but always getting stuck as they hit the concrete piles under the bridges. Usually no one sees them until midday or late afternoon, as people are more preoccupied with work in the morning. In the afternoon, recreational activity in the water increases, as does the traffic of little rowboats. Thus not a month goes by without a corpse turning up, but it is rare for three in a row to turn up, as had happened in recent days. The corpses were always women and girls.

None of that crossed Rushdi's mind when he met Camilla and suggested to her that they take a boat ride together on Mahmudiya in the morning, contrary to what all lovers did. She always liked this contrariness in him, but she was afraid that he might ask that they begin at Karmuz. He smiled and said they would begin at Nuzha, far, far away from the city. Usually Nuzha was the last destination for rowboats, then everyone went back westward. But they would rent a small rowboat and go east, where there was no one, just agricultural land and peasants in the fields, no buildings or workers or anyone related to her or to him.

The sky was clear, to the lovers' delight. A light rain fell as they were getting off the streetcar at the last stop, but it lasted only a few seconds. They walked under the huge camphor trees, whose branches embraced and whose leaves made quick dancing circles of shadow on the ground below. He took her hand as they went down the three steps to the colorful rowboat dock. Apparently many young men and women had the same idea. "See, we're not alone here. Most of them have more courage—they'll take the boats to Raghib and Karmuz."

She said, smiling, "Let's be cowards today. Just today."

She sat in front of him in the narrow, sleek rowboat, and he sat and began to row. Once again it rained, which bothered them a little, but the rain was only a drizzle and it soon stopped. "How about if we get ahead of all the others? We want to be alone. Row with me."

She took hold of the two oars. He put his palms on her hands and their warmth warmed him. They began to row fast.As his hands pressed down on hers, she felt pain and began to shift her fingers, so he moved his hands from hers, but they kept rowing and laughing.

After Nuzha, Mahmudiya had wild grass growing on the banks. As they rowed, swallows flew up from the vegetation. Now they were really alone. On both sides huge vegetable fields extended, and on the banks they began to see camphor trees, castor-oil plants, eucalyptus, and willows, known among the people as "bride's hair," as Rushdi told her. Camilla had read about it, but had not seen one before. There were a few peasants in the fields, a few scattered men, women, and children. They came across only one water wheel, a few sycamores, and a mighty oak standing alone in the middle of the fields.

"We've gone too far, Rushdi," she said, then looked at her watch. "We've been rowing for two hours. We only rented the boat for one hour."

"Don't worry, I have fifty piasters, my monthly allowance. I'll spend it all today."

They stopped rowing. The rowboat stopped in the middle of Mahmudiya, and a light current carried it to the bank, where it rested.

"We can get off here. Don't be afraid, the boat will not move," he said, and as he stood up the boat swayed under his feet. He almost fell, but he kept his balance. She laughed. A long time had passed, and he had a hard time stretching his legs. She also stood up, and the boat shook, but she had given him her hand, and he was now on land, so he helped her off the boat and pulled her up. They were standing on the edge of a huge expanse of green fields, over which the sun was smiling kindly.

"How wonderful! What more could we ask from the gods?" He exclaimed as he stretched his arms fully. "Let's run!"

He ran and she ran behind him. He stopped running only when he heard her having difficulty breathing. He threw himself to the ground next to a big sycamore, stretching out his legs and leaning back against the trunk of the tree. She did the same thing. They were breathing fast. Her legs glistened above her short white socks. When she saw that her knees were showing, she placed her leather school bag on top of them. He raised his left arm and embraced her, pulling her toward him. She clung to his thin, fragile chest.

"This is the best place in the world for madness!"

She drew back, apprehensive of what he had just said, and moved her chest away, but he said, "Don't be afraid of me, ever. I only felt that I would die in front of you."

Once again he was saying strange things.

She heard the sound of a crow, and she was startled. He told her that the crow was a poor bird; it was the crow that taught man the greatest secret, that of burial, and yet it was the most maligned of the birds. He asked her if she had read Sophocles' Antigone, and she said she had read it last summer in the holiday reading program.

"All Antigone did was bury her brother's body. Humanity can't have dignity if the dead aren't buried."

She fell silent for a few moments.

"Did you bring me here to talk about death?" she finally asked.

"The problem is, I only read literature," he said with a laugh. "I haven't come across a funny story yet. If you find one, please let me know."

He got up. "Don't move," he told her. "Today I'll read you some brilliant, crazy poetry."

He took a small notebook out of his bag. "I translated it for you just this week." Then he began to recite:

O clock, sinister, impassive, frightening god,
Whose threatening finger says to us, "Remember!"
Soon the vibrant sorrows, like arrows,
Will hit the target that is your heart.

Pleasure, ephemeral, will take flight toward the horizon
Like a sylph making a hasty exit to the wings;

Each instant gnaws a piece of the delight
Given each man for all his life.

Three thousand six hundred times every hour, the second
Whispers: Remember! In an insect voice,
The Instant says: I am the Past,
I've sucked out your life with my loathsome proboscis!

. . . .

Soon the hour will strike when . . .
Everything will tell you: Die, you old coward! It's too late!"

She admired his performance and his recklessness, with his
half-closed, perpetually sad eyes, his fragility in the midst of the
great, green space, that very tender being who could be carried
away like a feather in the wind, never to return. And yet it was to
that same being that all the open space and all the greenery
submitted. He was the master that the gods had made, not
knowing that he would be rebellious, always aiming to play their
role. That also would be the cause of his perennial anguish.

He reached out and held her hand, and she left her bag next to
his and stood up. He leaned her against the trunk of the tree. Three
egrets flew from the tree when he started kissing her neck, as she
made faint gestures of resistance.

"I'm sorry. I really don't know why I'm speaking about death
today," he said.

"Enough," she said as she placed her hand on his shoulder. He
had gotten used to her doing that, and she had gotten used to his
backing down. She took his hand in hers as they walked along the
edge of the field.

"I liked that a poet should write about a wall clock," he said.
"The poem is by Baudelaire and is called "L'Horloge." I didn't
realize it's tone was so dark until I had worked on it and I did not
stop. Next time I'll translate cheerful poems for you—I'll translate
crazy poems by Rimbaud and Verlaine."

She did not say anything. They walked in silence. A peasant,
his wife, and two children emerged from a cottage and watched

them in surprise; they had never seen anyone so clean, young, and beautiful.

"Don't be afraid. Don't talk to them," he said and gripped her hand. When they reached the peasant and his family he said, "May peace be upon you," and they quickly replied, "And upon you peace. Please come in."

He smiled and she smiled, and they headed back to the tree as the peasant and his family continued to watch them in surprise. The clear day and the gentle breeze had added to their glowing looks. They heard the peasant woman saying, "City folks are so pretty!" They laughed and hurried to the tree. They must have rowed a great distance, if the woman spoke of them as city folk. They had gone deep into the countryside, or so they thought. Rushdi raised his head toward the sky and looked at the sun overhead. He said to himself, "The clock, always the clock," and took her by the hand to the rowboat, still where they had left it. They sat facing each other, with the oars between them. He started rowing and as soon as he got to the middle of the canal, she placed her hands on his and said, "I'll help you."

She smiled and the world looked even more brilliantly beautiful. What happiness! Where did he get the courage that day the two schools had the contest, and how did his daring bring him to this point beyond reality? His body was shaking. He wanted to enter her to the point of no return. He needed to tear her up every which way, to lose himself completely in her, and she in him. Who would believe this was his first love experience? It began at an incredible speed, with an incredible girl in her simplicity, beauty, and religion. Who remembered religions now? She was laughing as the sun behind her lit the world around her delicate body. Next time, he would choose a spot farther away. He would not listen to her gentle appeal to stop as her body shook. He would go further.

"She is a beautiful girl with a magnificent neck who lets her hair drift languidly in the wine of her complexion. She walks like kings and sits like sultans. Her eyes invite humanity to explode, to dissolve in her open arms and her full breasts. The beauty of her flesh is a heavenly gift."

"What did you say?"

"I was remembering some beautiful poetry. But unfortunately, it doesn't seem like I'll get to see France."

"I was making a lot of progress in French until you came along and slowed everything down."

"Were you going to continue?"

"Yes. You've made me fall in love with France."

"But unfortunately we won't see it."

"Don't be such a pessimist. The war will surely end soon. We've got enough time."

He fell silent for a moment then asked, "You really think so?"

She smiled and did not answer. In the distance, there were some sailboats coming toward them, filled with sacks and some southern sailors in their blue and gray gallabiyas.

"They make a long voyage from south to north," he said.

She smiled more broadly.

"Did you know I was from the south?" she asked him.

"A white southerner! You must be a southerner from heaven. Do you know the song that says, 'You're a houri from heaven/You sneaked in and opened heaven's gate'?"

"I listen to it a lot and laugh. I also listen to Abd al-Wahhab and Sayyid Darwish. I love them. Last night they were playing Sayyid Darwish's songs and I cried."

He looked at her for a while.

"Was it when he sang, 'You deserve it, my heart. Why did you ever fall in love?'"

"How did you know?"

"I heard it. Listen."

He began to sing to her, and she laughed at his husky voice. A sailboat had come alongside them, and one of the sailors was standing there watching them and smiling. When he heard Rushdi's singing he sang to them:

O Captain of the sea, take me with you
To learn a trade before I shame myself,
To leave my land and live far away.
I send my greetings morn and night
To one whose love has brought me woe.
I looked up and saw the sail in the wind

And I said, Maybe I'll stay on land instead.

Rushdi smiled and shouted to ask him if he wanted to hear him make up a mawwal, an Alexandrian rhyme song. The southern sailor said that would be great. So Rushdi thought for a moment, as Camilla smiled, not believing what was happening, feeling elated at her lover's beautiful madness. Rushdi sang:

My eyes saw a galleon adrift on the sea,
Its captain valiant but his rudder, alas, lost
His eyes could not see, the water swept him.
Even his sail was broken, what was left was tossed.

Camilla nudged him gently in the shoulder, impressed, then applauded in admiration. The sailor sang again:

Two gazelles riding a camel
Have smitten me.
She, the sun; he, the moon
The abode is the heart; the door, the eye.

Rushdi laughed and began to row away as he said to the sailor, "But we're riding a boat!"

"And the abode is the boat," the sailor sang back.

Rushdi understood, and he began to explain to Camilla, who was surprised that the sailor could handle such concepts. The last thing the sailor said to them as he sailed away was, "Blame not the wounded one if he groans."

Suddenly her face turned ashen. She pointed to the water and stood up, screaming. The boat shook and almost capsized. Rushdi stood up quickly and held her arms as she screamed hysterically.

"Don't be afraid. Don't be afraid. Close your eyes. Close your eyes."

She closed her eyes. He went closer to her, and took her in his arms as the boat shook. Then he sat on one side and made her sit on the side of the boat close to the bank of the canal. He grabbed the oars and began to row at a frenzied speed.

"Don't look at the water. Look at the bank."

In the water was a swollen sack. From a small opening, a purplish human hand protruded, one finger bearing a ring that shone in the sun—a small, delicate hand of a girl or a woman. He also could not look at the floating sack and kept looking in front of him, rowing frantically to get as far away as possible. When he arrived at the docks in Nuzha, he thought she was conscious and only leaning on him and looking at the bank of the canal. He had not looked at her while he was rowing. As soon as he stood up at the dock, though, she fell to the side where he had been seated; she had been unconscious the whole way without his knowing it. She needed several minutes to come to. Dozens of girls offered her bottles of cologne and cheap perfume. She needed a whole hour of rest before she could stand and return home with him. That day she was out too late for a girl like her. At home there was a firestorm waiting: the school had sent her father a letter informing him of her repeated absences. Yvonne could not lie any more to her parents. She told the whole story, crying and shaking the whole time.

If they divulge the secret, their lives would be forfeited
As would be the lives of lovers.

Suhrawardi

19

The spring offensive started in Europe. The ice had begun to melt on the mountains, and the fog had dissipated over the land. Fires burned, and Berlin and Hamburg suffered devastating air raids by the British. English cities in turn were devastated by raids as Germany began to carry out a new offensive against ports. British ports were subjected to intensive raids, some of which lasted three consecutive nights, as happened in Portsmouth and Manchester, where casualties reached more than two thousand. At the same time, German submarines began to use the wolf-pack method: a group of submarines would simultaneously attack a single target and destroy it. Lieutenant Guenther Prien, one of the most famous German U-boat captains, and others followed this horrific method developed during the previous world war. But Prien and all the other men on U-47 were drowned when the British destroyer Wolverine sank their submarine. U-99 and U-100, whose captains, together with Prien, were the most influential leaders in the German navy, were also sunk in heavy fighting, thus handing German U-boats a serious blow. Focke-Wulfe 190 planes, better known as 'Condors,' were even deadlier than the U-boats, as they flew great distances over the ocean in search of British ships. The United States began to export military equipment to England, in accordance with the lend-lease

program. The States sent Britain seventy-five destroyers and a
fleet of boats together. Roosevelt addressed the American people,
declaring that no race had the right to subjugate another and no
nation to enslave another. There were heavy raids against Cairo
and Giza; Alexandrians were no longer the only target. The trains
carried large numbers of Indian soldiers coming by boat from
their country to Suez. They were mostly under twenty, happy
with their uniforms and equipment, unmindful of what it meant
to die away from home. Cinema Metro in Cairo screened Mutiny
on the Bounty, starring Clark Gable and Charles Laughton.
Cinema Studio Misr in Cairo screened *The Triumph of Youth*,
starring Farid al-Atrash and his beautiful sister Asmahan. People
in Alexandria continued to complain about adulterated flour. The
young men in Karmuz and other native quarters discovered that
small military cars were roaming the streets at night during the
raids and shooting their anti-aircraft guns at the raiding planes.
They realized that those cars were the reason the native quarters
were singled out for bombing. Their purpose was to divert the
attention of the raiding planes away from the English camps in the
suburbs and away from the harbor, where British destroyers and
French boats, seized by the British without a fight before the
surrender of the Vichy government, were anchored. Groups of
patriotic young Egyptian men formed to chase those cars, first
with Molotov cocktails, then with hand grenades—an action that
limited their appearances during the raids, until they completely
disappeared. After that, the raids on the center of Alexandria and
Dikhayla and Maks in the west and Sidi Bishr and Bacos in the
east diminished. The defeat of Graziani, whose army completely
collapsed, contributed to the diminishing scope of the raids.
Graziani's defeat was too big to hide. Il Duce gave a speech in
which he admitted defeat: "We do not lie like the British. A whole
army, the Fifth Army, with almost all of its units, has been
overrun, and the Fifth Air Force has been almost totally
obliterated, but we were able to offer strong, sometimes violent
resistance." Mogadishu, capital of Italian Somalia, fell into the
hands of the British, then Berbera, winter capital of British
Somaliland, also fell. Graziani was ousted from all his posts.
General Cavallero was likewise removed from his command of

the Albanian front after the sweeping victories of the Greeks. General Italo Gariboldi was appointed to the command in Libya. Britain threatened Bulgaria not to give up its neutrality as the Germans amassed troops at its borders. British paratroopers landed in southern Italy, and Genoa was bombed from the sea. The English paratroopers were captured. King Idris al-Sanusi, in full Islamic regalia and round beard, visited the camp of the Libyan battalion made up of Libyan refugees in Egypt. In Libya, the new military governor's warning was broadcast: "I, Henry Maitland Wilson, commander in chief of the British forces in Libya, hereby warn all inhabitants of the region formerly under Italian control to cease and desist from any action that disturbs public security." Haille Selassie entered Ethiopia and spoke to his people, congratulating them on the victory. The Nile boat *Puritan* hosted a party for RAF pilots returning from the battlefields on a one-night furlough at its anchoring place in Gezira in Cairo. During the party Hikmat Fahmi, the number-one dancer in Egypt and all of the east, danced, and Abbas al-Bilaydi, Muhammad Amin, and Aqila Ratib sang. A charity gala party was held at Studio Misr Cinema to raise funds for the Egyptian Red Crescent and Red Cross. Her Royal Highness Queen Nazli and Her Royal Highness Princess Fayza attended, in the royal box seats. The name of the armored division commander who led the attack on Sidi Barrani the previous December, wreaking havoc on the Italian forces and defeating them, was disclosed. It was Lt. General Richard O'Connor. Yugoslavia joined the Axis, but demonstrations erupted, and a coup d'état ended the monarchy there. Yugoslavia declared its neutrality. In the month of February, Italy lost 364 planes. Yusuf Wahbi celebrated the nineteenth anniversary of the establishment of Ramses Theater by showing the play *The Madman*, in which the brilliant actress Rose al-Yusuf co-starred with him. The British foreign secretary Anthony Eden came to Egypt and met with Egyptian leaders as well as the Eighth Army.

Usta Ghibriyal announced that the railroad authority needed two workers to work at the al-Alamein railway station. He had been summoned to the administration office that morning and was charged with the task, to be completed within a month. "So, whoever wishes to go should come to me, and I will convey his name to the administration." Then he added, "I know that you're all married with children, and that you don't like to stay away from home for a long time. But you have time to think. I hope to find someone who volunteers to go because if that doesn't happen, I will make the choice myself and, I am told, my decision is final." Magd al-Din and Dimyan felt they might end up being chosen for that. If no one stepped forward, Ghibriyal would choose them to minimize the problem as much as possible, for they had the least seniority.

Ghaffara began to stay away from Ghayt al-Aynab and Karmuz after most houses there had become vacant. He started working in the neighborhoods of Ghurbal, Paulino, and Muharram Bey every day in the early morning, but would return in the middle of the night, desperate and tired since he had earned hardly enough to feed his donkey. One of the pieces of glass that he used as an eyepiece had fallen off his fez and he did not replace it.

As for Zahra, she had grown big; her seventh month was almost ending, and sitting with Umm Hamidu was no longer a welcome distraction. How could a pregnant woman sit at the entrance of a house on the pavement? Therefore she was deprived of her stories at a time that she needed them most, for now Sitt Maryam's door was only opened to let someone in or out. It seemed the whole family wished to avoid speaking to anyone. The priest's visits increased— they became almost a daily occurrence. Zahra would always hear mumbling, muffled quarrels and groans, and sometimes silent weeping. She did not know what to do for the good family that suddenly seemed not to want to talk with anyone.

Umm Hamidu also needed Zahra more those days since Hamidu, her only son, had been arrested and moved to Sinai together with criminals who threatened the security and safety of the country during wartime. The few inhabitants still left in the street were depressed. When a man or a woman would come to buy fruit or vegetables, they would come in silence and leave in silence, their eyes fixed on the ground, as if carrying a mountain of shame. It was feeling the emptiness surrounding everything and expecting death at any time during an air raid that made people so fragile. The only one left for Umm Hamidu to talk with was the vegetable wholesaler each dawn on his cart drawn by a strong horse. As for the Territorial Army soldier who sang and proposed to her, he had been transferred to Damanhur. Zahra told Magd al-Din, "The priest is coming everyday now. I don't see either of the girls. I don't know when they leave in the morning. Apparently they sneak out quietly so I won't see them. Sitt Maryam doesn't open her door during the day."

She was surprised when Magd al-Din told her, "And I've met Dimitri more than once on the stairs, and he hasn't stopped to speak to me—he just says hello and goes on. Today he politely asked me if I could move down to Bahi's room. But I felt he wanted to tell me to move out of the house altogether."

Right away Zahra said, "There are so many vacant houses, and thousands who want to rent rooms."

"No. We won't leave the house. We'll go downstairs. Dimitri's in a tight spot. Today he doesn't want us to know anything, but tomorrow he might need us."

Dimyan helped him move the few articles of furniture to Bahi's room. As soon as Zahra walked in and opened the window looking out on the street and saw Umm Hamidu in the entrance of the opposite house, she felt relief. Here she was not going to suffer the silence that seemed to have taken root on the second floor. She would hear people and children coming and going and talking. After they moved the furniture, Dimyan took Magd al-Din to the café far away on the Mahmudiya canal near the lupino bean vendors. They had not been here in a very long time.

"Why did you bring me here, Dimyan?" Magd al-Din asked him. "We'd almost forgotten this place."

"Well, first, I've made great progress in reading and writing. In a few days, I'll be able to read the newspaper."

"Praise the Lord!"

"Second, I wanted to tell you that Khawaga Dimitri is going through a big crisis."

"I know that, but I don't know what kind of crisis, and he doesn't talk to me."

"I think it's a crisis that one doesn't talk about," said Dimyan after a pause. "It's also preoccupying the priest at the church. I've heard a few things in church about the subject, but I'm not sure whether they were talking about Dimitri or somebody else." They both fell silent for a long time. Magd al-Din was not the inquisitive kind and never made an effort to know what people were doing. Even secrets that came his way, he did not divulge. He hated scandal-mongering and gossip of all kinds.

"There's talk about a Christian girl's love for a Muslim boy," Dimyan finally said.

Magd al-Din's eyes opened wide in surprise. That was the first time he had heard about that.

"This is something that happens rarely, Sheikh Magd," Dimyan continued, "and it always fails, but only after causing crises at home and in the church. For you in Islam, there's no problem. In our case, there is."

Magd al-Din made no reply. "Of course, I don't know whether this has anything to do with Dimitri's family or not. But in any case, Dimitri has a problem that only time will reveal."

Magd al-Din returned home dejected. Zahra asked him why he was down, and he could find no excuse but Hamza to get him out of the sticky situation. He said Hamza had not yet returned— and that was true. She said he had already told her that. He told her there was much talk about his possibly being a prisoner of war, held by the Germans. She could not imagine how he knew that. He also did not know how and why he said that. Hamza's disappearance a few days before had caused him and his colleagues a great deal of worry. Usta Ghibriyal notified the railroad administration, which notified the Alexandria police department, which informed them that it in turn had notified the military command of the Eighth Army in Marsa Matruh and was waiting for news. Hamza's wife and his three young daughters never stopped crying at their home in the railroad housing compound. Hamza's relatives came from Rosetta. They turned out to be well-off and quite respectable. It also turned out that one of his cousins was a notable who held an important position in the Wafd party and that he was pulling all the strings he could to get news about poor Hamza.

Ordinarily when Hamza's colleagues spoke in disapproval and surprise about what had happened to him, a silent sadness would fall over them. But the matter was not without its humorous aspects. One of them would say that Hamza would suffer most from silence because he would not understand English or Indian, and the few words that he knew would not really help him. He would not get a chance to say that he had seen what the soldiers said they had seen or that it had happened to him before it happened to them. Neither Bayram's poetry, nor anyone else's, would do him any good. But in the end they would express total disbelief. Who would have thought that this had been preordained for Hamza?

Now they were more careful when they approached the troop trains; they did not come too close to them any more. In many instances, they no longer spoke to the soldiers or cared to get what canned foods they used to get. They realized that those things were worthless compared to the disappearance of their colleague, abducted in the dark. Yesterday Dimyan sobbed. He and Magd al-Din felt the loss the most once his disappearance was confirmed the day after his abduction. Dimyan felt sorry because he had always argued with him and was happy to expose his delightful little lies. Magd al-Din felt sorry because he had insulted him once and because he himself had thought about the possibility of being abducted, of being pulled up by the hand to the train and taken to the front, as had happened to his brother Bahi in the previous war. Had he known Hamza's fate beforehand, but was not aware of it, or was he the cause of it, with this crazy thinking of his?

Hamza had been pleasant with Dimyan and gentle with Magd al-Din; he was kind to children and loved everyone. He was worthy both of pity and love, and that was how everyone felt, especially Shahin, the tallest and strongest among them. He was very muscular and could carry a crosstie with one hand, and usually during work he carried two on his arms. He was the most dejected, but in reality it was for another reason—when Magd al-Din went to tell him that Hamza was smart and would know how to come back, he was surprised to see Shahin's eyes well up with tears as he said in a soft voice, "You're a good man, Sheikh Magd. You know God's Quran by heart. Please come with me to cure my son with the Quran, or show him the right path."

❖

In the afternoon of the same day, Yvonne had come back from school shaking. No sooner had she got upstairs to their apartment than she went running back down with her mother behind her. Zahra was coming in from outside as Yvonne ran into her at the end of the staircase and let herself fall in her bosom, crying, "Camilla's gone, Tante Zahra! Camilla's never coming back!"
The girl's tender heart was pounding and her eyes were filled with tears, her whole body quivering. The mother appeared behind her looking very angry and grabbed her daughter's arm and pulled her. Zahra had let the things she had bought drop to the floor and placed her arms around Yvonne, patting her on the back.

"Please let the girl be, Sitt Maryam," she said. "We've eaten bread and salt together."

"Zahra, don't come between us." Sitt Maryam spoke so harshly that Zahra's arms pulled away and she let Yvonne go. The mother dragged her daughter upstairs. Zahra went inside, oblivious to the things she had bought and dropped on the floor. In her room she sat and cried.

Dimyan went to the right as Magd al-Din turned left toward the railroad houses with Shahin and the other workers. There were a few clouds heralding rain that might fall after midnight, the rain that lasted for a short time but usually took Alexandria by surprise once or twice in the several weeks after winter had ended.

Shahin, with his powerful build, walked briskly, taking long strides as Magd al-Din barely kept up with him. All the workers except Dimyan were walking toward the houses. They had started out together, but after a short while, they spread out as some walked fast and others at a more relaxed pace. As they were crossing the gate separating the houses from the railroad tracks, Shahin told Magd al-Din, "These are old houses from the first war—they used to be warehouses and barracks for the English forces. You should apply to get one of them, since several workers are going to retire soon."

"I'll do it, God willing," Magd al-Din said with genuine hope. If he got a house here, that would be his best accomplishment in

Alexandria. He said to himself that he would tell Dimyan to apply with him, for they had been lucky together so far. As they left the narrow dusty road, the Mahmudiya canal and the road parallel to it came into view. Magd al-Din knew that place well from the days of looking for work. He had come many times to work for the oil and soap company a short distance past the houses. They turned left and passed a few yellow, one-story houses with closed windows.

After a few steps, they crossed the main gateway, which used to have a double door framed with tree trunks that was locked at night when the soldiers were there. Now the door was gone.

In front of the houses were some tin shacks that made the alleys even narrower, barely enough for two persons to walk side by side. From the shacks rose the smell and sounds of goats and sheep and chickens. Shahin led Magd al-Din to a short, wide street between two rows of houses that showed only their closed windows, since the doors were on the other side. After turning right at the end of the street, they stopped at the door to one of the shacks. "This is the house, Sheikh Magd." Shahin knocked on the door of the tin shack. From inside came a light and a voice asking who was there. The woman opened the door, carrying the small kerosene lamp. She stood behind the door as Shahin entered, then Magd al-Din. The chickens in the corner moved, and in another corner, a little goat moved, kicking its feet as it lay on its side. Shahin entered a big hall, empty except for a mat and a few scattered cushions, a few books lying around, an old wooden table with a few books in no particular order, and behind the table, a straw chair. Then Shahin went into a large inner room that had a bed of medium height and a sofa on which Rushdi was lying down. As soon as Rushdi saw his father and his guest, he sat up. He was wearing a clean gallabiya. The walls were clean and painted sky blue. The ceiling was painted white, and the room was lit by a big number-ten kerosene lamp placed on a shelf on the wall.

"My son Rushdi, Sheikh Magd." Shahin said then, addressing Rushdi, "Your uncle, Sheikh Magd al-Din." The woman, Shahin's wife and Rushdi's mother, did not come into the room but stayed in the hall, thinking about this Sheikh whose face glowed with light and serenity and about whose piety Shahin often spoke.

Would he succeed in curing her son of his sudden ailment? Magd al-Din sat next to Rushdi. Shahin sat at the other end of the sofa. Magd al-Din saw many little books in the corners of the room and a small unsteady wooden bookcase attached to the wall. He realized that he was in the presence of a young man who was different from what he had expected. He spoke first.

"What's wrong, Ustaz Rushdi?" he addressed the boy respectfully. "What's your complaint exactly?"

"Have you come to treat me, venerable Sheikh?"

Rushdi was deathly pale, with profoundly sad eyes. He had not been shaving, but his beard was not long, just a few clumps of hair here and there on his cheeks, hardly reaching the line of his jaw. His face was so gaunt one could see the bones under the skin.

"Only God cures, Ustaz Rushdi."

Rushdi calmly shook his head and said, "Your task is impossible, venerable Sheikh." He started to cry and was soon sobbing deeply. The mother too was heard sobbing outside.

His father embraced the boy and told him, "Don't kill me, my son. Don't kill your mother. Tell us what's wrong."

Rushdi turned and looked at Sheikh Magd al-Din for a long time then said, "The Quran will not cure me, venerable Sheikh. Please forgive me. I mean no disrespect. I have very strong faith and my problem is that my faith encompasses all people and all religions—therefore, I have fallen in love with a Christian girl. This is my ordeal, venerable Sheikh."

Rushdi spoke in a choking voice, trying to prevent himself from crying. Magd al-Din was now sure that he was in the presence of a very intelligent young man. The father was at a loss for words. Outside, the mother could be heard saying, "God protect us. Why, my son, do you want to waste your life falling in love with an infidel?"

Magd al-Din could not tell Rushdi that he was too young to fall in love, for while he looked gaunt and fragile, he seemed to be widely read, and it would be difficult to convince him of anything that he did not understand. That was why Magd al-Din remained silent as Rushdi continued, "I know how afraid my father and my mother are for me. I'm not insane, and I will not let insanity get to me. I just haven't seen her for ten days. I think her parents have found out and killed her. She doesn't go to school any more. Even her sister—I don't know if she's quit school too, or what, but I don't see her any more either. I've gone to their house and stood there during the day and at night, but I didn't find out anything, and no one's told me anything."

The boy's lips quivered in the pale yellow light as he spoke. His tears flowed ceaselessly. Those made miserable by love die young, Magd al-Din said to himself, as he remembered Bahi—he was certain of the end. The boy's pale face gave off the same aura of the sacred that Bahi had. The only difference between the two was the difference between the village and the city. City people gave themselves willingly to love, and did not leave themselves at the mercy of the wind.

"What do you think, Sheikh Magd?" the poor father asked after Magd al-Din's long silence. Magd al-Din looked at the boy, then reached out his hand to the boy's shoulder and pulled him to his chest. The boy rested against Magd al-Din's chest as the latter began to recite verses from the Quran. The mother sobbed outside, and the father prayed for a cure for his son in silence. Magd al-Din was the only one who realized that the boy had been preordained to feel this agony, that his end was near, and that he was no match for this age. He lifted the boy's face from his chest and began to dry his tears with his handkerchief, saying, "If I were to ask God for anything, Ustaz Rushdi, it would be for a boy as intelligent and wise as you.

"Listen Shahin," he said to the father, "Islam permits Muslim men to marry non-Muslim women, Christian or Jewish. The Prophet enjoined Muslims to treat Egypt's Copts well. He was the husband of Maryam the Copt, mother of his son Ibrahim. But the problem, Ustaz Rushdi, is that you are at the beginning of your life and you need time. You've also chosen the tightest path. Neither your father nor your mother will object to your marrying the Christian girl." The mother was heard muttering outside. Magd al-Din continued, "But do you know what her family is like? There are good Christians and there are bad Christians, exactly like all human beings in this world. If the girl has disappeared, as you say, then it is your duty to disappear also, to give her the opportunity for a normal life. I have learned from your father, Ustaz Rushdi, that you are in the last year of secondary school, that you are a poet, that you forgo food sometimes to buy books and learn languages, that you are preparing yourself to travel to Europe where, God willing, the war will be over this year, and you may become a genius like Taha Husayn. Love and marriage now would put a stop to all of that. Besides, Ustaz Rushdi, don't be afraid for the girl. We have a proverb that says 'Break a girl's rib, she'll grow two,' and women usually forget quicker than men. They rush to love and rush to forget."

Everyone was silent for a long time, until Rushdi said suddenly, "I will go to her family to tell them that I'll stay away from her."

The mother came into the room in panic, saying, "No! Don't go! Nobody's going anywhere! Everything will end on its own."

Noticing the anguish on the boy's face, Magd al-Din said to him, "Let me go in your place. Give me her address and her name, and I'll make sure she's all right and put an end to the problem."

After some reluctance Rushdi said, "Her name is Camilla. She lives on Ban Street, house number eighty-eight. She once told me that a man who worked for the railroad lived in their house, but she didn't tell me his name." Magd al-Din said nothing. He got up, his face pale. His hands shook as he gripped the boy's hand and patted him on the back. Shahin walked with him to the Mahmudiya canal, but Magd al-Din was oblivious to his presence.

Magd al-Din hurried away as if something were chasing him. Was it the boy's languid eyes or his pale, tormented face?

He sauntered along the dark street by Mahmudiya Canal, barely seeing his way, since there were no street lights, just the feeble glow of a little moon, sneaking through the occasional gaps in the clouds, reflected faintly on the small, shallow ponds on the unevenly paved road—just enough light to enable him to either jump over or walk around them. On the canal itself, there were some faint lights from a few torches on the barges and ships anchored far apart in the dark, with the white sails of the ships furled on the masts. The ships looked like giants, made only of darkness. The factories on the other bank were also dark, though their high windows gave off muted violet rays. The smokestack emitted white smoke that was quite visible in the dark, even though it was intermittent and thin. The streetcar moving on the other bank also cast pale yellow lights that enabled him to see a man climbing up from the canal. He must have been relieving himself, or perhaps he was an inhabitant of that godforsaken area. He could not quite make the man out, but saw him as a mass of black moving upwards. To Magd al-Din's right were the big warehouses of Bank Misr, which extended for a long stretch. He saw one of its gates was open; he could tell only because the area beyond it was darker than the sections on either side of it. Then he saw two cigarettes glowing for a moment, revealing two indistinct faces. They were almost certainly two guards from the Territorial Army.

"Greetings," said Magd al-Din.

There was no response. The cigarettes glowed again for a few moments, two little circles of fire in front of two circles of translucent skin. He hurried on until he was beyond the warehouses, and there he was in total, absolute, pitch dark. No houses, no lights; thick clouds must have completely blocked out the moonlight. On the canal there were no more ships, and on the other bank, no factories and no streetcars. Then to his right there rose an uneven, very dark wall that smelled of grease and soap. He could barely make out thousands of barrels, very close to him, stacked very high—was it possible that they would come tumbling down into Mahmudiya Canal right in front of him?

In every space, no matter how big or small, packed in between the mounds of barrels, were piles of scrap metal that smelled of solder. In the midst of these heaps were gleaming strips of brass, aluminum, steel, chrome, and zinc. He could not exactly see the metals, but they must be the ones gleaming, he thought. Then he saw a wooden kiosk, painted bright yellow, revealed by a ray escaping from the clouds. As he approached it, he heard muffled voices and what sounded like someone snorting, then a nervous female voice saying, "Easy," and a man's voice saying, "It's easy—what could be easier?" then the sound of intermittent laughter, so he hurried away, praying for God's protection against Satan's work. His footsteps must have been audible, for he heard a long laugh in which the man's and the woman's voices were intermingled. Then he saw in front of him something huge, a real giant, standing there with a lit cigarette in his mouth, blocking his way. Where did this giant come from, and what did he want? The giant took the cigarette from between his lips and said in a harsh voice, "Don't be scared. You can join him—it's only one piaster." Magd al-Din felt brave enough and strong enough to reach out his hand and push the giant aside. The latter stumbled and almost fell to the ground. Magd al-Din heard him saying, "Watch it! I curse your house! You think you're some hero, some Antar ibn Shaddad?"

Magd al-Din, who had been terrified only a few moments earlier, smiled as he started to walk briskly again, then all at once had the sensation that he was stumbling over many colorful, tangled rubber threads. Several balloons became caught between his legs, impeding his movement. He remembered the story of the man who went down to Mahmudiya Canal to perform his ablutions and got the rabbits caught in his underpants. His heart started pounding hard, but then the white stones of a long, low, neglected fence provided some light for him and reminded him that he was on a well-known street that led somewhere. Had it not been for that fence, fear would have completely unnerved him, and he might have started to run screaming down the street. He hurried along the fence, and Karmuz Bridge loomed closer. There were four metal lampposts, two on either side of the bridge, topped by a lamp with a shade of dark blue glass. And although they did not illuminate the place, at least he could see them, and he fixed his gaze on them until he arrived at the bridge, and there he breathed calmly for the first time. Next to the bridge, he noticed many push carts with goods left over from the day, covered with tarpaulins or cardboard. Children sleeping under the carts were covered in pieces of blanket, and he realized that he had stayed a long time at Shahin's house. He walked down the slope to the right, which would take him to Ban Street, which would take him home.

Where had he been exactly? He had a growing feeling that he had just come from hell, or nothingness. Was the boy really telling the truth, or was he just humoring him to end the meeting? In any case, Magd al-Din could not forget that sense of an ending in the boy's eyes. He belonged to an era different from ours and he won't be long for this world, Magd al-Din thought. His poor father! He walked on Ban Street—'Willow' Street—thinking of that happy person who had given that and the other streets around it the names of trees and flowers. They were named Narcissus, Jasmine, Sweet Basil, Vine, and Carnation, when in fact, they were shabby, sickly streets filled with tired, lost people whom no one realized belonged to the big city, where everything moved except this place. Alexandria, the white, gay, provocative city, was oblivious to them, the refuse discarded by faraway towns and villages. When did anyone ever pause for the sake of refuse? And who ever believed that from such refuse could come lovers, poets, lunatics, and saints? Only murderers and criminals deserved to stay in this rotten southern part of the city.

"Why are you so late, Magd al-Din?"

"Tuck me in, Zahra. Take my shoes off. Cover me over."

*The gods perceive future things, ordinary people perceive
things in the present, but the wise perceive things
about to happen.*

Philostratos

20

"I've chosen Magd al-Din and Dimyan for al-Alamein," said Usta
Ghibriyal during the break. Everyone fell silent and looked at the
floor. True, it was not their doing, but none of them had stepped
forward to move to al-Alamein. So it was only fair for Usta
Ghibriyal to choose those two workers who had not yet
completed one year on the job. Magd al-Din and Dimyan were
sitting next to each other at the time. They had been expecting to
be chosen. Magd al-Din said to himself that now Zahra had to go
back to the village. As for Dimyan, he smiled, but his face still
looked ashen.

"Al-Alamein, Sallum, it's all in Egypt," he said, pretending
contentment.

There was news of the arrival of a large German force in Libya,
that the Axis was regrouping its troops and had started attacking
Benghazi. Thus it seemed that the desert war would not end as
everyone had predicted, following Graziani's defeat. After Usta
Ghibriyal made his announcement and the break was over,
everyone went back to work. Magd al-Din went over to Shahin
and asked him about his son.

"He disappeared for three days," the man told him, tears in his
eyes, "then came back for one day, but then yesterday he disappeared
again. I don't know where he goes or what he's doing to himself."

"Did you tell him what I told you?'

"I did, and since then he's stopped speaking to anyone."

Earlier that week, Magd al-Din had gathered up his courage and gone upstairs to Khawaga Dimitri, who opened the door for him, surprised. Magd al-Din asked him to go with him to the café for a little while. Dimitri welcomed the idea right away, but could not hide his anxiety.

At the café Magd al-Din told him, "Nobody chooses his own religion, right, Khawaga Dimitri?"

"Right, Sheikh Magd."

"Please pardon me if I tell you that I know Camilla's story with Rushdi, the Muslim boy."

Khawaga Dimitri said nothing for a long while, then asked, "And you also know the young man's name, Sheikh Magd?"

"His father works with me," he said and fell silent.

"Listen, Sheikh Magd," Dimitri said abruptly, "your late brother lived with us for years and never felt that we were different. And you have lived almost two years with us—did you ever feel that we were prejudiced against Muslims?"

"No."

"Not only that, but sometimes we pay for the mistakes of some Muslim tenants. Lula, for instance, was a Muslim, and she lied to us and brought shame upon us."

"You're right, Khawaga Dimitri."

"I know that nobody chooses their religion, and I'm not surprised that my daughter has fallen in love with a Muslim boy. She is rash, and he is rash, and with a little wisdom everything can settle back in its place."

"That's what I wanted to talk to you about."

"We tried to make the girl come back to her senses, but we failed—me, her mother, and the priest. We had no choice but to send her back home to keep them away from each other for a while. The girl will lose a school year but that's better than losing herself. She's my daughter, Sheikh Magd. Would you agree to your daughter marrying a Christian?"

Taken by surprise at the question, Magd al-Din thought for a while then replied, "If he converted to Islam, I would have no objection."

"And if this young man converts to Christianity, neither I nor anyone else would have an objection. Can he convert?"

"He'd be killed, Khawaga. In our religion this is apostasy."

"Are we wrong because we don't kill those who abandon our religion?"

They were both silent, until Dimitri finally said, "How could I beget my daughter, raise her, and then have some young man just come and take her and cut off all her relations with us? When a girl gets married, of course it deprives her of her family's kindness, and deprives her family of her tenderness. So can you imagine if she's married to someone from a different religion? How can anyone ask me to be deprived of my daughter forever, Sheikh Magd?"

Magd al-Din nodded, thinking how sincere Dimitri was.

"I think you understand me now," Dimitri went on. "I don't care if he's Muslim or Christian. What matters is, how can my daughter, after marriage, remain my daughter? Either he converts to Christianity, or we all convert to Islam, and both are impossible options. So, there's no alternative to agony for a while, just a little while, Sheikh Magd. Then the problem will be solved. Or do you want us all to suffer forever?"

Magd al-Din remained silent.

"Please help me. Can you?"

"I can and I will, brother Dimitri."

"And please forgive me. I asked you to move downstairs so we could discuss our catastrophe freely, so that if we spoke loudly about religion, you would not misunderstand us, also so that the priest could come and go without embarrassment. He was embarrassed coming in and leaving, with a Muslim neighbor so close to us, a neighbor who undoubtedly knew the reason for his visits. He told me, and these were his words, 'The neighbors might think I hate Muslims, but I am only trying to cure the girl of her rashness.'"

"And I didn't leave the house, so I could be ready if you needed me. We've spent a beautiful time with you in these difficult days, brother Dimitri."

They got up and returned home together. Khawaga Dimitri went upstairs, saying loudly to Magd al-Din, "Zahra can come upstairs any time and sit with Maryam and Yvonne, like she used to."

What Dimitri made Camilla do was exactly what Magd al-Din had suggested to Rushdi, that they stay away from each other for some time. So now she was staying away, or had been made to stay away. It did not matter which. The main thing now was for them not to meet, so the wound would heal.

On the day following that meeting with Dimitri, Magd al-Din informed Shahin, who in turn informed his son. Magd al-Din felt this was an easy and natural end to the matter, and that the problem would resolve itself without Rushdi taking the trouble to go to Camilla's family. There was no sense in Rushdi declaring that he would stay away as he had promised. What happened afterwards did not bode well. The boy started to leave home for extended periods. Once, Zahra went upstairs and found Yvonne crying and her mother working on the sewing machine in silence. Both the mother and her daughter tried to appear less dejected. The mother asked Zahra about her pregnancy and how Sheikh Magd was doing at work and when she was expected to give birth. All the time Yvonne would stop crying, only to begin again. So she had to go into the other room, the one in which Zahra and Magd al-Din used to live, and there her sobbing continued. Zahra asked Sitt Maryam, "Yvonne loves her sister this much and cannot bear to be separated from her?"

"She's afraid that she won't come back," the mother said. I don't know where she gets these ideas."

Zahra noticed the mother also struggling to hold back her tears.

Once news of the German army's arrival in Libya hit town, the railroad station was crowded again. At one point Alexandria had appeared to be empty of inhabitants; therefore the crowds were a surprise to both Magd al-Din and Zahra as they sat on the floor of the station, in the sweaty, close atmosphere. Around them everywhere sat hundreds of black-clad women and men wearing all manner of clothing. Children were everywhere, running amid people sitting on the floor and baskets, suitcases, and boxes, or crying or sleeping on their mothers' laps. A state of melancholy

permeated the whole scene but, from time to time, a long, loud laugh
rose from a man or a woman somewhere. The quiet was also broken
whenever a train pulled into the station. Everyone would run to it
and stand in confusion, asking the railroad workers about the
destination. Then everyone would get aboard. Then everyone
would get off the train when they realized it was the wrong one.
Because of the crowding and the commotion, it seemed that
everyone was doing all these contradictory things at the same time.
Earlier, Zahra had gone upstairs to bid farewell to Sitt Maryam, who
appeared calm and collected. She kissed Zahra on both cheeks and
wished her a safe journey and a safe delivery. Yvonne, on the other
hand, could not help crying on Zahra's bosom as she told her, "I'll
miss you very much!" For the first time Zahra realized that there
was no difference between Yvonne and Camilla. Both girls were as
gentle as a breeze and as delicate as invisible angels. Zahra could not
prevent her tears, mixed with black kohl, from flowing down her
cheeks, and she said without thinking, "Please convey my greetings
to Camilla if you see her soon, or even not so soon. Please, Sitt
Maryam, don't be hard on the girl, for the sake of Jesus and Mary."

"Of course, don't worry, Zahra," Sitt Maryam answered, as
Yvonne ran to her room, crying.

Zahra went downstairs with a heavy heart. She had not realized
she loved her neighbors so much. She felt no joy going back to the
village, for she was leaving behind that prince among men, good-
hearted Magd al-Din. After she dried her tears, she crossed the
street to say good-bye to Umm Hamidu, who insisted on standing
up and saying as she laughed, "I stand up every evening. For your
sake, I'll stand up an extra time today." She took Zahra in her arms
and kissed her in the beautiful manner of the local women: she
placed her puckered lips against Zahra's cheek and made many
long kissing sounds, then did it again on the other cheek. She told
Zahra, if she came back to Alexandria, not to come back to that
house, for in less than two years, Bahi was killed, Lula was caught,
and Camilla disappeared. She said it had an unlucky threshold.
"Houses are their thresholds, Zahra."

She told her she knew the story of Camilla and the Muslim
boy, that everyone did. She said Dimitri was in a pitiable position:
"The Christians don't like him because he didn't know how to

bring up his daughter, and the Muslims don't like him because he broke the poor boy's heart. The real victims in the story are Dimitri and his wife—all their lives they've been respectable and minded their own business. But no one can figure out God's ways." Zahra left wiping her tears. Umm Hamidu did not sit down until Zahra and Magd al-Din had gone quite a distance.

Magd al-Din was able to climb into the train and sit next to the window, then Zahra handed him the only basket she had, which contained nothing but her clothes and a box of candy from the Gazar candy store. When she got into the car, she sat in Magd al-Din's place, and he got off and stood next to the window, not wanting to leave before the train moved. Shawqiya, the little girl, stood next to her mother, who said to her husband through her tears, "Take care of yourself, Sheikh Magd."

He did not answer, only looked at her. He really wanted to go with her, but it seemed that he was destined to move even further away from her. He would go to al-Alamein in a few days. Before he had arrived in Alexandria, he had not heard that name, not even before he worked for the railroad. Now he was always hearing the strange name of this desert town. He had never lived in the desert, but after all, it too was God's country, and God undoubtedly would look after it. He bought four hard-boiled eggs and two big soft pretzels and handed them to Zahra, who placed them with the basket on the shelf. "Maybe the train will be late, you might get hungry," he told her.

He remembered how Zahra had baked crackers to last him at least a month and filled little jars of dry mulukhiya leaves, tea, sugar, and ghee, and cleaned the Primus stove, and placed everything in two baskets: the food in one and the rest in the other. She did not forget to fold his clothes and place thread and some needles with them. She even packed some matches and candles in case of emergency. All Magd al-Din had to do was to carry the stuff to the cart that would transport him to the desert train at Qabbari in three days. As the train started to move he said, "Don't forget to let me know after the birth."

"Don't cry, Sheikh Magd. Don't cry," she told him.

He had not felt the tears as they formed in his eyes. He held her hand and ran along with the train, which had not yet begun to gain speed, and kissed her hand quickly, surprising the people standing on the platform and sitting near Zahra. She said in a soft voice, "Good-bye, my love," and let her tears flow. He felt his heart wrenched. The world had become a vast, white shaking mass with a distant sky, and he was a little child, crying sadly, like an orphan.

The distance from the platform to outside the station was the longest distance a man could walk, had Dimyan not appeared, standing among the seated masses, looking in every direction. Magd al-Din saw him and felt some consolation. He went toward him. This friend of his was the only one who could dispel his sorrow. He wondered what had brought his friend to the station at that time. Did he come to send his wife, mother, and two daughters to a village?

Dimyan had come directly from the church after passing by Magd al-Din's house and being told by Sitt Maryam that he had gone to the station to see his wife off. He could not wait, and took the streetcar to meet his friend before his return. Actually, he could have waited. Only now did he realize that there was no need for his going to the station nor for all that hurry. It was the dream he had seen, the nightmare he had had on the saint's anniversary, which he had attended for the first time in many years. The courtyard of the church had been filled for the last two days with people standing, lying down, and sitting. Many families brought their floor coverings and their food. There were some mats in one corner, sheets in another, a woolen blanket here, and a cotton kilim there. There were men in cotton gallabiyas, men in silk gallabiyas, men in woolen gallabiyas, men in old or new trousers and eyeglasses, women with bare shoulders, sitting in their house gowns, women covered with silk shawls and children of all ages and sizes, naked and in gallabiyas, barefoot and in light sandals. The only light came from the candles in the chandeliers hung around the pillars or on the walls under the darkened dome. Everyone under the dome or in the courtyard in front of it was praying devoutly, as the sounds of the mass found their way to

Dimyan's heart. In front of him, right under the center of the
dome, he could see the large, famous icon of Mari Girgis slaying
the dragon. That was Mari Girgis, his patron saint, taking care of
him in this world in such a way that gave Dimyan a joy that made
him forget the crowded courtyard and peoples' sorrows and the
crowds around the church. Among them were Muslims and
Christians who came to watch and participate in popular games or
congregate around the carts selling seeds and peanuts or macaroni,
or to sit on the wooden benches of improvised cafés set up by
vendors who made tea on Primus stoves placed next to the walls.
Generally those people appeared only once each year, during
saints' anniversaries. There were tattoo artists, who used red-hot
needles to make blue and green tattoos, marks of the cross for
women, young men, and also some middle-aged men, and pictures
of the martyr on men's shoulders, arms, and chests. For the
Muslims they made pictures of the legendary Abu Zayd al-Hilali
brandishing his sword as he attacked a lion, or riding the lion in
many cases, in addition to tattooing names and places of birth on
men's forearms. Most of those artists and vendors were the same
ones often seen during the anniversaries of the Muslim saints
Mursi Abu al-Abbas, Sidi Bishr, Sidi Gabir, Abu al-Darda, Sidi al-
Adawi, and other saints in Alexandria. They also were the ones
who went to the nearby villages to help celebrate the anniversaries
of famous saints. It is a beautiful occupation that affords the
people the chance to experience some joy and to break the laws
and taboos a little by pursuing love and flirting with women and
girls. Celebrating the anniversary of Mari Girgis outside the
church is identical to celebrating Mursi Abu al-Abbas's.

The smell of onions filled the inside and outside of the little
church, and the streets were filled with seated people all the way to
the Mahmudiya canal on one side and Ban Street on the other, as
well as up to Sidi Karim. Before the war, the lights had extended
all the way to Raghib and the railroad station, the Kom al-Dikka
station, which the Alexandrians called Masr Station because they
could not conceive of any other town outside Alexandria except
Cairo, which was called Masr. Dimyan slept in the courtyard of
the church for the first time in his life. In his youth he had heard
adolescent stories about how some women behaved at the

anniversary celebration, and he had always thought them to be
adolescent stories. That night he thought of finding out for sure,
but he quickly asked forgiveness of his patron saint, Mari Girgis,
and went to sit on a bench outside, amid the crowds. In the
middle of the night, he went into the church courtyard and found
most men and women awake. He took his place next to his wife
and mother, who were asleep. He lay down looking at the sky.
His eyes closed for a few moments, and he saw a great fire
engulfing Mari Girgis, his friend and patron, who with his horse
tried in vain to get out of the circle of fire. Dimyan got up in great
panic and left the whole place. It was shortly after dawn. He
crossed the adjacent streets, where people were asleep on the
sidewalks, and went to the canal to breathe some fresh air. He did
not go back until he had cried alone on the bank of the canal.
Then he took his wife, mother and, two daughters home and
went to Magd al-Din's house. But he did not find him, so he
came looking for him at the station.

The two of them had now left behind the station gate, the
crowds fleeing the city, and the stench of sweat and dung of the
horses and donkeys in front of the gates. They sat on the first
bench they came across in the garden. The sun was up, and the air
was fresh, neither cold nor warm. Dimyan realized that the open
space above the square was vast and soothing.

"Did you really come to see me, Dimyan?" asked Magd al-Din.

Dimyan did not respond to the question.

"I am afraid of al-Alamein, Sheikh Magd," was all he said. "I
am very frightened."

He raised the hem of his gallabiya to wipe some tears that had
suddenly formed in his eyes. Magd al-Din was quite astonished at
his friend, whom no one would believe had the soul of a lonely
little child. Dimyan told his dream to Magd al-Din, who in turn
was afraid, but for Dimyan himself.

"Where can we go, Dimyan? There's nothing for us except the
preordained, which no one knows. As the Quran says, *"No soul
knows what it will earn tomorrow, and no soul knows in what land
it will die."*

Dimyan felt sorry as he saw the traces of tears in his friend's
eyes. He really should not have caused him additional worry now,

but should now find a way to take his mind away from worries. He said he had learned how to read and write and would buy the newspaper for the first time and read it. Magd al-Din, still sad over his separation from his family, said nothing.

Magd al-Din and Dimyan's last night was Easter eve, on which Dimyan went with his family to church, as did Khawaga Dimitri, Sitt Maryam, and Yvonne. Magd al-Din stayed in his room. Had all that really happened since he left the village more than a year and a half ago? Had the world changed to that extent? Had all those catastrophes and events really taken place? Had he really met all these people? It seemed to him that the time that had passed between his leaving the village and this night was no more than one day and one night, or maybe just one day, or one night, one hour, or the blink of an eye. But that day, the day he had left, had sailed far away into memory. So it must be much longer than it really was, not shorter than a day. The short man who had come with him on the train had said the raids might reach Alexandria if Italy declared war, and that he and his friend were coming to Alexandria on the very day the war had broken out. Where could he find the short man and his friend now? They must have gone back. He had heard them saying that they would not spend more than a year in Alexandria, but the raids began before a year was over. Were they alive, or had they been killed in the heavy raids on the city? There Magd al-Din was, having seen all the raids, now going to al-Alamein, to the desert where fighting was going on. Al-Alamein, 'the two flags,' is a strange name, but it sticks in the memory, imposes itself indelibly on the ears. When he arrives at al-Alamein, will the war continue? When he arrived in Alexandria, the scope of the war grew larger and engulfed the whole world. They say the German army that landed in Libya was different from the Italian one.

Several events had taken place in the world the last few weeks. Bulgaria joined the Axis, and German troops entered the country to attack Yugoslavia and Greece. Italy lost seven battleships in one maritime battle with British warships in the Eastern

Mediterranean, and nine hundred Italian sailors were taken prisoner. Miss Denise Musiri donated bonds at a face value of thirty thousand Egyptian pounds as an endowment to be administered by the Royal Endowment Department for the funding of educational projects. That prompted King Farouk, who had recovered from a long spell of indisposition, to issue a royal decree accepting the endowment and Miss Musiri's conditions, and conferring upon her the Order of Perfection in order to encourage her and others like her to keep making such donations for scientific and humanitarian projects. Miss Musiri said that she could not forget the kindness of the late King Fuad I toward her father, Elie Musiri, which enabled him to achieve what he had achieved in industry and agriculture in Egypt. At the same time, a branch of the Egyptian ministry of justice announced the vacancy of three positions; four hundred persons applied for the jobs. King Farouk donated one thousand pounds for the Day of the Poor, which was chosen to commemorate the death of his father at the end of April. The film *The Mark* of *Zorro* was screened for the first time in Egypt. The birthday of the Prophet Muhammad was celebrated with Quranic recitation at the Young Muslim Men's Association. Once again streetlights were not permitted on the occasion. The British and Indian armies advanced on Asmara, where the Indian soldiers staged great victories. The United States seized sixty Axis ships in its own and in South American harbors on the pretext of protecting them from sabotage by their sailors, then arrested the sailors. General de Gaulle arrived in Cairo for the first time from Khartoum, after visiting the Free French troops, which had contributed to the liberation of the town of Keren in Eritrea. Together with the Indian forces, the Free French were largely instrumental in liberating that town in particular, after seizing Asmara, the capital. The general was received at Cairo airport by General Wavell, commander in chief in the Middle East and a representative of Sir Miles Lampson and Baron de Benoit, chairman of the National French Committee in Egypt, together with key committee members. Afterwards, De Gaulle visited Abdin Palace, where he signed his name in the guest book, then held meetings with the prime minister, the British high commissioner, and the military commanders of Free France in

Egypt. He traveled to Alexandria, where he spoke before the Free French Club on Nabi Danyal Street and visited the camp of the Polish forces, praising the support that the Free French were receiving from the Poles. The band played the French, British, and Egyptian national anthems, then de Gaulle left Alexandria for Cairo and London. There was a shortage of sugar in Alexandria, and the local population complained bitterly, whereupon the governorate of Alexandria intervened by bringing in large quantities of sugar from the south. The shortage was over in a few days. A coup d'état was foiled in Italy. The coup was engineered by Marshal Badoglio, who sought asylum in the king's palace, where the king kept him under his own royal guard, so it was more like a prison, but at least he was safe from Mussolini's wrath. Mussolini arrested Badoglio's men and sent them to the Albanian front. The comedian Ali al-Kassar screened his film *One Thousand and One Nights* in Cairo. Another crisis erupted in Alexandria, where the shipments of grain from the countryside to flour mills were delayed. Once again, as it had done in the case of the sugar shortage, the government acted quickly, setting aside special freight trains for grain shipments. Four young men robbed a poor cart driver who was out late at night and took his cart and donkey. A young man stabbed his friend, a barber, and almost killed him. He admitted to the prosecutors that he had been unemployed for a long time and that the barber, an old friend, knew his situation so he gave him free shaves and haircuts. The perpetrator got used to that. One day he brought a friend of his that the barber did not know and asked the barber to give him a free haircut too, for the sake of their friendship. But the barber let him down in front of his friend, and so the man became enraged and stabbed the barber with a knife. When the prosecutor asked him why he had brought someone to the barber for a free haircut, he said he was also unemployed and could not find a job. Then he added that in reality, he planned to take a half-piaster secretly from his friend, instead of the full piaster the barber would have charged him. The Hungarian prime minister, who could not acquiesce to German wishes and could not resist them, committed suicide. Germany deployed twenty-two divisions on the borders with Yugoslavia, then the planes bombed Belgrade, and Germany declared war on

Yugoslavia and Greece simultaneously. German planes first flew
over Belgrade on the morning of the sixth of April, and for three
days methodically dumped their bombs on the capital in such a
tactically meticulous manner that they flew fearlessly close to the
roofs of high buildings. The city was so devastated that on the
third day, when the raids ended, the bodies of twenty thousand of
its citizens filled the streets or were under the rubble. The wild
animals, set free when the zoo was hit, went on a rampage,
devouring bodies of the dead and the living in a city that
experienced horror at its worst. At the same time, the German
troops were overrunning Yugoslavia from all sides, and the
country surrendered after seven days. Hitler had called it
"Operation Punishment," after which he moved immediately to
attack Greece, successfully implementing his policy of "one enemy
at a time." The British forces could not protect Greece. The British
troops, which had gone in from the east to aid the Greeks,
numbered fifty thousand soldiers, of whom eleven thousand were
killed, wounded, or taken prisoner, in addition to the casualties on
the Greek side. The English, however, managed under the pressure
of the German offensive to safely evacuate the rest of their force,
in addition to ten thousand other Greek, Yugoslav, and Cypriot
nationals. At the same time, the British army retreated before the
new German forces in Libya, and the battles reached the vicinity
of Sallum after the British lost their former strongholds. The Axis
forces began attacking the base in Tobruk. The vice bureau
recorded the following arrests throughout Egypt: 850 beggars and
cigarette-butt collectors, forty-six thugs and pimps, fifty women,
including twenty minors, for incitement to vice on the street.
There were thirteen cases of gambling and wagering, eight
suspected brothels, fifty-three employ-ment offices suspected of
being fronts for prostitution, and fifty boarding houses accused of
the same. The British forces in Tobruk stood their ground and
took thirty German officers and one thousand soldiers and petty
officers as prisoners of war. They were shipped by train to
Alexandria, where the workers saw them for the first time. They
had seen many Italian prisoners of war before, but that was the
first time they saw the Germans, who had remained an enigma
since the outbreak of the war. They saw that they were very white,

with blond hair and blue eyes, and tall and healthy. From the cars of the freight train, they looked at everything in indifference and disbelief. The king of Greece and his crown prince moved the capital to Crete, and the king sent his people a message asking them to remain united, undivided, and free. The German forces entered Athens, and a young man in Alexandria committed suicide by throwing himself from the top of the Icarus Hotel, and two young women threw themselves in front of the Raml streetcar on Alexander Street. Sadness gripped Alexandrians, who sympathized with their Greek and Cypriot neighbors. Gold relics were discovered in Greek tombs in Kom al-Shuqafa. The film *Forever*, starring Fatma Rushdi and Sulayman al-Gindi, was screened at Cinema Concordia and Si Umar, starring Nagib al-Rihani, at Cinema Majestic. The United States decided to build four hundred battleships, nine hundred ships, and a huge number of airplanes for the Allies that year. Dimyan bought the weekly *al-Akhbar* and went to Magd al-Din at home the day following Zahra's departure and asked him to hear him read the news written in small print, not just the easy headlines. He read, "Death of a Well-off Maharaja in London," then paused for a moment and resumed, "Our correspondent in London informs us that a well-off maharaja has died in London." Then he paused, looking at Magd al-Din, who asked him to finish, but Dimyan said, "That's it—there's just a headline and a news item."

"Congratulations! You can read, Dimyan," Magd al-Din told him.

"What do you think of that, Sheikh Magd?" asked Dimyan after a second.

"What do you mean?"

"I mean, how useful is it?"

"To tell you the truth, Dimyan," said Magd al-Din with a smile, "I was puzzled too when you read it to me."

"Is this why I learned to read—for these newspapers?"

Magd al-Din laughed silently and Dimyan said, as if to himself, "What stupid newspapers! Why should I care about a maharaja, well-off or broke?"

Dimyan threw the newspaper out of Magd al-Din's window and left without bending to pick it up. Churchill gave a speech in which he announced Britain's options: victory or death. Nothing new was learned about Hamza. Shahin no longer spoke about his son to Magd al-Din. The verdict was announced in the case of the defective helmets, which was declared to be a case of commercial fraud rather than high treason, so the defendants got off with light sentences and everyone was happy. As of April 20, the sale of liquor in Alexandria was restricted to those with permits issued by the military. This was due to the many accidents resulting from drunkenness, and also because alcoholic beverages were used to make explosives. In their new raids on Alexandria, the German planes started dropping small incendiary bombs, and the people were instructed on how to handle them if they had not exploded. The military courts in Alexandria also heard seventy cases against Italians living in the city who had not heeded a previous military order to surrender their radios to the police. The radios were confiscated, but no spies were uncovered. It was announced that on the last Monday of the month, Charlie Chaplin's film *The Great Dictator* would be screened in several cinemas in the capital and in Cinema Royal in Alexandria. When it was shown, record crowds in wartime were observed in front of the cinemas. It now seemed that Dimyan had never expressed a strong desire to watch a Charlie Chaplin film; he found out about the film but did nothing about it—he did not even allow himself to think of it. Ghaffara met Magd al-Din on the street and reproached him for taking his wife to the station without asking him to give them a ride on his cart. Magd al-Din smiled and thanked him, telling him that that they left in the late morning, when Ghaffara was nowhere to be found on the street. Then he told him about his trip to al-Alamein the following day and asked him if it would be possible to pick him up at five in the morning to take him with his friend Dimyan and their luggage to the station. Ghaffara said he would then asked him where al-Alamein was, and Magd al-Din told him.

The night was long. His life passed in front of his mind's eye. He felt as if a whole lifetime had passed since Zahra left. Had Dimitri not come to visit him and sat with him a long time, the night would not have passed. Dimitri asked him if he would come to Alexandria during vacations, and Magd al-Din said that he would not, that if he got a vacation he would go to the village.

He said that with great emphasis, which baffled Dimitri. Then Magd al-Din told him that he would give him three months rent, and would send him the rent every month after that with Dimyan, who would surely come to Alexandria to see his family. Dimitri asked him who Dimyan was. Magd al-Din was surprised, and after a pause started to remind Dimitri of him but the man, who could not remember, said, "Oh yes, I remember him," but he was not telling the truth. This perplexed Magd al-Din, who began to wonder what might have happened to his landlord's mind. They spoke a lot about people, the country, and the war. Dimitri suddenly asked him if he had found out anything new about Rushdi, and Magd al-Din told him the truth, namely that his father no longer spoke about his son in front of him. Dimitri said with regret that he hoped the young man realized the gravity of the situation and would let it pass peacefully, that he personally would not have liked to stand in the way of his daughter's wish but that it was a difficult wish. He was sure time would heal all wounds. Magd al-Din thanked Dimitri for the time he had spent in his house and told him that both he and Dimyan had applied to the railroad authority for housing if a vacancy should occur, and that he was hopeful. Dimitri reassured him about his furniture in the room—"exactly as if you are here, Sheikh Magd"—and shook his hand warmly, then went upstairs and left Magd al-Din, who wished to get some sleep that night. He began to recite silently some of the short chapters of the Quran to calm his nerves.

The previous day's newspapers had announced that the country was ready for Hollywood's new masterpiece, produced by David Selznick, starring the famous actors Clark Gable, Vivien Leigh, Olivia de Havilland, and Leslie Howard, as well as more than thirty-five hundred new actors and actresses. That masterpiece was based on the famous novel by Margaret Mitchell, *Gone with the Wind*. The papers also published the name of the German officer commanding the Axis forces in Libya. It was Erwin Rommel, who came from the French front and who had shown great skill in desert warfare. The public health office in the governorate also announced that births in Alexandria that week numbered four hundred locals and twenty foreigners. As for deaths, they numbered 120 locals. The causes of death given were old age, a variety of fevers, malaria, tuberculosis, dysentery, whooping cough, tetanus, and air raids. Deaths among foreigners numbered ten. Causes given were drunkenness, insanity, and suicide.

*The time that my journey takes is long and
the way of it long.
I came out on the chariot of the first gleam of light and
pursued my voyage through the wilderness of worlds . . .*

Rabindranath Tagore

21

The Maryut coast—or the Libyan coast, as the ancient
Carthaginians called it—extending from Alexandria to Sallum,
before it enters Libya, is the forgotten coast in Egypt. It is where
Magd al-Din and Dimyan were going this morning. Off the coast
lies the Mediterranean, bluer than in Alexandria, with clear water
that reveals rocks and sand, enticing you to hold out your hands
and scoop up water to drink, and forget that the water is salty. The
coast, for whoever hears of or sees it, is the desert itself. It is a
barren coast, beyond which the desert extends endlessly, with a
horizon in every direction and a mirage on every horizon. On this
deserted coast many large armies have marched. The Libyan
Shishak I was the first to use it to invade Egypt in 945 B.C. At that
time, pharaonic glories had reached the high heavens: the pharaohs
sat on the gods' throne, and one dynasty followed another,
twenty-one of them, until the inevitable decline set in. Eventually,
though, it was the Egyptians' turn to march on the coast, this time
to Libya. That was in the reign of Aprieus, the fourth king of the
Twenty-sixth Dynasty. He set out to Cyrene to rid it of Greek
rule, but failed to do so. Ptolemy I, however, was able to reach
Cyrene and annex Libya, from which the worship of Isis spread
west. The Libyans built a temple for her. It is still standing today
in Cyrenaica, as is the bath of Cleopatra VIII (Selene)—daughter

of Cleopatra VII, who ruled Egypt—just like her mother's bath in Marsa Matruh. Both baths are carved out of the rocks in the sea. Were the two of them daughters of Poseidon, god of the sea, or were they both goddesses of the sea?

The road was not completely deserted then. Alexander took it to Marsa Matruh before turning into the desert to head for the temple of Amun in Siwa. The Arab tribes of Bani Salim and Bani Hilal took the same road a thousand years later, migrating from Najd to Morocco, then came back bearing the name "the Fatimids." The Fatimids were the last to take that road before troops from England and the Commonwealth, from India, Australia, Scotland, Ireland, New Zealand, and Cape Town marched on it, as did troops from southern Italy and Germany, in the opposite direction. The northern coast has been a road of war and death. In times of peace, the Christians took it to escape Roman persecution, and they built small monasteries in the farthest depressions in the desert. They reached all the way to al-Wadi al-Jadid and built churches and monasteries in Bagawat and near Alexandria in Bahig, Ikingi Maryut, and Burg al-Arab. During times of peace, the road was taken by the Bedouin tribes of Ali al-Abyad and Ali al-Ahmar of the Awlad Ali of the Saadi Arabs, and the sedentary Murabitin tribes of Jamayat, Qawabis, and Samalush, who were usually charged with guard duties and took up their positions among the settlements of the different tribes to provide them protection when the Saadi Arabs were busy fighting.

Amiriya is the closest city to Alexandria on that road, thirty kilometers to the west, and southwest of Lake Maryut, which bounds Alexandria and keeps it pressed to the sea. In the days of Muhammad Ali it was know as Ikingi Uthman, named after the ruler's majordomo. During Abbas Pasha's reign it came to be known as Biringi Maryut, that is, "First Maryut," thus Ikingi Maryut was the second city. Amiriya is a hodgepodge of a market town where the Bedouin of the Bihayra governorate meet with the Bedouin of Maryut and some merchants of Alexandria once a week. Beyond that, nothing much: a few scattered houses, an old railroad station, and a train that carries water once a week to the desert, where the few inhabitants go out to meet it and fill their jerry cans and load them on their donkeys' backs.

Ikingi Maryut is the more famous of the two. It is dry year-round, both a summer and a winter resort. It seems that God has given it the gift of wondrous, enchanting air. Beautiful windmills can be seen pumping pure water that has stayed underground for millions of years, in order to water fig, almond, and pomegranate trees, grapevines, and the memories of visitors. When you enter Ikingi Maryut, you forget all other towns and you feel your life simplified to serenity. Time and space cease to exist.

Amiriya is different. It seems at all times to be a town without an identity, choked by the dust that gathers from all directions, because it has no gardens and because the sun seems to linger above it always, day and night. This is one of the curious things about Amiriya, for despite being close to Alexandria and the lakes, it is always hot. It is said that it got its name from the ancient Greek city of Marea, which is buried near the sea and which used to be a great spot for wine-making, dance, and love. "Alexandria is Marea, a happy city, and its earth is saffron," as the saying goes. It is also said that the tribes of Rabia and Hilal ibn Amr settled here for some time before moving westward, thus the town got its name from these tribes. This is more plausible, as you could smell the hair of the Bedouin tents in the air; the few scattered dusty houses in Amiriya look from a distance like tent pegs, sometimes screaming with the desire to move in search of water and grass.

Not far from Amiriya is Burg al-Arab, which used to be no more than a guard post. In 1918, Major Bramly, police inspector in the Western Desert governorate, chose a high hill where he built a big palace in which he collected all kinds of artifacts and surrounded with a beautiful garden and fitted with windmills to raise fresh water. At the foot of the hill, several houses were built to serve the alabaster palace, whose Greek and Roman pillars Bramly had moved from the nearby area of Abu Mina. Abu Mina was a site that held scattered Greek and Roman relics as well as the church of Abumna, built by the emperor Arcadius in 405 C.E. on top of the tomb of Saint Menas, who had fled the persecution of Diocletian. But the latter sent troops that captured and killed the saint. Diocletian did not know that the Lord's children or disciples would not die; none ever truly died. As always happened, Diocletian died and Saint Menas lived on. Bramly died and his palace was taken over by the overseer of royal possessions. The soldiers who guarded it told the few inhabitants of the area stories about the luminescent alabaster walls, about beautiful singing sounds that filled the palace at night together with the sea wind. They spoke of a state of ecstasy that came over the soldiers every night, making them laugh for no reason, inebriated on a wine they had not drunk. They turned at night into happy children and spent the day surprised at what happened during the night.

Figs in the palace garden had the sweet taste of honey, almonds gave off the scent of apples, and the pomegranates were as cool as ice. Beyond this small settlement of Burg al-Arab, to reach al-Alamein one had to pass by the town of al-Hammam, established on the ruins of the Greek town of Kaminos, famous for its natural baths. It was built around an old market frequented by merchants of the west who went there to meet with merchants of the Delta. Al-Hammam was settled by Moroccans a long time ago and contained the Mosque of Ziyad ibn al-Aghlab, which he built while on his way to conquer North Africa. It is a desert town smelling of camels, goats, and sheep, where people moved fast whether going to it, leaving from it, or staying in it, as if everything suddenly has turned into a mirage. It is difficult to retain the memory of a face you come across in that town, where you pause only to push on, a town created for quick commerce. Leaving it and going west means going to al-Alamein, that deserted spot, a small railroad station with a mere half-meter-high platform topped by two wooden rooms for the stationmaster and the telegraph operator. The platform ends at a primitive barricade consisting of a wooden pole with a rope attached to one end and a weight of stone at the other end. When the operator pulls the rope, the pole is lowered, blocking the way. After the train goes through, he lets go of the rope, and the counterbalance causes the pole to be raised so that nonexistent cars and the few people may cross the tracks. That was before the war; now there were many cars and soldiers. That road across the tracks is the only road in al-Alamein. It starts at the sea and goes through the village, which is no more than two rows of houses built of limestone cut from the mountain of al-Hammam.

The houses stood empty. The same Bedouin who had left their encampments built them, but when the war broke out, they moved away again, leaving behind the limestone houses and going back to their tents and encampments on the edge of the Qattara depression. The distance between Alexandria and al-Alamein is one hundred kilometers, and between the sea and the Qattara depression is twenty-five kilometers, thus making it a bottleneck unsuitable for military maneuvers, but a good last line of defense if the armies had to retreat before the Axis. That area was now a repository for weapons, ammunition, and supplies and a training ground for troops. Al-Alamein is six hundred feet above sea level, and the land slopes southwards to the Qattara depression across an area of sand dunes and perilous salty swamps. On the edges of these dunes and swamps live a few Bedouin, Bani Ahmar and Bani Abyad, Saadis and Murabitin who have been at peace for such a long time that their dialect no longer has words for "war" and "fighting."

Beyond al-Alamein there were no other inhabited towns worth stopping at except Sidi Abd al-Rahman and Marsa Matruh. The dunes of al-Alamein are characterized by their off-white limestone color that continues to Sidi Abd al-Rahman, a little-noticed summer resort next to a small village that is nothing more than a mosque the Bedouin built to honor Abd al-Rahman, of watermelon fame, who had become a saint.

Abd al-Rahman was a handsome young man who was walking with his ugly friend, a barber who had evil designs on him. They had gone far into the desert when the barber took out a razor he had been hiding in his vest and severed Abd al-Rahman's head, then left him buried in the sand. A year later the barber took the same route, which he had forgotten. In the desert, the land and the dunes looked alike. He saw a watermelon patch bearing a big ripe watermelon lying on the ground. He could not resist; who could resist a watermelon in the desert? He picked up the watermelon, and on his way back, he thought of giving it as a gift to the chief of the tribe. That was more beneficial than eating it, he thought.

The chief of the tribe was happy with the gift. But as soon as he plunged the knife into it, blood gushed forth. He plunged the knife again, and again the blood gushed forth. The wise old chief looked at the barber, who by now was terrified in front of all those present. He had remembered everything. He asked the chief for an assurance of protection, and the chief gave him that assurance. So he started telling everyone how he had killed his friend on that very spot. The Bedouin built a tomb for Abd al-Rahman on top of the watermelon patch, and they buried the watermelon, which they realized contained Abd al-Rahman's head. The tomb became a shrine around which the little village came into being.

There are no more stories until you get to Marsa Matruh. Daba is a small village deserted by the Bedouin who moved to Sidi Abd al-Rahman and al-Alamein. Fuka is a strategic depression where forces and vehicles gathered to be deployed later on at the Libyan borders. Marsa Matruh, Cleopatra and Antony's historical city, was now the headquarters of the Eighth Army command through which military vehicles careened all day long. Marsa Matruh was the city of love and death where Cleopatra betrayed Antony by fleeing from Actium and where Antony worshipped at the altar of Cleopatra's body. It was in Marsa Matruh that both committed suicide. It used to be the capital of the Western Desert governorate; now it was the headquarters for General Wavell, who had defeated Graziani a few weeks earlier. Now the German Rommel came to command the Afrika Korps, now mostly German. What was that new commander who came triumphant from the French front going to do? He had an easy name, apparently destined for fame, like the names of the famous, be they good or evil; Napoleon is just as easy a name as Robin Hood, and Judas as Jesus, and Yazid as Husayn, and Umm Kulthum and Asmahan's names are just as easy as the serial-killing sisters, Raya and Sakina.

Celebrity makes everyone equal, and as time passes the evil might attain the same status as that of the saintly.

"Good morning. Ready, Sheikh Magd?"

"Good morning. Ready, God willing."

Magd al-Din had slept only one hour, after dawn. Before Ghaffara called out his name, Magd al-Din had heard the sounds of the creaking wheels and Ghaffara's voice as he stopped the donkey. Sheikh Magd came out carrying one of the two baskets he had packed. Ghaffara took it from him and put it on the cart, which Magd al-Din noticed now had two donkeys.

"It's a long ride and a heavy load. I had to get another donkey, so I rented one," Ghaffara said.

Magd al-Din smiled and went back to his room to bring the other basket. He noticed that Ghaffara was not wearing his mask.

"It's early. The air's still clean," said Ghaffara.

It was a little after five o'clock, with the day still trying to break away from the night. A cool breeze wafted in the dark, and the coming light exuded a pleasant smell. The eyes opened with the coming of day just as flowers opened up to the light.

Magd al-Din jumped up to sit next to Ghaffara on the cart. His eyes caught a glimpse of the little house. He wished he had gone up and said goodbye to Khawaga Dimitri and his family even though the man had visited him the previous night. Was he destined to see them again? Ghaffara started on his way to Dimyan's house.

That was the first time that Magd al-Din had seen the Qabbari railway station. It was indeed a long ride from his house. The cart covered the road extending along Mahmudiya Canal all the way to Kafr Ashri, then beyond it to the Maks road up to Qabbari Street, and ending at the station. For more than an hour the cart went without seeing anyone else on the road, even at the canal. Then suddenly light burst forth like pouring water. There was no movement to the right; the boats lay still, their sailors asleep. To the left were the warehouses of Salvago and Bank Misr, which Magd al-Din had seen the night he met Rushdi, who had gone crazy on account of his love for Camilla. Who was that figure that Magd al-Din saw sitting before Mahmudiya, his back turned to the railroad houses? That person seemed to be a thin, lost young man. Then it occurred to him that he had not met any of his co-workers going to work. A short while after they passed the houses Dimyan asked Ghaffara, "Isn't it strange that we haven't met anyone on the road?"

"It's early, Dimyan."

"I feel like God has just created us this very minute. Yes, I think we've just descended from heaven—you, me, and the two donkeys."

"And the two donkeys too?" Ghaffara said, laughing.

"And the two donkeys, Ghaffara!"

"You have a very fertile imagination, Blessed Dimyan."

A silence fell during which Dimyan thought that no one had called him "Blessed" before. Why was it that no one had shown him such respect?

The cart wobbled along the cobblestone road. It crossed Tigara Street, which went right through Kafr Ashri and Sheikh Abd Allah al-Nadim's school and his deserted house and entered Maks Street. It was then that they saw some traffic, a few cars and a slow-moving streetcar with hardly any passengers. The streets were bathed in light. Ghaffara stopped the cart and got off it for a few moments and picked up his air-raid mask, which was in a bag hanging under the cart. He put it on his face, then got on the cart again and began gently to prod the donkeys to hurry. Magd al-Din and Dimyan both smiled at Ghaffara's strange fez-mask but said nothing.

At the station they did not have a long time; the train would arrive soon. There were only three Bedouin men standing far apart on the platform. When the train arrived, each of them got into a separate car. It was an old train, its colors faded and its paint peeling. A thick layer of dust and sand covered it. Magd al-Din and Dimyan got on the car directly in front of them, placed their baggage on the shelf, and sat facing each other. The broken windows to their left were covered by shutters, which they did not think to open, for it was still chilly and they knew it was going to get colder as the train moved and as the air blew through the broken glass and the holes in the shutters. Like any other passengers, they turned their heads to see who else was there. They saw only one middle-aged man, almost their own age, wearing a clean, tan-colored gallabiya and a white silk turban and, showing through the gallabiya, a traditional woolen vest. The man had clasped his hands in front of his chest and rested his head on them and fallen asleep, emitting loud snoring noises. But he would wake up suddenly with a startled gesture, wipe away the saliva running from his mouth, then go to sleep again for a few moments, only to wake up again, startled, and wipe his saliva.

The train proceeded at a tottering speed with no concern for time before or time after. It left Alexandria in the morning, arrived at Marsa Matruh the following day, and started on its way back the third day. There were no other trains except the 3 p.m. train that stopped at al-Hammam and turned around at 7 p.m. The movement of trains on this military route had been limited, and now the only trains one saw were trains transporting military equipment, prisoners, or soldiers. Magd al-Din and Dimyan saw to their left, for the first time, Lake Maryut, which extended for a great distance. On it they saw small feluccas and fishermen who had gone to work early. They were now busy casting their small nets, then pulling them in filled with fish that glimmered like pearls in the sunshine, which now illuminated everything. To the right also were stretches of Lake Maryut, the dry, reddish salt basins that would turn white as the summer advanced. Then cranes and workers would begin to scoop up the coarse salt and transport it to the nearby plant, where it would be refined and packaged. Here the water collected during the winter and began to dry up by the beginning of the spring, then turned into salt in the summer. Huge stretches of the salty, rose-colored land dazzled and delighted the eyes. Dimyan left his seat in front of Magd al-Din at the left of the car and moved to the right to look out the window, spellbound.

"This is salt and these are salt basins. In one month it turns white," said the sleeping man and wiped the saliva running down his lips with his sleeve. He rubbed his eyes and coughed several times and his voice became clearer. "From here comes the salt for all of Egypt."

"Really!" Dimyan exclaimed, still dazzled.

"Egypt is full of bounty, of plenty, brother. Yes—look at God's might. On this side the water evaporates and turns into salt, and on that side, no matter how much it evaporates, it never runs out, and the lake stays full of fish."

Magd al-Din had begun to follow the conversation, and he let himself turn around to see from where he sat the glorious rose-colored salt basins extending in the distance.

"Where are we now?" Dimyan asked.

"In Maks," said the man.

"So we are out of Alexandria."

"Where are you going?" the man smiled and said.

"Al-Alamein."

"You have a long way to go," the man said with a gentle laugh. "God be with you."

As he said that he stood up. He was on the short side, with a squarish build. He put his hands in the side pockets of his gallabiya and moved over to sit down next to Magd al-Din. Dimyan came back and sat opposite them. The man took a gilded metal cigarette case from his pocket and offered each of them a cigarette.

"Is this your first time in the desert?" he asked.

"Yes," Dimyan answered.

"I have been traveling the desert all my life. I don't know any other place."

"Do you work or live there?" Magd al-Din asked.

"Both."

The train had started to stop so they were all silent for a while.

"Murgham station—the first stop," the man said.

A young man got onto the car wearing a loose Bedouin garment topped by a loose wrap over his shoulders and a woolen blanket-like scarf and a cap with a small tassel on his head. He looked around the empty car and at them, then hurried to another car after a very quick greeting.

"All the Bedouin here speak fast and walk fast. I've spent all my life asking myself about the reason for that and I have yet to find an answer. The desert brings serenity and calm, but the Bedouin here talk and walk as if they were on horseback."

Dimyan laughed and Magd al-Din smiled at the man's strange words.

"My name is Radwan the Peasant," continued the man. "Actually, my real name is Radwan Ahmad, but the Bedouin here have given me this nickname. But most of the time they call me Radwan Express!"

"I'm Magd al-Din."

"And I'm Dimyan."

The man's eyes grew wide and he asked, "Dimyan?"

"Yes, it means I'm a Christian," Dimyan said to spare the man any surprise or confusion. The man looked closely at him for a few moments.

"How strange!" he said.

"What's so strange, brother Radwan?" Dimyan asked. Radwan looked at him even more closely.

"Nothing, brother Dimyan," he answered. "You just reminded me of a friend of mine whose name was also Dimyan and who used to sell Pepsi here on the trains. He was a sweet man of sweet talk and sweet disposition. I don't know where he is now. God damn the war and the English and the Germans!"

There was a long interval of silence until Magd al-Din asked, "You didn't tell us what you do in the desert and where you live."

"I told you my nickname was Radwan Express. Actually, I work as an *abonne*. Do you know what that is?"

"I think an *abonne* is like a postman, except that he works on the train."

"Very good, brother Magd al-Din. He's like a postman but he doesn't work for the post office or for any office. He works for himself. He gets a permit from the railroad to ride the trains, and abonne means a pass that exempts him from buying tickets. He delivers peoples' mail and goods at different stations. I used to be the abonne of the desert trains until Mussolini entered the war. I had my own corner at the door of the car—the abonne corner—and at every stop people came and gave me letters and bags and baskets and bundles and boxes and everything that could be sent, big or small, and the name of the person they wanted them sent to, and the name of the station. And at every station everyone who wanted to receive a delivery would come to me. If I didn't find the addressee, I would leave the letters and parcels with the stationmaster. But people used to come and ask about letters and other things just on their own. Many times they would find that I had letters for them from their loved ones. At every stop I saw peoples' faces light up when they received their letters and the eagerness with which they took the letters. At every stop I saw the kindness and goodness in the eyes of those sending things to their sons or relatives or loved ones. A lot of times they would cry just because they'd gotten a letter. Of course a letter in the desert is something else! I could figure out the contents of the letters from the eyes of the senders and recipients. Now, as you can see, the train is empty. Business in the desert has dried up. The desert is now a battlefield. Nobody is left except armies and the Bedouin. Armies don't send their letters with the abonne, and the Bedouin don't send anything. The peasants and people from the Delta have returned to their villages, and nothing is left but me and this train."

They fell silent. Magd al-Din and Dimyan exchanged glances. The train had stopped at a station. The *abonne* stopped talking then stood to look out the window at the platform.

"Nobody got on. Nobody got off," he said. "The station-master didn't even leave his room."

The train moved on.

What do the armies of the Earth amount to?
Look at the moon in the sky.

Jalal al-Din Rumi

22

Magd al-Din had never before seen such an arid expanse before. True, there is open space in the countryside, but it is an expanse of soft green fields teeming with birds flying and humans playing or working peacefully. Next to the water wheels you can see children having fun, animals sleeping, women talking, old men playing tic-tac-toe, and ducks splashing in the water on which willows cast their shadows, while on the land, camphor, sycamore, and oak trees cast theirs. Now as Magd al-Din stood on the short, low platform of al-Alamein railway station next to Dimyan, he was seeing nothing but a wilderness, with no birds and no trees. Dimyan likewise was staring incredulously at the awesome, vast expanse. The train had started again slowly, then moved away, looking like a green worm spotted with yellow, wiggling away into the endless beyond. In the distance was military equipment, some scattered, other pieces arrayed close together. Among them were a few wooden kiosks and half-naked soldiers, their bodies above their khaki shorts gleaming in the distance, and other soldiers whose black bodies did not gleam. The train that sped away like a wondrous yellow-spotted worm, the high faraway sky, the mysterious groupings of soldiers, and the all-engulfing wilderness gave both Magd al-Din and Dimyan a sense of being lost. Five or six Bedouin had gotten off the train from the other cars, but they had not paused for a moment. Waiting for them were a few others, who spoke in loud, fast rattling voices, of which Magd al-Din and Dimyan could not understand a word. The two of them watched the Bedouin hurrying away down the narrow road next to the station between two rows of low, limestone houses deserted by their inhabitants. The Bedouin stirred up little eddies of dust, as if they were a herd of goats scurrying around. The stationmaster had gone out of his room to meet the train and spoke briefly with the engineer. As soon as the train began to move and the stationmaster turned around to go back to his room, he saw Magd al-Din and Dimyan and recognized them, for only a railroad worker would be wearing a green suit when he got off the train at the station. He approached them slowly. On the platform were two wooden rooms with pitched roofs also made of wood, painted a dull gray in several thick, clotted layers, betraying the painter's lack of skill.

"Welcome," said the stationmaster once he had come very close to Dimyan and Magd al-Din. Either they were still too awed by the expanse to respond or he did not wait for a reply.

"Are you the new workers?" he asked.

"Yes."

"Come on in."

He walked and they followed him to his room. At that moment, another man appeared at the door of the other room and stood there, staring at them. The stationmaster told him that they were the new crossing workers. The man welcomed them. Before they got into the stationmaster's room, Dimyan said, "Our stuff's on the platform."

The stationmaster smiled and said calmly, "Don't worry. Nothing gets lost here."

In the stationmaster's room they all sat, Dimyan and Magd al-Din on a small wooden bench and the stationmaster and his colleague on another one facing them.

"My name is Hilal," said the stationmaster. "My colleague here is Amer—he's the telegraph operator. His work is extremely important. Being late sending or receiving a telegram can have serious consequences." He paused for a moment and looked at Amer as if he needed confirmation for what he had said, then continued, "There may come a time when neither he nor I will be needed. Perhaps only the two of you will remain to handle the army traffic at the crossing. Military trains will not stop, which means your work is very important. Here we are working directly under the British command, supervised by a young English officer who knows a little Arabic. He's a little arrogant but quite sympathetic. There's an old housing compound, which is vacant now. Amer and I live in one of the houses. You can take the one next to it. The water train comes only once a week, and if it's late we get some water from the soldiers. There's no one in town except a few Bedouin in a settlement to the south. Some of their men sometimes show up when the water train arrives. They fill their jerry cans, but they don't mix with anyone. They walk fast and they look like camels. Every one of them is so tall you'd expect them to keel over any minute." He laughed by himself and continued, "They never feel hungry. They live on the fat of their bodies, exactly like camels. And they guard their dignity fiercely. Sometimes a young shepherdess comes with her sheep and her little brother. I hope no one will give her any trouble—but I haven't had the honor of your names."

"Magd al-Din."

Dimyan was a little hesitant to say his name. He had had it with the man's chatter, but politeness, especially because this was the first meeting, compelled him to listen on. "Dimyan," he finally said.

Resentment showed on the face of Amer the telegraph operator. Hilal was silent for a few moments, then said as if to rebuke Amer, whose resentment was visible, "In any case, Jesus is a prophet and Muhammad is a prophet, too."

But Dimyan was still thinking about what the man said in his long talk and was amused by the thought that the stationmaster's name meant 'crescent,' while his face was as round as the full moon.

It was noon. There was a big clock in the stationmaster's room, and Magd al-Din thanked God for that, otherwise how would he know prayer times when there was no mosque calling the faithful to prayer, for neither he nor Dimyan had a watch. He did not know that he would soon meet Muslim soldiers of the empire on which the sun never set.

The stationmaster got up to show them the house where they would stay. No sooner had they made it to the platform than they saw in front of them the young English officer wearing khaki shorts and a short-sleeved shirt. His knees were dark, which meant that he had spent a long time in the desert unlike new soldiers whose knees looked white and red, with the exception of the Africans, naturally. The officer wore a green cap.

"Hello Mr. Spike," the stationmaster called out. The officer pretended not to hear him and asked Magd al-Din and Dimyan in English, "Do you speak English?"

They understood the question but did not answer. Magd al-Din was at a loss for words; he thought immediately of Hamza, who knew a little English, actually a lot of English compared to the two of them. Hamza was lost.

Magd al-Din felt his face cloud over and sadness came over him as if ants were crawling all over his hot cheeks. He bowed his head and looked at the floor and almost asked the officer if he knew anything about Hamza. He heard the officer ask the stationmaster in annoyance, "What happened, Hilal?"

Dimyan blurted out, "Yes, sir, *afandim*?"

The officer stared at him in confusion. Now everyone was confused. Magd al-Din realized the mess that Dimyan's comment had created. The officer was now muttering audibly, "A pair of stupid Egyptians!"

Then he said to the stationmaster in a mixture of Arabic and English, "What a bunch of jackasses!"

"You know Arabic wonderful, General!" Dimyan said to the officer, smiling and blushing.

The officer, still staring, could not help smiling himself. Hilal, Amer, and Magd al-Din were visibly relieved.

"Give them some blankets, tins of food, and anything else they need," the officer told Hilal.

Hilal accompanied them to the housing compound, then left them after opening the door of the house where they would live. Magd al-Din had been inside a railroad-authority house the night that Shahin had invited him to see his son Rushdi. Magd al-Din and Dimyan had both applied to get homes in that compound at the earliest opportunity—and now they were getting a house not much different from the ones in Alexandria. But here there were no tiles, and the walls were not painted. The big white stones were now dirty and no longer white. Spiders and little insects were in the cracks. The wooden roof here was old and unpainted. Magd al-Din knew that when a human arrived in a place, he became the master of all beings in that place. So he would have to clean the walls and get rid of all the insects, even if he had to apply the flames of the kerosene stove to them. From the soldiers, he could probably get some substance that would get rid of the insects for good. Perhaps Dimyan was having the same thoughts: neither of them would spend the rest of his life here. This was a land of war, a land of death. This horrendous wilderness would swallow everything. Magd al-Din opened the little window of the inner room and saw the stark desert looking him in the face. Dimyan was in the outer hall looking closely at the filthy walls and wondering at the smell rising out of the dry bathroom that had no faucets and no pipes. He went into the room and found Magd al-Din standing, transfixed, in front of the window looking at the endless emptiness.

"What's the matter, Sheikh Magd? Do you miss Umm Shawqiya?" Dimyan asked.

Magd al-Din took a long, deep breath. "I am a peasant, Dimyan. I've never seen the desert before."

"And I've never seen the desert before either, even though I'm from the city."

He was silent for a few moments during which Magd al-Din thought about the work arrangement. They would have to split the day at the crossing: if he worked days, Dimyan would work nights and vice versa.

"You think the time can pass here, Dimyan? It seems like the world has come to a standstill."

Dimyan looked at him in surprise while Magd al-Din was overcome with shame, as he appeared, for the first time, awkward and impatient.

"Leave creation to the Creator, Sheikh Magd," Dimyan said sheepishly. "God has the power to make a whole lifetime pass in the twinkling of an eye." Then he laughed boisterously and said, "Do you know what I was thinking just now, Sheikh Magd? I was thinking of the *abonne* Radwan Express. He doesn't seem normal."

"Just because he never leaves the train?"

Dimyan did not answer. He fell silent and so did Magd al-Din. It looked like Dimyan was about to cry.

"I feel like I'm going to die here, Sheikh Magd," he said suddenly, tears welling up in his eyes.

Quickly Sheikh Magd al-Din assumed his old confident posture and patted his friend on the shoulder.

"People like you don't die so fast, Dimyan. Yes, it's only right that the world keep the few good folks it has."

❖

Time waits for no one. There was a light air raid on Alexandria, where many Libyan refugees from Cyrenaica had arrived. They were placed under quarantine then moved to the Maks and Wardian neighborhoods. Dimyan and Magd al-Din had seen them on the train coming from Marsa Matruh, which stopped for a long time at al-Alamein. Magd al-Din got on the train and went through the cars but did not see anyone he knew except Radwan Express, who was sitting with a group of refugees, talking to them enthusiastically while they listened, enthralled by what he was saying. Why did he get on the train that day? He did not know. Perhaps he was hoping to come across Hamza. He still felt that his insult to Hamza was behind his getting lost. Hamza's forgiving nature was not enough for Magd al-Din to forget. Five years had passed since the coronation of King Farouk, so the country celebrated for a week beginning on the sixth of May. A gala event was held at Cinema Metro in Cairo for *Gone with the Wind* to raise funds for the war victims. The papers were filled with pictures of Vivien Leigh under which were ads for all kinds of Egyptian and foreign products: perfumes, furniture, clothes, shoes, food, cars, cigarettes, matches, aspirin, and sports and health goods. A new airport was inaugurated at Nuzha in Alexandria to receive civil aviation at a time when all civilian flights from Europe and America had stopped. The Greeks celebrated over a bottle that a Greek soldier had filled with dust from Athens. The celebration

was held at the Greek Orthodox church of Saint Saba, close to
Cavafy's deserted home. The Greeks wrote on the outside of the
bottle, "Free dust for a free people." An elementary school teacher
won the Muwasa hospital lottery grand prize, a twenty-five-
thousand pound apartment building. But a colleague of his named
Muhammad Ismail claimed that he had paid half of the fifty-piaster
price of the ticket and therefore he was entitled to half of the prize,
but that the teacher who had possession of the ticket refused to
give him his share. Thereupon he sued the teacher to force him to
give him his due. The story spread throughout Alexandria and all
over Egypt. So Umm Hamidu clicked her tongue and said, "Now
that somebody with an un-aristocratic name wins, they make
trouble for him." Rudolph Hess flew a plane to Scotland, where he
landed and was found by a Scottish farmer who recognized him
from his pictures in the papers.

The world was all abuzz with Hess's flight. He was said to be
mentally unbalanced. He was also said to be the third man in the
Nazi party after Hitler and Goering. It turned out that Hess had
spent his childhood in Egypt and had studied at one of the English
schools there. His father had lived in Alexandria before World
War I and had a big office on the street later named Saad Zaghloul
Street. He was an agent for German marine, pharmaceutical, pen
and pencil, and chemical equipment companies. He had lived for
some time in Zifta before settling down in Alexandria. From Zifta,
Rufail Masiha, B.A., sent a letter to the editor of al-Ahram in
which he said that of all Egyptian villages, Zifta was the most
closely related to Hess, that he had spent his childhood there with
his father, who had owned a mechanic's shop and flour mills and
whose farm was still referred to as the Hess Estate. He added that
some inhabitants of Zifta still remembered the fifteen-year-old
Hess boy walking in the streets of the village. The author of the
letter concluded by wondering whether that humble village on the
bank of the Nile knew that it had been home to a personality who
would one day be talked about by the whole world as it was living
the most colossal war that humanity had ever known.

The newspapers outdid each other trying to prove that Hess
was born in Alexandria in 1886, then met with Hitler in 1914 at
the western front. The two young men, weary of life and the war,

were united by a feeling of injustice done to Germany and became comrades in arms. The problem, though, was that the Germans were now saying that he was crazy. Drunkards in Alexandria bars agreed that he was crazy, not because they believed Nazi propaganda, but because he had spent his childhood in Zifta, and they laughed. A poet even wrote a short poem about Hess's flight:

> *Was it flight, a ruse, or insanity*
> *That enabled Hess to evade mortality?*
> *If flight, then flight is bad—*
> *There are so many ways to be mad!*

Aziz al-Masri, together with the pilots Abd al-Munim Abd al-Rauf and Husayn Dhu al-Fiqar Sabri, flew a plane to meet Rommel in the desert, but the plane crashed near Qalyub, and they hid in the countryside. The government announced a one-thousand pound prize to whoever led to their capture.

German airborne troops landed on Crete in huge numbers, in a unique assault hitherto unknown in the world. The landing was preceded by intense aerial bombardment for hours, and Goering said that the assault on Crete was the greatest that paratroopers anywhere in the world could accomplish. Faced with this massive attack, the English had to evacuate the island and save as many of their troops as they could by transporting them to Alexandria. The Greek king and his ministers left the island for England. At the end, there were thirteen thousand dead, wounded, and prisoners of war, in addition to two thousand Royal Navy troops. Sixteen thousand troops made it to Alexandria. Crete was only one of the marvels of German victories that seemed as if they would continue forever.

Dimyan went to Alexandria at the end of the month and returned the following day after receiving his and Magd al-Din's salaries and spending a night with his family. He told Magd al-Din that he could not stay away from him, then he laughed and said, "Maybe I'm also attached to Brika." Brika was the young Bedouin girl that the stationmaster had told them not to give any trouble. Dimyan had seen her every day late in the morning with her sheep and her little brother and could not help starting a conversation with her. She spoke with him with spontaneity and sweetness, and he gave her some goodies, especially cookies and chocolate, that the Indian soldiers, whose acquaintance he had made, had given him. When Brika left, she left behind a smell of sheep and their wool that never left his nose until the evening when to his astonishment he carried the smell home with him. He realized that something was going to happen between him and the little girl, and he felt fear mixed with a strange kind of joy.

A girl in southern Egypt had died and been buried, then six days later came back to life. It was a miracle that people kept talking about. One poet urged her to go back to the grave where everything was quiet, instead of this deadly world. Cairo was divided into a number of wards, each of which was to be serviced exclusively by a certain number of undertakers who were not to operate outside the borders of their wards. This led to a widespread protest on the part of the undertakers, who submitted a petition to the Department of Internal Lawsuits in which they claimed that there were too many of them to be restricted to specific wards. Besides, the petition said, the dead in Heliopolis were not like the dead in Sayyida Zaynab. " Such a division would place the dead in each ward at the mercy of that ward's undertakers, who would exercise a monopoly of burials and shrouds and would charge exorbitant fees due to the absence of unrestricted competition." A number of detainees were released form the Tur detention camp in Sinai. Among them were twenty persons from Alexandria, including Hamidu, whose mother strung decorations at the entrance of the house on the now almost-deserted street. Very few people came to congratulate him upon his return, once they found out that he had been detained for his acts against the British and not for being a menace to security, as the government had said. Magd al-Din and Dimyan heard the German planes as they flew over at night, and they saw their red lights. There were shots from anti-aircraft batteries from several spots in the desert, but the planes were flying too high and none was hit. Neither Magd al-Din nor Dimyan slept that night. They sat for a while in front of the house. The moon was almost full.

"Who's the new German commander here?" Dimyan asked.

"Rommel."

"A frightening name."

They could hear some noises, some movement of troops far off or some shots fired in the air or the sounds of crawling, invisible night insects. After a considerable interval they saw the planes returning and the anti-aircraft artillery chasing them in the sky in vain. The planes went back and forth more than once that night.

They flew high over the desert, but as soon as they entered the air above the city they fearlessly went close to land, as if they knew their targets precisely. The most important target that night was the huge gun at Bab Sidra, which previous raids had not been successful in silencing. It was an anti-aircraft gun with three strong searchlights that lit up the sky. The planes kept firing throughout the raid, during which the gun was silenced and dozens of homes were destroyed in Bab Sidra and Karmuz. Two days later an even more intense raid was launched and lasted all night long against the Egyptian and well as the European quarters. That raid targeted Greek and English ships and frigates anchored in the harbor. The bombs fell in the sea, causing huge columns of water to break the darkness of the night. The raid did little damage to the ships, compared to the havoc it wreaked on the poorer quarter of the city. People left in panic with only the clothes on their backs, leaving everything behind. They arrived in Cairo in their gallabiyas, pajamas, even in their underwear. Many women arrived in their nightgowns. Alexandria became an inferno that consumed its people. Many families died, and in some of them there remained only a child or a girl or a mother—all alone. For the first time, the problem of single women and girls and homeless children arose. Tent shelters were hastily set up in Abu Hummus, Kafr al-Dawwar, Damanhur, and the villages of Gharbiya and Manufiya for those without family in the countryside. As for those that had family, their families stood waiting for them at the railway stations all the way to Aswan, welcoming them as they arrived without food or money or clothes, the men looking pale, the children with panic on their faces, and the women with tragedy and profound grief in their eyes. It seemed like Germany had decided to destroy the city. Rescue workers worked hard in the disaster areas. Fruits and vegetables stopped coming, and the slaughterhouse stopped slaughtering after a short raid during which the slaughterhouses received a direct hit, as they were close to the ammunition depot. The flesh of the vendors and buyers mixed with the meat of animals—a lot of blood flowed that day. It was said that Germany was trying to empty the city of all inhabitants so it could enter without resistance. The English launched an offensive against Rommel but two days later, on the seventeenth of June, everything turned topsy-turvy and the Allies started to retreat under air cover, pursued by Rommel. Churchill removed General Wavell, transferring him to India, where he became commander in chief of India and replaced him with Auchinleck, the former C-in-C India, who now became C-in-C Middle East command. Four major incidents took place on one night, the twenty-second of June. A woman, Badriya by name, was arrested on charges of having multiple husbands. At midnight two violent air raids were unleashed against Alexandria, which led to a mass exodus at dawn. At dawn also, Germany's foreign minister Rippentrop was presenting an official declaration of war on the Soviet Union to the Soviet Ambassador in Berlin. At the end of the night Magd al-Din had gotten up, performed the dawn prayers, and sat jubilantly reciting the Quran. He noticed that Dimyan's eyes were gleaming in the dark so he told him, "Tonight my wife gave birth, Dimyan."

Dimyan made no answer. "I saw her, Zahra, waking me up and offering me a glass of warm milk. Do you know what she had?"

Again Dimyan did not reply.

"A boy. I told her if that happened to name him Shawqi. She must have done that."

The day was when I did not keep myself in readiness for
thee; and entering my heart unbidden . . .
unknown to me . . .

Rabindranath Tagore

23

Before the offensive against Russia, the Führer had told his
military commanders that Russian soldiers were not to be treated
as prisoners of war, but that they were to be killed. After the attack
the world heard Churchill's speech on the BBC, and his words
were spread far and wide: "We shall not flag or fail. We shall go on
to the end, we shall fight in France, we shall fight in the seas and
oceans, we shall fight with growing confidence and growing
strength in the air, we shall defend our island, whatever the cost
may be, we shall fight on the beaches, we shall fight on the landing
grounds, we shall fight in the fields and in the streets . . ."

The massive German armies were sweeping across the vast
Russian front that extended from the North Pole to the Black Sea.
German planes were destroying the Russian air force on the
ground. Five million German soldiers were invading cities and
villages. Riga, the capital of Latvia, fell after just one week of
fighting. There was a decisive battle in Minsk, and the Russians
began to retreat in great numbers before the Germans. Intense
British air raids on Germany did little to relieve the Russians.
British air raids here in the desert against the Tripoli harbor
managed to destroy several German and Italian ships, but that too
was of little consequence. German and Italian planes responded by
launching a raid on Alexandria, where the only persons you saw

were those fleeing the city. Stalin broadcast a message to Hitler warning him that he would be defeated, just as Napoleon Bonaparte had the previous century. But the Russians retreated even further to Stalin's defense line. An artillery war began on the Egyptian borders between the Afrika Korps and the Eighth Army. King George II came from England to Alexandria, reviewed the Royal Hellenic Army, and decorated some soldiers. Safiya Zaghloul, nicknamed 'the Mother of Egyptians,' visited Alexandria. There was a call encouraging men to marry single Alexandrian women before the forces of the vice market got to them. New fire and rescue stations were established. The taste of drinking water in the city changed. It was said that was because of the many bombs that fell in the Mahmudiya canal; it was also said that it was because of considerable growth of moss in the Nile. The country celebrated Queen Nazli's birthday at the same time that a peasant woman gave birth to a baby that was more like a monkey, but was stillborn. Premier Paderewski, Poland's first prime minister after World War I and one of the most acclaimed pianists in America after he resigned, died. Sitt Badiya Masabni staged the revue *We Must Laugh*. The Germans reached the outskirts of Kiev and crossed the Dnepr river. The number of air raids on Alexandria during the month of June was fourteen, in the course of which 725 were killed, 850 wounded, and more than forty thousand displaced. The number of troops fighting on both sides on the Russian front was nine million, in the most vicious war that humanity had yet seen. The Germans succeeded in occupying Smilensk and Bessarabia and continued moving toward Leningrad, where fierce fighting took place. Two thousand new shelters were built in Alexandria, even though many people had fled. The Japanese intensified their activities in Indochina and occupied new bases to send their armies to the French colonies. Strangely enough, the beaches in Alexandria were crowded this year, and there was a call for government employees who had evacuated Alexandria to return and run government operations. German casualties in one month in Russia reached 1.5 million soldiers, three thousand tanks, and twenty-three hundred planes. Russian resistance guerrilla war operations began. The first air raid on Port Said in Egypt killed seventeen and wounded sixty. Said Ghazi's height reached two meters and 65 centimeters. The doctors gave up on trying to stop the fast growth of his bones, and he became the talk of the patients in the hospital. Visitors of patients in the hospital took pains to pass by the orthopedics section to catch a glimpse of Said Ghazi, if only from a distance. The hospital gave Said a wheelchair, as he was no longer capable of standing up, let alone walking and hitting door frames.

The trains carrying soldiers to Alexandria increased; the soldiers were English, Irish, Scottish, South African, and Australian, in addition to Greek, French, and Jewish volunteers. The trains emptied their troops in al-Alamein, from where they were sent on to Marsa Matruh and Sallum, where intermittent fighting was taking place at the borders. When a band of Scottish soldiers, with their distinctive uniforms and bagpipes on their chests, arrived, they lined up on the platform and began to play merry, boisterous music, which Dimyan heard in the house, so he hurried to the station. There he was amazed at the beautiful sight of the happy performing soldiers. The train started to leave the station, and the players proceeded on the narrow asphalt road to the north where the barracks and the headquarters were located, half a kilometer away.

"What are these musicians doing here?" asked Dimyan, who was now standing between the stationmaster, the telegraph operator, and Magd al-Din.

"They are Scottish soldiers who play music during the fighting," Hilal, the stationmaster, replied. Magd al-Din and Dimyan looked at him in astonishment as he continued, "The last Scottish band to come here was last year. They marched with the troops and went into Libya at the time of Graziani. None of them came back."

"So they fight with the soldiers?" Magd al-Din asked.

"They play during the fighting to raise morale," said the stationmaster.

Everyone fell silent and dispersed to tend to their business, while Dimyan stood alone in the glare of the brilliant daylight reflecting on the Scottish soldier-players who had disappeared among the barracks, the sound of their instruments lost in the great glare of silence. For the first time, Dimyan could see clearly, the vast arrays of military equipment scattered as far as the eye could see. There were hundreds of ocher tanks covered with greenish-yellow netting amid artificial cactus and thorn trees for camouflage, hundreds of vehicles in ceaseless motion, the roar of their engines muffled by the distance, rows of giant guns not yet in use, similarly covered with netting and branches. There were also little scattered kiosks and incessant movement of soldiers going in or out of them or the trenches. Suddenly Dimyan felt his sense of smell aroused. It did not take him long to figure that it was Brika on her way with the sheep and her brother and her desert sweat. Out of nowhere there appeared three jeeps driven by bare-chested soldiers; the jeeps were speeding jerkily along the bumpy road from the north. Brika's little brother could be seen scampering among the sheep, saying, "Herr, herr" to guide their movement on the asphalt road, anticipating mistakes on the part of the jeeps, which were coming toward him as he and the sheep came from the south, and skillfully evading them. Brika meanwhile was standing following the movement of the speeding cars and hurling unintelligible words at them. Dimyan knew that she tended her sheep behind the station so he went there ahead of her and saw her tender little frame approaching, her clothes glittering under the sun. It was the first time he had seen Bedouin costumes. He later found out from her that the top part was a *hawli* made of silk spun on a manual loom with gold brocade. Under it one could see a cotton *maryul* covering the whole body. On top of the *hawli* was a leather wrap covering the chest down to the waist, which she would soon take off when it got too hot. On her head was a silk burnoose covering the whole head and ending with flowers made of colorful threads and gold and silver spangles that shone in the light, leaving only a soft round wisp of hair on the forehead, which drew attention to the smoothness of her brow and to her delicate eyebrows, her big dark eyes and her long, killing, eyelashes. He could see at her feet, above her little shoes also embroidered with golden and silver threads, the ends of pants with tiny crinkles.

He wished what happened the first time they met would happen again today. For some reason, a little ewe had stopped next to his foot and stuck to his leg and when Brika came close and began to prod it with a long, thin stick, the little ewe stuck even closer and did not budge. Dimyan laughed and so did Brika and he smelled musk wafting through the smell of sheep wool of her clothes. It did not occur to him that such a young woman wore musk or some other perfume. He thought it was the smell of her sweat. And on that day he first met her, it also did not occur to him that ten days had passed since he had arrived here, and that his desire for a woman was becoming aroused. He found himself staring at her big, dark eyes and her slightly pale brown face and the two beautiful dimples on her cheeks. He saw her lips tremble when she did not speak but also when she spoke. Above the upper lips was fine fuzz that was truly exciting. He saw her hands under the sleeves of her gallabiya, small and delicate, their bones almost visible under the skin.

"Herr, herr," she said, trying to dislodge the little ewe that had attached itself so closely to Dimyan's leg that he had to spread his legs to give a chance to the ewe, which was enjoying their proximity, to pass through them.

When the situation became awkward, Dimyan said, "Leave her be. Don't break her heart."

But Brika bent down and picked up the ewe and raised it to her chest, and it rested there meekly, turning her muzzle toward Dimyan and bleating thinly. Dimyan laughed and so did Brika, who said, "She knows you."

She kept laughing as she hurried to the sheep and left the ewe with them, saying, "Herr, herr," as did her brother. They all left Dimyan, who found himself the following day waiting for Brika with cookies and chocolate. They kept meeting like that every day for a short while.

Today he found himself saying to her, "Brika, I know your name from Hilal, the stationmaster, but you haven't asked me my name."

"What's your name?" she asked with a smile.

"Dimyan."

After a pause, she repeated the name, "Dimyan, Dimyan, Dimyan" and said, "Nice."

Dimyan left her for a little while, went home, then returned carrying more chocolate. She was waiting for him behind the station, and a short distance away her brother was keeping an eye on the sheep. Brika ate a piece of chocolate with obvious relish and gave her brother two pieces.

"You like chocolate?" Dimyan asked.

"Yes. My father buys me some when he goes to Amiriya. This is better."

"What does your father do in Amiriya?"

"He sells and buys."

"Is he a merchant?"

"No. He just sells and buys."

There was an awkard silence, then she added, "He sells the sheep and buys what we want. Nothing more. He doesn't make a big profit."

Dimyan understood; it all made sense. He found himself saying without thinking, "And the little one?"

"What about him?"

"Would he tell your father that you sat with me?"

She laughed and said, "I'll tell my father."

"Aren't you afraid?" he asked, surprised at her courage.

"Afraid of what? We are Arabs, Bedouin. We are not afraid." After another pause, she said, "Your name is Dimyan?"

"Yes."

"It would be a good name for a girl."

He figured that that meant she liked the name. It surprised him that she did not realize that he was Christian. Perhaps she did not dwell on it. Perhaps she herself was Christian. Yes. Some Christians had fled here as they had fled to southern Egypt. But what good would all these illusions, or even facts do him?

They met many times. Dimyan found himself holding her palms and turning them over as she laughed gleefully. Her hands were not warm, but little by little warmth came into them and to his own hands. But was it not possible that this young Bedouin woman was simply treating him like a father, nothing else? Could he not think about that? But the look of profound happiness in her eyes betrayed something else, and he was not going to let anything rob him of his happiness, which the good desert had given him unexpectedly.

❖

At night in front of the house as they lay stretched out on the ground smoking, their eyes gleaming in the dark, Dimyan asked Magd al-Din, "Tell me, Sheikh Magd—can someone like me fall in love?"

A soft breeze was blowing slowly in the desert, softening the intense heat of the day. There were not many trains at night, just one that usually came at dawn, so they always had the chance to spend most of the night together. In fact they had not been able to divide the day into shifts except for a few days at the beginning. After that they sat together at the crossing rather than spending the time alone in the house. And so they became inseparable at work and at home.

Amer had passed by them a short while earlier, leaving the telegraph office to sleep early as usual since no one sent any telegrams at night. No one sent any telegrams during the day either any more. The Bedouin were not in the habit of sending telegrams, and the soldiers coming from overseas had their own military ways of sending telegrams.

Amer stopped after they exchanged greetings, then asked them, "Do you know who sent the last telegram from the office today?"

They looked at him for a while in confusion, then Dimyan laughed and said, "Muhammad Abd al-Wahhab, the singer!"

"No."

"Then it must be King Farouk!"

Magd al-Din smiled, but Amer did not. Scorn appeared in his eyes at what Dimyan had said, and he said calmly, "It was me who sent it."

Dimyan looked at Magd al-Din, who had a pitying look in his eyes and said, "Sit down with us for a while, Amer. You must be upset about something. Sit down and talk."

They were surprised to see Amer sit down in front of them. Magd al-Din offered him a cigarette, and he took it with trembling fingers. Dimyan lit it for him. He began puffing the smoke calmly and talking as if to himself, "Yes, I was the sender. I sent it to my wife. I asked her to talk to me about the children."

"Do you have children, Amer?" Magd al-Din said after a silence.

"I don't have any children, Sheikh Magd," was Amer's reply, after another long silence.

A more profound silence fell. Magd al-Din had received an actual telegram announcing that Zahra had given birth to a boy, whom she named Shawqi, as Magd al-Din had wanted. Magd al-Din had told Dimyan, proudly, "Exactly as I saw in the dream!" And much as he felt regret that he could not go back to the village, he felt content that God had granted him his wish for a son. He thought about all that as Amer got up and left in the dark. As they watched him go, Dimyan said suddenly, "You haven't answered my question, Sheikh Magd."

"What question, Dimyan?"

"My question about love."

"What're you saying, friend? Put some sense in your head. We're poor, Dimyan. Besides, you're married with children."

They both fell silent. Dimyan seemed unconvinced by what his friend had said. He thought, why should poverty prevent love? Why must a man love only his wife and his family? His heart has stirred toward Brika, and he could not stop his heart.

"What happens when a Christian man falls in love with a Muslim woman?" Dimyan asked.

Magd al-Din did not reply. He instantly recalled the story of Rushdi and Camilla, the story that Dimyan knew was coming back, in reverse, but the same story, no question about it. So why was Dimyan going to hell with his own two feet? He heard Dimyan exclaim, "Life is a bitch and time a traitor."

"Life isn't a bitch, and time is no traitor, Dimyan," Magd al-Din replied. "We bring trouble on ourselves. How can you be so weak in controlling you heart?"

"My heart defeated me, Sheikh Magd. My heart has grown attached to torture, and I can't stop it. I didn't do it deliberately. I never did anything intentionally in my life. Did you or I intentionally get transferred to work here in al-Alamein, in the middle of the desert? Did we intentionally meet in the first place?"

Magd al-Din did not have an answer, and he tried to think of some way to say, "A man over forty craves young girls—if one was a little patient, the crisis would pass in peace."

But Dimyan was thinking of another reason for his love of Brika. Perhaps because she comes from a vast expanse. Where does she come from? He did not know. He would ask her and she would say, "From Ghadi" and point south. Where does she go with her sheep and brother? She doesn't seem to go to a specific place, a tent or a house or a village. She always seems to have ascended to the sky or descended to the bottom of the earth. She comes from God and goes back to Him. She always comes from the vast expanse, and when she does, his chest grows bigger and fills with air from an unknown source in such heat.

"Our life in Ghayt al-Aynab is too tight, Sheikh Magd," said Dimyan, as if to himself. "We hardly have enough air to breathe on the banks of Mahmudiya—it's heavy air, most of the time made rotten by a corpse floating in the water. This girl is an enigma, Sheikh Magd. As she comes, so she goes. God has sent her to me to preoccupy me. I cannot refuse what the Lord sends, can I?"

They both fell silent. Magd al-Din saw Dimyan wiping a tear away with his fingers.

And make us all, O Lord, deserving of exchanging
a pure kiss with one another.

Coptic prayer

24

Dimyan announced that as of tomorrow he would not eat corned beef, meat, eggs, cheese, or anything of animal origin except fish. As of tomorrow the fast of the Virgin, which lasts two weeks, would begin.

The morrow was the seventh of August and the first day of the Coptic month of Misra. Dimyan noticed that Magd al-Din was a little lost in thought so he added, "Remember what I told you about the big fast, our holiest one that ends with Easter? This one about to start is the fast of the Virgin. There's also the Nativity fast, which lasts forty-three days, and ends with Christmas on January seventh. Then there is the fast of Jonah, three days. Do you know Jonah? He is mentioned in the Quran. He stayed for three days in the belly of the big fish and came out to preach to the people of Nineveh and guide them to faith."

Magd al-Din was thinking that he had forgotten the Coptic months, which he thought he would never forget. All peasants know the Coptic calendar because it is timed with the seasons, and keep up with it. And there he was hearing from Dimyan that tomorrow would be the first of Misra. "He is the Prophet Yunus, peace be upon him," he said to Dimyan, as he finally paid attention to his words.

"Well, do you know Nineveh? A beautiful name, but its people were evil," Dimyan said.

"I think Nineveh is in Iraq. I also think it is the city of the prophet Ibrahim, peace be upon him."

"You know many things, Magd al-Din, many, many things. In the Jonah fast, we completely abstain from eating for three days. Some of us fast it one day at a time. We also fast Wednesday and Friday of every week of our life, with the exception of the fifty days immediately following Easter, the time of khamsin sandstorms in Egypt, which is the period that Jesus Christ spent on earth after His rising. We fast Wednesday because that was the day the Jews agreed to crucify Christ, and we fast Friday because that was the day He was crucified. They are days of holy fasting on which we only eat fish, exactly like the big fast."

Magd al-Din was lost in thought again. Where does his friend get this religious information, when he had led a vagabond's life until just a year ago, when he first started going to church? "But you don't fast on Wednesdays or Fridays," he said with a smile.

"It's difficult for me, Sheikh Magd. I don't observe the Jonah fast either. It's not intentional—I'm just not used to it. I've also told you that all our days are not much different from fasting days. I fast more than I'm supposed to."

Dimyan fell silent for a short while, then asked suddenly, "Are all the stories of the prophets in the Quran?"

"Yes."

"They're also in the Old Testament. Praise the Lord. Anyway, I just wanted to let you know about my fast so you wouldn't be restricted to my food."

"I'll fast with you, Dimyan. I'll eat what you eat and abstain from what you abstain from."

As usual, time passed. Magd al-Din wrote a letter to Zahra and sent it with the abonne Radwan Express. He asked him to put it in the nearest mailbox in Alexandria. Dimyan asked him to pass by his family in Ghayt al-Aynab to see if they were all right after the heavy raids of the last few days. Dimyan laughed as he told Radwan, "Finally you're getting a job and customers." He gave him a box filled with tea, cookies, cheddar cheese, corned beef, and chocolate to deliver to his family. He and Magd al-Din also gave Radwan some tea, corned beef, and cheese, and he was very pleased. True, they would not be able to send things with him every day or even every week, but at least it was something to do instead of this abject idleness. He did not meet any passengers after Magd al-Din and Dimyan, only a few Bedouin. If a Bedouin saw him sitting in the car, he looked at him suspiciously, then left the car for another one. If a group of them came into the car, they sat together and spoke so fast that he could not follow or understand their conversation, even though, before the war, when the trains were crowded, he could understand and speak the Bedouin dialect. So what had happened to him? Since the beginning of the war he had begun to succumb to idleness and fell asleep on his seat alone in the big car.

Dimyan's appearance had changed considerably. His face had a dark tan from the heat and the sun. He took off the railroad uniform and replaced it with a soldier's summer uniform: khaki shorts and a short-sleeved shirt. His legs looked very thin above his heavy black military shoes. Dimyan asked the stationmaster to do the same, and the following day Hilal was in a military uniform and so was Amer.

Magd al-Din, however, did not change. What astonished Dimyan was that Magd al-Din, who had a fair complexion just like him, did not tan, but his face grew ruddier. And if it had not been for the fact that the two of them lived in the same house, he might have said that he used a magical lotion on his face or that he drank a lot of alcohol. Yes, drinkers always have ruddy faces, like most Greeks and Italians in Alexandria, although it was also true that sometimes they lost their luster, as happened to many Cypriots. But the latter drank too much and did not eat well. They were the poorest foreigners in Alexandria, surpassed in poverty only by the Jews. But the Jewish girls were always beautiful, said Dimyan to himself, proud of all this knowledge rushing in his head. He felt a strong longing for his wife.

"Sheikh Magd, are we going to stay like this without women?" he asked suddenly.

Magd al-Din was truly taken aback by the question, but he said calmly, "It's God's will. Besides, at least you can go to your wife."

"And leave you here?"

"I can do your work until you come back. As you can see, we almost always work together. You can go to Alexandria and spend as much time as you like there. Nobody comes to check on us."

"How about Officer Spike?"

"He's an Englishman, after all. He's not going to address the Egyptian government about two workers. Besides, as I told you, I'll do your work."

"But I was thinking about something else. They gave the soldiers recreational parties. The ATS women come once a month to give them recreation. What do you say we ask Spike to provide us with two Jewish women for recreation?"

Magd al-Din laughed hard and said that if he made such a request, Spike might kill him. They both laughed. Dimyan thought how easy it would be for him to go to Alexandria, and that way he would not have any sexual problems. That Magd al-Din is a marvelous sheikh—he offers solutions to the toughest problems so easily. How was it that Dimyan himself had not figured this solution out when it was so obvious?

This was the difference between him and Magd al-Din. If Magd al-Din were not a peasant railroad worker, he would have been a politician, perhaps a military commander. But Dimyan realized that he would not be able to go. It was not easy for him just to leave Magd al-Din alone in this wilderness. What a beautiful feeling he had for his friend. He realized that every time he went to Alexandria to get their salary every month. He could stay only for one night despite his longing for his wife. But he also could not stop seeing Brika. Perhaps she was the real reason for his staying put. But his love for Magd al-Din was a strong reason, there were no two ways about it.

At night, on the eve of the Feast of the Virgin, after the last day of the fast, Dimyan awoke from his sleep to a soft sound echoing in the room. Magd al-Din had put out the kerosene lamp and it was pitch dark, but Magd al-Din's eyes were gleaming in the dark and the sound of his breathing was getting louder. He heard Dimyan's voice from the other side, "What's wrong, Sheikh Magd?"

"Nothing, Dimyan."

"But you're crying. Are you thinking of Zahra and the kids?"

Magd al-Din did not reply. That night he felt the terrible injustice visited upon him. How could he bear not to see Zahra after the delivery of his baby son? Why could he not travel? How did he allow himself to be a victim of all this injustice without fighting back? What in his chest was attracting him away from the village and accepting it, as if leaving the village was his own desire? In truth he had done himself an injustice as grave as the mayor's.

"Yes, Dimyan. I remembered Zahra and the kids, but I thanked God. I cried for a few moments, then I praised and thanked God for his grace."

"You know Sheikh Magd," said Dimyan, breaking the silence. "I sometimes think that we'll go crazy here. I'm in love with a young woman, I don't know where she comes from or where she goes, and I forget my family, and you remember your family but don't think of going to them. Was Qays, the man who went crazy over Layla, living in a desert like this one? If that were the case then he was right to go crazy." Magd al-Din found himself laughing as Dimyan continued, as if to himself, "Yes. If it happened that one of us went crazy, he must be right, and soon people will find excuses for you and me, Magd al-Din."

Magd al-Din smiled at Dimyan's quirky effusions, so clearly the thoughts of one who had just awakened.

"You mean it's the desert that will make us go crazy?"

"No, it's the dark around us. Nobody else in the whole world is talking in the dark except the two of us. Go to sleep, Sheikh Magd. I'm going to sleep myself. Tomorrow is the Feast of the Virgin. There must be some foreign soldiers celebrating it. In the morning I'll walk toward the barracks for the first time. Maybe I'll find a mass to take part in. Listen, Sheikh Magd, recite some verses from the Quran to help you sleep calmly."

They both were silent for a while, then Magd al-Din asked, "What do you say in the mass about our Lady Maryam?"

"We say many things, but I remember only a few lines."

Then he began to chant in a deep voice:

Mary's glory is growing
East and west.

Exalt her, glorify her,
Enthrone her in your hearts.
She shines on high.
Her light never sets..

❖

"Al-Safi al-Naim, a man whose name means 'Pure Bliss,' cannot but be a reminder of heaven," said Magd al-Din, addressing a Sudanese soldier as Dimyan stood there, puzzled.

"I thought you were saying that someone had died and moved to the abode of pure bliss," said Dimyan, and the tall, huge Sudanese soldier laughed, his white teeth sparkling in the light.

A friendship had developed between Magd al-Din and Dimyan and a number of Indian soldiers since the early days of their arrival. When Magd al-Din saw the wall clock in the stationmaster's room, he had felt confident that he would be able to tell the time of the prayers. But then that same afternoon he had heard the call to the mid-afternoon prayers reverberating in the desert, thin, plaintive, and noble, but he did not know where it had come from. He learned that among the Indian troops were many Muslims and that groups of them frequently came to the station to unload the military equipment from the trains. Magd al-Din found himself standing on the platform at sunset making the call to prayer. He knew that the wind would carry the call to the south, so he intoned in a very loud voice and stood to pray, with Hilal and Amer behind him. The following day an Indian soldier, young with a dark-complexioned, yellowish, square-shaped face and small, gleaming, intelligent eyes, with the traditional Indian turban on his head, came to ask who had made the call to the sunset prayers the previous day. He said that Magd al-Din had a beautiful voice and promised to come at noon to pray behind him. At noon he came accompanied by a number of his merry friends. It was they who were giving large quantities of cookies, chocolate, tea, cheese, corned beef, lentils, and rice to Magd al-Din, Dimyan, Hilal, and Amer. Magd al-Din heard names he had not heard before and stories about a country that he had not believed existed. Everyone knew there is a country called India, but to actually see someone from that country was a real miracle. He came to meet men with names like Muhammad Zamana, Muhammad Siddiqi, Wilayat Khan, Karam Singh, Chuhry Ram, Raj Bahadur, Ghulam Sarwar, Irshad, Jinnah, and Iqbal. They were Muslims and Hindus who could not be more than eighteen, most of them sixteen, mere children, transported by the British Empire to lands other than their own from Peshawar, Lahore, Karachi, Bombay, and Kashmir. No one thought the day they were born that they would be in the Egyptian desert, fighting armies from Europe, and that they would most likely die there.

Amer had entered a state of profound depression, spending the day in the telegraph office tapping his fingers on the table, no one bringing him telegrams to send, receiving telegrams from no one. As for Hilal, he slept most of the time, waiting for passengers, of whom only one or two Bedouin traveled on any given day. But in addition to his work was traffic control and making the ground switches, for there was an old rail line that ended in front of the station, the line on which the military equipment trains spent the night before going back empty the following day. He also had to operate the semaphore, lowering its black and white arms as soon as the train moved. He did that from a switch adjacent to the platform. He also had to change the oil in the lamps attached to the rear of the arm of the semaphore once a week and light it every evening. There was a reason for his being there.

Today al-Safi al-Naim joined the Indian soldiers. He came on his own; no one had invited him. He said he heard the call to prayer coming from the direction of the station and was surprised by it. Then he saw the Indians around prayer times sneaking toward the station. So he decided to follow them. It had taken him a long time, but he finally did it.

"You look as though you might be from Sudan," Dimyan said, laughing.

Magd al-Din smiled in surprise as al-Safi al Naim said politely, "I am from Omdurman."

"The kindest people," said Dimyan. Magd al-Din was still surprised. He was preparing tea on a fire behind the kiosk, which they had left to sit outside near the crossing. He offered a cup of tea to al-Safi, who took one sip and said, "Strong sweet tea!"

"English tea," said Dimyan.

"No, it's from Ceylon. The English only package it. But more importantly, it's made by Arab hands," said al-Safi al-Naim.

"You are indeed pure bliss," Dimyan exclaimed like a child, and Magd al-Din laughed happily. Then after some silence al-Safi asked Dimyan his name.

"Dimyan."

They were silent again as a soft breeze blew. The sun was about to set, letting the dark take charge. The horizon was lit up by the red flames of the twilight. It was the tenth of August, the fifteenth of Rajab, and so the full moon started ascending early. There is nothing more beautiful than the desert in full moonlight.

"Dimyan is a beautiful name, the name of a saint," al-Safi said.

Dimyan had fallen silent, thinking that his name had shocked al-Safi or rather his religion, but it turned out that he was wrong.

"Thank you, brother," he said.

A while later Magd al-Din asked him, "Is there a Sudanese group here?"

"A very large group. Can you guess how many?"

"A thousand."

"No."

"Five hundred."

"No. You'll never guess. I'll tell you—it's only two of us, me and Siraj Khalifa. Siraj is in Marsa Matruh, now working in the service of the commander in chief, Mr. Cunningham. I was wondering why the British Empire needed two Sudanese, but now they've separated us and I guess now the empire needs each of us far from the other. But wondering doesn't do me any good. It must be that I'm worth a battalion from New Zealand or India, otherwise they would not have kept each of us away from the other. You're here alone too. What do you do? Nothing that the army can't do, but you're here like us."

After a long silence during which they finished drinking the tea, Magd al-Din said, "Perhaps we're here to meet you and get to know you, and that alone gives us happiness and more."

❖

The desert cold came with black clouds racing like raging bulls to the east on the sea and on the land. "So this is where the rain, which comes to Alexandria like the raids, starts," thought Dimyan to himself, then suddenly asked Magd al-Din, "Who put Alexandria where it is?" Magd al-Din did not reply but looked surprised by his friend's random question. The soldiers' uniforms had changed. They now wore long pants and woolen jackets over long-sleeved shirts and thick, knee-high socks and suede boots. They placed rags into the muzzles of their rifles to prevent moisture from the damp desert air getting into them. Tongues of flame shot up here and there in the vast, dark expanse where clouds blocked the moon and the stars. These were fires that soldiers, especially Indians, made from scrap wood and cardboard boxes to keep themselves warm. There seemed to be a state of relaxation on the military front; the trains no longer brought equipment or soldiers from the east, or prisoners of war from the west. Magd al-Din and Dimyan did not see anything new for some time except for a huge Indian, over forty years of age, who walked as haughtily as an elephant and who wore a huge turban. He came several times with the young Indians but did not take part in the prayers, instead sitting at a distance with the few Sikh Indians who had come to the station with their Muslim compatriots. His name was Corporal Bahadur Shand, and he was from Kashmir, where Muslims and Sikhs lived in a state of discord instigated by the English. When Magd al-Din saw Corporal Bahadur he marveled at God's ability to create all these different nations and peoples. He was reminded of the Quranic verse, *And we have made you nations and tribes that you may know one another.* He wished he knew enough English and Hindi to understand what was happening in this wide world. How great the Creator who controls all of this and who had sent Dimyan his way to make his days easy, even though he was in a place that even monkeys would flee out of boredom. Dimyan came back every day after Brika's departure in a state of childlike happiness. With Dimyan it was possible for days to pass; without him, total silence. A month had passed since the Feast of the Virgin, and Ramadan would begin the following day.

"It's my turn to fast with you, Sheikh Magd," Dimyan told his friend.

Magd al-Din was too surprised to reply.

"Don't you believe me? I'll fast the whole month with you."

"Our fast is a difficult one. We have to abstain from food and drink all day long."

"That's better than each of us eating alone in the desert," Dimyan replied immediately. He had made up his mind beforehand and made a strong case. Magd al-Din was touched. The two friends were silent for a long time.

"When do we go back to Alexandria, Dimyan?" Magd al-Din finally asked.

"You mean, to the village. I know that Ramadan is a month that loves company. If only some Indians would join us, then we'd be an international family."

"I miss them so much, Dimyan," Magd al-Din blurted out despite himself.

"Why don't you go then?" Dimyan caught him off guard.

Magd al-Din had no choice but to tell him the whole story of his banishment. He felt the need to tell someone. It is a strange moment that comes over someone when he feels the need to disclose that which he has taken such pains to conceal. One can never really escape that moment when it does come over him. His chest is filled with a heavy sadness that rises to his eyes as he begins to tell the story and let out the heavy secret.

His story took up most of the night. Dimyan listened, spellbound. While eating the pre-dawn meal with Magd al-Din, he asked him, "And you've put up with all of that alone?"

"It's God's will, Dimyan."

"But God cannot be pleased with all that injustice."

"God forgive us, Dimyan."

"The best thing you can do, Sheikh Magd, is to take a rifle from one of the Indians, go to the village, kill the mayor, and come back. Nobody will think of you and nobody will know the source of the Indian bullets!"

"If only I had wanted," Magd al-Din finally said, "I would have killed him a long time ago. I left to prevent bloodshed and also because I wanted to leave. Yes, I wanted to leave—I don't know why."

"You must return, Sheikh Magd."

"I will return, Dimyan. I will. I must."

During Ramadan, Brika stopped coming for days on end. Until the feast, she only appeared five quick times. She told Dimyan that she was getting ready for the jlasa, but he did not understand or pay attention.

On the day of the feast the Indian Muslims and al-Safi al-Naim performed the feast prayer behind Magd al-Din. They wished him a happy feast and he wished them a happy feast as well. There was nothing for Magd al-Din to do except to send a telegram to Zahra and his sisters wishing them a happy feast. Amer was very happy with the telegram, and as soon as Magd al-Din left the room he heard Amer crying. That was Amer's last day on the job. He left on the evening train, just like that, without telling anyone, leaving his room open to the wind.

"What could he do? He was about to go crazy," Dimyan said, laughing, to Magd al-Din and Hilal, who was silent.

"We should do like him, escape," added Magd al-Din. "What harm would it do the Allies if three wretched Egyptians disappeared?"

The feast passed in silence, no trains of any kind. After the feast Brika appeared. It was an unusually sunny day.

"Why have you stopped coming as often as you used to?" Dimyan asked her in pain.

"Because of the rain," she answered with a laugh.

"But you came some days."

"On days when there's no rain," she replied in her Bedouin dialect.

"You can tell such days?"

"We Bedouin know which way the wind blows."

They fell silent.

"What do you do here, Dimyan?" she finally asked with a smile.

The question surprised him. How come she doesn't know what he does? He realized that he had not told her about his job.

"I work at the crossing," he answered.

"I know that. What do you do?"

"Nothing. When the train comes, I stop cars and pedestrians. When it leaves, I let the cars and pedestrians cross."

"That's amazing!"

"My job?"

"I don't see any cars or people. I don't see any trains."

Dimyan felt perturbed. What's this girl doing to him today? This girl for whom his heart beats faster whenever he sees her, like an orphan when out of the blue, two parents appear. This girl whom he loves, but doesn not know how to tell her of his love for her.

"Where do you come from, Brika?" he found himself asking.

"From the south," she said pointing to the south.

"And where do you go after you're done tending the sheep?"

"To the south. Haven't you seen me?"

"I saw you," he answered her in her dialect, realizing how silly his question, which he had asked before, must be. But he asked another question anyway.

"What's the jlasa that you told me about before?"

"Would you like to take part in it?" she asked, laughing.

"I don't know it."

"Listen, play with me," she kept laughing. "I ask and you answer, and you ask and I answer."

He gave up. "What's sweeter than honey and what's more bitter than colocynth?" she asked.

He had no answer.

"Nothing is sweeter than honey except a child playing in the sand," and she pointed to her little brother, "and nothing is more bitter than colocynth but carrying a man on a bier," and pointed at an Indian soldier who was passing before her by chance, smiling.

Dimyan thought that he should break his silence and play with her. Does he not love her? His body shook as he thought what to ask her.

"Okay, I'll ask you—what beats fire?"

"Water beats it," she answered, nudging him in the chest.

"Okay. You win."

"No. I don't win yet. It's my turn to ask you—what beats water?"

He thought for a little while and almost said the wall, but he realized that water could go around the wall or through it, in time. His silence and thinking lasted for some time.

"The hot wind beats it," she finally told him, laughing.

Dimyan realized that she was incredibly intelligent, and he really wanted to beat her at the game. He nudged her gently on the shoulder and asked her, "And what beats the hot wind?"

"The horses beat it," she answered quickly, still laughing, "and the horsemen beat the horses, and the women beat the horsemen. Do you know what beats the women?"

"Men."

"No," she laughed and laughed. "Death beats women, Dimyan."

She stood up to call her brother to gather the sheep. She pointed to the sky, which had begun to fill with clouds. Dimyan figured that she wanted to beat the rain.

"But you haven't told me what a *jlasa* is," he said.

"Today we did a *jlasa*, didn't you know? And you didn't beat me. We do the jlasa in the village. The young man who beats me marries me. Herr, herr herr," she shouted to help her brother control the sheep, then walked away laughing. Dimyan stayed in his place, motionless, looking at the black clouds gathering and realizing there was no way that Brika could be his, ever.

❖

It was raining hard on the Maryut coast and inside Libya when the Allied forces surprised the Axis forces in Sidi Rizq, but the Germans won after a vicious battle in the airfield area and they regained Sidi Rizq. The Allied forces lost many of their armored vehicles. The day after the German victory, at the end of November, Cunningham ordered the Eleventh Brigade to march on Sidi Rizq anew, and that brigade almost regained it. But Rommel, now well-versed in desert warfare, left the battle and took his armored force eastward, to the Egyptian borders. He went twenty miles inside Egypt and wreaked havoc in the rear of the English forces and their allies. He took many of their soldiers prisoner until the Royal Air Force stepped in with fierce raids that

forced Rommel to go back to Sidi Rizq, chased by the Fourth
Indian Brigade. No sooner had November ended than General
Auchinleck dismissed Cunningham, replacing him with Major
General Ritchie. Rommel laid siege to Tobruk, which was a
stronghold, the strongest in North Africa, with a brave and
obstinate British garrison thirty thousand strong. It is surrounded
from the east and the west by rugged rocky terrain and to the
south by a level plain. Before 1940, it had been an Italian
stronghold, but the English seized it and made use of the defense
lines established by the Italians around it: deep trenches in the
ground, housing guns, and machine gun batteries that could pour
fire on the attackers to the last moments of their attack, decimating
them. There were also several barbed wire barriers that slowed
down infantry attacks and a deep trench surrounding the whole
area to prevent the advance of tanks. Behind all these defenses
were massive British artillery units and dense mine fields. The
fighting was over by the end of November, and even though
Rommel did not succeed in capturing Tobruk, he inflicted very
heavy losses on the Allied forces, exceeding eight hundred
armored vehicles, one hundred planes, and countless small arms
and ammunition, in addition to more than nine thousand prisoners
of war. Rommel suffered heavy losses and a great number of his
soldiers were taken prisoner. The Allied forces began to transport
them to Alexandria with shaven heads, without helmets or head
cover of any kind in the bitter cold, but they had long, heavy coats.
When the British Command decided to engage Rommel in a
decisive battle code-named Crusader, one hundred thousand
soldiers from the Eighth Army charged forward. Rommel left the
road open for them and did not mount a counterattack,
withdrawing quietly westward until they fell into the trap.
Thereupon he let loose with his artillery from all sides, destroying
almost all the British tanks. The valley south of Sidi Rizq became
a sea of dust, fire, and smoke.

The Russians had retreated behind the Dnepr river and
fighting intensified in front of Leningrad. The raids on London
ceased and the Battle of Britain ended because the Germans were
busy on the eastern front. The American navy declared that it was
determined to rid the Atlantic Ocean of Nazi ships after Churchill

met with Roosevelt on an American cruiser in the Atlantic Ocean. Roosevelt announced the United States' resolve to defend the freedom to sail the seas and warned that Axis ships would face destruction if they entered US territorial waters. A German U-boat torpedoed the British aircraft carrier *Ark Royal* and sank it. Afterward, German U-boats also sank the British battleship *Barham*; all seamen on board were killed. An Italian submarine came close to Alexandria and torpedoed the British battleships *Queen Elizabeth* and *Valiant*, crippling them. When the British command tried to take its revenge against an Axis ship convoy going from Italy to Tripoli, it assigned the task to a British force comprised of three cruisers and four destroyers. But it was the British force that was ambushed at sea; two cruisers were hit, and the third was sunk with all seven hundred seamen on board, with the exception of one, who was taken prisoner. It was a truly painful end to the English fleet in the eastern Mediterranean.

In France, seventy-two French hostages were shot, execution-style, by the Germans in Nantes in retaliation for their participation in the Resistance. That prompted de Gaulle to declare mourning and called on all the people to demonstrate. The whole of France expressed anger. In India, Mahatma Gandhi's seventy-third birthday was celebrated in his quiet village where he spent most of his time with his spindle and yarn. Gifts of spindles and yarn poured in from all over the country. In the Pacific, Japanese planes and battleships launched a surprise attack on Pearl Harbor, destroying three hundred American planes and thirty battleships and killing seven thousand. For the United States, it was a day of infamy, and it was the day that the States officially entered the war. Japanese forces spread in East Asia and fighting extended throughout the eastern parts of Malaya and Singapore and to Hong Kong. Russia's winter began to take its toll on the German troops, whose vehicles stalled and they were unable to enter Moscow even though they had reached its outskirts. The Germans began to retreat. The Slavic nation had awakened. Marshal Voroshilov, commander in chief of the Partisan movement, made a moving appeal to the inhabitants of Leningrad. He said that the enemy was trying to enter the city and destroy its houses and factories and the freedom of the motherland, that

Leningrad was the industrial and cultural capital of Russia and it would not fall, and that "the enemies would not set foot in our beautiful gardens."

Since December the Germans had suffered many defeats. Sixty thousand were killed in twenty days at the outskirts of Moscow, a fact that forced the Germans to relieve Field Marshal von Bock of his command of the Rusisian front. A rumor spread in Egypt that Marshal Timoshenko, one of the most prominent commanders in Russia, was a Muslim and therefore never lost any battle.

In Egypt, the writer May Ziyada had died weeks earlier, as had Talat Harb Pasha, father of Egypt's national economy. His Majesty King Farouk and the royal family paid a visit to the Farafra oasis, thus completing visits to all of Egypt's oases, to make sure that his subjects there were all right. There was a big air raid on Alexandria that left a lot of destruction and dozens of casualties as always happened since Rommel appeared in Africa. Clothing was distributed to refugees in the countryside. The Egyptian film *Schoolgirl* and the American film *The Thief of Baghdad* were screened. The Shah of Iran abdicated the throne in favor of his son Mohammad Reza Pahlavi, so Princess Fawziya, King Farouk's sister, was the first Egyptian princess to sit on the throne of Iran. The vice department celebrated the success of its call for the marriage of single refugee women by having a wedding ceremony for twenty couples on the same night. Two hundred thousand pounds worth of narcotics were seized in the coastal area. There was a surge of interest on the part of Hijazis in the Egyptian *takiya*, or Sufi lodge, in the Hijaz, and the newspapers called for increasing the budget of the *takiya* to be able to perform its charitable work. The Feast of the Sacrifice coincided with Christmas, and Dimyan went to Alexandria for two days and returned quickly to keep Magd al-Din company. Measures were taken to protect the bronze statues in Ras al-Tin palace from the air raids. And Rushdi walked along Mahmudiya Canal.

He had decided to make it to the Nile then go south until he arrived at Asyut, and on his way would examine all the corpses that he came across. He was certain that Camilla had been killed and that her body was dumped in the Nile. He was determined either to find her dead or alive. A rumor had spread in the country about a young nun with an aura around her head and face who was healing the sick in Asyut, and people started converging on her place from the surrounding villages. A butcher was arrested and faced a military tribunal for refusing to sell meat. There was meat hanging in his store, and a customer came to buy a kilo, but the butcher refused, saying the meat was not for sale, that it was for display only. The customer felt that he was mocking him so he went to the police station and lodged his complaint. Prices for birds rose: a nightingale was priced at twelve piasters, a canary at thirty-five piasters, and likewise for a parrot. The fighting powers pledged to observe a ceasefire on the last night of the year to celebrate the new year, but most houses in Alexandria were closed, destroyed, or deserted.

Traveler, must you go? . . .
Is the time for your parting come? . . .
Traveler, we are helpless to keep you.
We have only our tears . . .

Rabindranath Tagore

25

The new year started with a big commotion in al-Alamein. German and Italian planes conducted raids on the desert all the way to Alexandria. Anti-aircraft artillery scattered all over the desert kept firing, but no planes were hit.

The number of German and Italian prisoners of war being captured dwindled. It was Rommel now who was trans-porting more prisoners to Germany via Italy and the Mediterranean. Rommel's name now struck fear in the Allied troops. In the middle of January, in the early hours of the morning, Rommel turned off the little reading light and lay down on the bed in his command post, asking his private secretary, Staff Sergeant Boetticher, to wake him up in an hour. When he got up he held his morning briefing with his officers and told them, "We will attack at once." Then he explained to them that the British would exploit any relaxation to make use of the huge supplies that they had started to receive. That would give them vast superiority over the Axis forces, hence their lines and their plans should be penetrated to make it all the way to the Delta.

A major operation to deceive British intelligence from Rome to Libya began. Strong rumors were spread that the Germans were withdrawing. Rommel began to blow up mock ships and mock camps. The rumors were so strong in Alexandria that the Allied soldiers started drinking toasts to the withdrawal of Rommel, who was now reduced to blowing up his own ships. But only the belly dancer Hikmat Fahmi in Cairo knew that this was just a ruse. She lured high-ranking English officers to her houseboat, and gathered information and secrets and conveyed them to the Germans by a secret transmitter with the help of the two spies, Johannes Eppler and Hans Gerd Sandstetter.

After pretending to withdraw, Rommel began his daring and sudden offensive by dividing his armored force into two divisions, one for the coast and the other for the desert. He seized Ajdabiya, then Antalat and Sawinnu. British armed forces retreated in a state of great disarray toward the Egyptian borders. The road to Benghazi on the one hand, and to al-Makili on the other, was now open to Rommel. Toward the end of January he pretended to launch an offensive against al-Makili, so Auchinleck moved his armored force and his infantry there, but, making a tiger-like leap, Rommel changed direction to the coast, cutting off the Indian Fourth Division and taking Benghazi. The Führer promoted him to general. The British had lost their morale and ran away as if bitten by a snake. Rommel had unleashed his eighty-eight-millimeter anti-tank guns on their armored vehicles, then overran them with his heavy Panzer tanks.

At that time the Russian forces had smashed six German divisions and a big Russian offensive extending from Sevastopol in the south to Finland in the north. Hitler admitted for the first time that the Russians were advancing. Germany prepared by deploying five million soldiers, Russia by deploying ten million. The United Sates allocated the largest budget for the war, fifty billion dollars for military industries and operations. The French ship *Normandie* caught fire as it was anchored at the harbor of the Houston Ship Channel in the United States, resulting in forty dead and 165 injured. The Japanese landed in Java, and the Kingdom of Siam declared war on Britain after it was captured by Japan. Indian leaders Nehru and Gandhi rejected anything less than total independence from England. The city of Alexandria established fifteen new shelters. The Coptic Church celebrated Christmas in the first week of January amid prevalent sadness because of the raids. A woman died in Karmuz, leaving behind three children. As the people carried her bier, they were forced back to where the children stood in front of their house, crying. That happened three times, and every time the bier would turn and take the men carrying it back to the house. Men, young and old, cried out "God is great!" and women and girls cried. The world was bathed in a brilliant light as the heavy clouds lifted over the city and a gloriously beautiful sun shone. People knelt down and kissed the ground and prayed and cried. The mother could only be buried after the children were carried away. Alexandria spent the night in a state of amazed wonderment. Stones surrounded the statues of Muhammad Ali Pasha and Ismail Pasha to protect them from the heavy raids. The cabinet ministers began to prepare headquarters in Luxor and Aswan, away from Cairo, because of winter, it was said. In reality they wanted to get as far from Rommel as they could. His Majesty the King went on a trip to the Eastern Desert, in which he visited the mines and the Bishariya, the inhabitants of Halayib. Epiphany coincided with the Islamic New Year; a newspaper reader observed that Christian and Islamic feasts were coinciding with, or occurring closer to each other these days. Another reader said in reply to it that that happened only every few generations and that this generation was luckier than others because of this divine blessing. Nahhas Pasha became prime minister after great pressure on the king from the English. Husayn Sirry Pasha resigned, or was forced to resign by the king. Demonstrators chanted, "Forward, Rommel." The people expressed their love for their young king. A poet poked fun at the English by writing,

They came into the lion's den
Armed to the teeth.
Losing their way to Benghazi,
They arrived at Abdin.

Blood and Sand, starring Tyrone Power and Rita Hayworth, was screened in Cairo. Taha Husayn published his beautiful novel, *The Call of the Curlew*, and kosher meats were included in the official price lists in Alexandria, a move Jewish butchers resented. The sisters of Abd al-Fattah Inayat, who had been convicted of killing

Sirdar Sir Lee Stack in the twenties, petitioned Nahhas Pasha to pardon their patriot brother, who had served three-quarters of his sentence. The parliament session opened with the speech from the throne delivered by Nahhas Pasha before the king. A thaw began in Moscow. The population increase in Egypt for the whole of the previous year was calculated to be forty thousand. Dimyan and Magd al-Din began to see soldiers coming back from the front, tired, dirty, and in a state of shock and fatigue, to be replaced with fresh, rested troops from Alexandria. The soldiers whose eyebrows and eyelashes were burned by the sun and the cold looked no different from the prisoners of war, so much so that Dimyan mistook them. Every time he saw them he would tell Magd al-Din, "Look! Here's another batch of prisoners!" Magd al-Din would assume they were Allied soldiers, since prisoners of war did not carry rifles. Dimyan would laugh, but he would make the same mistake again and again.

Rumors increased about Rommel's advance on the Egyptian borders. Rommel by now had become the unrivaled champion of the desert wars, the "Desert Fox" whose blows no one could anticipate. For the first time, English soldiers began to see their comrades coming back from the battlefield with eyes that had lost all hope. But in the evening the music played from the battery-operated radios in the trenches and the rooms: *Bolero, The Wizard of Oz*, Beethoven, Strauss.. And there was laughter.

"I wish we had a radio here," Dimyan said to Magd al-Din.

Magd al-Din liked the idea, but said nothing.

"I'm fed up with sitting with the Indians and al-Safi al-Naim," added Dimyan.

Actually, it was Brika's absence that bothered him and gave him the crazy idea to go to the village and ask about her. Al-Safi al-Naim's English was quite good, and he conveyed to Dimyan and Magd al-Din the heated discussions that the Indians were having about independence. The Muslims from Peshawar and Lahore supported Mohammad Ali Jinnah, who called for Pakistan's secession from India. The Sikh, on the other hand, considered Jinnah a traitor and did not believe the Muslims should establish a separate state. The arguments raged back and forth, but eventually subsided. Dimyan kept wondering, "Shouldn't they get independence first, and then argue?" Magd al-Din did not comment. Once al-Safi al-Naim, who was siting alone with Magd al-Din and Dimyan, told them, "India will gain its independence before Egypt and Sudan."

"Why?" asked Dimyan.

"India is a large country," al-Safi al-Naim said in a confident tone. "It has about three hundred million people. True, they have many religions, but they also have Gandhi."

"The guy with the goat and the spindle?" exclaimed Dimyan.

"Exactly. He's the one who's fighting the English. He's fighting them without weapons. He tells the Indians to fast, and they all fast, to stop dealing with the English, and they all stop, not to trade with them, and they all refrain, to stand on one foot for a whole month, and they do. They are like one strong man. Gandhi doesn't have any army, but he has a whole people."

"In Egypt too, the English will leave after the war," Magd al-Din said after a short pause. "The people support Nahhas Pasha."

"But it was the English who brought Nahhas Pasha to power," said al-Safi al-Naim.

"True, the English brought him, but the people are against the English, and he will side with the people as usual," replied Magd al-Din quickly.

After a short while Corporal Bahadur Shand joined them. Now al-Safi al-Naim had to interpret for them and the corporal, or at least convey the gist of what was being said. It was in the afternoon with a hint of spring in the air, interrupted from time to time by a short quick *khamsin* storm, heralding the real *khamsin* that was due in a few days. Suddenly Dimyan told al-Safi al-Naim not to translate his words, as he was going to speak English himself. Magd al-Din looked at him in surprise, thinking that Dimyan was heading for a catastrophe. The young Indians who had come to perform the mid-afternoon prayer behind Magd al-Din joined them. Dimyan began speaking in 'English,' but he was actually wondering aloud in Arabic, "Are there really people who worship cows in India? If a cow crossed the street, do traffic and people actually come to a standstill?"

Dimyan was saying these words in such a way that every word was separated from the other and was pronounced very distinctly, also softening the pronunciation of his vowels. When he was done everyone was silent, but Magd al-Din and al-Safi al-Naim burst out laughing. As for Bahadur Shand, his face grew pale, because Dimyan was pointing at him while he spoke, so he thought he was making fun of him. The three young Indians smiled, and their eyes gleamed as they exchanged glances in polite bewilderment.

"You think when you emphasize the words and soften your vowels that you're speaking English? You're speaking Arabic, Dimyan," Magd al-Din said.

Dimyan came to, his eyes growing wider, then burst out laughing and told al-Safi, "Translate for the Indians that I was asking whether they will really get their independence after the war. Don't say anything about the cows."

Al-Safi al-Naim translated what Dimyan told him and Bahadur Shand nodded confidently and proudly. The three young Indians said, "Of course."

"Sudan also must gain independence from Egypt after the war," al-Safi said.

Dimyan and Magd al-Din looked at him in surprise. "Don't you mean independence from England?" corrected Magd al-Din.

"From both, Sheikh Magd."

"All my life I've known that England occupies Egypt and Sudan," said Dimyan. "This is the first I've heard of Egypt occupying Sudan. Perhaps it's because of this that we have too many monkeys in Egypt nowadays."

Al-Safi al-Naim growled, or rather made a gentle roaring sound.

"Egypt and Sudan have always been sisters," Magd al-Din said.

"Exactly, Sheikh Magd," said al-Safi al-Naim, "What sweet words!"

Everyone laughed with the exception of Bahadur. Even the young Indian soldiers laughed when they saw Magd al-Din, Dimyan, and al-Safi al-Naim laugh. Perhaps that was why Bahadur felt awkward and told al-Safi al-Naim to translate. Al-Safi thought a little, then said quickly, "Sudan, like India and Egypt, is under Britain's control."

Bahadur nodded and al-Safi added, "They will be independent as quickly as possible."

Once again Bahadur nodded gently, and the three other Indians smiled. Magd al-Din suggested that they stop talking politics. They looked at him in surprise and asked why. He hesitated before answering. Actually he did not know why he had made the suggestion or how to answer.

"Because we're in the desert," he finally said.

He never understood, even later on, what the desert had to do with not talking politics. But that's what happened. Everyone fell silent, unconvinced and a little bewildered, then they stared at the vast expanse of the desert.

Faint lights came from the trenches, and from the scattered rooms above ground. In the morning the officers and soldiers came out of their holes and went to the great sea. Spring had arrived and nothing remained of the winter except the bitter cold of the night. Summer uniforms came out anew, and the scorpions and insects came out of their holes. Every morning the soldiers went into the sea, naked except for their dirty underpants. The bodies of the soldiers were no longer white, they had turned bronze-colored. The new soldiers exposed their bodies to the sun as long as possible so they would look more awe-inspiring, as if they had had a long fighting experience. In truth, as Magd al-Din said of them, they were all poor children, "God's little children who have come down from heaven for this difficult test," in exactly the same way he had been driven out of his village, and perhaps just as easily.

"Do you still carry the snake in your pocket?" Dimyan asked Bahadur.

"It's with me all the time during the war."

He took the snake out of his jacket pocket, a small, thin, yellow snake with dark speckles that coiled itself on his fingers. He returned his hand to his pocket and took it out easily without the snake.

Al-Safi translated what Bahadur had said, to the effect that in India they domesticated large and small snakes, even cobras, that certain Indian sects worshipped snakes, cobras in particular, that

Indians in general were skillful at domesticating snakes and handling them, that the snake in his pocket had not come from India but that he had caught it in the desert the previous summer. At night he placed the snake in a tin can with some food, like chopped eggs and corned beef. The snake had not escaped, or even thought about it so far.

That was not the strangest part of what Bahadur had said. Al-Safi al-Naim translated and no one believed that the world could be so small. Bahadur said that his father also served in the cavalry in the British army in Egypt during the Great War. When the war ended there was a big revolution. Dimyan interrupted him to say that was in the days of Saad Pasha. Al-Safi did not translate what Dimyan said, and Bahadur continued to say that there was an uprising in a town named "De-rut." Bahadur paused to look at the faces of his listeners and Dimyan told him, "You probably mean Dayrut." Bahadur continued to say that its name was "De-rut." No one commented, and he added that in a village near De-rut there was a big rebellion attacking the British forces, so the English sent the Indian Sikh cavalry to the village. "My father was among them, and their commanding officer was an Englishman. He ordered his men to rape the women of the village before the eyes of their men, who had been bound with ropes."

Magd al-Din closed his eyes in pain. Dimyan looked shocked, his lips trembled, and he said nothing. Bahadur smiled and added that his father had told him how the women ran and threw themselves into the Nile, preferring death by drowning to rape. "My father lived in pain because he had done that, and especially because he had seen the English rape Indian women also." Bahadur fell silent and so did everyone, until Magd al-Din said calmly, "That's a strange story; we didn't hear of it during the revolution. We took part in the revolution. We attacked the English and sabotaged the railroad, but we never heard that any force from any army raped the women of any village—no English army or Indian army."

The young Indians had been smiling at first, but now were bowing their heads, looking at the ground.

"I've seen the Indians in Sudan walking arrogantly as peacocks," said al-Safi al-Naim, "as if they owned the earth with everything on it. But I didn't see them beat anybody or rape any woman."

Bahadur did not understand what al-Safi said and naturally the latter did not translate it.

"I'm from Dayrut and I know the story," Dimyan joined the conversation. "I've heard it—it's a true story."

"They also killed the men," said Bahadur loudly.

"The whole village was eradicated without a trace," added Dimyan. "I remember that it was called Kom Gahannam, 'Hell Hill.' The men who survived disappeared, dispersed all over the country. Most of them died of shame."

Everyone fell silent. There was a wide range of reaction, sorrow on al-Safi's part, sadness in Magd al-Din's case, despair in Dimyan's, and awe in the case of the young Indians.

"In many countries foreigners have raped the women," said Magd al-Din.

"In Egypt there are many villages that bear that out. Rosetta by the English, and in the deep south there are blond girls of Mamluk origin," Dimyan said nonchalantly.

Al-Safi al-Naim said, "Thank God you can't find a single white man in Sudan. Our women are still black, and giving birth to black babies. Blackness has protected our women against rape."

He wanted to make light of what Bahadur had said. He realized that Magd al-Din and Dimyan, or at least one of them, would explode. It was Dimyan who spoke.

"But Mr. Bahadur, if you look all over Egypt for any trace of anyone Indian, you would find none."

He fell silent and Bahadur waited for al-Safi to translate. Al-Safi hesitated, but Dimyan told him to go ahead.

"You mean I'm a liar?" Bahadur asked.

"No. You're telling the truth. It's your father and the Sikh cavalry that are liars. They didn't do anything. On the contrary, it was the Egyptians who mounted them."

Magd al-Din could not laugh, nor could al-Safi al-Naim, whose face turned ashen with fear. He stopped playing his role as interpreter, but Bahadur ordered him to translate at once.

Actually al-Safi liked what Dimyan had said; he got some satisfaction out of it. After all, he was an Arab like Dimyan and Magd al-Din, and they all came from the Nile valley. That was why he translated precisely and slowly what Dimyan had said. The dark of the twilight was descending upon the desert as the night breeze was stirring. The moment al-Safi finished the translation, Bahadur's hand was on his revolver. He stood up, hurling curses in Hindi at Dimyan, who had jumped up to flee the moment Bahadur got up. Shots rang out in the air behind Dimyan, but he was not hit. The dark helped him escape. Bahadur stood for a few moments fuming with rage, then roared in Hindi at the young soldiers and they all left. He looked askance as al-Safi and Magd al-Din, who in turn got up and moved away. As soon as they were at a safe distance they burst out in jubilant laughter.

What Dimyan did could have cost him his life. How easy it would have been for a bullet from Bahadur's revolver to hit him! Shooting was going on all day long, trying out new arms, killing scorpions, snakes, and desert rats, or hunting foxes. Sometimes rifles went off, hunting birds that appeared suddenly in the sky. In addition to the sounds of gunshots were the noises made by the planes dashing off from time to time to bomb Alexandria or to return to their airfields in Tripoli and Benghazi, with anti-aircraft guns following them, going and coming. A bullet shot by an angry Indian would not make anyone pause. Who would pause at the killing of a worker at a small, almost deserted crossing in a tiny, little-known village that no one had ever heard of before? That was what Magd al-Din and Dimyan spoke about until midnight. Dimyan asked Mari Girgis to protect him from the wretched Indian Sikh and he pledged that if he did that he would himself burn frankincense at the martyr's church in Ghayt al-Aynab, would light seven candles, and would stay for a week in the service of the church. He fell asleep only after he felt that Mari Girgis would grant him his request.

In the morning Magd al-Din asked him not to leave the house until he had seen Bahadur and tried to calm him down. At noon al-Safi al-Naim came to Magd al-Din in the wooden kiosk next to the crossing. He was smiling, and as soon as he got close to Magd al-Din he burst out laughing. He said that Bahadur had left with a battalion early in the morning to join an Indian division at the border where fierce fighting was taking place. Magd al-Din smiled in relief and felt his body sharing in his joy, so he could not stay put. He left al-Safi al-Naim and hurried to Dimyan to give him the good news. Dimyan was so overjoyed that he felt he was being lifted from the ground, but he stood scrutinising Magd al-Din. Had the love between him and the martyr grown so much that he would never let him down? He let two tears drop, and went out with Magd al-Din, ecstatic at seeing the desert—vast, white, beautiful, and brilliant—with a sky so purely blue, like a faraway sea, and the world expansive and without end.

At night several days later, as they both lay on their government-issue mattresses on the floor in a corner of the room, Dimyan said, "I'm longing for Alexandria, Sheikh Magd."

In the morning, Dimyan had seen the sheep coming from a distance, with the little boy strolling in their midst and Brika walking behind them. She looked small, but as usual he thought that she would grow as she got closer. His heart started pounding. There she was, appearing after a long absence. He had thought seriously yesterday and the day before of going to her village himself. He even walked a long way south, but when he could see nothing in front of him except vast dunes in every direction, he feared getting lost. Quickly he returned, retracing his steps, and when the railway station loomed in the distance, he took a deep breath and thanked Jesus Christ, the Virgin, and Mari Girgis and all the martyrs and saints he could think of. He had almost forgotten that he had a pledge to fulfill. It was now time for him to forget Brika and to go to Alexandria to fulfill his pledge.

Yet Brika would not let go of him, appearing just at the time that he had decided to get used to forgetting her. But she was not getting bigger as she got closer. His heart kept pounding even more. When she got closer still, he realized that it was not Brika, and the gleam in his eye faded, as did the joy in his heart. He had thought of running to the house to bring as many of the gifts he used to give to Brika as he could. But he forgot about that. He saw Hilal from the door of his room, and he thought he was the rival he did not know, come out to see him and gloat at his misery. Magd al-Din was at home and Dimyan missed him. He wished he could rest his head on his chest like a little child.

As soon as the girl stopped with the sheep and her brother behind the station, he approached her and asked her about Brika. Laughing she said, "You're Dimyan!"

"Who told you?"

"Brika. She loves you, and she asked me to give you greetings."

This girl, who could not be more than ten years old, was talking with the matter-of-factness of an experienced female. What kind of people are these Bedouin, and what is the secret of their being so candid and straightforward?

"Where's Brika?"

"She made a jlasa and got married to my cousin, a horseman who reads and writes and has a good head on his shoulders."

He left her and walked to his house from which he brought as many gifts as he could.

"For me?" she asked.

"For you and Brika," he said.

He went home and asked Magd al-Din to go to work in his stead. He lay down facing the wall, finding the room to be completely empty. After reaching forty a man yearned to be young again. He should have realized that and gotten over it in peace. Besides, could he have counted on this wretched love to succeed? Brika was a Muslim, and he a Christian. Even if Brika was Christian he still could not divorce his wife. Every way he looked at it, it was doomed to fail. He should not have laid his heart open. But that was what happened, anyway. The only thing he could do was to fulfill his pledge to his shepherd and comrade, Girgis the Martyr.

In the evening he asked Magd al-Din, "What happens if I go to Alexandria and don't come back? Would anyone ask about me? I don't think so. And you too, you can come with me. Us being here doesn't make any sense. Mr. Spike no longer asks about us. The inspector who visits us every month hasn't come in two months. The trains are few and far between. Hilal or any Indian, African, Australian, New Zealander, Egyptian, or English soldier can handle the crossing. Us being here is meaningless, it's absurd, amid all these soldiers from all over the world."

Magd al-Din could not get into the discussion with him. He was not used to Dimyan having this tone of despair. Something must have gone wrong in Dimyan's mind, nothing less. But Magd al-Din started to think about their strange situation here and about his own situation, his being so late in seeing his son Shawqi, far away in the village. This was too much for a human to bear. But he said calmly, "You go, Dimyan, and don't worry about it. I'll wait for you until you come back."

You won't find a new country or a new sea.
The city will pursue you
You will walk the same streets . . .
There is no ship for you, there is no road.

Constantine Cavafy

26

Dimyan arrived in Alexandria on the second of April. On that same day the Jewish Agency and the General Council for the Jews of Palestine issued an appeal. It called on Jewish men and women to volunteer in the Jewish units working with the British army in the Middle East, since there was a dire need for a large number of volunteers of both sexes to serve in the auxiliary regional force. The appeal stated that the first step was to recruit childless unmarried persons between twenty and thirty years of age. "Let the response of the Jews of Palestine be worthy of our great task and the gravity of the situation," read the statement issued by the council. At the same time, Dr. Ali Ibrahim, chairman of the Society to Save Homeless Children, was issuing an appeal to the country to come to the aid of its children. The newspapers were filled with stories about Hitler's connection with the month of April. He was born on the twentieth of April, 1889. On the seventh of April, 1939, he allowed Mussolini to invade Albania. On the twenty-eighth of the same month and year, Hitler delivered his famous speech in which he denounced the Anglo-German naval treaty of 1935. On the ninth of April, 1940, Hitler's armed forces invaded Denmark, and on the sixteenth of April, 1941, he attacked Yugoslavia and Greece. The newspapers wondered what Hitler was planning for April of this year. Was he

going to cross the Caucasus to Iran and Iraq or penetrate Turkey
to Iraq and the Levant?

On the fifth of April, the Cathedral of Saint Mark celebrated
Easter by holding an elaborate mass that began with a prayer
imploring God to bestow his mercy on the world. In al-Alamein,
prayer services were held and some priests appeared among the
troops during the day, but at night there were parties at which
beautiful ATS women sang and danced with the soldiers. Two
days earlier, Alexandria had been subjected to a heavy air raid, and
rescue operations were still going on. The government hospital
was filled with casualties. Dimyan's family moved out of the house
to live in the church courtyard. It was there that Dimyan met
Khawaga Dimitri, who looked miserable and oblivious. He
silently shook his hand. As usual, many pashas visited Alexandria
in the company of the governor to comfort the victims. The
casualties of that air raid were fifty-two dead and eighty wounded,
each of whom was given two Egyptian pounds in temporary aid.
On the seventh of April, Alexandria suffered an even worse air
raid. The prime minister, Nahhas Pasha, visited Alexandria after
delivering a speech on the Egyptian Broadcasting Service in which
he said, "Dear Alexandrians, I address you with a heavy heart for
what you have suffered. Alexandrians, I am fully confident that
you will withstand this ordeal with the patience I have known you
to have. You have given the whole of Egypt the most splendid
example and proved yourselves most capable of withstanding
catastrophes. It is no wonder that your city has become the object
of admiration, appreciation, and respect."

Meanwhile the prime minister signed a decree abolishing
prostitution, except in capitals of provinces and governorates as of
May, and banning the establishment of new brothels immediately.
Nahhas Pasha played host to about three hundred convalescing
soldiers from Pakistan, New Zealand, and South Africa, who spent
the day enjoying pleasure cruises and recreation in the parks. The
air raids on Alexandria continued to intensify, so the civil defense
distributed leaflets advising the public to remain calm during the
raids, to go to the nearest shelter, not to look at the sky or watch
the anti-aircraft artillery, to avoid crowding, to stop running,
because no matter how fast, no human can outrun a plane. It said

it was best to prostrate oneself on the ground if one could not find a nearby place with a roof, and to move away from glass surfaces and if in a car, to leave the vehicle, turn off its lights, and park it on the side of the road. Dimyan kept one of the leaflets and memorized it. He thought whoever wrote it was mocking him and people like him. He began to run during the raids to see if he was faster than airplanes or bombs and reached a conclusion that was at variance with the instructions, as he generally was able to move from one side of the street to the other before a bomb hit the ground. In reality bombs never hit the ground, because they usually fell somewhere else, and he could only hear their impact after he had reached the sidewalk. Whenever there was a raid, Dimyan would leave his family at the church, which he had served longer than he had pledged, and go out to watch the people to see for himself whether they really headed for the shelters and the entrances of houses as they used to, before he was transplanted to al-Alamein, or whether they no longer bothered to do anything. He saw that they did not care any more. Those who had stayed in the city no longer feared for their lives.

Dimyan started walking aimlessly from Ghayt al-Aynab to Karmuz to Khedive Street to the Alexandria station. Sometimes he would walk on Muharram Bey Street and at other times he would go to Raml Station, crossing Nabi Danyal Street and from there, on the coastal road, to Ras al-Tin palace. Then he would go back, oblivious to Alexandria's breeze, the clear light of the day, or the blue sea and faraway sky. There was more emptiness around him than at any other time. He did not venture out late at night and so did not run into the drunkards. He must have seen foreign soldiers, but he was not aware of their presence. The cafés of Manshiya were still filled with merchants, brokers, and strangers, but he saw nothing and did not know why he went on these mysterious walks. He realized that he only made a point of doing this after each raid, and there were many raids. He became like a madman who could see only the destroyed houses and not the houses that had been spared, craters where the bombs had fallen and not the smooth pavement, smell only the smoke of burned flesh and wood and not the fresh breeze coming from the sea. He thought to himself, this was not the city that he knew; it was more like a movie reel. For quite some time he had not been to the cinema and had not seen any new Charlie Chaplin films. He discovered that he was barefoot once again, as he used to be. He did not wear shoes at the church and would go around there all day serving those who had taken refuge in it, offering them food and water, cleaning the walks, the alabaster columns, and the mirrors, and adoringly dusting the huge icon of Mari Girgis. He remembered seeing him from the middle of the fire but did not believe it. He remembered Magd al-Din, who did not believe his vision either. He wanted to go back to his friend, but he also wanted to stay in the city, which had become so large now that so many of its inhabitants had left, and so old now that so many of its buildings had been destroyed. There were still big crowds around the railway station, and fear began to find its way to his heart. Could the day come when there would be no one but him in this city that he no longer recognized?

He did not have any desire for his wife. Every time he looked at her he thought, how could she live after him? He would realize that this meant he would die and, shaking, he would think how wretched the world would be without him. Could people really continue to live after he had died? Kyrie eleison. How he needed Magd al-Din to give him confidence in longevity!

Some Junkers bombers were shot down over the city. Hamidu was released from detention with several others, and he wrote on the wall of the house, "Either take me for good or let me be forever." The few passers-by knew what he meant and laughed. The city was showered with charitable donations from Salvatore Cicurel and Their Royal Highnesses the Princesses and Queen Nazli. Karmuz remained the target for German air raids, but the neighborhood of the martyrs insisted on remaining in its historic location. Even German Junkers and Heinkel and Italian Savoia bombers were being shot down over it. The spring holiday of Shamm al-Nasim, however, was observed in a normal manner. People went out to Nuzha and the waterfall gardens. The Mahmudiya canal was filled with colorful feluccas adorned with flags, on which boys and girls danced and sang. Alexandrians went out to the beaches unconcerned by the raids. It was a mild day, and the sea, with its blue and white water, was calm. Many people from

Karmuz converged on the Anfushi beach, the women carrying trays filled with fish. They went down into the sea with all their clothes on. The boys and girls engaged in horseplay as usual. In Manshiya, however, the children could not go into the sea, as the eastern harbor was now filled with British battleships. In Raml Station people sat around the statue of Saad Zaghloul on the grass of the small garden and began calmly to eat their fisikh, the traditional salted mullet and sardines, without a thought in the world. That day, fifty carloads arrived from Cairo to spend the day on the beaches of Stanley, Glymenopoulo, and Miami. The English ATS women and their friends went into the sea in their bathing suits at the Mustafa Kamil beach. Many people spent the day at the zoo and were very generous in feeding the animals. In the evening, they all went back home exhausted, filling the streetcars, horse-drawn carriages, and carts of all kinds. There was silence everywhere, as their voices had grown hoarse from shouting and singing all day long. When the air-raid siren sounded, no one bothered to move. The cars stopped, but most people were fast asleep. The raid did not last for a long time. One plane was shot down over the city.

A few days after Shamm al-Nasim, a royal decree was issued appointing Abd al-Khaliq Hassuna Bey governor of Alexandria. He succeeded Muhammad Husayn Pasha, who had requested to retire. Another royal decree was issued placing the beautiful Ras al-Tin palace at the disposal of the British embassy to use as a military hospital for the duration of the war. One of the most important initiatives undertaken by the new governor was putting an end to the use of adulterated flour in bread. The archaeological discovery of the temple of the god Apis in Kom al-Shuqafa was deemed auspicious for the new governor. Dimyan was walking in front of Pompey's Pillar when he saw a crowd of notables and learned the story of the archaeological find and was amazed at the mysteries of this land. The month of April ended with a heavy air raid that killed sixty persons and wounded more than a hundred. Four Axis bombers were shot down. As usual, the wounded were taken to the area hospitals, and those who had lost their homes were taken to shelters in Damanhur and Kafr al-Dawwan, since Alexandria could not provide shelter any more. In this raid the Jewish synagogue on Nabi Danyal Street was destroyed. It had been built in 1870, and renovated only ten years before to accommodate five hundred people. It was said that the synagogue had cost ten thousand Egyptian pounds, at a time when one Egyptian pound could buy two feddans of land. There was a rumor that the German planes had been looking for the synagogue for quite some time, and when they found it they destroyed it, and that explained why the raids stopped for a week afterwards. But when they resumed after a week, they went even deeper into the Lower Egyptian provinces, a fact that resulted in food supplies, especially wheat, being cut off from Alexandria. But the new governor soon solved the problem. It was said that the people were eating more because of anxiety and fear. An order was issued by the commander in chief of the British army in Cairo, General Sir Claude Auchinleck, to all senior officers in the general Middle East command, that there was a real danger that the name 'Rommel' had become a bogeyman dreaded by the forces, that his name had become the subject of many endless discussions, and that no matter how capable and efficient he was, he was not a supernatural man. "Even if that were true, it is not proper for our forces to describe him as such. Therefore," the commander in chief added, "you should do your utmost to erase this idea of Rommel. He is no more than an ordinary German commander. Therefore his name should not be used when referring to the enemy in the Western Desert. Instead, we should say 'the Germans' or 'the Axis forces' or 'the enemy,' and not 'Rommel.' I ask of you that you make sure that this order is carried out and that junior officers are instructed to do the same. The matter is of the utmost psychological importance."

Charitable donations for Alexandria continued, and several new donors joined the effort. They included Prince Umar Tusun, Prince Yusuf Kamal, Princess Samiha Hasan, and Salim and Samaan Sidnawi. Once again people complained about adulterated flour and were told that solving the problem required more time. Civil defense distributed helmets to volunteers, and Ghaffara got one since he had joined the volunteers, using his cart to transport the wounded. He was late with some wounded who were bleeding, so they died, and he was relieved of that duty. His cart was now set aside for transporting the dead. So he wrote on one side, 'The Chariot of Divine Mercy.' On the other side-panel, which he had attached to it, he wrote in a very clear hand verses from the Quran and sayings about death such as, "The living should take precedence over the dead," and also "God might give you a reprieve, but he never forgets you."

On the fifth of May, Coronation Day was celebrated, as it was every year throughout the country. Mass was given in the churches and prayers performed in mosques, literary festivals were held, music played in the streets, and free restaurants opened for the people. Cinema Olympia showed *I Love Sin*, starring Tahiya Kariyuka and Husayn Sidqi. Local communities began to combat barefootedness by distributing twenty-five thousand pairs of shoes. The ministry of social affairs distributed eight thousand pairs of shoes to the peasants in the villages, which they sold in the nearest town for twenty-five piasters a pair. The British military governor banned all lights at night, even in celebration of Coronation Day. Army and police bands toured the streets and the parks playing music. Alexandria was appalled by a horrendous murder that took place after a fierce air raid in which thirty persons were killed. Used to air raids by now, people forgot about the raid and talked about the murder: the body of a woman was discovered in a garbage bin next to the fence of Nuzha Gardens. The corpse was identified as that of Fathiya Gab Allah, about twenty years old. People stopped going to Nuzha, especially in the late afternoon and at sunset. The romantic lovers stopped going during the day, as did the pleasure seekers who used to go at night, to take advantage of the pitch dark on the tree-lined road adjacent to the garden. Everyone knew that plainclothes policemen were now all over the place. For some reason, Dimyan got up early in the morning, walked to Ban Street, crossed it and the two streets south of it, and arrived at the railroad wall. From the spot where the wall had given way the first day he went to work, he crossed it, as he always did, and walked over to the post. When he did not find the man who used to sit at the Raven, he felt apprehensive but kept on walking. As soon as he went into the post, his co-workers, who were drinking tea, leapt to their feet in disbelief, and one after another embraced him. Usta Ghibriyal shook his hand with a broader smile this time. He sat down with them. Not finding Hamza there, he realized that the man had not come back. He did not see Shahin either, so he asked about him and was told that his son Rushdi had left Alexandria to walk all the way to Upper Egypt in search of his beloved, Camilla, and that the man was sick at home, waiting for his son to return. Dimyan went afterwards to Shahin. The man's eyes were bloodshot from crying. He sat a long time with Dimyan, who told him that he had learned at the church that Camilla had entered the convent—that there she would be all right and would forget. If it did happen that Rushdi met her, he would recover from his love for her, because he would find that she had recovered.

On the twenty-eighth of May, Ibrahim Ata, who had killed the woman found in the garbage bin at Nuzha—who turned out to have been a dancer—was arrested. Romantic and 'practical' lovers started going back to Nuzha in the daytime and by night. Ration cards were distributed to the people to counter merchants' price-gouging. A new offensive by the Axis forces began after Rommel received massive reinforcements. It became clear that a major battle was in the offing. Major General Ritchie sent a message to the Eighth Army to raise its morale, reminding the troops that they were defending freedom and democracy. Auchinleck sent a similar message. A major battle took place in Bir Hakim in which the French acquitted themselves valiantly. German prisoners of war began to arrive in Alexandria. But the Germans were able to capture Bir Hakim, from which the Allies and the Free French, who fought with unparalleled courage, withdrew. Communists in Europe clamored for opening another front against Germany to alleviate the situation in the Soviet Union, and an agreement to that effect was reached by Russia, England, and the United States: it would be a front not in Europe but here in the Western Desert. That was Churchill's vision: to expel the Axis armies from Africa, then invade Italy from the south and get rid of Mussolini, leaving Hitler isolated. From there, the French front would be breached and the English

Channel crossed. But the Germans were advancing in the desert
and deploying millions in Russia.

The French left Bir Hakim after twenty-six days of fighting,
their morale still high. The troops of the Eighth Army withdrew
from Adm and Sidi Rizq. The fighting moved to the south and
west of Tobruk. Rommel bypassed Tobruk, leaving it behind, and
made a dash for the Egyptian border.

By June first, the British Grant, Crusader, and Stuart tanks
stood here and there on the hot sand. General Ritchie also stood,
powerless, not knowing where Rommel would strike. Rommel's
winning card was the eighty-eight-millimeter anti-tank guns,
which he used by baiting the British tanks to a killing field, then
letting those mighty guns loose on them from every direction,
blowing them up. Then the Panzer tanks finished off the rest.

At dawn on the twentieth of June, the German bombers
attacked Tobruk so intensely that the barbed wire was blown to
smithereens and the Indian division's post was leveled. Waves of
planes bombed the defensive posts continuously. Then the
German armored offensive began, with the Twenty-First Panzer
Division preceded by the artillery. Another division overran the
harbor, and a third one crushed the British naval forces there.

Forty thousand men stayed in the garrison to fight. German
engineers built a bridge over the deep anti-tank trenches, and after
the bombers had softened up the defenses, Panzer convoys headed
for the garrison, supported by mechanized infantry units.

It was 8:30 in the morning as Rommel followed the battle,
taking delighted pride in his men. The German engineers opened
several breaches in the minefields. Another wave of German planes
came, and British resistance in the front lines was crushed. The big
surrender had begun, and the world shook, and Alexandria shook
even more. Everyone realized that Rommel was coming to the
Delta. At the end of the battle Rommel himself led a light mobile
armored group. He personally took part in removing 'Satan's
eggs,' or landmines, from the anti-tank trenches.

The British head of the garrison sent a cable to Cairo that it
was no use, then he and thirty-three thousand soldiers surrendered
and were shipped to Italy. A thousand armored vehicles, four
hundred guns, and other British equipment were added to

Rommel's arsenal. Rommel gave a speech thanking his men and asking them to move toward the ultimate goal, Egypt. Hikmat Fahmi performed the Tobruk dance at the Kit Kat nightclub, where the patrons were singing a song popular in Europe at the time, "The sun had a date with the moon, but the moon hasn't shown up." To the delight of Johannes Eppler and his colleague Sandy, news of the fall of Tobruk broke. The Egyptians requested that Hikmat Fahmi do the Tobruk dance, not knowing that she was a spy for the Germans.

Thus Rommel reached the peak of his glory. He wrote to his wife, "Dear Lu, it was a magnificent battle. Tobruk! I must sleep after all this effort. I think about you a lot. The fall of Tobruk is the crowning point of our victories in the desert." At the same time the reputation of the British army was greatly diminished, since Singapore also fell to the Japanese, and a force, eighty thousand strong, also surrendered. Churchill was in America visiting Roosevelt, who showed tactfulness by asking Churchill what the United States could do. So he requested large numbers of the new Sherman tanks. Immediately ships carrying three hundred tanks were dispatched to the Suez canal.

Dimyan stayed a long time in Alexandria. He loved to serve the church and those who had taken refuge from the raids and the difficulties of life in it. Stories were told about the young saint performing miracles in Asyut, how a girl who had entered the convent only a few months earlier was now healing people of all satanic diseases by a touch of the cross or her hand on the head. She was often seen in the convent talking to herself or to beings that no one could see and always praying and fasting, but the light never left her face. People began to come from the neighboring villages to see her, bringing their children who suffered from smallpox or intestinal or chest problems. They themselves would also come, and she would cure them of asthma, fever, heart disease, and epilepsy. Barren village wives also went to her. There were lines around the convent. The young saint went out two hours in mid-morning and two hours in the afternoon, and people fought each other to get near her. Rushdi was still walking against the current of the river, eating whatever vegetable he came across in the fields—eggplant, tomatoes, cucumbers or whatever people who had pity on him would give him. It became known that there was a crazy young man walking against the current and whenever he saw a corpse in the water he screamed to summon the people of the village, not stopping until they had taken the body out of the water. Every time that happened, his eyes would grow wider and he could not stay still until he had found out all he could about the dead person's particulars of age, sex, and shape. He never came across Camilla, so he continued his journey to the south. His journey had started four months earlier, and he was getting very close to Asyut. He was starting to hear about the young woman who had entered the convent a year earlier, and had already become a saint, performing miracles that surpassed those of Saint Theresa. His eyes grew wider and his tears flowed when he heard the name Camilla. That also happened to Dimyan when news of the saint reached Alexandria. He kept looking for Khawaga Dimitri but could not find him at the church and learned that he too had fled with his family to Asyut. Dimyan thought to himself, could he have become a saint? His love story with Brika had ended in failure, and Mari Girgis had saved him from certain death more than once. He was loving the church and working in it, and serving its people and visitors, and choosing the most menial jobs and doing them with joy. But his love story with Brika was nothing but the whim of a man over forty, as Magd al-Din said. Why did that whim not happen with a Christian woman? Why was the woman in question a Muslim? It must be that Mari Girgis did not want him to commit any sin. A Muslim woman meant that it was a hopeless case. That protected him from sinning, but it also meant that he had to crush his heart, his mind, and all his senses. What injustice!

Rushdi walked fast. He knew that she saw him, whether she was asleep or awake. She liked to clean the room in the convent in which the Virgin Mary had stayed with her child. The ancient Egyptians had hollowed out the cavern, a hundred meters above the fields, to take refuge in at the time of the flood. The Virgin and her son and Joseph the carpenter had stayed there during their flight into Egypt. The cavern became a church of the Virgin and a convent visited by people. Houses for nuns were built around it. Camilla liked to clean the Virgin's room. One night she saw the light, the light that no one could imagine, a light that had the color of honey, that was as pleasant as a cool breeze on a scorchingly hot day, and had the taste of the purest water. She saw it emanating in the room, small as a candle at first, then growing, its brilliance increasing, lighting the whole room, then spilling out to light the whole cavern, which, despite its thin candles, looked as though it were bathed in sunlight. Then one corner's gleaming stood out. It was the Virgin Mary appearing in the form of light everywhere. Camilla saw her pass in front of her, smiling her ever-present smile, and felt her anointing her hair with a sweet fragrance. She told Father Mikhail that the Virgin had appeared to her and now she was seeing her all the time. She had received the blessing of eternal holiness. She saw Rushdi walking exactly as magicians used to see what was happening in a magic crystal ball. She was never afraid for him. She was certain that he would reach her safely. She was just waiting for him and praying to the Virgin to preserve him from any harm. It was he who had imparted this tenderness in her, awakened her transparent soul, and brought out this angelic nature in her. He deserved her prayers to the Virgin to preserve him. She knew he would arrive. He kept walking. The young saint was his beloved, his heart told him that with every beat. She had not been killed. She was not dead. His own spirit grew stronger, his languid eyes lit up, and his feet carried him down to the river to bathe more than once. He would not meet Camilla in his present condition, barefoot, with tattered clothes and a dusty face and hair. He realized that he had seen in the countryside a world more brilliant and verdant than the one he had left behind. The land was green, the sun kind, and the people meek and sweet, walking peacefully, the children playing in the streams. True, the peasants looked poor and neglected, with pale faces and emaciated bodies, but they appeared content. People in the fields, next to the waterwheels, under the old acacia, oak, and sycamore trees appeared happy and serene. The birds flew freely in the sky, then calmly came down to feed on grains or insects, then soared back up, unfettered by anything. He tried working in the fields. People knew that he stayed in a village no more than a day or two then disappeared without warning. People were mystified about him but said he was a blessed young man. He worked in silence and ate and drank in silence, but in reality he was in a trance, like that which prophets experience at the time of revelation. The spring of poetry in him had welled up, and he found himself reciting his own poetry mixed with that of French poets and others whose poetry he loved. The joy and élan of creation appeared in his eyes. What beautiful pain had awakened the poet from his deep sleep? He was certain that he had been saved for a mission. He would carry the burden of knowledge off the people's shoulders and would give them joy with his chants. Those intoxicating pains! But he also saw the peasants humiliated and spurned, beaten by the masters of the land. He saw them sharing the animals' sleeping quarters, eating the lowliest of food and drinking, like animals, directly from irrigation canals. But they praised the Lord, in any case. He realized the Egyptians' secret power: they left the unjust ruler to the Just Ruler, who never failed them no matter how long they had to endure. How the Egyptians have survived from the ancient past to this day! What a miracle this people represent, enduring injustice more than rebelling against it. As he walked further he got closer to Asyut, his joy increasing, and he felt his body shaking with a mysterious ecstasy. Was it the poetry or the promised meeting with her? It did not make any difference; both poetry and the meeting represented a new birth of the spirit. He would only see her, then go back, now that she, like him, had penetrated the unseen, had become as tender as he and had not died, just as he was alive. He was a poet and she, a saint. Both had attained prophethood.

He saved the price of clean clothes and a pair of shoes from his occasional jobs. The first thing he did in Asyut was to go to an inexpensive hotel to bathe and sleep after shaving his beard. He slept for a long time, and when he got up he looked at himself in the mirror. What a beautiful face and what anguish were reflected! He started crying for what he had done to himself and for what love had done to him. He thought of going back, his heart having been reassured that she was alive. But he also needed to see her. He walked leisurely in Asyut's hot streets, then went back and slept. He had decided to go in the morning to the convent, which he had located that day.

On the way he thought of going back and contenting himself
with the changes they had both undergone. But he was strong
enough to go and see her without suffering a relapse or coming
unraveled. He told himself that she too must have become strong.
Both were somewhere between the divine and the human: he was
a poet; she, a saint.

He saw the great crowd of men and women, sick, bereaved,
and afflicted, in love and in life, in soul and in body on the stretch
of land between the mountain and the valley, all the way to the
village of Drunga. He stood at a distance until shortly before her
departure. He was penetrated by the halo around her head and
face, by the movement of her little lips that spoke mysterious
words that no one heard, by her white habit, by her body that was
as fragile as a sparrow's. Then he approached. The moment that
had seemed as distant as Judgment Day finally came. She raised her
face to him. The small silver cross shook in her delicate hand. Her
lips quivered without words. His smell filled her nostrils and she
could scarcely stand, and when he was directly in front of her she
almost collapsed, but she collected herself and let the tears flow
down her cheeks in front of him, to the amazement of the
assembled sick, bereaved, and afflicted. 'Rushdi' was the word that
he had longed to hear.

"I am cured," he said.

"I knew it. I saw you walking through the fields. I am also
cured," she said.

"I will go to France after the war. God has given me the gift of
poetry," he said.

"And I will not leave the convent. God has given me the gift of
helping others. Love is the Lord's path, Rushdi."

They both fell silent. His tears also flowed.

"Will you bless me?"

She nodded and he knelt. She placed her hand on his head and
murmured an incantation, then took his hand to raise him to his
feet, and in front of everyone she stood on tiptoe and kissed him
on the forehead and said, "Good-bye, my love."

He made his way back through the crowd, and she went back
to the convent and did not finish her blessings that day. She
stayed inside for three days, during which time the people slept

outside the convent until she came out again, preceded by the light of her face.

His Holiness, Thrice-Blessed Abba Yuannis, patriarch of the Orthodox Copts and pope of St. Mark's mission, had died in Alexandria, and the Most Venerable Abba Usab, archbishop of Girga, was elected to succeed him by the Public Church Council. Saint Mark's Cathedral opened its doors for the people to view the body of the departed patriarch before he was buried. Dimyan went and came out in a daze—why do people die? It was the first time that he asked himself that question. He was afraid that the all-powerful faith, which had possessed his heart in the previous months, had dissipated in the desert and was no longer enough. But he did not stop asking himself. At night, as he slept in the church courtyard on a mat among his family and other poor families, he once again had a vision of Mari Girgis on his horse, surrounded by fire on all sides, unable to extricate himself from it.

The famous new American Grant and Sherman tanks were now arriving at the Suez harbor and pouring into Alexandria and then to the desert as the British forces were retreating before Rommel to the Egyptian border, then Sallum and Sidi Barrani. The Eighth Army stopped at Marsa Matruh, waiting for the battle. It did not have to wait long. The Axis forces pursued the army, and it withdrew from Marsa Matruh, which was taken by Rommel as the Allies continued to retreat. At Daba there were battles with cold steel in which the soldiers from New Zealand acquitted themselves brilliantly, showing great courage. But who could stop the legendary Rommel, whose very name inspired fear in the hearts of his enemies and was enough by itself to win the war? al-Alamein was the spot where retreating and advancing armies had to stop. It was a bottleneck not more than twenty-five miles wide from the sea to the Qattara depression. It was far from the bases of the Axis forces in Libya. Rommel needed to rest there for some time. For the Allies, it was the best defense area since it was close to their supply lines and because it was too narrow for the kind of military operation that Rommel was so good at. Here he would have to attack directly. There was no room for maneuver.

❖

Rommel! Rommel! Rommel! The name was carried by the wind and repeated by the people associating it with power, cunning, genius, and miracles. Rommel could not be defeated, could not be killed. The armored vehicle in which he was riding exploded as soon as he left it. Shells poured on the trench that his soldiers had left only a short while earlier. An English commando force landed on the Libyan coast from its submarine and reached his headquarters, but he was not there; he was attending a friend's wedding. The commandos were taken prisoner after a battle during which some of them were killed. His car stalled in the desert so he, accompanied by his staff, accidentally entered a British camp that had a field hospital. He ordered the commander of the hospital and the doctors to stand in front of him and behaved as if he had occupied the place. He asked them if there was anything he could get for them after getting the land he had occupied under control and promised to comply with their requests. After he left, they realized that they had been tricked and that the prize catch had gotten away.

Panic increased in the country and large numbers of Jews left, and their property was sold at ridiculously low prices. The Alexandrians heard the racket of guns at al-Alamein, and confusion reigned in the city. The foreign consulates began to burn their documents, as did the embassies in Cairo. The British embassy thought of evacuating five hundred ATS women to Luxor on the grounds that such a delightful bounty should not be left for the Germans. There was a strong rumor that the English had asked the Egyptian government to flood the Delta in case the Germans occupied Alexandria so that the land would turn into a sea of mud in which the German armored vehicles would be stuck. The people's resentment of the English grew.

For their part, the English insisted that it was necessary to evacuate the popular singers Umm Kulthum and Muhammad Abd al-Wahhab, voluntarily or involuntarily, from Cairo so German propaganda could not exploit their songs.

People mobbed the banks to withdraw their money. They were gripped with fear and stayed at home, venturing out only when necessary and in groups because of news of the arrival of stray animals—lions, tigers, wolves, foxes, and monkeys—from the desert, driven into the city by the war. And indeed people found that several monkeys had climbed some trees, so they chased them with stones and killed them. At night dogs turned into foxes and wolves that everyone fled from. As for the lions and tigers, no one saw them. There was news, however, of an old lion that appeared in the Mina al-Basal neighborhood, went to sleep on the streetcar tracks, and was killed by the first morning streetcar, which almost overturned. Thus people began to expect to see lions and tigers at any moment. The military commander of Alexandria, an Egyptian, fell into confusion since he had no specific instructions about what he should do in case the Germans entered the city. So he sent a letter to the war ministry asking what he should do if such an eventuality came to pass: should he resist or surrender? The letter was brought to the attention of the minister, who ordered that no response be sent. But the confused commander sent another letter to the same effect, whereupon the war minister yelled, "Transfer the son of a bitch!" The minister was afraid that if he ordered resistance, the Germans would try him if they were victorious, and if he ordered surrender the British would try him for treason! An air raid on the city leveled the whole of Manasha Street in one night. The inhabitants of Karmuz, Raghib, and Ghayt al-Aynab ran in panic to the banks of the Mahmudiya canal, but the German planes dropped many bombs on Mahmudiya that night, setting many ships on fire, sinking them and killing dozens of people on the banks. A great exodus to the countryside began by train, car, taxi, carts drawn by horses and donkeys, carriage, bicycle, and on foot, choking the main road out of Alexandria. The women went out in panic in their housedresses or nightgowns. Dimyan made the rounds to see the damage, as he did after every raid. He found that many houses had been destroyed and among them was Khawaga Dimitri's house. The second floor had fallen in on top of the first, and the facade wall had collapsed, blocking access to the pavement in front of the locked door, which remained standing. There had been no one at home at the time of the raid, no tenants, and Dimitri had gone to Upper Egypt. Dimyan thought of taking his family there, but he remembered that he had been out of contact with his sisters for quite a long time. So he decided to take his family to the shelters set up by the government in Kafr al-Dawwar.

On the road Dimyan ran alongside the cart driven by Ghaffara, who had the fez on his face. On the cart sat Dimyan's mother, his wife, and his two daughters. Ghaffara had once again removed the walls of the cart so people could easily sit on the long migration route. He no longer transported the dead. He could not stand it. Now he was moving the living to Kafr al-Dawwar, outpaced by the taxis and the horse-drawn carriages and the long carts drawn by healthy mules. But it was all right. The two sickly donkeys did the job, and people were poor, having left their houses with nothing. So he did not charge much. He asked Dimyan to climb up next to him, but Dimyan, who saw how slowly the cart was moving, and how poorly the donkeys were, was content to walk or run alongside the cart. Why did he not see the scene around him as well? That misshapen line of people fleeing in different garb, nakedness, loud voices, crying, too much baggage, too little baggage, clean, dirty, the sun above exposing them, the trains dashing past them, near them and more crowded, everyone looking at everyone else, moments without meaning. Dimyan thought of Brika. Rommel has made it to al-Alamein, and she and all the Bedouin must be gone by now, having fled before the stupid armies. God Almighty! Would Brika appear in the shelter camps? He did not think so. If that happened, he would marry her. She is married. He is married. He would kidnap her. He could not see her again, just let her go. The mere memory of her almost lifted him from the ground. His service at the church and his undertaking the most menial of jobs was not enough to make him forget, even cleaning the toilets and taking a long time doing it was not enough. But the vast, wide open space in which people and vehicles ran said there was no way that Brika would come back to the vast expanse. The Lord had sent her and the Lord had taken her back. Bedouin did not sleep in government houses. Brika was a grain of sand carried by the wind. He must go back to Magd al-Din.

In Kafr al-Dawwar, Queen Nazli's tents provided temporary shelters for the refugees until real houses were built. Nothing was more beautiful than living in houses built by royalty, even if they were mere tents! He had to convince himself also that nothing was fancier than being transported by Ghaffara on whose cart he had loaded some belongings and the whole family and which moved ever so slowly on the main road, so crowded with refugees that you could not see ahead or back, and Dimyan was in the middle of it all.

The strange story that surprised the people of Alexandria was the story of the Jewish lady Miss Samhun, who lived in a small villa on Manasha Street with dozens of cats. She came from the famous Samhun family, which was among the first to live on that street in the time of Ismail Pasha. No one knew her name, so they used her family name. No one knew when she was born or the day she had first appeared on the street, but she became well known during the previous world war. She had been in love with a young Jewish man who went to the Eastern front with Lord Allenby and entered Palestine with him and did not come back. He had promised to write her to join him after victory, but he did not. He was killed in the fighting against the Ottoman Turks and their allies. In turn she chose not to go to the land where her beloved was killed. She discovered that she could never leave Egypt. She stayed home alone after the death of her mother and father and after her brothers and sisters married and moved to Saba Pasha. No one remembered her except on Saturdays, when she would go to the synagogue on Nabi Danyal Street. Since the temple was destroyed, she no longer went out on Saturdays. No one knew how she lived. It was said that she had a maid who came from Hadra every day. But the servant was seldom seen, and unlike most servants, she did not speak with anyone. She bought everything from the bazaar in Hadra and brought it in the morning. She rarely bought anything from Manasha Street or from Paulino or Muharram Bey. During an air raid, the Samhun villa received a direct hit, and it fell into rubble like the other houses on the street. Rescue teams came, and crowds gathered around the remnants of the villa. Where had Miss Samhun, the most famous resident on the street, gone? The rescue teams worked, and as they made some progress, small and big cats ran out meowing from the rubble, not believing what happened to them. Miss Samhun was found on her side in a corner surrounded by strong walls and covered with some pieces of wood from the ceiling. She was dusty and her eyes were closed and she did not move. There is no power or strength save in God! What an end for a true lover! She was the most beautiful woman, but loneliness brought her an early old age. She must have had heaps of money. People talked and waited for the money to appear. It took three days to remove the rubble, and jobless and poor people from all over Alexandria pitched in. They had come to look for the buried treasure of the Samhun family. No one asked why no one from the family had appeared, except for a few moments, to take the body of their sister, then disappeared. In the end they found a few old utensils and some decayed pieces of furniture and some incense sticks, many colorful bundles of incense sticks, that the beautiful Miss Samhun had kept.

We praise you, Lord
Calamities are generous gifts,
Catastrophes a sign of munificence.
We praise you, no matter how long the ordeal
Nor how overwhelming the pain.

Anonymous

27

Magd al-Din's heart beat fast as the train approached. "Until when will you lie to me, my feeble heart?" he said to himself. This was happening every day and still no Dimyan, still nothing filled the wilderness around him. Even the great commotion of the armies around him did not fill that emptiness, not the retreat and panic before Rommel, not the long queues of the wounded, transported by trains, not the sorrow in the different-colored eyes of the soldiers, the occasional crying, the silence of the bagpipes, not the dust that filled the air, the planes that came and went, went and did not come back, then returned, nor the devilish bombs. He stayed home for days on end, suffering pangs of hunger since the Indians and al-Safi al-Naim had stopped coming. Hilal the stationmaster fled to join Amer, who had left the telegraph room open, ravaged by the wind. All of that did not succeed in making him forget Dimyan. Was Dimyan the reason he stayed? He would never again find events more compelling than those he had just witnessed to cause him to leave the place. It must be Dimyan. He was waiting for him to return, and he would return. And there he was. He saw him getting off the last car of the train, which was carrying military equipment.

He saw him standing there in the middle of the platform, looking exactly as he had when they first came to that place together. Dimyan seemed not to believe that he had come back to his friend, and Magd al-Din also looked incredulous. They rushed to embrace each other.

In the stationmaster's room they talked and talked. Magd al-Din described the soldiers' miserable retreat before Rommel, and Dimyan talked about Alexandria's misery, no one staying, no one sleeping. Magd al-Din could not take his eyes off the aura surrounding Dimyan's face. This was something that Dimyan did not have before.

"Why are you staring at me so much, Sheikh Magd?"

"Nothing, Dimyan. I just missed you. I didn't believe we'd meet again."

Dimyan became lost in thought. The priest, Father Ibshawi, had stared at him a lot. He had taken him to the confession booth and sat him down and stared at him. "What's the matter, Father?" "Don't leave the church, Dimyan. Don't stray far." The deacons and the other priests also stared at him long, then met and talked. Something, he was not sure what, was happening to his face. But why was his family not staring at him? Or those that sought refuge in the church? What made Magd al-Din like Father Ibshawi and the priests and deacons?

"You should have left this place and joined me," said Dimyan, lying. In the last few days he had felt that he no longer knew Alexandria and that she no longer knew him. He had no life away from Magd al-Din, and now he was feeling that he could not stay here.

"Yes, I should've joined you," agreed Magd al-Din.

"Why didn't you, Sheikh Magd?"

Magd al-Din did not have an answer. He realized that he had almost lost all sense of time, that the world was larger than al-Alamein. He kept staring at the face of Dimyan, who continued talking about Alexandria. When Magd al-Din learned that Dimitri's house had been destroyed, he felt depressed and was able to recall the smell of the home, that calm, sweet smell that induced sleep and rest, a house where you did not hear the noise outside. That was Khawaga Dimitri's house. He remembered Bahi and immediately recalled the aura that had surrounded his face for so long. He wondered if Dimyan was going to meet the same fate as

Bahi. When Magd al-Din recalled the little house, it brought back all the images that he had lost: Lula, Camilla, Yvonne, Sitt Maryam, Ghaffara, Bahi, and Zahra, the love of his soul, who must be withering away in the village grieving over their separation. He felt a sudden jolt of joy that almost lifted him off his feet when he remembered Shawqiya and Shawqi. That meant that he would soon return, a secret magical voice in his heart told him.

"I didn't know they'd canceled civilian trains," Dimyan said.

"Since the withdrawal they no longer come here. They stop at al-Hammam now."

"Yes, I took one of them, and at al-Hammam I boarded this train in the rear car. There were no soldiers there—they were on top of the cars and the equipment."

"Nothing can stop you, Dimyan! Come on, let's go home."

In truth Magd al-Din wanted to confirm the aura of light around Dimyan's face and find out if it appeared in the shade indoors, and whether Dimyan knew about it or understood what it meant. Dimyan was unknowingly joining the ranks of the saints.

On the way Dimyan asked him, "Do you have any information on Brika?"

"All the Bedouin have left this area for al-Hammam or Amiriya."

By nightfall Dimyan had tired of Magd al-Din's staring at him, but he considered it to be a new phase that his friend was passing through temporarily. Magd al-Din talked about how they had to stay there until they received instructions to leave. Dimyan asked about the kind of work that they could do now. Magd al-Din said they had to switch the train onto the old tracks and spend the night there to accommodate another train that usually arrived at the station during the night. He said it was an important job that they should not neglect, even though the crossing was now useless and the semaphore irrelevant, since the trains no longer went farther than the station. The aura of light grew brighter in the night. They heard footsteps approaching. They were in the inner room, but the outside door was open. The footsteps grew louder and were now

at the door, then in the hall, then they saw the two of them
standing in front of them. It was the English officer, Mr. Spike, in
person, after a long absence. Next to him was a short man with
disheveled hair and a long beard that covered his whole face; his
face was dusty and looked extremely tired, his khaki shorts and
shirt tattered and the legs tanned black. Mr. Spike stood staring at
Dimyan and Magd al-Din then said, "This man is Egyptian. We
found him in the desert. Please help him."

He left the tired man with them and went away. The man
stood staring at them, then said in a trembling voice, "Don't you
know me, Sheikh Magd? Don't you know me, Dimyan?"

"Who? Hamza!"

They both shouted and pounced on him, embracing him and
lifting him off the ground. In a few moments he was sitting
between them crying and laughing and telling his story.

"Where can I begin, Sheikh Magd? What do I say, Dimyan? This
story of mine could be the subject of epics recited by professional
storytellers! Yes, I swear! Coming back to Egypt was the farthest
thing from my thoughts. Where was Egypt? From the moment
that stupid African son-of-a-bitch soldier pulled me up, I lost all
hope of ever coming back. May God forgive him—I saw his belly
blown up before my very eyes. May God forgive him. He took me
away from you, from my children, from my people and my
country. You all moved away from me. I saw you running
backwards as the dust blinded me, and I couldn't see anyone any
more. I found myself in Marsa Matruh. I spent a whole night in the
train, with the soldiers mocking me and making fun of me. They
didn't give me a chance to get near the door. I would have jumped,
I swear, even if it meant I'd die. All night they mocked me,
Australians, Indians, Africans, and Englishmen, the whole world
was mocking me, and I was lost in their midst. They asked me
what my name was. 'What's your name?' I said, 'Hamza,' and they
said 'hamsa,' 'amsa,' 'gamza,' and they laughed and tossed me
around from one to another, and I was frightened as a mouse,
looking them in the eye and begging them, 'Please help me, please

let me go home.' But it was no use. I wish I hadn't known a word of English or had just shut up, but I did know some. I asked and persisted that they let me go. I knew they understood, but they didn't care and didn't move. It hurt. If I had been mute or ignorant I would have waited in silence, but I got down on my knees and begged them. 'Please let me go back, let me go home, please, my home, home.' And they laughed and said, 'Home? What's home? We are homeless. You're like us, homeless, Hamsa,' and they laughed, 'Hamsa is homeless,' and kept on laughing until a young officer, who apparently liked my helplessness and my fright, patted me on the shoulder to reassure me. Then he talked with the soldiers, and they laughed even more boisterously. I realized that he wasn't going to help me either, but he pointed to a corner of the train car, and I went and sat there. I put my hand on my cheek and realized I was a goner, no doubt about it. I heard the officer say as he pointed as me, 'Like a monkey!' and the soldiers laughed, and I just gave up all hope. I remembered you, Sheikh Magd, and you, Dimyan. But strangely, I was afraid that if I came back and told my story that you, Dimyan, would not believe me, and that made me smile, despite the ordeal, and I said to myself, 'If only I could go back. I wouldn't care whether anybody believed me or not.' Then, like Sheikh Magd, I said to myself, 'May He who never sleeps take care of me!' And He did. Praise the Lord, but He really took His time! It must have been a test, surely, but a hard one. 'Anyway, praise the Lord for everything,' I said to myself and fell asleep where I was, and when I woke up I found myself in Marsa Matruh in the middle of a heavy raid on the town, the station, and the train. I saw soldiers running in the desert, and sometimes I was ahead of them and at other times behind them. I saw a bomb falling near that stupid African soldier who had abducted me, and I saw him fly more than ten meters in the air, then land with his belly torn wide open, and blood gushing from it. I saw his stomach and his guts. I went close to him and saw that he was still alive but not in pain, but he looked hard at me as if he felt I was gloating over his misfortune and didn't want to appear weak in front of me. But really, I pitied him. He just turned once and groaned, then gave up the ghost, and I covered him with sand, right there in the middle of the bombing, I swear I did. Anyway the raid ended, and we were back in the middle of the barracks. I stood there, at a loss for what to do. I expected them to let me go, but they pushed me toward the kitchen. I saw the same officer that was on the train and heard him say to a black soldier, 'Take him to the kitchen. He's a servant.' The black soldier with white teeth dragged me over and asked me what my name was, and when I told him, he said, 'What is Hamsa?' And I said to myself, 'My God! Must a man know the meaning of his name?' And I told him, 'Jackass,' but I said it in Arabic, just 'Humar,' so he asked me, 'What's humar?' I said 'Hamza,' and he looked at me for a time in silence, then said, 'Very good, Hamsa.'

"All day and all night I worked in the kitchen, carrying food and washing the dishes and pots and pans and saying to myself, 'It's okay, at least I'm being fed, and one might hate something that is good for oneself. In the end, someone is going to find out my true story and will let me go to the station, get on the train, and go back to my children,' but nobody paid any attention to me. I kept looking around the barracks for a way to escape, but I couldn't figure out which was east and which was west. There were soldiers of every color and nationality and arms of all types out there in the middle of the desert. I just resigned myself to the will of God and prayed that a German raid would come and level the barracks. I dreamt I was going back by myself. The officer kept looking at me and laughing and talking with the other officers, who laughed too. One day he signaled me to follow him, and my heart sank. I followed him to a large car full of soldiers. There were many cars full of soldiers with their weapons. He told me to jump, and I stood there, at a loss—the car was too high, and I was too short. But a soldier, another black one, extended his hand to me and pulled me up. In a little while the cars began to move, surrounded by tanks and guns. I was very frightened, as frightened as an orphan puppy, so I asked the black soldier, 'To where we go, soldier?' Laughing, he said to me, 'To the war,' and laughed like a crazy man. I knew already, of course, that it was the war, and that meant the end of me. I was sad, and implored God for one thing, that he defeat the English and the Allies in all their wars against the Germans and the poor Italians and that I end up being a prisoner of the Germans or the Italians, who, if they knew my story, would let me go. The whole way, the officer was yelling at the soldiers. It turned out he was a vicious son of a bitch. I heard the officers calling him 'Shakespeare,' which was his name, apparently. But the soldiers used to call him 'Macbess.' It seemed that was his nickname. That's what I thought. So once I said to him, 'Mr. Macbess' and he gave me such a look, I was completely terrified. I knew the soldiers had duped me, and that the word 'macbess' must be a bad word, otherwise why would he be so upset? It must be an insult or something. I said to myself, 'May God take Shakespeare and Macbess the same day!' After that I found it really hard to serve food to the soldiers at their posts. They gave me a uniform, of course. The battalion I was taking food to was all Indian soldiers. I said to myself that perhaps serving them would be easier, since they were enslaved like us, but serving them was the pits. There was not a single Muslim among them that I could talk with. They were of course all taller than me, wearing turbans that always looked like they were about to fall off their heads. They didn't bother wearing helmets. All their orders to me were gestures. They treated me like I was a deaf-mute. At night I slept in the kitchen and amused myself with poetry, singing and crying:

> *Look at time and what it has done to people:*
> *One day it smiles at them, the next it frowns.*
> *The days of joy are gone, bad times are upon us,*
> *The lowest of all now lords it over the noblest.*

"In the first battle with the Italians, I was taken prisoner. The Italians took me with some English, Indian, and Australian soldiers and marched us a distance through a red desert with fine sands that blew in our faces and blinded us, a desert that appeared endless, until we saw a big camp surrounded with barbed wire. To tell you the honest truth, I was gloating, especially because I hadn't seen the battle before being taken prisoner."

"How were you all taken prisoner, then?"

"We just found, out of the blue, an armored German division in the middle of the camp, surrounded by infantry soldiers that looked like demons. Everybody knew the Germans had arrived, so they surrendered. The fighting was far away from the camp, and since the Germans and the Italians appeared, it meant that the English had been defeated. Later, when Rommel came, he drove the English crazy. He drives them nuts, because as soon as he begins a battle, he leaves the scene, and in the blink of an eye, he's back behind the English lines, and they surrender right away. But this time, he hadn't appeared yet. Why do you think they call him 'Rommel'? The word must mean something like a fox. Yes, Sheikh Magd. I swear by God, Dimyan!"

"Your story is very long, Hamza!"

"I'm still at the beginning, Dimyan. I can't believe it's over."

"Okay, okay. Don't cry, Hamza. Tell us, don't hold it inside."

"I missed you very much, Sheikh Magd."

"Okay. What did you do with the Italians?"

"Yes, Dimyan, they took us to a huge camp filled with prisoners from all over the world and from all religions. We slept outdoors. It was hot during the day but cold at night. And just as I had seen the English treating their prisoners, I saw the Italians doing the same thing. They threw the food to us over the barbed wire fence, and we ran to take it like animals. But, truth be told, after the soldiers picked up the food, they redistributed it among themselves. They were respectable, even though war is hell, and survival is very important. I saw the German and Italian prisoners before that in Marsa Matruh doing the same thing, no one demeaning themselves or losing their dignity. So why had they tried to demean me and take away my dignity? Anyway, every day the Italians took a few prisoners to interrogate, then shipped them to Italy. When it was my turn, I was afraid. I said only one word, 'Egyptian,' and one sentence, 'I am Egyptian.' They looked at each other, the Italian officers, and spoke loudly and as fast as a train, and laughed. Suddenly one of the officers got up and walked around me, looking at me, and said 'Egyptiano.' I wanted to tell him that I wasn't a soldier, that I was an Egyptian railroad worker abducted by the English. But I lost all the English words I had learned all my life, and only the word 'Egyptian' was left. I started to cry. They took me back to the camp. I couldn't believe it. I had seen them ship all the other ones they'd interrogated to Italy. I thanked God and kept pacing next to the high barbed wire fence, wondering why they had let me stay, what they had in store for me. I looked at the distant sky and the wide world in front of me and said to myself that it was unlikely that God would hear my prayers here. Yes, I swear, Sheikh Magd, but God is great, and He heard me.

"I saw among the soldiers on guard duty a soldier who looked like an Arab. I spoke to him in Arabic, and he responded. It turned out that he was a Libyan who had been conscripted against his will. I told him my story and saw in his eyes a sincere desire to help me. He said to me, 'Wait a few days. I'll see what I can do for you.' I waited. I remembered the raid on Marsa Matruh, with the bombs exploding before my very eyes and the racket of the guns at the border and the shells raining down on the soldiers and cutting them to ribbons. I also remembered the cries of the wounded all night long in the field hospital near the camp. I was always in the rear of the English lines, but I saw hell more than once, because sometimes they pushed me up to the front with the supply team. Yes, what is hell? Isn't it fire? You know, Sheikh Magd, I think those foreigners are actually from hell. They have hearts of iron, and every day they drop a trainful of bombs on each other. Oh God! Do you think we Egyptians could ever fight like that? We are a kind people, and we cry a lot. If we got into a war and the enemy confronted us with a sad song, we would cry and get out of the way."

"Okay, Hamza. Don't cry. You don't have to finish the story today. You should rest."

"I am rested, now that I've seen you again. War is very bad, Sheikh Magd. I've seen many soldiers get their heads blown off as they stood behind the guns. I've seen guns blown to bits in the air. I've seen soldiers suddenly go crazy and run and scream as if possessed by demons and jump up and down. Their comrades would tie them up and give them injections that put them to sleep, then ship them back to their countries. I saw so many crazies that I thought England, Italy, Germany, India, and Africa had all become great madhouses. I saw soldiers look at the sky and scream and others run and fall into the fire, committing suicide. I saw soldiers break down and cry like grieving women. The soldiers are very pitiful, Sheikh Magd. They all cry alike. They are all children that you pity. War is very bad, Dimyan. Anyway, a few days later I found them setting up another camp and a field hospital, and I saw cars carrying hundreds of wounded soldiers and big storms of dust and commotion, like it was Judgment Day. I asked the Libyan soldier, and he told me, 'It's your good fortune, Egyptian. The English have defeated Graziani. Wait for them. They must come here.' And that's exactly what happened. The English came, and they took me with the other prisoners and shipped us back to the Egyptian borders. See how the Lord works! I found myself once again in Egypt, but as a prisoner this time. But praise the Lord, I was back. They handed me over to a tall Australian corporal, very tall, so tall his legs alone were my height, I swear. He took me to the commanding officer. It was then that I learned that my height made me look suspicious to anyone who saw me—I didn't look like a soldier, and no officer would be that short, so I must be a spy. That was the whole story, and the reason for my ordeal.

"The officer asked me who I was and what I did. I told him, 'I am Egyptian, ghalban.' I didn't know how to say 'I'm just a poor little Egyptian' in English, as my English was still lost. The officer looked at me in annoyance, but I felt stronger than I did before. Now I was on Egyptian soil, anyway. The officer had his suspicions about me, so he locked me up in a wooden room all by myself. An African soldier stood guard, and I would tell when it was night when I looked out through the cracks and couldn't see his face, only his teeth. You know, Sheikh Magd, I felt very valuable in that locked room. I rejoiced for the first time in a long time and I remembered my wife and my children and my friends. But I still felt a need to cry. I held back my tears and remembered the sad songs:

> *Look at this broken, humiliated peasant*
> *In the jaws of a crocodile from ancient times*
> *Tell me your story, friend, and how that came to be.*

"A month later they released me, and I said to myself that they must have investigated and found out I'm just a poor Egyptian, and that they were going to let me go. But it didn't happen that way. They put me in the kitchen to cook for the soldiers, and again with the Indians—as if they knew what had happened before. I said to myself that it was okay, I had to be patient, and asked God to give me patience and He did, and I waited until I saw, with my very own eyes, the English soldiers come back from the borders, crushed by Rommel. It was the first time we heard of Rommel, who had replaced Graziani. I heard that the big English general Ritchie went crazy. I now felt that my rescue would be at the hands of Rommel. It felt strange. I was in my own country—why should I need a German commander to rescue me? But that's what happened. I was in the kitchen one day when I saw the smoke coming out of the officers' rooms. They were burning everything quickly and driving off in their Jeeps and clearing out. I could hear only one word: 'Rommel.' Soon the camp was full of Germans, and everything around us was fire and smoke.

"The Germans took me to a high-ranking officer. I was inspired to say 'Rommel.' They asked me in German, I said 'Rommel,' in English, and I still said 'Rommel.' I said to myself, there must be one sane person who will get me out of this mess, which has gone on too long, and the only sane person is Rommel.'

"And they knew that you wanted to see Rommel?"

"Yes, and I did see him. He's a strange man with a round face, green sunken eyes and thinning hair. He didn't say much. Three days later they took me to see him—three days of terror."

Dimyan looked at Magd al-Din, saying to himself, "Hamza's back to his old ways!"

"And in Rommel's room, I saw a Bedouin man standing next to Rommel, who was sitting down. I told them my story from the beginning and heard the Bedouin translating it into German as Rommel smiled in surprise, his face looking like that of a little child, I swear. He said one sentence, which the Bedouin translated for me. He said that I would stay with them while they chased the English and the Eighth Army, until they reached Alexandria, where I would guide them through its streets, and then they would let me go. At that time I prayed to God that they reach Alexandria quickly. I wondered how the Bedouin knew German and said to myself he must be a spy, dressed like a Bedouin."

"Okay, Hamza. That's enough for today. Go to sleep."

"Wait, Dimyan, the story is about to end. I'm sure you don't believe me."

"No, Hamza. It looks like you've suffered even more than what you just told us."

"Afterwards, the Germans advanced to Marsa Matruh. I was at the rear with the supply crews. They assigned me to a jeep driven by a crazy driver who broke my bones by speeding over potholes, and whenever he saw me in pain, he laughed and said 'Aegypter!' which means Egyptian in German. I kept saying to myself, 'Dear God, let it end well.' I was afraid of the landmines. In Marsa Matruh I saw the big battle. I saw the tanks firing, and I saw the tanks blowing up, and I saw the big guns recoiling as they were fired and the planes going and coming from the sea, and at night I heard the moans of the dying and the groans of the wounded. The whole world became a big dusty mass, all black and red. At night I sat in the dark, shrinking in on myself in fear and saying, 'Please, God, take me now. I've had enough.' But the Germans won and they entered Marsa Matruh and Daba afterwards until they came here. Alexandria was near and no one paid any attention to me. I said to myself that it did not make any sense that Rommel needed someone like me to guide him through the streets of Alexandria. I sat at night singing sad songs:

> *Time has given me catastrophes that aggravated my*
> *   ill health.*
> *I was so frightened I did not know what to do.*
> *My heart told me my time was so contrary.*
> *I sat down and wept, my eyes shed tears of blood.*

"All the time I was still the crazy jeep driver's charge. One night he drove me around for more than half an hour and pointed to the stars in the sky, then got off the car, and I followed suit. He pointed forward with his hand and said 'Alexandria' several times and gestured for me to go, so I walked like somebody under a spell. I quickly identified a star in front of me. I knew that the sea was to my left and that the soft steady sound I was hearing was that of the waves that I could not see. I kept walking, but after a little while I didn't hear the sound of the sea, and the stars all looked alike. Then I remembered that armies usually laid land mines when they retreated, and I figured the English must have done that as they retreated before Rommel, and I knew that my end was near and that I would probably step on a landmine in the dark—or even in the daylight! So I sat down on the ground like a lost child and looked at the faraway sky and I said, 'God, you can see me, and I can't see you, you can hear me but I can't hear you. God, I complain to you about my weakness and my lack of options. If you're with me, please give me a break. I have suffered enough. Almighty God, all I did was stretch out my hand to get a box of cookies for my children. Do I deserve all this torture, most merciful God? Please give me a helping hand. Why are you abandoning me, once to evil enemies who have tortured and demeaned me, and now to the desert, the landmines, and the wolves? Yes, if a landmine doesn't blow me up, a wolf will surely eat me. Where is your mercy, which encompasses the whole world? Please forgive me and help me.' I was so tired, Sheikh Magd, that I slept where I sat. Did I sleep long? In a minute, I saw his radiant face, the face of the Prophet. He was wearing green and sitting with his companions, with radiant faces, wearing white. I greeted him, and he returned the greeting. He asked me who I was, and I said to him, 'I am Hamza, O Messenger of God.' He smiled at me and made room for me to sit with him and said, 'Come and sit with my friends Abu Bakr and Umar, Hamza, for your name is very dear to me.' I sat with them, and then I woke up from my sleep rested, as if I'd slept for a hundred years. I was sure that God would help me. I felt a kind, warm hand holding mine and started to walk confidently as his voice—the Prophet's—told me to walk to the right, and I did, then to the left, and I did. And whenever my feet sank in the sand I would be frightened, and he would tell me not to fear, and my fright would go away. I walked until morning. It was the first time I had seen the day so beautiful and sweet, and the sun so happy—yes, that's how I saw it. I said, 'Please God, bestow your full favor upon me,' and as soon as I said that, I saw an Indian soldier coming from out of nowhere. It was he who took me to the English headquarters, where they wondered how I survived all the minefields. They were suspicious, but I finally remembered all the English words that I had forgotten and I told them the story. They kept me for three days until they were sure I was telling the truth, and then the officer brought me to you, praise the Lord—I've missed you so much!"

Then Hamza could speak no more.

O thou the last fulfillment of my life, Death, my death,
come and whisper to me!
Day after day have I kept watch for thee;
for thee have I borne the joys and pangs of life.

Rabindranath Tagore

28

Hamza left them after two days of rest. He started on his way to Alexandria, going on foot until he reached al-Hammam. He refused to get on any train that had soldiers on it.

"It's forty kilometers to al-Hammam, Hamza."

"I'll walk. I'm not riding with any soldiers, ever." He said that he wanted to take the regular passenger train from al-Hammam.

Hamza walked on the railroad tracks that reached all the way to Alexandria. This was the only way to arrive safely. When Hamza disappeared in the distance, Magd al-Din and Dimyan thought about the big world and all the stories that were taking place in it. How could the world cope with all these painful stories? For several days they spoke only in whispers and said very little to each other. One evening al-Safi al-Naim came and told them that he would not be seeing them again. He had been away for a long time. He told them that a new commander named Montgomery had taken over command of the Eighth Army and that he was very strict with his troops and had devised a rigorous training program. He told them that a new war between Rommel and Monty, as the soldiers nicknamed the new commander, was imminent.

Al-Safi brought them large quantities of cheese, corned beef, tea, and cigarettes and conveyed to them the greetings of the young Indian soldiers. He told them that Bahadur Shand had been killed. Then he smiled, looking at Dimyan and telling him, "Bahadur was intent on killing you upon his return. It seems the Germans love you, Dimyan."

Dimyan was distressed to learn that Bahadur Shand had died. He knew that it was Mari Girgis who was protecting him, but he wished he had protected him in a different manner this time, like by sending Bahadur back to India, for instance. But he quickly apologized to Mari Girgis and made the sign of the cross and said to himself that it was the war that ate up the soldiers.

Churchill had visited Egypt and met with General Alexander, the new commander in chief of the Middle East, who had replaced Auchinleck, and together they visited the Eighth Army in al-Alamein after meeting General Montgomery at his command post in Burg Al-Arab. Churchill saw for himself the changes that Monty had brought about in the soldiers. He saw a number of soldiers go down into the sea in the morning in dirty underpants. That distressed him and caused him pain, but he did not order new underpants for the soldiers. He wished the war would come to an end, and so end the soldiers' misery. He returned with Alexander to Cairo and visited the caves at Tura, those caverns hollowed out in the mountains when the ancient Egyptians built the pyramids and which had now become secret recesses for the repair and hiding of military equipment. Churchill wished the ancient Egyptians had taken larger stones so that the English would have more secret depots for their equipment. He reviewed the preparations for the defense of Cairo if Alexandria fell with Alexander. Foremost among those preparations were the plans to flood the Delta and hinder German advances by opening the barrages and dams. He ordered that British employees all over the country be issued rifles. Then he returned to England.

Alexander promised to send him the word "zip" if fighting broke out. "Zip" was the label of Churchill's clothes.

It was well known that Rommel would not stop at al-Alamein, and preparations were made to meet him there. Al-Alamein had to be the last post he would reach and the first step of his retreat westward—the day should never come when plans for the defense of Cairo were implemented. The topography of the place did not leave Rommel with any room for maneuver. There was only one way—he and his armored force had to cross the minefields south of the front, in order to go north to encircle the British forces and their right flank. To do that, Rommel would have to occupy the hills of Alam al-Halfa. Therefore Monty deployed his troops in such a way as to make the capture of those hills impossible.

There were preparations for attack and preparations for defense around Magd al-Din and Dimyan, who felt increasingly isolated. One afternoon Dimyan saw the door of the telegraph room open, and he entered the room. Actually the door had been open since Amer had left, but Dimyan saw it as if for the first time. There was nothing in the room but an old, open wooden cabinet containing dirty yellowish notepads of all sizes and scattered pieces of paper on the shelves and the floor. There was also a dusty, faded table on which sat the transmitter and receiver, which suddenly came to life and began to make successive clicking sounds. Magd al-Din was nearby on the platform, and Dimyan quickly called him over, and he did, just in time to see and hear the last clicks of the machine. Then there was silence.

"I wonder who was sending a telegram?" Dimyan asked as Magd al-Din's thoughts strayed far away as they walked over to their house. The days were now passing in silence, a silence that enveloped the whole desert, on which a heavy ominous gloom descended, making the very air heavy. The long lines of armored cars moving all day did not succeed in dispelling the silence, nor did the movement of the planes which came out, then went quickly back to the sea and the east, the English and American planes that apparently were training for the coming battle. The traffic of armament trains driven by Indians increased, and the trains were now going back without soldiers—there were no sick leaves or furloughs. The soldiers milled silently around the trains carrying tanks, guns, and ammunition, taking their equipment to the vast desert that seemed to swallow everything. Silence was now the sensation that wrapped itself around Magd al-Din and Dimyan and permeated everything around them, living and inanimate. Even the sun began to move farther away, opening up the vast expanse around them to even more silence and devastation. Magd al-Din saw the dusty clock in the stationmaster's room, which had stopped working. He stopped making the call to prayers. Everything here had grown old, foretelling the end. But, so as not to lose track of the time, he planted a stick near the kiosk at the crossing. It was noon when its shadow disappeared, and midafternoon when a long shadow formed to the east, and sunset when the length of the shadow doubled. As for the time of the last prayer at night, he did not need to find that out, since he usually prayed late at night. One night, close to dawn after the desert night had set up its tent to cover the whole world without a sound except the indistinct noises of unseen insects, Dimyan, who now realized that he had been harboring a desire not to stay there in the desert, suddenly asked, "What's happening, Sheikh Magd?"

By that he meant the increased movement of the trains carrying armament and of the planes during the day and sometimes at night. Magd al-Din was reciting the Quran, and now he raised his voice, "*We surely shall test you with some fear and some hunger and loss of wealth and lives and crops, but give glad tidings to the steadfast. Those who, when a calamity befalls them, say 'To God we truly belong and to him surely we shall return.'*" He stopped to respond to Dimyan, "It must be that the war is about to break out, Dimyan."

Dimyan sensed a little irritation in Magd al-Din's tone of voice, an irritation that he had not noticed before. Was that the first time that Magd al-Din realized there was a war going on?

"If the war breaks out while we're here, we will die, Sheikh Magd," Dimyan said.

Magd al-Din, quoting the Quran, said, "*And when my servants ask you about Me, I am surely near, and I answer the prayers of every supplicant when he calls unto Me . . .*"

Dimyan fell silent and Magd al-Din continued, "*Say, 'I have no power to harm or benefit myself except as God wills.' For every nation there is an appointed time. When its time comes, they can neither put it off for an hour nor hasten it.*"

"You're scaring me tonight, Sheikh Magd. I see Mari Girgis every night saving himself from the fire, and now you're scaring me too. Besides, why won't you stop staring at my face? What's in my face? I've looked at it in the mirror several times and saw it was pale and yellow. Am I going to die here? We've got to run away.

If you don't run away with me in the morning, I'll go alone. I came back for your sake, but you're letting me down. Do you know what the telegraph clicks that we heard mean? That was a message for us to leave this place. It couldn't have been anything else. If that message didn't come from the Railroad Authority, it must have been from God. Do you have any other explanation? Why don't you answer me?"

The answer came from a distance, sounds of successive colossal explosions, as if the whole sky was tumbling down to earth, and a vast flash of red lit up the sky. "Oh my God! What's that, Sheikh Magd?"

There were sounds of thin sharp lengthy screeching, the sound of missiles flying from the ground and falling from the sky. The ground rose and fell under Magd al-Din and Dimyan, so they got up in a panic and moved away from the house, looking at the fire lighting up the night, as the earth shook under their feet.

Rommel had just finished writing a letter to his wife, "Dear Lu, we have some severe shortages and disadvantages, but I took the risk. If our blow is successful, it will determine the outcome of the whole war."

General Alexander had sent the word 'zip' to Churchill from Cairo. Monty was confident about his defense plan. There were four hundred German tanks, half of which were equipped with the diabolical seventy-five-millimeter guns. Awaiting them were seven hundred British and American tanks. Rommel's usual tactics were to attack the enemy forces quickly with a small force, encircle them, then try to liquidate them. The German planes began their raids on the forces in front and at the rear simultaneously to confuse and disorient them.

"The shelling is far away, Dimyan. Don't be afraid."

Dimyan was busy reciting prayers or incantations, of which Magd al-Din would make out only a few words: 'Kyrie eleison,' 'Georgius,' 'Jesus,' 'Yuannis,' 'Yusab,' 'Kirullus,' and 'the Virgin.' Dimyan, shaking, made it back to the house, followed by Magd al-Din. As soon as they were there, Dimyan collapsed and stretched out on the floor with his back against the wall. Magd al-Din stretched out near him and lit a cigarette for himself and one for Dimyan, pretending to be composed.

"There's a lot of light," he smiled. "I don't think the Germans will notice a cigarette in the middle of all this shelling."

They kept smoking is silence. Magd al-Din noticed that neither he nor Dimyan had taken off their work clothes. They even had their shoes on. They had been returning from the station a short time ago when an ammunition train arrived just before the shelling began.

The formations of Royal Tanks and Royal Scotch were defending the Alam al-Halfa plateau against the German armored offensive. The German planes had stopped for a while, but as daylight approached, they returned with a vengeance and started bombing everywhere again. From the north and the east, British and American planes came, and an intense air battle ensued and ended soon. The planes of the Allies went back to their posts in Alexandria and the Delta and to the American aircraft carrier in the Mediterranean. The German and Italian planes went back to their airports in the desert, only to return after a short while in greater numbers, going deep to the rear lines of the Eighth Army, extremely close to the railroad station and the abandoned houses, and to Magd al-Din and Dimyan. A wind swept them off their feet, and they hit the ground hard. A powerful bomb had fallen from the sky, making the air convulse around them and hurling them off their feet. Magd al-Din saw Zahra's face, which he had almost forgotten, and he heard her scream. He shouted in a hoarse voice "Dimyan!" but did not hear an answer. Dimyan was some distance away, looking around for Magd al-Din. When Magd al-Din saw him he went over to him.

"Are you all right?" Magd al-Din asked him.

"No."

"Were you hit?"

"No."

Magd al-Din understood what Dimyan meant, and he fell silent.

"Does our presence here make any sense any more?" asked Dimyan in despair.

Another shell fell near them, and even though it was not strong enough to knock them off their feet again, Magd al-Din shouted,

"Come on, Dimyan."

❖

They found themselves hurrying up near the station between the tracks going east. From behind they could hear the falling bombs and the airplanes, and they went even faster. When they had moved quite a distance away from the station, they heard a harrowing explosion that shook the air and caused them to lose their balance. They fell on the crossties, and hellish flames lit up the whole world. They realized it was the end. Dimyan remembered his nightmarish vision, and he resigned himself to death. Magd al-Din longed for his son Shawqi, whom he had never even seen. They saw, however, that the flames were far away, and when they were able to see the red sky, they realized that the explosion was at the station. After they regained their balance and could see more clearly, they saw the train that had stopped at the station. All its cars were turning into a river of fire that the German planes kept fueling. They saw the two wooden kiosks—the station-master's room and the telegraph room—burning and flying in the air and turning into ashes. Everything was turning into ashes. Most merciful God! Eternal, living God, help us! Jesus, Mary, Prophet of God, help us, save us! They started running again.

They kept on running, never feeling hunger or pain from wounds or bruises they had suffered when the explosions threw them to the ground. And what a beautiful new day! This river of milk that was beginning to light up the dark and wash away the night. This world that God has created was so beautiful, why was it that people were destroying it? The planes kept on coming from the east and from the west, engaging in short dogfights, then disappearing only to appear again and again. The German planes bombed everything in sight until a new dogfight started. In the meantime Magd al-Din and Dimyan kept on running, sweat pouring out of every pore of their bodies and their skin and chests burning, their feet almost giving way, but who could stop in the midst of all those fires?

"I am flying, Dimyan!"

Dimyan heard and saw Magd al-Din next to him.

"And I am flying too, Magd al-Din!"

"My God, I am not running—I am flying, Dimyan!"

"And so am I, Magd al-Din!"

What bird was now carrying them on its wings! It must be the angel Gabriel, the very one who brought the good tidings to the Messenger of God. It was he who also brought the Virgin Mary tidings of her immaculate conception. Their breathing was now inaudible, they were almost anesthetized, asleep on calm waves. The bird was carrying them gently into space, their sweat was drying, and they were drinking a magic potion that imbued their veins with a secret delight. Was Gabriel taking them to Alexandria or to God in the high heavens? They were both certain of a safe end.

The distance from al-Alamein to al-Hammam is forty kilometers. Throughout that distance a god-like strength possessed Magd al-Din and Dimyan. The bombing and shelling behind them would stop, only to resume again. The battle for the hills of Alam al-Halfa was not over yet. Rommel knew that Monty's headquarters was in Burg al-Arab and that his strategic cache of vehicles and equipment had to be attacked.

The sun had ascended the sky and gone past Magd al-Din and Dimyan and now to the German Front. All the time they felt nothing other than being carried on the wings of Gabriel. They even fell asleep while running. Had there been no train waiting at al-Hammam they would have kept on running all the way to Alexandria. How was it that they felt no hunger and no thirst? The bombing and shelling had subsided as evening settled on the second day. The civilian train stood empty at the station, which also was empty of people. The last car of the train was the one closest to them, and they got on and sat down on the first seat. The sounds of the guns roared again, and the train got ready to depart as they heaved a long and deep sigh of relief. What a good omen! They looked at each other in contentment and fell into a deep sleep.

Was it one moment? An hour? A whole lifetime that they slept? Whatever it was it was long enough for them to feel somewhat rested. It was impossible for them to remain asleep in the midst of the roar of the guns that were let loose with the new evening. Dimyan was thirsty, so he went through the other cars to look for water. In a corner he found a tap and turned it on. The water was yellowish and rusty, but he drank it anyway and went back. The train was completely empty and dark except for the moonlight coming through the broken windows.

"We've won, Sheikh Magd. I now realize that the nightmare in which I saw Mari Girgis engulfed by flames was nothing but the devil's work."

"The Lord be praised for everything, Dimyan."

The train began to rattle, and the sounds of explosions drew nearer and fear returned to their eyes, but then the train started to run smoothly, and the sounds of explosions grew distant as the train's speed increased.

"The train engineer must be Indian!"

"The Indians don't operate civilian trains."

"But he's going at a crazy speed."

"If only he'd go faster, Dimyan. Where did you find the drinking water?"

"In the fifth car. It's been standing for a long time, but I drank it."

"I'm going to get a drink of water and I'm coming right back. Wait for me."

Dimyan smiled in surprise. Where could he go?

Magd al-Din hurried to get a drink. Why was he hurrying? He was being rattled hard between the empty seats as the train kept swaying unevenly. He reached the tap, turned it on, and filled his cupped hand with its yellow rusty water and drank it. The sound of explosions drew near, the train shook so violently that Magd al-Din lost his balance and fell on a nearby seat, his head hitting the back of the seat so hard it almost split open. He could not keep his balance seated either. He got up and the train was swaying violently from side to side, so he kept tumbling down and hitting the seats on either side. He shouted, "Dimyan," and from the open windows he saw shells landing not far from the train and stirring the dust and stones, which hit the sides of the train. He fell down between the two rows of seats. The aisle was narrow, so he stayed down, stretched out and holding on to the underside of the seats so the rattling of the train did not hurt him. He realized that assuming a crucified posture was the best option for someone in his situation. Dimyan had also come to the same conclusion, but the car he was in shook more violently since it was the tail end of the train. At the same time that Dimyan was saying, "Merciful Lord and Savior of all who was made flesh for us here for our salvation, who lit the way for us, sinners, who fasted for us forty days and forty nights, who saved us from death," Magd al-Din was reciting from the Quran, ". . . *that man can only attain that for which he strives; that his striving will be noted; that it will be fully rewarded; that your Lord is the ultimate goal; that it is He who grants laughter and tears; that it is He who gives death and life; that it is He who has created in pairs, male and female; from a seed when it is poured forth; that it is up to Him to ordain the second coming to life.*" The train swayed violently, shaking, its wheels thundering, as the shells kept coming, landing not far from it now. "*This is one of the early warning signs; the threatened hour is near; no one but God can disclose it.*" The light of the bombs entered the train car, which was already lit by a faint moonlight. The train swayed more violently than ever. A crash was heard, then something heavy being dragged on the ground and hitting against the crossties and the tracks. The train jumped up several times and swayed to right and left. One of the cars that had received a direct hit, and resisted being separated from the rest of the train, was being dragged along the ground. "Dimyan! Dimyan!" Magd al-Din could not stand up. The train could overturn if the car did not separate or if the train did not stop. But it did not stop, and the car did not separate.

Did that take a long time? Probably a fraction of a minute, but it felt to Magd al-Din as long as a whole lifetime. The train was now steady, and the terrible noise was over. Everything was smooth and calm after the heavy, turbulent movements. The rattle was over, and it was possible to breathe again. Even the lights of the bombs had now moved away in the distance, and once again the moonlight entered the car, and the winds, which a few moments ago had been buffeting the train, subsided into a breeze. The train was now balanced again, and the sounds of its wheels were once again monotonous. Magd al-Din could stand up again without fear, and so could Dimyan. Dimyan? If it was the last car that was hit, then

Dimyan was lost. If it was the one before the last car, then he was also lost. Quickly Magd al-Din left the car, oblivious to whatever harm might come his way. Then he left the next car, then the third and the fourth, and the last car did not seem to be there, just a mass of red flames in the middle of the black night and the silence that now enveloped the world. Nothing else was there but the fire. "Dimyan!" he shouted, but then he saw him rising through the fire with a golden body and a golden face, holding in his golden hand a long golden lance, riding a golden horse and transfixing the heads of the fire-spewing dragons, and he heard the neighing of the golden horse. "Dimyan!" The lance was planted into the head of the dragon, which spewed forth more fire, then into the other head as the fire kept coming. The besieged knight fearlessly pulled his lance from one head after another, striking again as the fire rose and surrounded Dimyan's pale face and the neighing of the horse continued. "Dimyan!" He saw him rising on horseback to the highest heavens, pursued by the fire, which was rising behind him, almost singeing his feet. Then the neighing stopped, and Dimyan carried on rising radiantly into the vastness. "Dimyan!" The golden flame now diminished into a dot, which finally vanished, then the dark prevailed. The train had gone quite a distance without Magd al-Din noticing it. He sat down on the nearest seat, sweat pouring from his skin as if a fire were burning in his chest. He stretched out on the seat and took off his shoes, leaning against the wall of the train car, realizing for the first time that he had become an orphan. Did he have to come to Alexandria and meet Dimyan? "Dimyan!, Dimyan!" He began to shiver. It must be the desert cold coming early, otherwise why was he shivering? But his sweat was still pouring forth. It must be a fever. "Dimyan! Dimyan! Dimyan! *The Most Gracious. He has taught the Quran. He has created man.* Dimyan! Dimyan! *He has taught him speech. The sun and the moon follow their courses punctually. The stars and the trees bow in adoration.* Dimyan! Dimyan! *And the sky He had raised high and He has set the measure.* Dimyan! Dimyan!" Magd al-Din's voice rose suddenly, then subsided, and trembling he said to himself, still reciting from the Quran, "*Which of the favors of your Lord will you deny? Everyone on earth will perish and the countenance of your Lord, Almighty and Glorious, shall abide. So which of the favors of your Lord will you deny?* Dimyan! Dimyan! *All who are in the heavens and the earth entreat Him. Every day He exercises power. So which of the favors of your Lord will you deny?* Dimyan! Dimyan! *We shall dispose of you, both worlds. So which of the favors of your Lord will you deny?* Dimyan! Dimyan!" His tears poured down his cheeks. "Dimyan! Dimyan!" The train came close to Alexandria but did not enter it; it cleared through on its way to Cairo, as heavy raids were still bombarding Alexandria and the battle for Alam al-Halfa was still going on. The train went past Kafr al-Dawwar, leaving Alexandria behind. Magd al-Din sensed that they were in the country again from the total darkness surrounding the villages, the different breeze, and the tall white dovecotes, and he sighed, unable to believe that it was God returning him to his village. Did he have to lose Dimyan to go home again? "Dimyan! Dimyan! *When the sky is rent asunder, becoming red like ointment; so which of the favors of your Lord will you deny? But those who fear the time they will stand before their Lord will be granted two gardens. Dimyan! Dimyan! So which of the favors of your Lord will you deny? Of spreading branches; so which of the favors of your Lord will you deny?* Dimyan! Dimyan! *In them two fountains flow.*" His tears continued to flow. "*Blessed be the name of your Lord, Almighty and Glorious.* Dimyan! Dimyan!" Dimyan did not die; he was not burned. God had lifted him up to heaven, and he had seen him, otherwise who was ascending on the golden horse, moving away into space from the fire of the dragon? "Dimyan! Dimyan!" And he kept reciting that beautiful chapter from the Quran, the only chapter he could still remember, punctuated by the name of his friend, until he was overcome with sleep.

The cold air coming lightly through the windows awakened him. From the window he saw the darkness, deep in a long gap, and realized that the train was crossing the Nile and that the lights were coming from the little houses of Kafr al-Zayyat. He could not mistake the smell of the trees along the river bank, near the villas and small houses. He was now very close to his village, and he had to get up and focus his eyes to jump when he reached the platform. He had no other choice. The train had not stopped in the city of Kafr al-Zayyat—was it going to stop at a small village? The engineer undoubtedly had some contraption giving him orders to proceed fast, to Cairo. The train had moved away beyond the range of the air raids, yet the engineer was still speeding along. Magd al-Din stood near the open door of the car, the cold air drying his sweat. He realized that he was standing barefoot. He had left his shoes near the seat. He did not think of putting them on. He had left the village barefoot, and here was the white platform, approaching fast. Blessed be the name of your Lord, Almighty and Glorious. He stepped forward to get off the train as if he were under the influence of some narcotic drug, and he flew into the air. "Ah!" It came out deep, slow, and faint.

The stationmaster stayed late at his post because of the continuous evacuation of refugees from Alexandria. He heard a hard, heavy thudding sound, a deep, muffled sound. He even saw something hurtling over the platform and landing on the dusty soil a short distance from the platform. It was not the sound of a bomb exploding, anyway. It must be a ghost that he had seen. The groan reverberated. The human sound encouraged the stationmaster to approach, gingerly. The sounds of grasshoppers and frogs came from the canal along the tracks. The stationmaster approached, carrying a lamp shielded with blue, held back by all the rural legacy of fear of ghosts and demons. But the green eyes glowed in the dark. Most merciful God! This is a real human being! He went closer and shone the lamp on the human's face and exclaimed, "Sheikh Magd al-Din?!"

It was the same old stationmaster, Abd al-Hamid, his classmate in Quran memorization class a quarter century earlier, the very man who stood bidding him farewell when he left the village. Magd al-Din heard his voice and closed his eyes in relief. He was now certain he was not going to die.

And he said to me:
What kind of life will you have in this world
After I appear?

al-Niffari

29

Rommel did not succeed in breaking through the front in al-Alamein. For six days he tried, to no avail. He lost three thousand officers and soldiers, either killed, wounded, or taken prisoner, and seven hundred armored vehicles, including fifty tanks. The Allies lost sixteen hundred officers and soldiers, and seventy tanks. Air superiority and short supply lines ensured victory for the Allies. That was Rommel's first defeat in the desert. Soldiers in the Eighth Army now realized that Rommel was not a legend, but a military commander who could win or lose.

Montgomery took advantage of the situation and contin-ued to train the soldiers and conduct huge maneuvers in the desert from Alexandria to al-Alamein. The raids on Alexandria stopped for some time. Panic continued to prevail in the foreign consulates. Jews carried on lining up at the British consulate to get entry visas for Palestine and South Africa. Magd al-Din, who had been moved by the stationmaster to Tanta hospital on the first car that had arrived on the scene, was still in a cast. His legs and several ribs and other bones had been broken, but he had miraculously survived. The stationmaster brought word back to the village, and Zahra, his sisters and their husbands, and his mother, whose days were numbered, visited Magd al-Din. He was told he had to stay in the cast at the hospital for three months. Meanwhile in Cairo the belly-dancer Hikmat Fahmi and the two spies Eppler and Sandstetter were arrested on charges of spying for Germany. The German armies entered the outskirts of Stalingrad, and cold steel massacres took place. They surrounded the city, which they were determined to capture because it was the military industrial city named after Stalin. The Soviets were very determined to stand their ground because the city was named after Stalin. The Muslim general Timoshenko advanced to the river Don in an attempt to cut off German supply and communication lines. Egypt silently celebrated Queen Farida's twenty-second birthday, but there were no public decorations or lights marking the occasion in Alexandria, her birthplace. Montgomery was busy establishing a new corps, the Tenth Corps, to counter the German Afrika Korps. American Sherman and Grant tanks and self-propelled 105-millimeter guns poured into the front. British and American bombers continued to pursue German army supplies on land and on sea. Rommel's blood pressure shot up, and pain in his liver forced him to go back to Germany to seek treatment. General Stumme, who had arrived from the Russian front, replaced him. The month of Ramadan had begun, and the sorrows of Magd al-Din, who lay helpless in bed, increased. True, he had his family around him now, but he could not forget the previous Ramadan in the vast desert with its awesome sunsets, and breaking the fast with Dimyan. Dimyan! Dimyan! How could life go on without Dimyan! Magd al-Din had found out that his sisters had sold his land to themselves in his absence, but he did not even comment on the matter. The mayor sent the village chief to visit Magd al-Din and let him know that the mayor himself was going to visit him soon and that he, the mayor, was sorry for what had happened in the past, but Magd al-Din did not comment on that either. He considered everything preordained by God.

Stumme was six years older than Rommel and, like him, had high blood pressure, which usually afflicted commanders. Egypt had great strategic importance in creating a huge pincer movement from which the German forces, if successful in occupying it, would advance eastwards to meet the forces coming from Europe and the Caucasus. Hitler had promised Rommel to send him the dreaded new Tiger tanks and multi-barrel mortars, but he did not keep his promise. Rommel had felt disappointment after his failure at Alam al-Halfa and decided not to be on the offensive again, but to resort to defensive military tactics for the first time since he took command in the desert. So he set up dense minefields, huge devil's fields, between his position and those of the Eighth Army. Churchill was under great pressure to open a second front. If Stalin and Roosevelt were convinced that that second front would be the African desert, he had to start. The normal English plan would be to take out the German armored vehicles, then deal with the infantry, but Montgomery suggested the opposite. He had greater confidence in the infantry, especially the Australians and New Zealanders, and expected them to acquit themselves valiantly. The same was true of the Fifty-first Highland battalion, which had been recently re-formed to replace the First Highland battalion, which had been decimated in France in 1940. The Fifty-first was intent on vengeance.

The Eighth Army had to advance through half a million German mines. That required a new high morale among the soldiers, and that was one of Montgomery's top priorities for the two months between the battle of Alam al-Halfa, which was over, and al-Alamein, which was about to begin.

There were 230,000 Allied troops versus 77,000 Axis troops; 1,400 Allied tanks, including 400 Sherman and Grant tanks, versus 600 Axis; 1,500 Allied anti-aircraft guns versus 1,000 Axis; 900 Allied aircraft versus 400 Axis. More important than that, the Allies had short supply lines, one hundred kilometers from Alexandria, versus long Axis supply lines, one thousand kilometers from Tobruk.

The foreign consulates had finished burning their papers in Alexandria. Emigration from the city slowed, as only a few of its original inhabitants or those who had fled to it from their villages were left. Sometimes it made sense for some to take refuge in fire if it meant a chance to escape death!

❖

The month of Ramadan had come and gone and so had the days of the feast. On the eve of the middle of Shawwal and October 24, with a full moon and a refreshing breeze, everything was portending an imminent explosion. It was inconceivable that the desert could witness such a majestic night at a time full of loathing and madness. At exactly 9:40 p.m., all at once a barrage of shells and missiles was let loose from one thousand guns at the faraway enemy and at the minefields in front of them. At the same time, planes came from Alexandria and the Delta, dropping gigantic bombs on the well-fortified Axis defenses. The Thirtieth and Thirteenth Battalions advanced, followed by two armored brigades from the mighty Tenth Corps. The soldiers marched at a hysterical pace brought about by the sound of bombs and shells exploding in the midst of the minefields, destroying the mines and sending off dazzling flashes of light that danced in the middle of the no man's land—flashes descending from the sky, and flashes ascending from the earth, flashes coming from the east and flashes coming from the west—a carnival of fire diabolically, unimaginably beautiful. Twenty minutes later, at exactly 10 p.m., was Montgomery's bedtime. He serenely went to bed, and fell asleep as the whole world stayed up waiting for the outcome of the decisive battle. People in Alexandria could hear the guns and see the planes. Cairo shook, and the rest of the country stayed up and watched.

Dressed in their shorts and woolen shirts, infantrymen advanced through the dust and the fire. The cold of the desert night was gone in the midst of the fire. The men carried on their shoulders their rifles with bayonets at the ready and all their possessions: cookies, canned corned beef, and cigarettes. Some carried a light mortar or a submachine gun. They all had hand grenades and empty sacks that they would fill with sand to fortify their positions when they gained ground. Each attack group was commanded by a navigating officer, who carried a small compass and a roll of tape, which he uncoiled behind him to guide those coming after him to the right path through the mines and the dust. Many navigation officers died that night and the following nights. As for the Scottish bagpipers who played on in the midst of those volcanoes, their music was considerably subdued as the landmines blew them away, or the dust choked them, or the guns destroyed them, or the bombs and airplanes drowned out their valiant efforts. Teams of engineers went ahead of everyone, trying to detect anti-tank and anti-personnel mines. They lost many of their men. The Australians were to the right, the New Zealanders to the left, and the bagpipes in the middle, falling. Soldiers were jabbering, their nervous laughter mixed with crying. The offensive turned into near-chaos. Everyone was oblivious to everyone else. The Axis firepower unleashed flames from hell on the Allies. By morning the bagpipe music had been totally silenced. The Thirteenth Battalion had made a large breach in the Axis front. General Stumme had died of a heart attack, an Australian squad having managed to break through the German lines and attack his car.

Montgomery woke up early the following morning. Air Force sorties were still flying. The RAF had flown a thousand sorties during the night in addition to a hundred and fifty sorties flown by the USAF. The Luftwaffe disappeared from the sky, and the Allies had total control of the air. Monty was pleased.

On the third day of the battle, Rommel arrived at the front, cutting short his medical leave. On the fifth day Monty decided to launch his main offensive, which he dubbed 'Excess Baggage.' Rommel wrote to his wife, "There's still a chance today. Perhaps we can still stand fast, but we might not, and that could have dire consequences for the whole war."

Rommel decided to retreat to Fuka, sixty miles to the west. Monty postponed "Excess Baggage" until the second of November. Hitler issued orders to stay and fight, but it was no use. The Axis army was exhausted, and the whole matter was already out of Rommel's hands. The Fifth Indian Brigade had launched a lightning attack five miles south of Tall al-Aqaqir, after which the way was open for the armored corps to pursue the Axis in the desert. The jubilant fakir boy soldiers, followers of Ghandi, Nehru, and Muhammad Ali Jinnah, were now on top of their armored vehicles pursuing an army that only yesterday had been an invincible legend. It was now an army in disarray scattered in the vast desert, beyond the minefields that the Indians had managed to penetrate. Rommel began his quick and total withdrawal. He did not have sufficient means of transportation, and suffered a fuel shortage. There was chaos in the ranks, and the Germans took their vehicles and ran away, leaving behind six Italian divisions, lost in the desert without food or water, their only option to be taken prisoner. The Allies could have turned the defeat into a major killing field, but the rain was Rommel's ally. It began falling suddenly, and hard, and the Allies were stalled until Rommel left the Egyptian borders. The desert was now a graveyard for wrecked and burned tanks, cars on fire, cars totally burned out, corpses both complete and disfigured, helmets with heads with open eyes, shoes with feet, arms with no bodies attached, legs, burned uniforms. The smell of burned flesh was all over the desert. Scorpions and snakes came out, and blue flies appeared after the rain. Kites and old vultures flew overhead. The smell of death filled the air.

Rommel wrote his wife, "Our neighbor has simply crushed us. I made an attempt to save part of the army. Will my attempt succeed? At night I lie down, my eyes wide open, racking my brain trying to find a way out of this ordeal for my poor soldiers. We are facing difficult days, the hardest that can happen to anyone. The dead are lucky, it is all over for them."

Churchill ordered that the church bells in London be rung for the first time since the outbreak of the war, and peals were heard all over London and other English cities, and people took to the streets in jubilation. There was jubilation in Alexandria, too. The streets were lit up for the first time in three years. The lights, which were turned on suddenly before midnight, turned the city into an immeasurable mass of amber. The blue paint covering the tall lamppost fixtures had vanished with the passage of time, and the weather conditions changed, giving the city a new, endless phosphorescent ceiling. Those out on the street shouted in jubilation, and those indoors came out to admire the pearls and diamonds newly studding the night sky. How could it have been possible for Alexandria to remain darkened for so long? Owners of closed stores came out and opened them in the middle of the night. Men went out to coffeehouses that decided to stay open until the morning. Women let loose ululations of joy from the windows of their homes, and children were allowed to play in the streets despite the chill in the air. It seemed everyone had agreed to stay up till morning. Music played on at the Monsignor, the Louvre, and the Windsor nightclubs. Soldiers exchanged kisses with ATS women on the streets. Whiskey and champagne flowed in the posh brothels, now roaring with laughter, and so did rum, brandy, and arak in the poorer brothels, which were suddenly bustling with business again. It was as if everyone, the whores and the pleasure-seekers alike, was just around the corner, waiting for the lights to come back on. Horse-drawn carriages carrying lovers galloped along the corniche, as the sound of the waves became more regular because of the light wind. The destroyers and military ships turned their lights on and started shooting fireworks over the city. Thousands of people went up to the roofs and released balloons into the sky. Cannons started to discharge, and for a moment people were scared, but they soon realized that they were shots of celebration. On the corniche a man who saw the sky lit up with phosphorescent missiles and the surf rising, shouted, "Dance, Alexandria, dance—Hitler had no chance." Another man heard him and repeated what he had said. The words spread throughout the city, then became a song. People kept talking and telling stories, which everyone knew, about the days of the war, which had ended only the day before. The city administration decided to have decorations everywhere, and the streetcar company decided to give everyone free rides for several days. Celebrations were held at schools. Refugees began to return in droves. Army and police bands played their music in the streets and the squares. The autumn sun rose gently, filling the city with a white glow. Hamidu was released. He had been arrested again, despite what he had written on the walls. As usual his mother celebrated, and he stood there laughing amongst the happy well-wishers. Ghaffara took off his fez, deciding never to wear it again. He was surprised that after losing the glass part, he had also lost the filter, and realized that he had been breathing regular, unfiltered air. He could not figure out how he had not noticed the loss of the heavy filter. Anyway, he laughed and reattached the wooden side panels to his cart, writing on them, "Sawdust cart. Capacity: four tons. Will deliver all over the country," and got ready to go back to his old job. Khawaga Dimitri reappeared in front of his house with some workers, who immediately started removing the rubble in preparation for rebuilding the house. The Territorial Army soldier who used to buy tangerines from Umm Hamidu reappeared. She saw him standing over her head, laughing, shaking his head and saying, "Oh tangerine vendor, tell me how much for a dozen."

Umm Hamidu laughed loudly, saying as she shrugged her shoulders, "A dozen tangerines, darling, are free—and then some."

He danced in front of her and held her hand and told her, "I want that 'and then some' in holy matrimony."

She did not answer but bowed her head and closed her eyes. He fell upon her, embracing her head and kissing her as she sat there. Alarmed, she pushed him away, looking up and down the street.

This time she agreed to marry him. She did not believe that he would come back, and he did not believe that she had agreed. Rushdi realized that if Germany was defeated once, it could be defeated every time. He was certain that the war would soon be over, and that he would go to Paris. The public health office in Alexandria announced that there were only one hundred Egyptian births that week because of the flight of so many of the inhabitants, and only one birth among the foreigners for the same reason. Deaths among the Egyptian Alexandrians totaled fifty because of old age, different types of fever, dysentery, tetanus, and whooping cough; five foreigners died of drunkenness. There were no suicides, but the public health office registered five deaths among Alexandrians because of heart failure during sexual intercourse. The time for Magd al-Din's discharge from the hospital drew near, and he and Zahra exchanged lengthy glances. He had come back to life, and Zahra's face glowed like a rose. Each understood the feelings of the other.

"I am not staying in the village," he said.

"I know."

"Will you come with me?"

"Of course."

They both fell silent. She saw that he was dejected, that a touch of sorrow shaded his face. "I don't know what Alexandria will be like without Dimyan, or how I will be able to go back to work without him."

He wiped away his tears. She did not want to dissuade him from going back to the city to which she had first gone against her will, and which she later left also against her will when she left him behind. This time she was going to go in contentment and happiness, even if she did not find the people as carefree and cheerful as they had been. The white city with a blue sea and a blue sky would revive the spirits of its people.

"This time we'll leave early in the morning," she said.

"Of course. Arriving in a city at night is hard," he said.

Harbingers of winter had come in a hurry. It rained hard day and night for several days, but no one complained. Life did not come to a standstill, stores were not closed, and coffeehouses did not turn down the volume on their radios. It seemed to everyone that the sky was washing the city. The clouds were high and white, and that was a miracle. Where had all that rain come from? When black clouds settled over the city, the operator of the main power station in Karmuz forgot to turn the current to the street lights off during the day, so the city remained lit up day and night. People had removed the blue paint from the windows, storefronts, and car headlights. Everyone kept the lights on in the houses and in stores all day and all night long. Alexandria became a city of silver with veins of gold.

Modern Arabic Literature
from the American University in Cairo Press

Bahaa Abdelmegid *Saint Theresa and Sleeping with Strangers*
Ibrahim Abdel Meguid *Birds of Amber* • *Distant Train*
No One Sleeps in Alexandria • *The Other Place*
Yahya Taher Abdullah *The Collar and the Bracelet* • *The Mountain of Green Tea*
Leila Abouzeid *The Last Chapter*
Hamdi Abu Golayyel *A Dog with No Tail* • *Thieves in Retirement*
Yusuf Abu Rayya *Wedding Night*
Ahmed Alaidy *Being Abbas el Abd*
Idris Ali *Dongola* • *Poor*
Rasha al Ameer *Judgment Day*
Radwa Ashour *Granada* • *Specters*
Ibrahim Aslan *The Heron* • *Nile Sparrows*
Alaa Al Aswany *Chicago* • *Friendly Fire* • *The Yacoubian Building*
Fahd al-Atiq *Life on Hold*
Fadhil al-Azzawi *Cell Block Five* • *The Last of the Angels*
The Traveler and the Innkeeper
Ali Bader *Papa Sartre*
Liana Badr *The Eye of the Mirror*
Hala El Badry *A Certain Woman* • *Muntaha*
Salwa Bakr *The Golden Chariot* • *The Man from Bashmour* • *The Wiles of Men*
Halim Barakat *The Crane*
Hoda Barakat *Disciples of Passion* • *The Tiller of Waters*
Mourid Barghouti *I Saw Ramallah* • *I Was Born There, I Was Born Here*
Mohamed Berrada *Like a Summer Never to Be Repeated*
Mohamed El-Bisatie *Clamor of the Lake* • *Drumbeat* • *Hunger* • *Over the Bridge*
Mahmoud Darwish *The Butterfly's Burden*
Tarek Eltayeb *Cities without Palms* • *The Palm House*
Mansoura Ez Eldin *Maryam's Maze*
Ibrahim Farghali *The Smiles of the Saints*
Abdulaziz Al Farsi *Earth Weeps, Saturn Laughs*
Hamdy el-Gazzar *Black Magic*
Randa Ghazy *Dreaming of Palestine*
Gamal al-Ghitani *Pyramid Texts* • *The Zafarani Files* • *Zayni Barakat*
The Book of Epiphanies
Tawfiq al-Hakim *The Essential Tawfiq al-Hakim* • *Return of the Spirit*
Yahya Hakki *The Lamp of Umm Hashim*
Abdelilah Hamdouchi *The Final Bet*
Bensalem Himmich *The Polymath* • *The Theocrat*
Taha Hussein *The Days*
Sonallah Ibrahim *The Committee* • *Zaat*
Yusuf Idris *City of Love and Ashes* • *The Essential Yusuf Idris* • *Tales of Encounter*
Denys Johnson-Davies *The AUC Press Book of Modern Arabic Literature*
Homecoming • *In a Fertile Desert* • *Under the Naked Sky*
Said al-Kafrawi *The Hill of Gypsies*
Mai Khaled *The Magic of Turquoise*
Sahar Khalifeh *The End of Spring*
The Image, the Icon and the Covenant • *The Inheritance* • *Of Noble Origins*
Edwar al-Kharrat *Rama and the Dragon* • *Stones of Bobello*

Betool Khedairi *Absent*
Mohammed Khudayyir *Basrayatha*
Ibrahim al-Koni *Anubis • Gold Dust • The Puppet • The Seven Veils of Seth*
Naguib Mahfouz *Adrift on the Nile • Akhenaten: Dweller in Truth*
Arabian Nights and Days • Autumn Quail • Before the Throne • The Beggar
The Beginning and the End • Cairo Modern • The Cairo Trilogy: Palace Walk
Palace of Desire • Sugar Street • Children of the Alley • The Coffeehouse
The Day the Leader Was Killed • The Dreams • Dreams of Departure
Echoes of an Autobiography • The Essential Naguib Mahfouz • The Final Hour
The Harafish • Heart of the Night • In the Time of Love
The Journey of Ibn Fattouma • Karnak Cafe • Khan al-Khalili • Khufu's Wisdom
Life's Wisdom • Love in the Rain • Midaq Alley • The Mirage • Miramar • Mirrors
Morning and Evening Talk • Naguib Mahfouz at Sidi Gaber • Respected Sir
Rhadopis of Nubia • The Search • The Seventh Heaven • Thebes at War
The Thief and the Dogs • The Time and the Place • Voices from the Other World
Wedding Song • The Wisdom of Naguib Mahfouz
Mohamed Makhzangi *Memories of a Meltdown*
Alia Mamdouh *The Loved Ones • Naphtalene*
Selim Matar *The Woman of the Flask*
Ibrahim al-Mazini *Ten Again*
Samia Mehrez *The Literary Atlas of Cairo • The Literary Life of Cairo*
Yousef Al-Mohaimeed *Munira's Bottle • Wolves of the Crescent Moon*
Eslam Mosbah *Status: Emo*
Hassouna Mosbahi *A Tunisian Tale*
Ahlam Mosteghanemi *Chaos of the Senses • Memory in the Flesh*
Shakir Mustafa *Contemporary Iraqi Fiction: An Anthology*
Mohamed Mustagab *Tales from Dayrut*
Buthaina Al Nasiri *Final Night*
Ibrahim Nasrallah *Inside the Night • Time of White Horses*
Haggag Hassan Oddoul *Nights of Musk*
Mona Prince *So You May See*
Mohamed Mansi Qandil *Moon over Samarqand*
Abd al-Hakim Qasim *Rites of Assent*
Somaya Ramadan *Leaves of Narcissus*
Kamal Ruhayyim *Days in the Diaspora*
Mahmoud Saeed *The World through the Eyes of Angels*
Mekkawi Said *Cairo Swan Song*
Ghada Samman *The Night of the First Billion*
Mahdi Issa al-Saqr *East Winds, West Winds*
Rafik Schami *The Calligrapher's Secret • Damascus Nights • The Dark Side of Love*
Habib Selmi *The Scents of Marie-Claire*
Khairy Shalaby *The Hashish Waiter • The Lodging House*
The Time-Travels of the Man Who Sold Pickles and Sweets
Khalil Sweileh *Writing Love*
Miral al-Tahawy *Blue Aubergine • Brooklyn Heights • Gazelle Tracks • The Tent*
Bahaa Taher *As Doha Said • Love in Exile*
Fuad al-Takarli *The Long Way Back*
Zakaria Tamer *The Hedgehog*
M. M. Tawfik *candygirl • Murder in the Tower of Happiness*
Mahmoud Al-Wardani *Heads Ripe for Plucking*
Amina Zaydan *Red Wine*
Latifa al-Zayyat *The Open Door*